# LOLA FLORES

ALSO BY DAVID PERLSTEIN

Fiction

*2084*
*Big Truth: New and Collected Stories*
*The Odd Plight of Adonis Licht*
*Flight of the Spumonis*
*The Boy Walker*
*San Café*
*Slick!*

•

Non-fiction

*God's Others: Non-Israelites' Encounters With God in the Hebrew Bible*
*Solo Success: 100 Tips for Becoming a $100,000-a-Year Freelancer*

# LOLA FLORES

David Perlstein

# LOLA FLORES

iUniverse books may be ordered through booksellers or by contacting:

iUniverse
1663 Liberty Drive
Bloomington, IN 47403
www.iuniverse.com
844-349-9409

JPS Hebrew-English Tanakh: The Traditional Hebrew Text and the New JPS Translation — Second Edition. The Jewish Publication Society, Philadelphia, 1999 – 5779.

Myjewishlearning.com. "Genders in the Talmud" by Rachel Scheinerman.
https://www.myjewishlearning.com/article/the-eight-genders-in-the-talmud/

ISBN: 978-1-6632-3763-7 (sc)
ISBN: 978-1-6632-3764-4 (e)

Print information available on the last page.

iUniverse rev. date: 03/30/2022

For Yosi

And God created man in His image, in the image of God
He created him; male and female He created them.
*Genesis 1:27*


Rabbi Yirmeya ben Elazar: In the hour when the Holy One
created the first human, He created him as an *androgynos*
(one having both male and female sexual characteristics),
as it is said, "male and female He created them."
*Genesis Rabbah 8:1*

# FEBRUARY 1912

# THE LADY

As the SS *President Lincoln* pitched and rolled into New York Harbor, Yankev Sobel, his near-two-year-old son Anshel in his arms, stumbled by the upper-deck railing.

Rivka Sobel called to her husband in warning and rebuke. Anxiety sharpened her normally hushed voice into one as penetrating as the single-funnel liner's horn.

Anshel's older sister Tosia giggled.

Yankev frowned at his daughter, cast his wife an uneasy smile, widened his stance and buttressed himself against the railing. He had no intention of being dislodged. In his defense, he had spent nine disagreeable days crossing the Atlantic from Hamburg. Now, their native Warsaw having provided no frame of reference, he could not resist being dizzied by Manhattan's looming skyscrapers. At 170 meters, or as they said in America, 560 feet as he'd learned in a letter from his brother Mendel, the Metropolitan Life Insurance Company Tower all but touched the steel-gray winter sky. The new Woolworth Building would climb even higher.

Anshel's face remained deadpan, his composure serene. He was too young to imagine his father losing his grip and dropping him into the swirling, white-capped waters below. Nor could he conceive how America would alter his family's history and his own singular future. Still, he sensed his parents' nervous excitement.

The Goldene Medina offered Jews like the Sobels bright prospects. Yankev's brother Mendel, who left Warsaw for New York three weeks after Anshel's bris, had established the family's leather-goods business. If smaller than the one Yankev sold off, it offered far more promise. The

Sobels would enjoy security from pogroms like those several years earlier in Kishinev and Kiev, Odessa, Minsk and Bialystok.

A deck below, less-fortunate steerage passengers in ragged winter clothing huddled shoulder to shoulder. The best they could do was warm themselves with their dreams. Traveling in second class, the Sobels would be allowed to take a ferry from the dock in Hoboken to Manhattan. Officials assumed them to be healthy and so unlikely to impose a financial burden on their new nation. The authorities required steerage arrivals to undergo immigration procedures on Ellis Island accompanied by the risk of being sent back to Europe.

The *President Lincoln* advanced northward among tugboats and ferries clogging the Upper Bay. An inhospitable wind shot down the Hudson River. It flogged exposed skin as mercilessly as any gale that ever roared up the Vistula.

Rivka retreated further into her heavy wool coat, nestled her chin deeper into its fur collar.

Yankev, the picture of a Polar explorer—a Jewish Peary—pulled the the fur flaps of his hat further down over his ears. Again, he came close to losing his footing.

"Come away!" Rivka protested. "You'll drop your son."

"Drop my angel?" said Yankev. A white stream of vapor shot from his mouth. His eyes denying Rivka further objection, he hoisted Anshel higher. "The boy must remember." He pointed to the statue that dominated the harbor. "Look, Anshele. The Lady."

Anshel gazed at the Statue of Liberty with an unnerving intensity. He studied the verdigris patina overlaying the Lady's copper skin, her long flowing robe, her pointed crown. He noted her left hand holding a tablet upon which, he would learn in school, was inscribed the date of America's independence. He followed the Lady's right arm rising heavenward. Its torch of welcome bore its own crown—a golden flame.

Yankev brushed his lips across Anshel's and breathed deeply of his son's innocence mixed with salt air redolent of smoke from thousands of coal furnaces. Inspired, he whispered words he sought to lodge in the deepest recesses of Anshel's memory, words Anshel would recover only decades later. "In America—"

# HAVANA

# OCTOBER 1929

# THE HAVANA SPECIAL

Lola Torres, hoping she'd entered the near-empty chair car on the Havana Special unnoticed, pulled down the window shade. She could not be sure—at least, not yet—anyone was searching for her, but prudence demanded that she conceal herself from the platform until the train made its late-evening departure from Penn Station. She set her nondescript gray cloth valise on the window seat to ward off anyone who might wish to join her and chat before sleep overtook them. Atop it, she placed her weighty volume of Shakespeare's plays and the evening's *New York Sun*. Whether she would be able to sleep sitting up remained in question. More certain, she would make every effort to stay awake for the next several hours given the events of the past day.

Continuing to follow instructions, Lola burrowed into her seat to make herself as small as she could. At five-feet-five-inches, she was taller than the ideal woman, portrayed by the popular song as five-feet-two with eyes of blue. The blue eyes, she had. Also, a slender figure. According to Mama, too thin. Practically a scarecrow. Regrettably, Lola's feet more resembled a man's. About that she could do nothing. The same was true of her hands. Fortunately, they lacked any hint of masculine bulkiness and far from representing a minor curse, provided a major blessing. Long, supple fingers enabled Lola to play many of Rachmaninoff's most difficult chords, unreachable by some male pianists nearing or surpassing six feet. Accepting her physical limitations and fighting exhaustion, she made herself as comfortable as she could to begin the journey south to Key West. Two nights on a train represented a small price to pay for a new life free from the constraints imposed on her for most of her nineteen years.

A shiver spread across Lola's shoulders and slithered down her spine. Despite the car's warmth, a bone-deep chill clung to her fourteen hours after she plunged into the East River to emerge a new person. In the absence of a blanket, she draped herself in her heavy coat. In Cuba—a boat from Key West would take her to Havana—she would abandon the coat along with her identity.

Motionless, her breathing shallow, Lola held no illusions about the challenges ahead. Havana stood worlds apart from Manhattan and all she knew, but where else could she find refuge and resurrect herself? Novels and movies hailed the great American West—particularly California—as the place for new beginnings, but she'd never crossed the Hudson River and knew no one who lived beyond it. For that matter, she'd never been south of New York. The intimates who'd helped plan her escape had warned that the journey she was about to undertake posed constant danger. Making her way in Havana would be safer if not easy. Another plotter awaited her—the sister of her family's maid, who'd taught her to speak Spanish like a habanera and spun endless tales of island life. Lola might still confront the ridicule and violence she'd already experienced—no one guaranteed a return to Eden—but she'd chosen the best path available. She'd live or die following it.

A door opened and closed at the far end of the car revealing a middle-aged, brass-buttoned conductor. Imitating a Hollywood actress in the bygone talkies, Lola lowered her eyes and assumed an expression of feminine placidity. She'd been forced to play-act nearly all her life and considered herself well-rehearsed for the trip's crucial first leg to Washington, D.C. If her carefully orchestrated immersion in the East River failed to convince the authorities in New York of her death, a vast network of pervert-hating police and scoop-hungry reporters might lay in wait. No place would be more fraught with danger than Penn Station. Just as daunting, all along the line private detectives, as pitiless as relentless, would seek to claim what could emerge as a bountiful missing persons reward.

The conductor stepped forward.

Lola picked up the *Sun*, calling on newsprint to help conceal her from any railroad bulls or local police who came aboard. Earlier, she'd scoured the paper in a corner of the waiting room. To her relief, she'd found nothing regarding her disappearance. But if a story was to be filed, more likely it would appear the next day. Hopefully, it would be obscured by reports about the tottering stock market. Between stations, she'd return to *Hamlet*. After departing Washington, she would place the valise on the overhead rack, curl up across both seats and take shelter beneath her coat.

Despite her desire to hide in plain sight, Lola peered over the top of the paper and observed the conductor chatting with two of the car's half-dozen other passengers. One raised a flask no doubt filled with prohibited whiskey. The conductor flashed a broad smile to conclude pleasantries.

He approached Lola.

Absent-mindedly, she raised a hand to her hair—light brown and bobbed. She'd once attempted the popular finger-wave curls suggestive of the undulating ocean, but her hair virtually collapsed. As a child, her hair had been thicker. Mama kvelled receiving compliments from strangers. Then, in her mid-teens, it thinned out. Still, Lola knew herself to be sufficiently attractive to draw unwanted attention from men lacking control of their animal instincts. She was content that her current hairstyle might suppress unwanted male attention on the journey south.

The conductor peered over the newspaper. "Evening," he said.

Lola placed the *Sun* next to her Shakespeare then looked up to avoid making an impression of guilt. She attempted to take the man's measure. His stooped shoulders attested to the weight of his responsibilities. A paunch evidenced working-class prosperity. Beneath his cap, gray hair came close to matching the seagull white of his mustache. Pink cheeks and twinkling ice-blue eyes suggested Santa Claus as he might be illustrated in *The Saturday Evening Post*. She held out her ticket.

"Going all the way down to Key West and on to Havana, are you?" he said. His accent suggested an upbringing in a warm climate.

Lola's restrained smile intimated that she'd ridden the Havana Special before, although aside from a lone trip to see Mama's family in Europe, her previous travels consisted of subway rides to Harlem, Greenwich Village and occasionally Brooklyn.

The conductor winked. "No offense, miss, but you don't strike me as a Garcia."

Lola returned his comment with a renewed expression of nonchalance.

"I guess I got that wrong, huh? Your family, they came here from Spain is what. Lots of Spaniards, they look like white people. But I'll say this if you don't mind. Cuba became much better off when America took it over back in 'ninety-eight."

Lola nodded in agreement then explained that she was from right here in New York and going to Havana to see relatives. Lying came easy. She'd been forced to live most of her life as a lie.

The conductor reached into his vest pocket and extracted a silver watch like Papa's. "Ten-oh-two," he said. "We'll be leaving in three minutes, right on time." He nestled the watch back into the pocket. "I tell you what. You being a young lady traveling alone, I'll come back after Newark to make sure you're settled in for the night. How's that?"

Lola offered a neutral "Thank you."

The conductor went on to the next car.

At five past ten, the lights dimmed and the train pulled forward. As it plodded through the tunnel beneath the Hudson, Lola fingered Stravinsky's solo piano composition *Piano-Rag-Music*. Approaching the first stop at Newark, she again buried her face in the paper.

After departure, the conductor appeared from behind her. She couldn't help flinching. She hoped he hadn't noted her discomfort.

"Looks like you're doing just fine," he said and continued down the aisle to greet the stop's two new passengers.

Lola resumed fingering the Stravinsky piece.

In North Philadelphia, a man carrying a briefcase left the car. A yawning couple boarded.

The train's cradle-like rocking induced Lola to let down her guard and close her eyes. The sleep she doubted she'd enjoy—was afraid to enjoy—overcame her. She dreamed of the East River—a salt-water tidal estuary, Miss Staunton informed her sixth-grade class—as it rushed towards New York Harbor. Granite-colored swirls and eddies conveyed a bouquet of brilliant yellow daisies repeatedly dropping beneath the surface and rising. Choking off a small cry, she woke, turned on the overhead light and reached for Shakespeare.

As Claudius and Gertrude discussed Hamlet's strange behavior with Rosencrantz and Guildenstern, a finger tapped Lola's shoulder. "Hope you don't mind," the conductor whispered, "but I feared you might not be comfortable, a chair car being satisfactory for some but not necessarily appropriate for a young lady off to a foreign country unchaperoned."

"What time is it?" Lola asked.

"Near three. We'll be in Washington shortly."

She assured him she'd sleep soundly after that.

The conductor hoped so. He anticipated few, if any, passengers boarding, this being shoulder season before winter vacations and most folks choosing to stay home, the stock market heading south instead. "But don't you worry, they'll ride the Havana Special soon enough. People with money, seems like somehow they always manage to hold on."

Still chilled, Lola crossed her arms beneath her coat and clasped her shoulders.

The conductor's face registered concern.

Lola sought to put him off. "The excitement of the trip," she said.

"Just why I came by." A young girl—a young *woman*—oughtn't be sharing a chair car with strangers, few as the passengers were. No doubt at this moment, her parents also were awake. That was the natural state of things. He had a daughter around what her age might be, though a gentleman would never be so bold as to hazard a guess. Surely, she would prefer privacy for the remainder of the trip.

Lola thought her privacy substantially assured once they left Washington. On the other hand, she didn't fantasize herself Cinderella traveling in a magic carriage under the protection of a hovering fairy godmother. Or godfather.

It happened, the conductor explained, that the Havana Special's Pullman cars were even emptier than the chair cars. "There's this porter—Boy owes me a favor." He could put her into a bedroom all by herself. "A double, so it'll be extra roomy."

Lola offered no response.

The conductor played his trump card. "You'll have your own bathroom."

Lola weighed the delights of a Pullman against her limited resources. "I haven't enough money," she said.

The conductor rested his hand on her shoulder. "Don't you be concerned about *that*."

A low heat prickled along Lola's legs, rose to her stomach, flared through her chest and blazed across her cheeks. She wanted to admonish him that a gentleman never touched a lady, not even to shake hands, unless

9

the lady initiated such contact. But considering the risk the conductor was taking, that such kindness might jeopardize his job, she withheld her protest.

The conductor removed his hand. "Forgive my concern."

Lola understood. Newspapers and magazines reported with great frequency how girls and women—even married women—fell prey to men of low character. Now, she'd been offered shelter—more, a haven—until Key West. The heat that suffused her body dissipated. "Are you sure it will be all right?" she asked. She left unsaid, *Do you think we can get away with it?*

They could go to the Pullman right now, the conductor assured her. He'd even carry her valise.

Lola assented. Carpe diem. Wasn't that Horace? Life required adaptability given that so much depended on chance. She followed the conductor, glad to escape the snoring of passengers, indifferent to tempo and discordant. In the designated sleeping car, doors to the privileged accommodations lined the right side of the narrow corridor running to the far end where a porter sat hunched in a chair, asleep.

The conductor motioned Lola to wait. He took no more than three steps when the porter lifted his head, stood and walked forward. A white jacket defined his lanky frame. The dim light all but obliterated the features of his black face.

The conductor waved Lola forward.

"So, this is your niece, huh?" said the porter in a lilting voice tempered by wariness.

The conductor laughed. "Now we'll be square."

Lola wondered what the conductor held over the porter but accepted that the matter was between the two of them.

"Anyone finds out," said the porter, "cost me my job." But yes, they were square.

The conductor turned to Lola. "All this excitement, you alone on a grand adventure and all. Wouldn't be surprising if you found yourself having difficulty falling asleep even in the privacy of your own bedroom."

Lola, having drifted off earlier, said she would be fine. She kept to herself that an emerging case of nerves had banished her fatigue.

"And how many folks have said they'd drop right off before suffering a sleepless night?" the conductor countered. A young lady needed her beauty rest, and he knew just what would help—a hot toddy made from an old family recipe. It required bourbon—honesty compelled him to disclose that—but just a bit. Despite Prohibition—not that he lacked respect for the law—he'd brought the real thing aboard. "I don't mean to be forward," he said with a chuckle, "but you being a young woman from New York City, I can't help thinking you may have enjoyed a nip or two. For medicinal purposes, of course."

Lola, again chilled and increasingly uncertain about the possibility of sleep, offered no protest of innocence. That would pile one deceit atop another, although deceit was as vital to her survival as air. In New York, she'd played piano with Cuban and jazz bands in several small clubs and speakeasies. From time to time, she'd sampled whiskey and rum smuggled into the country from Canada or the Caribbean. Occasionally, a homemade variety.

The conductor pressed his hands together. "I'll be back before you know it. Meanwhile, George here will make up your room. You'll sleep like a baby, and he'll knock on your door before Fayetteville, so you'll have time for a hearty breakfast in the dining car." He reached into his pocket and withdrew two one-dollar bills. "I know your folks'd want you to eat right."

New York being home to many men contemptuous of a woman's honor, Lola had learned to erect proper defenses. But the conductor struck her as a different kind of man from a different kind of place. She accepted the bills.

The conductor gave Lola a fatherly kiss on the forehead then strode back towards the rear of the train.

The porter took Lola's valise into the bedroom and lit sconces above two large easy chairs on either side of the picture window.

Lola skirted the shallow wardrobe by the entrance and sat on the adjacent sofa.

"Sofa you're on, that pulls out for your bed," said the porter. He pointed to a narrow door. "Your facilities. Clean and shiny."

Lola slid a hand over the sofa's leather upholstery then stepped to the table between the two chairs and set down the dollar bills.

"You bring food?" asked the porter.

She had. White rolls, smoked fish, two piquant cheeses, half-a-dozen bright red apples.

"That's good," he said, "'cause goin' to the dining car? Given the circumstances, that could be troublesome." He removed sheets and blankets from the top of the wardrobe. "What I'd do if I was you is, I'd squirrel myself away in here till Key West."

As the porter finished making up the bed, the conductor returned and held out the hot toddy. "For medicinal purposes only," he reminded Lola.

Lola acknowledged to herself that a bit of fortification might finally warm her and provide for a sound sleep, if not until Fayetteville, hopefully until sunrise. The day's events had taken their toll. She might also be on the verge of a cold. She sipped from the toddy and shuddered. She sipped again.

"Tomorrow," said the conductor, "we'll enter sunnier climes with dispositions to match." He bid her sleep well and slipped out the door.

The porter fluffed two pillows and noted the train beginning to slow. "Washington," he said. He stepped towards the door to the corridor, stopped and pointed to a red cord. "You need somethin', you pull this. Only, it better be important."

Relieved to be alone, Lola finished the toddy. When the train eased out of Union Station and crossed the Potomac into northern Virginia, she showered, the entire bathroom composing the stall. Warm at last and drowsy, she put on cotton pajamas she'd not anticipated wearing on the train—a floral V-neck top with lace at the cuffs and flowing bottoms, floor-length and flared. After settling beneath the covers, she drifted off. Soon, she dreamed. The voices of two unseen men spoke. Agitated voices. "I'm just making sure everything's all right," said one. "What wouldn't be right?" asked the other. "Don't you forget, I could tell people some things," said the first.

A door opened and closed.

Her bedcovers flew off.

A great weight dropped onto the bed.

Her heart fluttering, Lola smelled a man's breath, suffocating and rank with alcohol. What kind of dream was this? How could a dream be so real? She struggled to open her eyes. Her lids resisted. A rough hand cupped her small breasts. She attempted to break free but could no more

12

move than someone in a dentist's chair incapacitated by laughing gas. The hand slid down to her stomach. Her body stiffened. The hand descended until it thrust between her thighs. "What the hell!" the intruder shouted. "Jesus, goddam—"

Lola attempted to scream. A gurgling sound erupted from the back of her throat.

The intruder slapped his hand over her mouth then withdrew it.

She again attempted to cry out.

His fist struck her jaw.

Lola sobbed. This time, she produced enough sound to be heard in the corridor.

"What's goin' on in there?" asked the second voice. It struck her as a real voice.

The intruder jumped up and flung the door open. It thudded against the wall as he fled into the corridor.

A burst of light forced Lola to cover her closed eyes.

Hands shook her shoulders. "Wake up!" a voice urged. She recognized it as the porter's. "You gotta wake up!"

Footsteps retreated then quickly returned. Water splashed her face, ran down her cheeks and trickled along the base of her neck. She sat up. Struggling to open her eyes, she squinted.

"Damn!" said the porter.

Her heart pounding, Lola realized that the first voice belonged to her attacker, the conductor. She scolded herself for being so naïve, so foolish to trust a stranger. Her reprimand gave way to a throbbing on the left side of her face. She raised her hand to comfort the aching flesh.

The porter bent over her. "Are you— Did he—?"

Lola's chest rose and fell as she struggled to free herself from the remains of her stupor.

"Be right back," the porter said. He returned with an icepack.

She shook her head. She couldn't bear to be touched.

He insisted. If they were to keep the swelling down, she'd have to lie back. Now.

She relented. The ice pack caressed her cheek. The porter's gentleness offered a small measure of reassurance in the existence of human decency.

"Now you tell me, you hear? Did he—"

Lola took a deep breath, a second, a third. "I don't think so," she whispered. "No, I'm sure." Had he violated her, she would know. She'd once experienced the pain men inflicted on women, the piercing, slashing pain a violated soul never forgot.

"This is bad," the porter muttered. Not so much her face, he claimed, praising Jesus. Allowing for the skill with which women applied their powders and rouges—he could not speak with any certainty regarding white women—no one might notice anything when they reached Key West. No, he had a greater concern. "You gonna report this?"

Lola, the ice slowly coaxing her mind her mind towards clarity, shook her head. The porter's job was safe. Speaking up would prove fruitless. The conductor would deny everything, and the police hardly could be expected to take the porter's word over that of a white man. They might even accuse the porter of being the attacker, which would upset her more than the attack itself. If she protested strongly enough and they let the porter off, her bruises would still provide evidence that an assault had taken place. But being subservient to the railroad's interests, the police would keep an attack on a passenger aboard the Havana Special under wraps, especially if a railroad employee might be involved. Instead, they'd point fingers at her, accuse her of being a hussy, a harlot, a temptress and—here she would be defenseless—a squatter without a Pullman ticket. The police would arrest *her*. At best, they would ship her back to her family to endure more of the shame she'd fled. At worst, she'd find herself savaged.

The train slowed.

Lola's vision came into focus. "Where are we?" she asked.

"Comin' into Richmond." The porter's eyes mingled repentance with fear. "I didn't know. God's honest truth. And your so-called uncle? He got me over a barrel. Anyways, this run he gets off here."

"I'll be all right and thank you," Lola whispered. She assumed that offering the porter those few words of consolation would bring the matter to an end but knew her answer represented at best a half-truth. She would survive, yes. But she would have to march on bearing her wounds, undaunted like the suffragettes who'd won American women the right to vote. Each day she would struggle anew to be the woman she knew herself to be, the musician she knew herself to be. Hadn't she, like every American, the right to life, liberty and the pursuit of happiness? She believed that she had, even if many others disagreed.

Making the best of a bad situation, the porter was all business. Lola would stay in the bedroom until Key West. Upon leaving the Havana Special, she'd put all this behind her. He handed Lola the icepack and returned to the corridor.

The bone-deep chill of the previous day returned with wintry fury. Lola collapsed back on the bed. Her hands shook as if playing an octave tremolo.

At six-thirty the next morning, the Havana Special arrived in Miami for a brief layover. Awakened by the tumult of passengers leaving and boarding what now would serve as a local train, Lola pushed off her bedcovers. Having slept for most of the past twenty-four hours, she found her head clear, her determination resolute. Admittedly, she'd let her guard down, been taken advantage of. She would register that as another lesson learned and go on. What choice had she? And she'd succeed. Women could be as brave as men. Her appetite stirred by her tenacity, she stared at the window table and the conductor's two dollar bills.

With the train's departure at seven-fifteen, Lola, dressed. Made up and scornful of any pretense at stealth, she entered the corridor.

The porter shot to his feet.

"I'll scream!" she warned.

He sat.

In the dining car, Lola occupied a table covered by a white cloth and set with gleaming china, silver and a crystal water glass. The few well-to-do breakfasters picked at plates heaped with bacon, eggs and hotcakes. While none took particular notice of her, Lola noticed them—eyes near vacant, cheeks pinched, voices, when they spoke, subdued as if in mourning.

A pale, white-coated waiter offered a menu along with a printed meal check and pencil, then poured coffee. "Would you like this morning's *Miami Herald*, Miss?" he asked, his voice somber. "Although this morning's news might unsettle a young lady's constitution."

Lola gave him a look tinged with disdain. "I read newspapers every day. And thank you, but my constitution is and will remain tip-top."

Chastened, the waiter stepped away.

At Cocoanut Grove, he returned, newspaper in hand, and took Lola's completed meal check. She'd selected the Combination Breakfast for eighty-five cents, muffins and coffee included. She would leave a ten-cent tip—fifteen cents if merited by service rendered—and still retain one of the conductor's blood-money dollars.

The *Herald*'s front page took her aback. Bold headlines blared: STOCKS PLUNGE. RECORD VOLUME. WORLDWIDE PANIC. *Variety*, the newspaper of stage and screen, had proclaimed what it termed Black Tuesday in its singular style: WALL ST. LAYS AN EGG.

After finishing her meal—Mama would at least be proud that she'd cleaned her plate—Lola left the dollar without expectation of change. It seemed selfish to deprive someone of a nickel in such threatening times. Forty-five minutes before Key West and grateful for the unexpected privacy that had exacted a terrifying price, she changed into the clothes that would facilitate the sea leg of her journey. She had no choice but to be a chameleon. *Camaleón.* To protect herself, she would have to think in Spanish.

At six-twenty—afternoon for some passengers, evening for others— the Peninsula & Occidental steamship entered Havana's Harbor Channel. Lola stood at the rail wearing an ill-fitting dark gray suit serviceable for a factory worker's Sunday, white shirt loose in the collar, tie striped black and dull blue. Her right hand clamping a battered gray fedora to her head, she studied Morro Castle and its famous lighthouse on her left then Old Havana on her right. Despite the warmth and humidity draping her like a second skin, she shivered.

Ashore, a boy carried her bags to a pink stucco building where a sign read CIUDADANOS DE USA / CITIZENS OF USA. A uniformed immigration officer beckoned her forward, gave a cursory glance at her bags and held out his hand.

Lola wiped perspiration off the back of her neck then presented her American passport. A cutout window in the stiff red cover displayed her unique number.

The immigration officer stamped the required page, returned the passport and said in heavily accented English, "Welcome to Cuba, señor Sobel. A man alone in Havana will find much to enjoy."

# NOVEMBER 1929
# CALLE LAMPARILLA

L ola peered through the arched window's cracked wooden shutters and
again surveyed Calle Lamparilla below. Except at noontime, the street,
narrow as a Manhattan alley, covered life in shadow. This provided shelter
from the blistering Caribbean sun for ground-floor shops meeting the
neighborhood's mundane needs and drab workers' apartments above like
the one in which she found herself confined. The scent of frying onions
entered the apartment along with music. Competing radios and record
players broadcast African rumba with its claves and congas, syncopated
danzón and a number Lola recognized from Eduardo Sánchez de Fuentes'
opera *El Caminante*. What proved festive about Havana left her scowling.

Habaneros celebrated life while she was practically punished rather than
rewarded for escaping New York and its stifling constraints. The cramped
apartment of Elena Mendoza-Torres, who'd met her at Immigration,
seemed more a cell. The living area barely contained a square, reddish-
brown Cuban mahogany table, one leg evidencing the amputation of a
clawed foot and propped up by a block of wood, and two chairs. Three
paces distant stood a small icebox, aged stove and leaking sink. A single
bare bulb hung from the bowed ceiling. Elena insisted that it be left off
during the daytime. Wedged into a tiny alcove was a loveseat with sagging
cushions. Offering little more space than the adjacent seats in the Havana
Special's chair car, it served as Lola's bed. Elena, the sister of Maribel, the
Sobels' maid, slept in a bedroom barely larger than an ample closet. Thank
God they had a bathroom.

Lola thought it past time that she venture out by herself—as herself. As
a woman, she'd explored Manhattan from Harlem to Greenwich Village.

Elena dissented. Lola did not appreciate the dangers lying in wait for a young woman in Havana, particularly one lacking papers. In a nation of volatile politics and frequent violence, Elena envisioned Lola being swept up along with Communists and innocents when the Sección de Expertos—the secret police—raided a crowded plaza or marketplace. For that matter, she could be singled out on a whim. God knew what might happen and without the intervention of Jesús, where would she be? Lola maintained that she understood the perils she faced but would not allow them to stand in the way of a bright future as a musician. And yes, she was prepared to ward off Cuban men.

Despite her bravado, Lola's brow furrowed seemingly of its own accord. Men always held the advantage. Albert Sobel, the male self she sought to abandon but on whom she still depended—for now—flaunted an American passport. She conceded that this offered Lola Torres a unique benefit. Albert—Alberto—could freely wander the Old City, study its rhythms, observe its people. In doing so, he could inform Lola as to how Cuban men approached women, their suggestive language, their insistent hands. Seeing life through Alberto's eyes would enhance Lola's ability to survive.

On this early Saturday afternoon, Calle Lamparilla appeared deserted except for a three-legged dog gnawing at a discarded bone and another mongrel savaging a rat. Residents and shopkeepers occupied themselves with the day's main meal, napped or defied the tropical heat by slaking their various thirsts, whether induced by love or lust. Lola looked up. A single white cloud sailed across a river of pale turquoise, peered down on peeling walls in faded pastels—green, blue, yellow, pink. Shallow balconies enclosed by black iron grillwork, some displaying flowers, added relief to endless planes of flat walls rising one or two stories above the shops.

Lola confronted a measure of guilt. How could she be so unkind to Elena, who owed her nothing? Had nothing. Forty-one and alone, the broad-shouldered, wide-hipped baker's assistant, whose muscular arms and thick hands implied she could rip a telephone book in half like a carnival strongman, worked long days just to get by. Yet after receiving Maribel's impassioned letters, she provided a haven to a young woman trapped in a man's body. No one Elena knew would understand what she'd agree to do let alone approve.

Maribel had hinted that there was more to Elena's desire to help. Years before, Elena gave birth to a daughter, who died days after. Her husband blamed her for their misfortune. Then she gave birth to a stillborn son. Her husband left. Lola believed that in offering compassion to a younger woman treated badly, Elena exercised her motherly instincts.

Elena was proving to be a conspirator as resourceful as willing. While she had little to do with her neighbors, she understood that curious eyes constantly observed the street and tongues wagged. In response, she had dropped a passing comment to the old woman upstairs. Within an hour, the entire street knew that Elena's nephew Alberto had arrived from America. His twin sister, visiting family in the countryside, would follow. When, Elena could not say.

Aggravated by her confinement, Lola closed her eyes and grit her teeth. Only Alberto remained free to explore. Admittedly, Lola hadn't felt restive during her first few days with Elena when she wished only to sleep and eat. She freely accepted the restrictions imposed upon her by a woman she took to as a loving but iron-willed aunt. She also conceded that despite the porter's best efforts, modest yellow and purple bruises had blossomed on her cheek and beneath her eye. They might draw little notice on a man's face—perhaps draw praise for his machismo, considering the blows he might have landed on the other fellow—but would bring unwanted attention to any young woman in the neighborhood, particularly a stranger.

Lola stood on the verge of rebellion. Two nights earlier, her frustration had surged like a turbulent sea washing over the Malecón, the boulevard lining the city's northeastern shoreline. Alberto had guided Lola along the Prado where, evenings and Sunday afternoons, men and women promenaded beneath broad trees and the towering dome of El Capitolio. Alberto noted the new capitol building's resemblance to the American Capitol in Washington. After they returned to the apartment, Lola proposed to Elena that she begin to explore the city on her own.

Elena disagreed.

A discussion followed in hushed tones, as opposed to the Sobels who, excepting Mama, argued in voices best described as fortissimo. Lola suggested a compromise. They would venture out together. Evenings provided an appropriate time for a young woman to take the sea air accompanied by her aunt.

Elena, wary of keeping a lid on a boiling pot, relented.

Of necessity, the outing proved brief. Elena went to bed early to rise at three-fifteen each morning except Monday for her job at the Hotel Santa Isabel across from the Plaza de Armas. Still, Lola delighted in the gentle breeze ruffling the hem of her skirt and fondling her legs.

Upon returning from work the following afternoon, Elena announced that she'd found Lola a possible job.

"I will play piano at the hotel?" Lola asked. She intended to play and sing with bands in Havana as she had in New York. In the interim, she would condescend to provide background music in proper bars like that in the Hotel Santa Isabel.

"Hotels and nightclubs will have to wait," said Elena. "When you have gone about Old Havana as Lola sufficiently, we will complete the fabrication of your story. Then you can pursue your musical career and not, God willing, seem a rabbit pulled from a hat."

"This job? Am I to work with you in the bakery?"

Elena took Lola's hands. "I would never allow *these* to be endangered." It happened that the manager of the hotel's restaurant mentioned to the baker that the general manager's young daughter studied piano. Her mother was displeased with her teacher. The child was sweet, but the mother imagined her another Ernestina Lecuona. "She is very difficult, the mother. I remarked that my nephew from America is an exceptional musician and a wonderful teacher. I am hoping the mother will speak with Alberto."

"I do not wish to teach children," said Lola. "Certainly not as Alberto."

Elena pointed out that the mother would pay well and might recommend Lola to her friends and the women at her church.

"I do not care," said Lola. How long would Alberto remain in Havana, forcing her to hide for all but a few minutes in the evening?

Elena offered a simple answer. "As long as necessary." She had promised Maribel that she would protect Lola, and while Lola spoke Spanish like a habanera, she was not one. Not yet. "Would you like coffee?" she asked.

Lola declined. Her voice feigned contrition. To be angry with Elena would display ingratitude.

As Elena puttered at the stove, Lola took clothes and a small bag from her valise at the end of the loveseat, entered the bathroom and locked the door. Even after Elena called to her, she applied makeup and slipped into a yellow cotton dress with an open-weave lace top and long sleeves. She studied herself in the cracked mirror. The dim light revealed her thinning hair—the single defect that could keep her from achieving success in a city famed for glamorous women. She leaned closer, frowned then smiled. While not a classic beauty—such women struck her as insipid—she had every confidence that her face expressed both a delicacy of feature and depth of character capable of charming an audience. She returned to the living area where Elena again sat at the table, held out her skirt and twirled like a ballerina.

Elena shot to her feet. "¡Dios mío!" she said, as if Lola had waved a sign demanding the downfall of President Machado.

"If I do not go out as Lola, by myself, I shall go mad," Lola replied with a dramatic flair she imagined worthy of the legendary Sarah Bernhardt.

"So now, not only Calle Lamparilla but all of Havana will enjoy the very visible presence of Alberto *and* Lola?"

"Why not?" Granted, Alberto embodied an affront to her true self. But Lola, even at the risk of being considered perverse, enjoyed playing the role of twins. Her distinctive nature long had demanded the skills of an accomplished actress, the ability to cloak reality in illusion. Hadn't she deceived the neighbors?

If they weren't careful, Elena insisted, the neighbors soon enough would uncover her—their—double game.

"You worry too much," said Lola. "Women in the comedies of Shakespeare often assume the identity of men and fool everyone."

Elena shook her head. "This is not your Shakespeare. This is *life*." She gripped Lola's shoulders as if to lift her off the floor. What about her protector's position did Lola not understand? Last month, the hotel cut the wages of the entire staff. It took all her strength to pay rent and put food on her table. Food for *two*. And God protect her in her old age.

"I will be famous and take care of you," Lola said.

"Until then?"

A knock on the door interrupted them.

Elena motioned Lola to retreat to the bathroom.

Inside, Lola bent down and peered through the keyhole.

Elena opened the door to a man wearing a soiled jacket and an open-collared white shirt badly in need of laundering. A green scarf coiled snake-like like around his neck. "Hector!" Elena said with a catch in her throat. She raised up on her toes and threw her arms around him.

Despite her limited field of vision, Lola noted a startling resemblance. Then she understood. Hector was the brother once mentioned by Elena, the very same for whom Maribel often wept, having not heard from him in years. Their differences also were striking. Ten years younger than Elena, Hector was tall and disturbingly thin, his cheekbones less prominent than exposed. His weathered caramel face set off eyes flashing a boyish impishness. They divulged the restless energy of a man defiant of the social order that placed him at its margins and the resilience of one who, despite his defeats, believed triumph inevitable.

Elena had not seen Hector in at least a year. "And not a single letter."

Hector collapsed onto a chair. "I have been in Camagüey under a different name. Mostly with a band playing in the hotels."

That Hector was a musician, Lola had not known. She barely avoided calling out.

Elena sat and placed a hand on Hector's lined cheek. She feared that such a ravaged condition resulted from something other than playing congas.

The life of a musician was hard, he reminded her. Bandleaders and managers made all the money, mostly by stealing from their musicians. "Also, there was a bit of a commotion."

"In Havana or Camagüey?"

Hector laughed. "Both." He laid his right hand over his stomach. He'd been in Havana three days without a decent meal.

Elena fried an egg with sausage, set down cheese alongside half a loaf of day-old bread from the hotel and poured coffee.

Hector asked for rum.

Elena produced a half-filled bottle and a glass. "The police? Again?"

As Hector ate, he answered that yes, the police were looking for him. And no, they would never find him. "They could reach into their trousers and not find their pitos."

"Hector! Such language!"

Lola found no reason for Elena's reprimand. Albert had heard such words in English and Yiddish. A more serious matter concerned her. What would happen if the police came? Would they arrest Elena, too? And what if their questions extended beyond a brother and sister?

Unaware of the additional danger he'd brought with him, Hector raised his hands in submission and offered a smile of accommodation. Then his mouth contorted in anger. He banged his hands on the table. What the police did, he insisted, was not seek out criminals but manufacture them by keeping people from making an honest living. He raised his hands and motioned around the apartment to point out the shoddiness in which his sister dwelled.

"My life is fine," Elena countered.

Lola conceded that if Hector seemed dramatic, his views were shared by others.

Hector tilted back in his chair then rocked forward. The front legs slammed the floor with the rage of a gunshot. "You still work six days a week, ten hours a day? Often more?" Her problem was that she let the government, the bosses and the priests tell her what to think. Anyway, she had nothing to fear. Before the police would consider coming here, he would be gone. He finished the rum and held out his glass.

Prudence yielding to curiosity, Lola stepped out of the bathroom.

Hector's eyes grew wide. He stood.

Elena collapsed onto the other chair.

Lola's breathing quickened. Standing close and without the limitations imposed by the keyhole, she found Hector potentially as handsome as her once-favorite Hollywood heartthrob, Rudolph Valentino, whose funeral three years earlier impelled her to join a hundred thousand mourners lining the streets of Manhattan. Clearly, Hector's life had diminished, although not obliterated, his striking looks. Did he find her appealing? Under different circumstances—he was Elena and Maribel's brother, after all, and something of an older man—she might be attracted to him. But towards what end? Romance and courtship? Or just sex. This was the Twentieth Century after all, and forward-thinking women insisted on their right to physical pleasure, an idea which, unfortunately, most men rejected. As Lola, she'd had only a single experience, horrible and confusing. Still, she often thought about physical intimacy even if she remained unsure as to what to expect. Albert knew nothing since Papa avoided discussing the subject. Well, she did know that a penis entered a vagina. Or other places.

The boys in school constantly whispered and giggled about such things, and in the absence of girls or adults, shouted insults relating to sex. These were crude and often related to Albert. But sex had to involve something more. Only, what if it didn't?

Had Mama acknowledged her as Lola, perhaps she would have enlightened her middle daughter. But Lola suspected, as all children did even as adults, that Mama knew little beyond the basics. Even that would have helped.

Now, despite her natural urges, Lola saw sex as posing serious risks. Did the particulars of her anatomy restrict her choice of people to sleep with? To love? She was a woman, so naturally she took an interest in men. But the term *natural* seemed abhorrent. What *was* natural? And what about women? Could she desire them, too? Men *and* women?

Hector smiled. "And who is this beautiful young lady?"

Elena glared.

Despite her unease, Lola radiated delight.

"This is Lola," said Elena, "our distant cousin from New York."

Lola waited for Elena to mention Albert. When she didn't, Lola hid a small sigh of relief. Either Elena's excitement overcame her or she feared revealing a complicated situation that might lead to Hector's discovering the truth.

"New York?" Hector responded. He knew that Maribel lived there, or used to, working for a family of wealthy Jews. "Is Maribel still there?"

Elena informed him that Maribel was well.

Hector examined Lola's fair skin. "I think our delightful Lola is perhaps a *very* distant cousin."

"Yes," said Lola. She couldn't help adding, "Also a musician."

Hector held out his arms.

Lola stepped into his embrace. The stubble on his cheeks grazed the soft skin of her own, coated by a fine blonde down that, in high school, provoked teasing from schoolmates and his cousins.

Hector released Lola and stepped back. If only he could stay in Havana, he told her. It was the only place in Cuba for a serious man with serious ambitions. He cocked his head. "And what do you play, Cousin Lola?"

"Piano," Lola said. She thought it pretentious to mention she also had mastered the violin.

Hector's hands mimed dancing over a keyboard. "I wish I could hear you play, but I cannot stay."

"You must leave Havana again?" Elena asked.

Hector smirked like a man with a secret.

Elena sighed. The simple act related a story with which Lola was familiar. After their father died so young, their impoverished mother sent Maribel to relatives in America. Then their mother died. Hector ran wild in the streets. He often disappeared not just for days but weeks. "Now I will lose you *again?*"

Hector had been given no choice. Life had not been kind.

Elena went to what served as her kitchen and returned with a white rag and three sugar cookies on a small plate, its rim decorated with tiny red roses and marred by a thumbnail-size chip. She wrapped the remains of the cheese and bread in the rag and tied it with a piece of string.

Hector accepted the package with a bow then slipped the cookies into his jacket pocket.

"Where will you go?" asked Lola.

Hector pressed a finger to his lips.

Elena took Hector in her arms.

"If God is kind, my dear sister, we will see each other again." He turned to Lola. "And *you,* my cousin."

An hour after the bells of the Baroque La Catedral de San Cristobal sounded noon on Sunday, Elena still at work, Lola strolled the cobblestoned Jewish Market. She wore the yellow cotton dress and a broad-brimmed white hat. Habaneros swirled around her. The men wore suits as ill-fitting and threadbare as Alberto's, their heads covered by tattered fedoras, homburgs and straw boaters. Periodically, one cast Lola a glance as if sizing up a potential conquest.

Lola paused to listen to a changüí tune playing in the distance. Its pulsing percussion suggested the secret police pounding on doors. At a small, umbrella-topped table filled with magazines, she picked up an old copy of *Social*. Its creased cover displayed an illustration in the style of a tiled mosaic depicting a bare-breasted woman carrying the emblematic masks of Greek theater. Her own life surely consisted of comedy and tragedy. Both reflected her daring escape from New York leading to virtual imprisonment in Havana. At last, she had won her freedom. On such a day with such a blue sky, the air filled with music, not even Elena could expect her to remain locked away like Rapunzel in her tower.

Around Lola, women in well-worn dresses combed through piles of shoes, men's ties, lingerie, table lamps, frying pans, fountain pens, cheap jewelry, hairbrushes and sewing materials. They searched for flaws that would enable them to drive down prices. The Polacos—Jewish merchants from Eastern Europe—were formidable bargainers like their brethren pushcart peddlers and shop owners on Manhattan's Lower East Side. From every direction, Yiddish rang out. Even non-Jews haggled with Yiddish words and phrases.

A piano drew Lola's attention. She walked towards a battered upright. A young boy in shorts and an oversized sailor shirt frayed at the cuffs struck the yellowed, cracked keys as if wielding a hammer. He produced random notes foreign to anything resembling rhythm or melody. A man and a woman, both dark-skinned, hovered over the boy. The mother turned to the father. The father made no effort to hide his pained expression.

A pale-skinned man Papa's age, his suit wrinkled and in need of cleaning, tapped the father on the shoulder. "A piano like this," he said in Yiddish. "Perfect for a young boy, he should become learned in music and also a scholar."

The boy used a knuckle to thump an A-flat and then another.

The merchant switched to Spanish constricted by a heavy Yiddish accent. "Such talent this boy has."

The parents exchanged looks as if they'd discovered their winning lottery ticket was counterfeit. The mother dragged the boy away. The father smiled and followed.

"A piano like this, so beautiful it makes music," the merchant cried after them. His voice registered dejection. "A price this good no one else will give."

Lola approached.

The merchant's eyes brightened. "A piano you want?" he said in Spanish. "Perfect for a young lady of obvious refinement."

Lola hid her disagreement out of kindness to a fellow Jew. The rickety piano offered no comparison to the brand-new baby grand Papa and Mama gave Albert for his fifth birthday. Still, Lola longed to caress the keys with her fingertips, play a brief tune. She hesitated. What if Papa and Mama suspected Maribel's involvement with Albert's supposed death and forced her to confess? What if at this moment a private detective was here in Havana asking questions? Wandering the Jewish Market? She scowled. What if? Should she spend the rest of her life asking that question? She'd come to Cuba to play piano as Lola Torres. How could she forge a new life if she gave in to her fears? Resolute, she sat on the mismatched bench and played an afrocubanismo tune to which she often listened on her family's Victor Orthophonic Victrola.

A crowd gathered.

As she played, Lola glanced around. She thought she recognized a familiar face at the crowd's edge, but it vanished just as a heavyset woman with bright red hair elbowed her way to the piano. The woman's left eye stared straight ahead, immobile, the creation of an artisan in glass. Her right scanned the area as if searching for someone disagreeable then fixed on Lola. It hinted of an unspoken recognition. Lola wondered if the woman knew she was Jewish. The woman appeared to be a fellow Israelite, her pale skin and facial features resembling those of the Sobels. More, the woman bore a likeness to one of Mama's favorite singers, Sophie Tucker, the self-professed "last of the red-hot mamas," who made popular both the tender "My Yiddishe Momme" and the lusty "Nobody Loves a Fat Girl, But Oh How a Fat Girl Can Love."

Disregarding the glass-eyed woman, as well as the piano's need for tuning, Lola played on. When she stopped, the crowd applauded. Elated, Lola stood and bowed.

"For *you*," the merchant said in Spanish, "I can give a special price." He placed his hand over his heart. "My family should forgive the sacrifice."

"Thank you, but I don't need a piano right now," Lola, without thinking, returned in Yiddish.

The merchant grinned. "A Yiddishe maidele! I knew even before you opened your mouth. From where you came?"

Acknowledging that she could no more recall her words than an archer the arrow he'd just loosed from his bow, Lola returned in Yiddish, "From *there*."

"More, no need to say. My family— We are *here* until we can go to America. If America again lets Jews enter."

"What is so wonderful about America?" Lola asked, having just abandoned the new Promised Land.

The merchant shook his head in wonderment as if he'd been asked whether God existed and watched over the people Israel.

A bearded man—another Jew—interrupted. He held up a violin, its varnish worn, its E string snapped.

The merchant turned towards his new prospect.

Lola stepped away.

A young man only an inch taller and slight of build cut her off. He tugged on his short-billed flat cap, the kind worn by golfers and newsboys. "You are very talented," he said in Yiddish. "But I wouldn't let it go to your head."

Lola took note of his sallow face. It attested to much time spent indoors. Yet highlighted by a prominent nose setting off gray eyes, it exuded a combination of energy and earnestness, both unrelenting. His erect bearing suggested a brashness like Hector's. He also dressed as badly. His striped, gray coat was hopelessly mismatched to checked gray trousers. His scuffed shoes seemed on the verge of disintegration. Under his left arm, he carried a brown leather artist's portfolio as worn as his shoes. In all, Lola found him lacking any pretense of charm although possessing a certain vague attractiveness. She smiled.

"I hope you know you have broken that poor merchant's heart."

Lola glanced back at the piano where the red-haired woman remained as if waiting for someone.

"The Cubans—" said the young man.

Lola turned back to her accuser.

"—think all Jews on this island are rich." He acknowledged that might be true of the Americans and most of the Turcos from Aleppo and Istanbul, but the Polacos from Europe like them—he'd overheard her Yiddish—were poor. *Most* of the Polacos. Given her obvious musical education, she was one of the fortunate ones. As such, she shared their guilt. "Your family became wealthy climbing on the backs of their own people."

Lola wondered if she'd overestimated the man's attractiveness. "Do you always introduce yourself to women in this way?"

"Do you always treat poor merchants with such disdain?"

Lola found herself tongue-tied. She'd never held the poor in contempt. Besides, despite the young man's gaunt appearance, she had to admit he was almost handsome.

Also, adamant. The majority of Polacos worked in factories or peddled in the streets. The Cubans blamed them for the bad economy and even banned Jewish street peddlers from selling at intersections, although God knew—this represented a figure of speech, God being a bourgeois concept—they made little enough money as it was.

Lola stuck out her chin in defiance. "And *I* am the cause of their problems?"

The young man looked skyward then shifted his gaze down and peered into Lola's eyes.

Lola found herself more disturbed—and more fascinated.

If a Jew failed to understand what he'd just told her, the young man insisted, what would become of the world? "If you are not with *us*, you are with *them*."

Lola returned his gaze. "And who is *us*?" She took a half-step back. Something in his eyes unsettled her. Elena had warned Alberto that the Sección de Expertos was not above recruiting an attractive young woman from the small group of Polacos who safeguarded their prosperity by kissing the backsides of those in power. Such spies would ferret out Jews sympathetic to the Communists and others encouraging revolution. On the other hand, Lola reasoned, most young Polaco men, unlike the Turcos, arrived in Cuba without families. His attentions towards a woman would be natural.

The young man, searching for an answer or unwilling to provide one, narrowed his eyes and clenched his jaw.

Lola remained unsure what to make of him. She didn't object to a passion for politics. Papa and Uncle Mendel discussed politics the way rabbis discussed Talmud—incessantly and often in furious disagreement.

"*Us*," the young man finally replied. He turned his head this way and that then took Lola's arm.

They strolled through the market like a young couple recently joined in marriage under the chuppah. Surely, these hardly were the kind of people to whom the Sección de Expertos would turn their attention. As they threaded their way through the crowd, he leaned his shoulder into hers. "*We*," he said, his voice hushed, "are the Sección Hebrea."

"And the Sección Hebrea is what?" Lola asked, her voice lowered sufficiently to impress him as an empathetic companion rather than an interrogator.

His eyes combed the crowd before answering. The Sección Hebrea struggled to free workers from their chains in Havana and in the countryside. Over centuries, the sugar barons imported a million black slaves. Then they brought tens of thousands of free blacks from Haiti, Jamaica and across the Caribbean to work for starvation wages. Justice demanded that someone free these victims of capitalism from lives of misery. Workers everywhere in the world must rise up and be freed!

"You are a Communist!" she whispered.

He raised a finger to his lips.

Lola almost stumbled. What if they *did* appear suspicious? What if, after they said their goodbyes, the secret police arrested this young man? Would he give in to their threats and provide information about his activities? If that proved insufficient, would he disregard her innocence and betray her? God help Lola Torres if the secret police discovered she was the American Albert Sobel. A stranger in a strange land, she could find herself in new and far more dangerous shackles. Who would serve as her redeemer?

He placed a hand on her cheek, exhibiting a surprising gentleness, then dropped it.

She wished he'd left it there.

"Look around," he said. "Not with your eyes but with your heart." Cuba was a Catholic nation, he explained, so the big department stores like El Encanto closed on Sundays. The Jewish Market had struggled to stay open since merchants who observed Shabbos on Saturday couldn't take two days off and make a living. The Sección Hebrea assisted their cause, although it had to plead with the Turcos and Americans for support.

Lola, consumed by music rather than politics, found herself uncertain. Papa and Uncle Mendel, who derided communism, employed dozens of men—mostly Jews—in their factory and paid reasonable wages. Still, they made their employees work on Shabbos. They invited anyone expressing dissatisfaction to open a business of his own, as her grandfather had done in Warsaw before his sons moved it to America. See how easy that was! She also wondered whether this young man and others like him did anything but talk. "Tell me, what exactly do *you* do?" she asked.

They circled back to their starting point. The young man untied his portfolio and drew out a pencil illustration of a nude woman with long dark hair covering her breasts.

Lola raised her hand to her mouth.

"Do I shock you?" he asked.

Lola lowered her hand. "*You* drew this?"

He was an artist. At least he hoped to be, which meant earning an honest living selling his art as did men and women—women played an equal role in the movement—who labored in stores, in factories and on farms. For bread, he worked for a Jew from Krakow who wholesaled textiles on Calle Muralla. As to the drawing, she should buy it now. Secret police were everywhere. If they were watching, they would think only that a struggling artist had taken great pains to make a sale, though spending time with her was anything but painful. "The next time we meet, I will return your purchase price."

Lola opened her handbag and found the conductor's second dollar bill.

The young man took it and turned to step away.

Lola grabbed his arm. Why should initiating a relationship be the privilege only of men? "And when," she asked, "will that be?"

"Next Sunday," he said. "The steps of El Capitolio. Four o'clock."

Lola had not anticipated meeting a man. Not so soon. But what purpose could be served spending a life she was free to invent as a recluse? "Yes," she said.

He pointed to the drawing in her hand. "Good choice," he said, too loud for a normal conversation but sufficient to be overheard by someone from the Sección de Expertos. He walked off.

Lola's elation turned to anxiety. Had she been foolish to make such a promise? Although that promise was hardly a vow. If she broke it, what were the chances he would find her again unless she returned to the Jewish Market? But she very much wished to see him. Her thoughts plunged from a great height back to earth when a Yiddish tune sounded on the piano, the music comfortingly familiar albeit played with little technique.

She turned to see the one-eyed, red-haired woman at the keyboard. The woman stopped playing and beckoned Lola forward.

Lola drew near.

The woman leaned close and whispered in her ear.

# NOVEMBER 1929

# CLUB GARDENIA

Seated at the white Bosendorfer grand on Club Gardenia's palm-flanked bandstand, Lola fixed her gaze just beyond the stage's apron.

Frida Herskovits sat at a small table. She wore a simple, long-sleeve white blouse and gray skirt, the outfit similar to the one she'd chosen for the Jewish Market. But now, a strand of expensive pearls curled around her neck and a silver broach encasing a large ruby over her heart drew attention from her artificial eye. Her right hand, the nails a bright crimson, twirled a long black cigarette holder with an ivory tip.

Next to her sat a short man with a barrel chest, the club's silver-haired bandleader Eduardo Ruiz. His left hand held a glass of rum. His right brandished a cigar at which he glowered.

In the wings, musicians and dancers stood silent except for the shuffling of feet.

Ruiz looked up. "So, you are the woman of mystery about whom Frida speaks with such enthusiasm." He waved his hand. A tendril of cigar smoke arced in the club's dim light. "You have come prepared?"

"Yes," said Lola, who considered her response anything but a falsehood. While having no opportunity to prepare for her audition over the past twenty-four hours let alone since boarding the Havana Special, she'd made herself ready for years.

"Yes, *Maestro*," Ruiz urged, his voice demanding.

"Yes, Maestro."

"Then show us."

To display her virtuosity—most leading Cuban musicians were classically trained—Lola played elements of Ravel followed by the young

Cuban composer Gonzalo Roig. The piano's bright treble, focused mid-range and clear bass supported both her technical mastery and her ability to express the passion the notes as written only suggested. To showcase her voice, she began singing Sindo Garay's *trova* anthem to women, "Mujer Bayamesa." A classic, she'd performed it hundreds of times. But after concluding the first stanza, the familiar lyrics slipped away. Her cheeks hot, her lips and tongue frozen, she envisioned her dreams stillborn. Yet her hands demonstrated a life of their own. She began to play Perucho Figueredo's "La Bayama," which three decades earlier had become Cuba's national anthem. Only later would she consider each title's reference to the city that played an important role in the war of independence from Spain.

As Lola sang "Hasten to battle, men of Bayamo!" Frida stood followed by the reluctant Ruiz.

Lola continued:

> *The motherland looks proudly to you;*
> *Do not fear a glorious death,*
> *Because to die for the fatherland is to live.*

When she finished, the wings erupted with loud murmurs of approval.

Frida said nothing. Ruiz's silence bellowed displeasure.

The wings went mute.

Lola's hands dropped from the keyboard. Her shoulders slumped.

Ruiz licked his thin lips. He appeared to relish his display of domination intended to humble a young pianist arrogant enough to believe herself worthy to play for the Eduardo Ruiz Orchestra. He puffed on his cigar, drained his rum then ran a finger along his trim silver mustache. After examining his polished nails, he cleared his throat and held up his glass.

A young woman in a white smock refilled it.

Ruiz sipped, contemplated his cigar then asked, "Do you read music?"

"Yes, of course," Lola answered.

"Yes, of course, *Maestro*!" Ruiz reminded her.

Recognizing the delicacy of her position, Lola demonstrated restraint. She'd come to Club Gardenia to secure a position with what Frida assured her was one of Havana's leading bands. The red-headed woman had failed to mention undergoing an inquisition conducted by a man surely

Havana's most difficult bandleader. But if launching her career required subordinating herself to Eduardo Ruiz, she would indulge him. "Yes, of course, *Maestro*."

Ruiz snapped his fingers.

The young woman handed Lola sheet music.

"A new song I have just written," said Ruiz.

Lola's eyes skimmed the page. She immediately transposed to a key better suited to her voice, played the introduction as if she'd done so at every club performance in New York and began singing.

> *A woman longs for a man.*
> *She surrenders her soul to his.*
> *She makes his strength her own,*
> *Pledges that he holds her heart in his hands.*

She thought the lyrics as pedestrian as they were offensive. Why did Latin men insist that women were inferior? Why did men everywhere think that? Still, she embraced each word, brought the Maestro's lyrics alive with the many colors of her voice and sophisticated phrasing, demonstrated a polished technique expected of a performer approaching forty rather than twenty.

Ruiz's cigar hand drummed the table.

The wings burst with applause and shouts of approval.

Ruiz held up his hand. Cigar ash scattered around him.

Yet again, the wings quieted.

Frida smiled.

Lola suspected that Ruiz struggled to conceal that same response.

"You have classical training," Ruiz said. "The Havana School of Music? With Roig himself?" He tapped his glass on the table in 6/8 time then proclaimed, "I would have heard of you."

Heat infused Lola's body as if she sat beneath the summer sun on Varadero beach. What accounted for the Maestro's hostility? Yesterday, Frida took her from the Jewish Market, whose noise and bustle offered her an odd sense of peace, to a café. There she explained the club's predicament and painted a picture of the new life Lola would enjoy, granting that she knew nothing of Lola's old one. Acknowledging that Ruiz required some explanation regarding her training, Lola said, "I have had several teachers. Here and there."

Ruiz drew another puff from his cigar and raised his meticulously barbered head to follow the smoke he emitted as it ascended to the ceiling. "We have here a woman of mystery," he said as if in conversation with God. He glanced down at Frida then returned his gaze to Lola. "You say you are called Lola, but you withhold your family name. You speak like a habanera, but one senses that your origins lie elsewhere." He smiled. "Or perhaps you are a goddess." He turned towards the wings. "Venus born fully formed from the sea."

The wings returned laughter.

"But," Ruiz continued, "Venus with a talent rarely encountered." He hummed several bars from his new song, emulating Lola's interpretation. "So let us review what we know."

Club Gardenia was redecorating and in the midst of producing a new show on a scale grander than any Havana had seen. This revelation prompted him to throw both arms into the air. "So why has God put all these obstacles in my way?" Two days earlier, a Cuban-American bandleader named Xavier Cugat stole his pianist, Guillermo Benitez, to make films in Hollywood. Later that same day—that very day—his vocalist, Teresa Aguilar, suffered terrible injuries in an automobile accident. Despite these acts of God—or the Devil—Club Gardenia would open in three days. "Nonetheless, hiring Lola Whatever-She-Is-Called would require an act of faith."

Frida ground the remains of Ruiz's cigar into a crystal ashtray. "Eduardo, rising from bed each morning requires an act of faith. When yesterday I heard Lola play, I knew she could replace Guillermo. And she is a better singer than Teresa." She mounted the bandstand, sat next to Lola and circled her arm around Lola's waist. "This young woman, this Lola, she is special."

"I agreed she has talent," said Ruiz.

"Then why have you a problem?" Frida asked

Ruiz stood and crossed his arms. Talent, he insisted, is like a boat sailing from the harbor to show its guests a day of pleasure. A good captain readies his vessel so that should Poseidon betray him, he will find his way back to port. "Is this one willing to learn what only the Maestro can teach?"

Frida held out her right hand and flicked it downward.

Ruiz dropped into his seat.

Frida pulled Lola close. "Yes, you are a mystery, my pretty Lola. But Havana will be fascinated as *I* am fascinated." She eyed Ruiz then turned back to Lola. In a voice seemingly intimate yet loud enough for everyone to hear she explained that while she and not the Maestro owned Club Gardenia, the club's renovation required assistance from several investors. These were men of importance, who would be displeased by any delay in Club Gardenia's reopening, scheduled with great fanfare for Thursday evening. Therefore, the matter was settled. Lola was a gift from the Almighty. She would step into rehearsals immediately and, like everyone else, work day and night to make this effort a success.

Lola beamed. She had met her redeemer.

Frida looked towards the stage's wings and snapped her fingers. "Fernando!"

The tall, slim man—older than Hector but much younger than Papa—led Lola down a short passageway behind the stage. They arrived at Club Gardenia's costume shop and wardrobe where two women, one gray-haired, the other young and dark, sat at sewing machines. He dismissed them and locked the door.

Lola tried to appraise this man called Fernando, evidently the club's costumer given the yellow measuring tape around his neck. In keeping with such a position, he presented the image of someone fastidious about even casual dress given his white shirt as spotless as Hector Torres' had been soiled, straw-colored linen slacks held up by suspenders striped aquamarine and magenta, and copper-and-chocolate brogues with two-inch heels creating the illusion of a six-footer.

Fernando stepped forward.

Lola rocked back on her more modest heels.

"It is important that no one disturbs us," he said. "We have little time to make ready our woman of mystery."

His reference to her unrevealed identity left her uneasy.

"But I must properly introduce myself," he said. "I am called Fernando Fallon."

"Fallon?"

"My grandfather came to Cuba from Ireland and married a woman of many bloods. And your family?"

Lola suspected that Fernando Fallon sought to disarm her to unearth the truth. Obviously, he was doing this at Frida's bidding.

He laughed.

She wondered if he'd read her mind.

"Oh, I know you," he said. "Frida has spoken with me, and observation tells me the rest."

Lola clenched her jaw.

His eyes expressed amusement. "What is it the American president Abraham Lincoln once said? You cannot fool all of the people all of the time?"

The reference to Lincoln chilled her despite the room's warmth. What did Fernando know? She could not believe that he understood her to be an American. To have *been* an American. Perhaps Frida had disclosed that she, like herself, was a Jewess, but that would be of little significance. None. This left the most frightening possibility. At either the Jewish Market or the café afterwards, she had betrayed herself, exhibited to Frida without knowing a telltale male mannerism. Was it possible? Alberto had left New York with her and remained in Havana, but she could deal with his presence. Lola Torres had made her way throughout New York without discovery, facilitated her deception with attention to the smallest detail. Although she balked at the word *deception*. She'd presented herself as a woman because she *was* a woman. It was Albert who drew attention to himself with his small displays of femininity. Yet none of her reasoning—her rationalizing—mattered. Lola Torres had tipped her hand. Frida Herskovits, despite their shared Jewish background, was playing with her, prodding her to confess, intent on punishing her for violating the commandment prohibiting men from dressing as women, and women as men. The invitation to audition for the club's re-opening served only as a ruse by which Frida pursued sadistic, self-righteous pleasure. And Fernando? Did he seek to gain her confidence so that he might expose her with a certainty she could never contest? In doing so, might he attempt to seduce her? Take her by force?

Fernando held his palms up. "So, a young musician of extraordinary talent suddenly appears in Havana like—" He scratched his chin. "What the Maestro said."

She saw in his eyes not malevolence but confusion, innocence. She now believed he knew nothing unless he was an accomplished actor. Still, she could not let down her defenses. She masked her apprehension with a jaw-jutting look of defiance. "Venus," she started to inform him. As the goddess' name flew from her lips, her new-found courage wavered.

Fernando shook his head. "Cariña, please do not tell me you come from Santiago, Santa Clara, Camagüey or even Bayamo. The island is small, and Fernando Fallon knows everyone."

Lola reflected on what she'd read about magicians, who performed sleight-of-hand by misdirecting their audiences. Having little recourse, she hurled a direct challenge. "Fernando Fallon knows every musician in all of Cuba?"

"Did I say only musicians?" he countered. He placed his hands on her shoulders.

Despite the lightness of his touch, Lola stiffened.

He scrutinized her from head to foot. "Take off your dress."

Lola quivered.

"Cariña," he said, "we have only three days. It is natural that despite your great talent you are nervous, but—" He brought her a chair and motioned her to sit.

She did.

He placed a second chair opposite, its back facing her, and straddled the seat. "Understand, cariña," he said, his voice lowered despite the closed door, "I know all the women in Cuba born as men."

Lola's jaw dropped. Frida and Ruiz *did* know. They were toying with her the way children torment a captive spider. Without doubt, they waited in anticipation for her to flee the costume shop and, all other exits locked, dart across the stage in tears. They would howl in derision. The musicians and dancers would join in. All of them would be heartened that unlike the deviant specimen in retreat, they were normal, decent people. Tomorrow, word would have raced across Havana, across the island. Elena would sob and scold, perhaps beat her. The police would come. She would suffer wounds forever defiant of healing.

Lola's chest heaved. Again, she stood at a crossroad but now with no one to come to her aid. She had to choose a path no matter how great the risk. Bolting the costume shop in hysterics would present a wordless confession that Frida and the others were correct. She was an aberration, an offense to the purpose and harmony of God's creation. But such an accusation was unacceptable. No one could make her believe that she was anything but a full and complete human being created in God's image. A different path would prove equally unpleasant, but it offered the opportunity to deprive them of their anticipated and contemptible victory. She rose to her feet.

Fernando pushed her down.

Lola turned away.

Fernando cradled her chin in his hand and brought her face towards his. "If I wished, cariña, I could have announced to everyone what you are. No. Forgive me. That is unkind. *Who* you are." He lowered his hand. "You are not the first woman I have met who was born what seemed a man. Or a man born a woman."

Lola's eyes widened. Curiosity displaced fear. "And how do you know such people?"

"I see them clearly because I do not hate them."

"Then you are an unusual man."

"I am who I am." He confessed that he was not an educated man—at least in terms of schooling—but he'd read articles in medical journals and books by doctors who studied the matter of men who knew themselves to be women, and women understanding they were men. These doctors believed that everyone should be free to live as they chose. "Look at our Lola. You are slim, you have breasts—yes, they are small but no matter—and hips." She also had no need to shave other than to keep her legs smooth. He himself shaved only every other day but nonetheless was a man. And yes, Frida had informed him that she was a Jewess. "But if I am to keep you safe, you must bare not only your body but also your soul."

Heart pounding, Lola saw herself standing before Fernando as the Israelites had confronted the Red Sea, Pharaoh's army at their backs, the waters not yet parted. Could she summon the faith, the courage, to exercise her only choice? She plunged ahead. "New York," she said. "I was not born in America, but I grew up in New York."

Fernando smiled. "Yes, you have secrets and for good reason. My task is to make certain that the patrons of Club Gardenia and all Havana fall in love with our mysterious Lola." He stood.

Lola rose and slipped out of her dress.

"But there is one challenge," he said. He brushed his fingers through her hair.

*On a March Saturday morning, Papa wraps Albert née Anshel's hand in his. Takes him from the warmth of their building on East 69th Street. A real home after a first American year in Harlem. The office can wait.*

*They survey Manhattan encrusted in snow. Already soot gray. Spotted dog-yellow. Follow the icy path shoveled by the super. Listen to the crunch of their footfalls.*

*Albert delights in seeing his breath. Reaches towards the silver mist. Startles as it eludes his grasp.*

*"An important day, Albert," Papa says. His limited English is hard-won. Albert née Anshel recognizes his American name. Mama never uses it. Papa insists. With Uncle Mendel, he runs Sobel Brothers. Leather handbags, wallets and belts for department stores and fine shops. An American businessman must speak English. An American boy requires an American name.*

*At Second Avenue, they stop. A Ford Model T passes. A Buick and a Chevrolet follow. They cross. Behind them a small procession. A Cadillac. Old Courier Roadster. New 1913 Locomobile. They turn left. Make their way to 65th Street. Arrive at a basement barber shop.*

*The barber displays a middle thick with American prosperity. Unshackled by old-country constraints, sports a broad, brushy mustache. Smooth cheeks. Beard discarded after Ellis Island. "Nu?" he asks. Radiates good cheer. Of course. America is the land of the free.*

*Papa went to the shop the week before. Knows that ten years earlier the barber barely survived the pogrom in Kishinev. Now, fancies himself a Yankee of long standing. Loves baseball. Papa confessed to knowing little. Promised to give the game his attention. His Albert will know everything.*

*Now, Papa's excitement is as self-evident as the red, white and blue pole outside the shop. "My Albert," he says. "This very day, three years old!"*

*The barber smiles. "His first haircut?"*

*Papa betrays discomfort. "Me? His hair I would have had cut long ago. My wife? Still with the old ways."*

*Confusion clouds Albert née Anshel's face. What is a barber?*

*The barber places a child's bench seat across the arms of his chair. Lifts Albert née Anshel.*

*The princeling sits on his throne. His eyes widen.*

*Papa grins. "Sit still like Papa told you."*

*Albert née Anshel complies.*

*The barber drapes him in a white cloth. Steps behind him.*

*Albert née Anshel stares into the mirror. Sees the raised comb and scissors. Shudders. Steel blades sever the first blond locks. He shrieks. His anguish approaches that of Kishinev's victims.*

"You will need a wig," Fernando said, "but that will not be enough. Our Lola must be glamorous. Special." He scratched his chin. A feathered headdress might do, but the dancers wear them. Perhaps a gardenia in her hair. *Two* gardenias. He shook his head. Conventional. Then his face shone. "Let us get started, cariña. We have little time to make Cinderella ready for the royal ball, and I am not a fairy godmother. Well, not exactly."

When Lola returned to the stage, Frida still at the table with Ruiz. Frida gestured to two typewritten documents. They bore her signature.

Lola reached for one of the copies.

Frida held out a pen. "You sign now and begin rehearsal. After, you can read your contract."

Lola took the pen.

Frida leaned closer. "And now the mysterious Lola will reveal her identity. Or whatever identity she wishes to provide."

Nerves interrupted Lola's brief late-afternoon nap. She dashed to the toilet and retched. She hadn't anticipated getting the jitters, but her moment of truth, long anticipated, was only hours off.

Following three days of rehearsal until near sunrise, Ruiz had awarded the musicians and dancers a short break. Lola returned to Elena's apartment confident. Buoyant. From the outset, she'd followed the charts he'd given her with unerring facility. More important, she brought alive the spirit of each tune. The musicians offered abundant praise. The Maestro's reticence—an unknown pianist forced upon him could not possibly play this well—had turned to grudging respect. Now, all that the evening ahead represented staggered her.

After washing her hands, Lola examined her face. The bruises had disappeared, but her mirrored reflection disclosed something more disturbing. Staring back at her was Albert. She blinked. He continued staring, refusing to cut the tether that bound them, threatening to anchor her to a past that would block her passage to the future. Applying makeup, she concealed him—at least temporarily. Whether she wanted him to disappear altogether she remained unsure.

As Lola slipped into a plain cotton dress, Elena entered the apartment. She placed a bag of day-old bread and pastries on the table and, panting, dropped into a chair.

"You worked overtime," said Lola. "I told you, you would not have to do that any longer. You know that Club Gardenia reopens tonight."

"And have they yet paid you?"

Lola approached her. "Are you ill?"

Elena closed her eyes.

Unable to contain herself, Lola went to the sofa and retrieved a large envelope. If the woman to whom she was so indebted was exhausted, this would revive her.

Elena studied a black-and-white photograph of four men in shirts with long, ruffled sleeves and flowing trousers surrounding a slim woman in a form-fitting gown. The woman's sparkling eyes and brilliant lips turned up ever-so-slightly. They hinted at naughty secrets awaiting Havana's discovery. Most striking, she wore a hat twenty inches high made up of gardenias, mariposas, roses, dahlias, gladioli and orchids. "Who is this?" Elena asked.

"This is Lola Flores."

A dozen dancers shimmied as Lola concluded the late show with the final stanza of the new song written by Eduardo Ruiz. His announcement of its composition produced an ovation even before the downbeat.

*I will lose myself in your heart,*

*A prisoner of my love for you.*
*I will wear these chains with joy,*
*Your captive forever.*

As the piano's last notes faded, Lola trembled. Throughout this show and the band's earlier performance, she'd thrilled to the attention directed towards her by Havana's rich and powerful joined by wealthy American tourists who shrugged off Black Tuesday. Yet she found her excitement diluted by apprehension. Despite their enthusiasm, she could not resist speculating whether the audience embraced or mocked her.

As earlier in the evening, applause swept away her doubts. A male chorus reverberated: "Lola! Lola! Lola!"

The Maestro stepped off the bandstand and approached the stage's apron. With his left hand, he raised his trumpet to acknowledge his triumph. With his right, he motioned Lola forward.

The applause and its accompanying chant intensified. Lola felt her heart approach bursting. She had endured so much, journeyed so far. Now, she had triumphed.

Ruiz motioned towards a ringside table where Frida sat with three men clapping each other on the back. Although the table was dimly lit, Lola thought two of the men to be in their twenties. More, they appeared to bear distinctive Jewish features while, as had Albert and Lola, appearing to be very American. The third man seemed several years older than Fernando. Handsome and broad-shouldered, he could have been taken for a movie star—perhaps he was—with his olive complexion, dark eyes and pomade-glistening black hair. He whispered into Frida's ear.

As the applause subsided, Ruiz announced, "Damas y caballeros, we cannot be more proud to have entertained you at the reopening of Club Gardenia." He raised Lola's arm. "We hope you will tell everyone you know that tonight you have witnessed the birth of Havana's newest star."

The audience stood and cheered.

Lola's skin tingled much as when Mama scrubbed her and her younger, American-born sister Sylvia in the tub. The torrent of approval washed away the last of her reservations. For the first time since arriving in Havana, she felt clean and new.

Ruiz grunted, dropped her arm and pushed Lola towards the wings.

Fernando met her with a green silk dressing gown adorned with flowers. "Cariña, you were magnificent!" he shouted. He led her to her dressing room, even smaller than Elena's bedroom.

"The men sitting with Frida," Lola asked. "Do you know who they are?"

"The two younger are from New York. As I understand, they are serious men of business seeking opportunities in Cuba."

"And the third?"

"Colonel Manuel Gallegos-Lucchese. His wife comes from a wealthy family close to President Machado."

A loud knock announced visitors. Without waiting for Lola's response, Frida entered followed by Colonel Gallegos.

Lola noted the absence of the two New Yorkers.

Frida grasped Lola by the arms, touched each cheek to Lola's then kissed her on the mouth. Her lips lingered.

Lola found the greeting confusing but hesitated to disrupt the evening's celebratory mood.

Gallegos stepped forward. "You are a remarkable talent, señorita Flores," he said. "Frida tells me you are new to the musical world of Havana. In my humble opinion, the name Lola Flores soon will be on the lips of everyone in this city. In all Cuba."

Lola looked down, not to convey humility but to avoid his dark eyes which threatened to penetrate her in a way that made her feel vulnerable and exposed. "Thank you," she said.

Gallegos took Lola's hand and expressed his regret—his sorrow—that he had to return home. His wife expected him, of course, and tomorrow he would have to attend to the grave responsibilities thrust upon him by the Cuban nation. If she would not think him forward, however, his driver awaited. He would be honored to first escort her home.

Lola thought his offer gallant yet forward.

Frida expressed her disapproval. "I was going to escort Lola myself. She lives not far from the club."

"Once, one would applaud such an act of kindness," said Gallegos, "but these days, one never knows when one may encounter troublemakers. Even Frida Herskovits must take precautions."

Frida smiled, her sighted eye both convivial and adamant. "Frida Herskovits always takes precautions."

45

"With your permission, Colonel," said Lola, "and with yours, Frida, Fernando has promised to take me home. I owe him much for the success of my performances tonight, and we have much to talk about to prepare for successful shows tomorrow evening."

Frida nodded her consent.

Gallegos bowed. "Señorita Flores, I look forward to the pleasure of seeing you again." He rose and squeezed her hand.

The gentleness of his grip displayed a capacity for kindness. His eyes revealed a desire of alarming ferocity.

# NOVEMBER 1929

# "WORKERS OF THE WORLD—"

On Sunday afternoon, Elena not yet home, Lola meandered through the Old City's crowded streets. Her left hand clutched the rolled-up drawing of a naked woman she'd purchased at the Jewish Market the Sunday before. A pink ribbon protected the subject, and her, from prying eyes.

At El Capitolio, the bells of La Catedral, tolling four, sounded a warning. The young artist had selected a perilous place to meet. If agents of the Sección de Expertos were stalking the young man, the broad, sunbaked stone steps rising to El Capitolio's columned entry would make him an easy target. Surely a Communist should have considered that. Unable to locate him, she crossed the street and stood in the shade of an elongated balcony.

At four-fifteen, Lola debated with herself, rebuffing Albert's attempt to intercede. Perhaps the young man now occupied a jail cell. More disheartening, he had decided she was insufficiently attractive despite the scarcity of unmarried Ashkenazi women. Whatever the case, his arrival now seemed unlikely.

Just as Lola decided to return home, she saw him. He not so much walked towards El Capitolio's steps as strode, a man of great purpose. Yet he wore the same coat and trousers, the same flat hat, and carried the same portfolio. She rushed to meet him.

"My apologies," he said. "Although why should I apologize? A pressing matter came up. The modern industrial world makes people slaves to time. Don't you agree?" Before Lola could answer, he half-dragged her towards the Prado. The tree-lined pedestrian walkway led north to San Salvador de la Punta Fortress overlooking the bay. Imposing buildings rose from both sides of the promenade, including the Grand National Theater and the Hotel Sevilla-Biltmore, which recently had added a ten-story tower and rooftop ballroom. Someday she would play there. He made no further comment.

Unable to endure his silence, Lola asked, "And what of this work you have been doing?"

He halted. "I am sorry I cannot take you to one of the better cafés," he said, leaving her without an answer. A man, he informed her, his voice betraying anger and frustration, should be able to buy a woman coffee and a pastry at a café worthy of her beauty. Without gauging her response, he went on that the bosses and politicians ground down working men— women, too—while reserving even life's smallest pleasures for themselves.

Lola tugged his arm. They resumed walking.

This is such a lovely place to stroll," she said. "Even the secret police cannot stop us from doing that. And as to a café, I can pay."

He halted again. His face reddened. Did she take delight in embarrassing men? Even if not Latin by birth, he had his pride. As to the pressing matter that delayed him, if she understood *that* she would understand *him*. Understand the agony of Cuba. He reached into his portfolio, glanced around as if appreciating the beautiful setting, and withdrew a small handbill. "I just received several dozen from a comrade." He first noticed she was holding his drawing.

"The one you sold to me," Lola said. "You wished to buy it back."

"A necessary pretense," he said. He took the drawing, untied the ribbon and placed it flat in his portfolio. Then he reached into his trouser pocket and pulled out the dollar she had given him.

"Keep it," said Lola. "You can pay for coffee. And pastries."

"The dollar is yours. I have done nothing to earn it."

"Consider it a rental fee. I have admired your drawing all week."

The young man refused the dollar then placed a handbill in her hand. A bold black headline proclaimed RALLY FOR THE DIGNITY OF WORKERS. The event would take place the following Sunday.

"Won't this be dangerous?" she asked.

He sneered. "Those who face danger are Cuba's oppressors—the business owners and bankers. Most of all, the government officials from the policemen who extort money from shop owners all the way up to

President Machado." In due time, the people would stop embracing their chains and throw them off. First, they had to be prodded with the truth. The protestors—the vanguard of revolution—faced risks. They accepted them. Theirs was a moral duty. "Also, the wealthy American Jews are embarrassed by their poor cousins but often they protect us." He snatched the handbill and returned it folded.

Lola slipped it into her purse along with the dollar. If this young man's pride seemed as massive as El Capitolio, so did his heart.

"It is settled then," he said. "You will come next Sunday."

"But I don't even know your name," Lola said.

"Moishe. Moishe Finkelstein. In Cuba, Moisés." He held out his hand to conclude a formal introduction.

Lola turned to walk home.

He followed. "Why are you leaving?" he asked. "And what is *your* name?"

She laughed softly. A touch of mystery made a woman more desirable.

The Sunday following, Lola sat at the table with Elena, who'd come home early. The chief baker had insisted she was not well enough to work. Elena, who'd just awakened from a nap, rubbed her temples.

"It hurts again?" Lola asked. "Shall I go downstairs to the farmacia before I leave?"

Elena dropped her hands. "You play piano and sing six nights a week at the nightclub, and now, on a Sunday afternoon of rest, you are going *where?*"

"Someone invited me to a meeting of working people."

"Someone? And this meeting— You will learn what?"

"How the bosses oppress the workers of Cuba and the world."

Elena rose on unsteady legs. "Maribel sent me Lola Torres, not Vladimir Lenin."

Lola sighed. She would be eternally grateful for all that Elena had done for her, but she'd never intended to cast off one parental yoke for another. She was Lola Flores, a musician of note. The shows at Club Gardenia played before enthused audiences. If her income was modest— for now—it was greater than that of a piano teacher. Soon she would rent an apartment, buy furniture—a proper piano, of course—and purchase a wardrobe appropriate to her rising station. For now, she considered it wiser to acknowledge Elena's pointless fears. Lola Flores had fooled everyone but Fernando, although she disliked the idea of having to fool anyone. "Thank you for your concern, dear Elena," she said, "but I will be well disguised and the meeting very educational."

Elena sat and buried her face in her hands. "This someone. What do you expect of him? What does he expect of *you*?"

*Albert closes his worn copy of* Pollyanna. *Takes up a small cast-iron racing car. Body and featureless driver painted red. Wheels and tires black. Pushes it in circles over the living room carpet. Frowns. Would rather be practicing Liszt's* Mephisto Waltz No. 1. *Didn't Mama and Papa purchase the baby grand "for the sake of the children"? For him?*

*Madame Bushinsky, successor to Madame Silberman, thrills Mama with praise. No eight-year-old—no older student—plays Liszt with such flair. Still, like her predecessor, she can take Albert only so far.*

*Albert devours her compliments. Equally enjoys the applause when he performs for Uncle Mendel, Aunt Agnieska, his cousins, his father's business associates.*

*Today he is ordered away from the piano. Papa and Mama have taken Tosia shopping downtown. Five-year-old Sylvia has a bad cold. Naps in Maribel's small bedroom off the kitchen. Albert tosses the racing car aside. Stares at the piano. Wishes Maribel could play with him.*

*He and Maribel converse in Spanish. Papa frets. Tosia scolds. America! Of course, Albert speaks perfect English. New York-born Sylvia only now grasps that Spanish, English and Yiddish represent distinct languages. Worships her big brother.*

*Albert retreats to the bedroom he shares with his sisters. After his bar mitzvah, he will take the guest room. Wear long pants. Restless, he thumbs through an old children's book. Dutch Twins, brother and sister, visit Grandma. Ignores the text. Stares at the pictures. Craves the little girl's clothing.*

*Dropping the book, Albert picks up one of Tosia's dolls. Bisque porcelain. An infant girl. Strokes her blonde curls. Examines her blue eyes, rosy cheeks, red lips. Sees in then his own. Admires her blue dress. White booties edged in blue. Fingers the delicate lace around her neck. Moves her head, arms, legs. Confides to her in Spanish. He desires a dress like hers.*

*Goes to the large wardrobe. Removes one of Tosia's dresses. The top emulates a sailor suit. Wide collar. Long sleeves. Down the right side, shoulder to hip, large brass buttons parade single file. A belt ties the dress below the waist. Albert can't remember when Tosia last wore it.*

*Takes off his white shirt and knickerbockers. Slips into the dress. Glances at the mirror on the wardrobe door. The dress is too large. No matter. He feels pretty. Feels like who he is. Deep down inside. Not Albert. Stares at his reflection. Fails to hear the bedroom door open.*

*Maribel appears.*

*Albert tenses. Has he been naughty?*

*Maribel studies him. "Do you like this dress?"*

*He nods.*

*"It looks very beautiful on you."*

*Albert feels a new emotion. Contentment.*

Elena shook her head. "Very well. I cannot stop you from going. But if something happens, the guilt will rest on *your* head."

Responding to Moisés Finkelstein's invitation—if thrusting a handbill at her represented a proper invitation—Lola entered Plaza Vieja. She wore her wide-brimmed white hat and held aloft a white parasol. The sun played hide and seek among the clouds, sharpening and blurring the late-afternoon shadows splayed across the plaza's stone surface.

Wishing to see rather than be seen—what if *Moisés* was a member of the secret police?—Lola strolled towards the plaza's periphery. Arched walkways beneath the two- and three-story buildings enclosing the plaza offered shade to groups of young men and women, couples, families. Boys darted among them hawking lottery tickets. Deep in the shadows, other men smoked. They exchanged words sparingly and in voices subdued.

Lola looked back towards the center of the plaza. A Carrara marble fountain displayed four leaping dolphins. Around it loitered a dozen police on horseback.

In a corner of the plaza exposed to the sun, a hundred or more men milled about. Many held hand-lettered signs on wooden sticks. The most common read WORKERS OF THE WORLD UNITE! Sheltered by the arched walkway, Lola drew closer and made out conversations in Spanish and Yiddish. The men's haggard faces, stooped shoulders, suits and shoes at best shabby bore witness to their grievances.

At the edge of the crowd—no one could call such an assembly a mob—several women chatted softly. A few held signs. Elena had said that most women in Havana were less fortunate than she was. They worked long hours in factories making cigars, clothing and shoes. They earned starvation wages and suffered many abuses. Lola was not unmoved. As a child, she'd learned about the 1911 Triangle Shirtwaist fire—over 140 dead, mostly women—and the survivors' struggle for better working conditions. Almost a decade later, she read in the newspaper about telephone operators in Massachusetts, all women, striking for the right to negotiate with the New England Telephone Company. And winning. Yet how could she consider herself one of the demonstrators in the plaza, fight their fight, coming as she did from such a well-to-do family?

Moisés, emerged from the shade. Smiling, he clapped a worker on the shoulder.

Lola walked towards him. Drawing near, she saw that his eyes were red, his cheeks even more drawn.

"I did not believe you would come, woman with no name," he said in Yiddish.

A police horse whinnied.

"Is gathering here not dangerous?" she asked.

Moisés' laugh seemed almost a growl.

A shoed hoof clattered against a cobble.

Moisés looked towards the police. "They have no reason to be here," he said. The demonstrators had not concealed themselves at midnight in some underground cellar to hatch a plot. They stood in the open, in view of man and God—again, the latter a figure of speech—to make known their simple demand for justice. Machado feared their words. And words could shatter steel. "Have you read *Das Kapital*?"

"No," said Lola.

"I will get you a copy. You will find it enlightening—if a woman of privilege dares open its pages."

Lola wondered how he could afford a book but not coffee for the two of them. Unless Cuba's Communists possessed copies provided by agents of the Soviet Union. Surely that would pose grave danger. Yet this proximity to politics in the flesh—revolutionary politics—was thrilling. Besides, she'd experienced considerable danger just being Lola. As to *Das Kapital*, she knew only that it was written by Karl Marx. Also, that Papa and Uncle Mendel condemned it as being against all that America stood for although they hadn't read it. "Will you speak this afternoon?" she asked.

A horse snorted. Another joined in.

"I will," said Moisés. "In Yiddish. One of the comrades will translate."

A chorus of whinnies broke out.

"¡Adelante!" a voice called.

"Carlos, our leader," said Moisés. Naturally, the demonstrators had no true leader, all workers being equal. "We try to be punctual, although I do not find this trait common among Cubans. It is also rare among Jews."

A short, robust man mounted a wooden box. "¡Bienvenidos, camaradas!" called Carlos.

The demonstrators gathered.

"Perhaps," said Moisés, "you should withdraw to the shade."

Lola pointed to her parasol.

"The sun may not be the only danger we face."

Acknowledging that she was ill-prepared for any sort of turmoil, Lola retreated to one of the near arches.

Moisés approached Carlos, who held out his arms. "Comrades, today we come together—"

"Steady!" a voice called from the mounted policemen.

"—to show the government and people of Cuba—"

A horse reared on its hind legs. Its companions stirred.

"—that the working people who are the lifeblood of this island—"

Hooves scraped the plaza's stones. They set off sparks.

"—understand their rights and will demand—"

The commanding officer blew a whistle.

From beneath the arches behind the demonstrators, brawny men in shirtsleeves ran forward. Their boots beat a terrifying rhythm. Their hands waved wooden clubs, baseball bats, metal pipes.

The demonstrators turned to face them.

Onlookers scattered.

Lola stifled a cry.

"Hold your ground!" Carlos commanded in Spanish.

Moisés bellowed the same in Yiddish.

The demonstrators drew closer.

Additional groups of armed men rushed them from the plaza's other three sides.

The police drew their pistols.

The armed men launched their assault.

Some demonstrators fought back with their signs' wooden handles. Others used fists.

Lola collapsed against a stucco-covered column.

The plaza resounded with the cracking of skulls, arms and legs, cries and moans. A woman shrieked, "Why do the police not protect us?"

Voices at the plaza's edge drowned out her plea. "Give the dirty Reds what they deserve!"

Lola saw Moisés struggle with two men, both considerably larger. A blow from a club buckled his knees. He rose and landed a fist between the legs of one of the attackers. The man swayed then collapsed. His companion stepped back.

Another whistle blew. The police urged their mounts forward.

The attackers scattered.

The police charged the demonstrators.

A shot rang out. Then another.

A demonstrator fell.

A fusillade followed.

Sharp echoes filled the plaza.

More demonstrators fell. Others staggered in place.

A third whistle blew.

The firing stopped.

A hush fell.

The police holstered their pistols. Then, as if performing in a circus, paced their horses around more than twenty sprawled bodies. A final whistle blew. They withdrew.

Lola saw Carlos drag Moisés towards the fountain. She ran after them.

A policeman blocked her path.

Lola froze then summoned the courage to chastise the policeman.

"Shame on you!" she cried. She skirted the animal, holding her parasol out like a shield.

The policeman laughed. "It is only Jew blood," he called after her.

Lola helped Carlos recline the unconscious Moisés at the fountain's rim then pulled a white handkerchief from her purse. She held it gently against his belly. The handkerchief turned red.

Carlos splashed water on Moisés' face.

Moisés' body jerked then went still.

Lola mumbled the Sh'ma—Hear O Israel, the Lord is Our God, the Lord is One. She fought to keep from collapsing. She'd never seen someone die. And she'd failed to give Moisés her name.

Two weeks later, the noontime sun lit the apartment as if the cracked and peeling ceiling had opened to the heavens. The cloudless sky upset Lola. This day, she would attend Moisés' funeral service—too long delayed— at the small Ashkenazi synagogue on Calle Jesús María. She finished knotting Alberto's tie, slipped on his wrinkled suit jacket, poured coffee and sat at the table. Elena had put out Lola's favorite guava-and-cheese pastries, but Lola had no appetite. She considered going downstairs for cigarettes. She'd seldom smoked in New York and hadn't yet in Havana, but she longed for comfort. Perhaps a glass of rum. But what would people think if they smelled alcohol on Albert's breath? Then again, Albert was a stranger in Havana, virtually nonexistent despite his passport and papers. Lola stayed seated. Fernando was coming. He'd insisted on accompanying her to the small shul.

How quickly he'd become her confidant. He knew her darkest secret, although she did not consider that Lola Flores embodied darkness.

If darkness described anyone, it was the police. Even before the blood had been scrubbed from Plaza Vieja's stones, they announced Moisés' death to be an accident. A shooting? Nonetheless, they delayed releasing his body. This affronted Jewish law, which commanded burial the day after death or, at the latest, the day following. Rumors spread that the government retained Moisés' body to discourage other Jews from further demonstrations.

Lola wished she could also go to the cemetery. Albert could help shovel dirt on the grave, the ultimate kindness performed for the dead. But the police restricted the burial to a rabbi and nine mourners approved by the government. This would provide the minyan—ten adult Jewish males—required for reciting Kaddish, the traditional mourners' blessing of God that made no mention of death.

Drumming her fingers to the rhythm of a zarzuela by Ernesto Lecuona, Lola pondered the wisdom of Albert appearing at the shul. Why expose herself to danger and a fate potentially worse than Moisés'? Who, after all, was he to her and she to him? Yes, he'd seemed drawn to her and yes, she found him appealing despite his revolutionary fervor. Or *because* of that fervor. This was all new and puzzling. What disturbed her most was that in a twisted way, Moisés death almost relieved her. Had they developed a relationship, what would have been the outcome? Surely, she would have disappointed him. Her small breasts might prove adequate, but when he ventured between her legs—

Lola thought of the famous Viennese psychiatrist Sigmund Freud, also a Jew. Would he find her a perfect patient? Parents made children ill, wasn't that what he wrote? Dr. Freud might conclude that her interest in Moisés signified her estrangement from Papa. Also, Mama. And, she supposed, Uncle Mendel. All feared that Communism in the new Soviet Union threatened their business in America. Where did Lola Flores stand? She'd freely enjoyed the fruits of her family's success if not their emotional support. Moisés had, to a small degree, involved her with the plight of Cuba's workers. Granting the merits of their cause, she felt no call to serve as a political agitator. Her career was in its infancy. She settled on the one reason she could embrace for attending the service. She was a Jew. It was a mitzvah.

A fist rapped on the door.

Lola shuddered. Had operatives from the Sección de Expertos followed her home after Moisés was murdered? Exhibiting the patience of the truly cruel, had the secret police bided their time before pouncing? Lola imagined being dragged off and raped before a bullet penetrated her forehead and men without consciences dumped her body into the sea. She held her breath.

The rapping continued.

Lola considered that failing to answer their summons would not deter but infuriate them. They would break down the door and return later for

Elena. She rose. Whether through boldness or folly, she flung the door open.

A tall woman in an elegant black dress gasped. "For God's sake, cariña, what took you so long?"

Lola lurched back.

Fernando entered and shut the door.

"Why are you dressed like that?" Lola asked.

"For the funeral!" said Fernando. He glowered. "A cheap suit does not become Alberto Torres." He glanced at the table. "You can offer me coffee."

Lola went to the stove. "I can heat some in a minute."

Fernando sat at the table.

"A funeral service is not a costume party," Lola said.

"And here the newest musical sensation in Havana wears the clothing of a man. Clearly, a costume *is* required."

"But you in a dress?"

Did Lola think he wished the secret police to recognize him? They would have one or two men present in the synagogue and possibly—probably—an informant among the mourners.

"Then you can let me go by myself as I begged you."

Fernando reached for a pastry. "Your hair—"

"I will wear a hat. In a synagogue, men cover their heads. Women also."

Fernando put the pastry down, opened his purse and withdrew a black headscarf.

Lola returned to the table with coffee and frowned. "Your dress is beautiful, but your shoulders. Your chin. And you are so tall." No one would believe him a woman.

Fernando's eyes widened. "But cariña, I *am*. That is, I *was*. I was called Josefina."

Lola's hands shot to her mouth.

Fernando pulled them down then stood. "If you wish to see—"

Lola shook her head.

He lowered himself back into his seat. "Believe me, when I pee, I must sit. Thank God, I have a bladder of iron."

"And that is how you knew—"

A person forced to live a life of deception learned to recognize people like himself and form alliances. Or perish.

"When did you know about yourself?"

When did he *not*? As a child, Josefina preferred playing with boys. Especially fútbol. Bigger than many boys her age, she used her size to great advantage. The girls teased her, but all the boys wanted her on their side. Embarrassed by their daughter's sporting talents, his parents scolded. Josefina must act the devoted daughter, wear dresses, play with dolls. This was God's will. They paid a seamstress to teach Josefina how to sew, a skill his mother lacked. Unknowingly, they did him a great favor. But Josefina could never avoid their disappointment and, ultimately, their anger. No boy, they assured her, would ever ask for her hand. "I have, however, come to know many boys," he assured Lola. "And girls." He touched the back of his hand to her cheek.

"Did you grow up in Havana?"

He had to learn the ways of the city. His father managed a tobacco farm in Pinar del Río west of Havana. Josefina ran away after her— Fernando's—fifteenth birthday. "My parents had eight other children. I do not think they expended much effort searching for me." He took the name Fallon, an Irish name, because he was born Josefina Reilly, grandson of an Irish immigrant. In Lola Torres—Lola Flores—he saw a reflection of himself, the anguish of the outcast. When her fingers skipped across the keyboard, her music touched his heart just as it hardened the Maestro's. The old man resented that a woman, and one so young, was the more accomplished musician. Yet despite the great talent of this Lola-from-nowhere—perhaps *because* of it—a difficult road lay ahead. He could not look away and let her fail. "That, and not any disagreement between your body and your soul, would be a mortal sin."

Lola placed her hand on his. "Are there many people like us in Havana?"

Fernando sighed. People like them could be found everywhere. Some in remote villages lived openly, esteemed by superstitious natives who believed them touched by their primitive gods. The vast majority hid in the shadows and emerged only on special occasions. They stood condemned by the Church, vilified by the government, menaced by both. "People who bully and intimidate others burn with a white-hot anger not because they see people like us as different but so much the same." But a few men and women like Lola Flores and Fernando Fallon lived as their true selves although always teetering on the razor's edge of discovery. "If you have the courage to endure the spotlight, cariña, I will render all the assistance in my power to safeguard Lola Flores and her music." As to Fernando Fallon, all anyone knew was that he created the most beautiful costumes in Havana. "Frida, of course, offers me her protection."

"Frida knows?"

Fernando adjusted his black, beaded-glass necklace. "There is nothing about men and women Frida does *not* know." She also had made the acquaintance of many important people—like Colonel Gallegos. "When you have powerful friends, people see what you *wish* them to see."

Lola blanched. "You frighten me."

Fernando waved his hand as if brushing aside a mosquito. They must forget about themselves for the moment and go to the synagogue to mourn her poor young man.

Lola returned that they could not. In the synagogue, men and women sat separately. Without her, Josefina would call attention to herself.

Fernando's eyes darkened then emitted a light rivaling the sunshine outside. "I will change into men's clothes and wear a hat low over my face. My apartment is close. We will go now."

Lola remained seated. "What will happen if the secret police see that you are ignorant of the prayers?"

The answer was simple, he countered. He would humble himself and confess to being an ignorant Jew but one of good heart. The secret police felt rewarded when people groveled. "After the service concludes, we will take a winding route back to my apartment. Then, after you perform this evening, we will return there to toast poor Moisés and get drunk."

# DECEMBER/JANUARY 1929-30
## A TALE OF TWO CITIES

B locks from the Harbor Channel, Lola and Fernando approached a drab doorway three steps below Calle Empedrado. While Christmas lights brightened the Old City, their destination revealed only a dim glow behind curtains covering two small windows. Along the narrow street, men and women celebrating Noche Buena scurried past, their clothing dated, the gifts they carried more modest than they wished. In three hours, many would attend Midnight Mass. Lola's sole experience with Christmas had been helping decorate the small tree in Maribel's room, a concession Papa and Mama granted to demonstrate their American good heartedness.

Fernando halted and inspected Lola. He'd guided her purchase of an unassuming dress of royal blue rayon, its shawl collar edged in cream lace.

She touched her hand to the wig he'd selected—a light-brown close in color to her natural hair, attractive yet conventional. She thought it ironic that many Jewish women after arriving in America abandoned their wigs, mimicking their husbands shaving off their beards. Of course, she understood the need to avoid drawing undue attention. Still, she resented having to limit her sense of style when, onstage, Lola Flores posed such a colorful figure.

"You look beautiful," said Fernando.

His earnestness set her at ease. In just six weeks, he'd become her big brother, her protector, a kindred soul. Papa, Mama, Tosia and Sylvia had never offered their support. Perhaps Sylvia.

At the top step, Fernando held up his right hand. "We must give you a name."

Lola looked at him in disbelief. "Of these, I possess an abundance."

Fernando shook his head. "Here, you must take on one more identity."

"Are there secret police inside?" asked Lola. Too late, it occurred to her that her flippant remark informed Fernando that she failed to understand the gravity of the situation.

Fernando's silence confirmed that given the economic and political turmoil in Cuba, even the joy of Christmas could not be taken for granted. The government watched everyone. The Sección de Expertos even exploited workers facing hunger and eviction, seducing them with small cash payments to sell their souls as informers.

"And so," asked Lola, "what am I to be called?"

*Albert welcomes the apartment's quiet. At his birthday party the day before, Papa raged against the recently passed 19th Amendment. Banning the sale of alcohol except for religious reasons? "This is America!" Now, Papa is at work. Mama has taken a protesting Tosia and a pliant Sylvia to Central Park. Albert sits at the piano. Wears one of Tosia's old dresses.*

*Maribel emerges from the kitchen. Hands behind her back. "You play wonderfully!"*

*Albert stands. Curtsies.*

*"You look very becoming," she says.*

*Albert smiles.*

*Maribel reveals a package. Pink paper. Pink bow.*

*"You gave me a present yesterday.* The Jungle Book.*"*

*Maribel holds the package out.*

*Albert accepts it. Assesses its weight. Light. Squeezes. Soft. Rips the paper. Holds up a dress. Also, pink. Ruffles circle the neck. Ring the cuffs of the puffy three-quarter sleeves. He beams.*

*"I made it myself," says Maribel. They will keep it under her bed. Take it out for special occasions. When they are alone. She runs a finger down his cheek. She has been thinking. Perhaps he would like a new name. Just for them.*

*Albert's eyes widen. "Alberta?"*

*She shakes her head. The female version of his name will not do him—her—justice.*

*Albert scratches his head.*

*"I had a friend named Lola," says Maribel. "God took her. Let us call you Lola."*

*Albert nods.*

*Maribel hugs him.*

*Albert inhales the scent of her eau de toilette. Violets.*

*Maribel takes Albert's chin between her thumb and forefinger. "This, only we can know."*

*Albert concedes the need for secrecy. Conceals his disappointment.*

Fernando stroked his chin. "It is Christmas Eve. Why not Maria?" He frowned. "Too obvious." He pursed his lips. "Concepcion! Concepcion Fuerte, because you are strong."

Lola shrugged her consent then followed Fernando down the steps.

He knocked.

Light shone through a peephole.

"Is this party for Communists?" Lola whispered. The intended gaiety of her quip turned to melancholy as she struggled with the image of the dying Moisés Finkelstein, a human fountain in Plaza Vieja spurting blood.

Fernando addressed the unseen person behind the door. "It is Felipe," he said. "Felipe de León."

The peephole shut. The door opened. Music drifted out. A slender woman with dark hair urged them inside and bolted the door. "Ah, Felipe," she said.

Lola thought the glimmer in her eyes a welcome contrast to Fernando's solemnity.

The woman kissed Fernando on both cheeks, then on the lips, then took his hand and led the new arrivals into a room strung with colored lights. Above a buffet table hung a poster of baby Jesus in the manger and the words FELIZ NAVIDAD.

Fernando smiled. "Let me present Concepcion Fuerte."

"I am called Victoria," the woman said to Lola.

Fernando handed her a small sheaf of pesos to cover their share of expenses.

Victoria accepted them, again kissed Fernando and drifted off.

Fernando escorted Lola around the room where small clusters of men and women, drinks in hand, engaged in animated conversation. Some balanced plates of roast pork, black beans and rice along with crisp-crusted Cuban bread.

Lola located the source of the music, a record player offering Louis Armstrong's "When You're Smiling." Near it, a couple danced.

Fernando took her aside. "So? What do you see?"

Lola returned his question with a stare. What did he expect her to see at a Christmas party? "Men and women eating and drinking."

"And?"

"Talking. Dancing."

"Exactly," he said. "Here we have a Noche Buena like any other. Except—"

Lola counted four beats then asked, "Except what?"

"Everyone here is just like *us*."

Lola's heart throbbed as if pounded by Louis Armstrong's drummer. Maribel had assured her that she was not an aberration and introduced her to a few others like herself, but they, even in their gayest moments, could not conceal their anxiety. Now, here in Havana—at least on this holy night—women and men, despite the stigma imposed on them and the fear it impelled, had abandoned their daily cares.

Fernando introduced her to a small group engaged in a serious discussion. A woman sporting a blonde bob glanced at Fernando then grasped Lola's arm. "Have you heard what they are doing in Europe?"

"I wish they could do it for men," said the group's lone man.

Fernando nodded.

Lola had no idea what they were talking about.

"To give someone a penis—" the man said.

The blonde drew Lola close. "That will have to wait. Felipe has informed us that a doctor in Europe believes he can create for a man the body of a woman."

A second woman, stout and dressed in a green skirt and matching jacket, her mahogany skin glowing, explained that a man from Denmark—a well-known painter there—had presented herself as a woman for years. Soon, if Felipe's reports were correct, a surgeon in Germany would remove her penis and testicles and construct for her a vagina. Imagine that! But the doctor also would implant in her ovaries. The woman wished to bear a child. Science was remarkable, yes, but was such a thing possible?

Fernando assured them that medicine was taking great leaps forward. The future would offer many possibilities they could not begin to imagine.

"Even without vaginas, we also are real women," insisted the woman with the blonde bob.

A small commotion sounded in the street. Conversation ceased. Someone turned off the music.

Lola trembled.

Fernando placed an arm around her shoulders. "Firecrackers," he explained. "Cubans loved to celebrate with firecrackers. Especially the young people. Even on such a holy night."

Quiet followed.

Louis Armstrong returned. A second couple started to dance. Conversations resumed.

Victoria approached with a glass. "Whatever troubles you, Concepcion, nothing calms the soul like rum."

Lola drank heartily. Her spirits reviving, she swayed with the music. "I feel like singing," she confided to Fernando.

"That would not be for the best, cariña," Fernando said. "Even among friends, you must remain Concepcion."

More firecrackers exploded. Then a rock shattered one of the small windows. Shards of glass struck several partygoers.

Lola collapsed against Fernando.

"The children," he said. "Do not be afraid of the children."

"¡Monstruos!" a voice called from the street. It did not belong to a child.

Revelers at Club Gardenia's New Year's fête swayed to the music of the Eduardo Ruiz Orchestra as if only dancing could usher them safely through the future on a tropical island become the gloomy wood of a Grimm's fairytale. Above them, twirling mirrored balls gave off a silvery light illuminating a ghostly blue haze of cigar smoke. Below the miasma, men in tuxedos and women in floor-length evening gowns, backs and silk-stockinged legs exposed, consumed French champagne, Russian caviar, Argentine beef and Maine lobster.

Just before midnight, the guests followed a tradition begun in Spain twenty years earlier and ate twelve grapes commemorating the months of the year. Then balloons of red, white and blue—the colors of the Cuban flag—ascended from each table. Noisemakers blared. Responding to the

Maestro's cue, Lola, wearing a gold lame gown, led the partygoers in singing "Auld Lang Syne." Ten minutes later, the club's patrons merrily oblivious, the Maestro allotted the band a break.

Frida approached Lola and whispered in Yiddish, "You will make 1930 a wonderful year. Later, you must come to my apartment for a drink. We are, in so many ways, sisters—even if I am an *older* sister."

A hand tapped Frida's shoulder. Manuel Gallegos stepped forward and sought Frida's permission to invite Lola to his table.

"Please do, Colonel," she said. "Our honored guests will be delighted to meet the newest star in Havana."

At the table, the two dark-haired men from New York whom Lola had noted at the club's reopening sat shoulder to shoulder, a striking blonde on either side. As she approached, the men stood. The taller rose to Fernando's shoeless height. His nose appeared to have been broken in a fight, but his piercing eyes and off-kilter smile suggested that his opponent had only managed a lucky punch and suffered far worse punishment.

The second man barely stood eye to eye with Lola. He displayed prominent ears, bushy eyebrows and the tight-lipped expression of an accountant.

"Señor Siegel and señor Lansky again have come to visit us," Gallegos said in Spanish.

Responding to the mention of their names, Siegel—the taller—and Lansky grinned.

Gallegos pulled out an empty chair and motioned Lola to sit. "My wife has left with a headache," he said. "Tomorrow, of course, she must supervise the servants and the nanny even though it is a holiday."

A waiter filled everyone's glasses with Scotch bottled at the turn of the century.

"You were terrific," said Lansky in English, unsure whether Lola would understand.

"Definitely," said Siegel. "They'd love you in New York. Ain't that right, Meyer?"

"Thank you," said Lola, masking her native English with an accent mimicking Maribel's.

Siegel looked at Lansky and said in Yiddish, "I don't know about this dame. She look Spanish to you? But if that's all the English she's got, I wouldn't mind givin' her a few lessons."

Lansky laughed.

Lola retained a poker face. She was unsure whether to feel flattered or offended.

"I hope," said Gallegos in English, "you have not said anything that would cause señorita Flores any embarrassment."

Siegel smirked. "Would it make a difference?"

Gallegos raised his glass. "¡Feliz año nuevo!"

Siegel directed Gallegos to stick with English and emptied his glass.

Lola sipped from hers. Although not fond of whiskey, having indulged only occasionally in New York to avoid giving offense, she embraced the small flash of heat that suffused her body.

Siegel grabbed the bottle and poured another drink. As he raised his glass, a wobbly merrymaker brushed his shoulder. Liquor showered the tablecloth.

"Lo siento," the man apologized. A drunken grin sprawled across his face.

Siegel reached inside his jacket and withdrew a gun.

The man's eyes bulged.

Lola's breath caught. She'd heard of such incidents in New York but never expected one to take place in Havana. At least, not in Club Gardenia.

Lansky, displaying the placid expression of a funeral director, pressed down on Siegel's hand. "Nu, Benny? It's New Year's Eve. And trouble, we don't need." He inclined his head to signal the man to return to his table.

Siegel slipped the gun back into his shoulder holster.

A waiter appeared with a new bottle.

Gallegos offered his apologies.

"Fuck it!" said Siegel. He refilled his glass and downed his whiskey in a single gulp.

Lansky glanced at the two blondes.

Siegel stood and yanked his companion to her feet. "Been great, Colonel, but the night's as young as the year. Meyer and me, we got other things to do, if you get my drift."

Lansky looked at the other blonde and raised his chin.

She stood.

"Give our regards to President Machado," Siegel said. "We'll sleep it off tomorrow and see him the day after."

Lola was glad to see Siegel leave.

When they were out of earshot, Gallegos turned to her. "Señores Siegel and Lansky may lack the upbringing of gentlemen, but despite what is happening in America and Europe, they see a great future for business in Cuba." He held his arms out. "A great future for Club Gardenia. For all of us."

Frida joined Gallegos and Lola. "Your wife must be growing impatient," she said.

Gallegos smiled. "She will be sleeping, but no doubt will keep open an ear."

"Given her family, she is not a woman one wishes to upset. But then, you are a man of great importance."

Gallegos preferred to see himself as a man of great *responsibility*. As such, duty compelled him to attend the party at the Presidential Palace. "I am sure you will not mind of I ask señorita Flores if I may have the honor of her accompanying me."

"Lola must play again soon," said Frida. "Our guests came to see her."

"And they have. The Maestro can entertain them."

Frida weighed her options then suggested that it might be ill-advised for Gallegos to be seen with another woman—a younger woman and one so pretty.

Their exchange confused Lola. Despite all that Maribel had told her about Cuba and what she'd read, she had entered a world still foreign and often unnerving. Had the Colonel simply expressed a man's natural desire to squire an attractive, newly celebrated woman to an important social event? Or had he intimated something less honorable? Lola regretted consuming the small amount of whiskey that seemed to have clouded her appraisal of the matter. But what could happen at the Presidential Palace? And why should she deny herself such an unimagined experience? Yet she held the Machado government responsible for the death of Moisés Finkelstein. Would her accompanying the Colonel betray Moisés' memory? But what memory was that? They hardly knew each other. Besides, her refusal might place an obstacle before her career, a career only just beginning and one for which she'd taken such frightful risks. She was not without pity, but she had no choice but to give her career precedence. Uncertain nonetheless, she looked towards the stage's wings where Fernando stood watching.

"Perhaps," Frida suggested to Gallegos, "Fernando Fallon, our costume designer and personal assistant to our talented Lola Flores, might go with you." This would preempt the nattering of small-minded people who saw evil in every innocent gesture.

Gallegos bowed his assent.

The gilt clock in the Presidential Palace's Hall of Mirrors chimed the conclusion of the New Year's first two hours. Above the festivities, the ceiling displayed Armando Garcia Menocal's twenty-two-meter-long painting *Triumph of the Republic*. Its winged, white-robed angel hoisted a red flag marked by a prominent white star. On the marble floor, several hundred guests flaunting wealth and power with little regard for the island's unsettled state danced the Lindy Hop to an American jazz band led by a bald Negro.

Lola and Fernando stood next to Colonel Gallegos. Although exhilarated, Lola repressed a yawn. She could not remember whether the glass she caressed contained the evening's second drink or third. Perhaps her fourth. Certainly, she had reason to celebrate. Over the past two months, she'd negotiated the voyage between lives in New York and Havana with skill and pluck. Not yet twenty, she'd transformed herself from Jewish refugee of sorts into a woman entertained by Gerardo Machado, fifth president of Cuba, and his wife Elvira.

Colonel Gallegos, like Ben Siegel earlier, reached into his jacket. Instead of a pistol, he withdrew a gold cigarette case engraved with a gracefully scripted *G*. The president and first lady declined, as did Fernando. Lola accepted. She'd found that an occasional cigarette relaxed her when a stray malicious thought threatened to untether her soul.

Machado held up a gold lighter. "A Christmas gift from the Colonel, a true patriot and loyal friend." He clapped Gallegos on the back.

Lola struggled to grasp the moment. The only other president she knew was Uncle Mendel, who assumed that title when he and Papa established their company in New York. Papa, the younger brother, became vice-president.

Señora Machado offered Lola a polished smile. "Gerardo and I must come to Club Gardenia to see you perform. Your talent makes you a treasure of the homeland."

"Thank you," said Lola. Mindful of the problems that goaded many ordinary Cubans to contest the government's authority, she avoided making any comment that could be taken as political. But discussing politics represented the least of the risks she faced in public. Professional and personal questions threatened to raise the curtain behind which she hid. To counter them, she directed her inquirers to their favorite setting—center stage: "I play piano and sing. What I find important is what *you* think."

The Machados nodded their approval.

"Lola Flores," said Gallegos, "is the finest pianist and singer in Cuba, a land famed for its musicians." His speech betrayed a slight slur but no depletion of energy. "A woman of mystery? Yes. This is part of what makes Lola Flores so exciting."

Machado smiled. He believed that señorita Flores would not remain a mystery for long. "Not to *you*, Manuel." He turned to Lola. "By nature and training, Colonel Gallegos uncovers secrets." Sadly, men of treacherous intent threatened the homeland. The Colonel's vigilance compelled him to peer into places dark and vile, and thus enable Cuba to maintain its honor. "Not that *you* have secrets, señorita."

Lola gritted her teeth. Had Machado disclosed that Colonel Gallegos worked in the Sección de Expertos? If so, he too bore responsibility for Moisés' death. This raised a more frightening prospect. Would he peer into her own hidden places?

Gallegos eased her fears with a self-deprecating laugh and a bemused smile targeting señora Machado. "Every woman is a mystery, no?" He would be honored, despite his natural curiosity, to respect—to *protect*—the mystery of Lola Flores.

Señora Machado turned towards her husband. "Darling, I see Ambassador Guggenheim looking in our direction."

Lola gazed out towards the ambassador, whom she'd met half an hour earlier. They had much in common, a matter she could not reveal. His grandfather, Meyer Guggenheim, an Ashkenazi Jew, arrived in America from Switzerland well before the Civil War and made a fortune in Colorado silver mining. The Sobels were well-off but not wealthy and represented another Jewish-American success story.

Following kisses and an abrazo between the men, the Machados strolled off.

Gallegos summoned a waiter for a fresh drink. "And you?" he asked Lola.

"No thank you," she said. "I have had enough."

Gallegos raised an eyebrow. "One never can have enough of anything." He suggested to Fernando that the British ambassador's wife, whose dress Fernando had complimented earlier, might love to have a word with him.

Fernando's eyes engaged Lola's. Then, accepting the situation, he zig-zagged across the room, He had no idea where the British ambassador's wife might be found—if the couple had not already left.

A sense of earnestness recomposed the landscape of Gallegos' face. "I meant what I said about offering you protection."

"From who?" Lola asked. The lighthearted inflection of her voice disguised her unease. "The Maestro? Frida Herskovits?"

Ruiz, he assured her, was a little man with an inflated sense of himself. Frida? Another matter. Señor Lansky, he believed, was a distant cousin. All Jews were related. "Scratch one and a hundred scurry out from the woodwork." Still, business was business.

Behind her back, Lola balled her right hand into a fist. Maribel had assured her that Cuba treated its Jews well. Moisés' death and how it represented the government's treatment of workers, Jews included, had created a measure of doubt. Gallegos had just rent the delicate fabric of Maribel's assertion. Lola considered it more important than ever to conceal her Jewishness while encouraging the Colonel's support. "I value your friendship," she said.

In time, Gallegos assured her, she would appreciate all he could do for her. Without him, the Machado government would fall. He gestured towards the crowd, fools akin to passengers on a boat far from shore, sipping cocktails while oblivious of storm clouds blackening the horizon. "They concede that sugar prices will continue to collapse but still express high hopes for the New Year."

"Why is that?"

"America, they believe, will be their savior." He shook his head. "Do you know that in the U.S., hundreds of banks already have failed? Farmers cannot obtain credit." The situation in Europe was worse. To keep the island's prospects afloat, the government had no choice but to call on men like Lansky and Siegel—Jews yes, but men whose greed would fuel the engines of state. He summoned another drink. "The Communists we will exterminate."

"Surely you have made Cuba secure," said Lola. She intended her brief reply, admittedly obsequious, to deflect the Colonel from penetrating her fragile emotional and physical armor.

He needed no more encouragement to continue. "Only steel and blood can maintain order in the Fatherland. Mussolini understands that and look at Italy. Il Duce is the greatest man of our time. Now, he is tutoring that fellow in Germany, Hitler." With the suddenness of a viper, he swung his right hand behind Lola's neck and pulled her to him. His tongue pried apart her lips and forced her teeth to yield.

Stunned, Lola offered no resistance.

With unanticipated suddenness, he pushed her away. "Forgive me. I am drunk. My car will take you and señor Fallon to your homes. For myself, I will summon a taxi."

Lola found herself shaken. She had failed to resist or at least protest. But didn't she have her reasons? Despite her fairytale success, her situation in a festering Havana remained tenuous. And she found the Colonel's advances not distasteful but thrilling. Did this make her depraved?

# MARCH 1930

# WOMEN IN DANGER

A knock on the door woke Lola, who'd fallen asleep browsing the latest issue of *Harper's Bazaar*. The pharmacist's assistant, a small young woman with close-set eyes, summoned her to answer a telephone call. Few of the Old City's residents had phones. In cases of emergency, they used those of local shops. Lola went downstairs.

Fernando reported that a matter of great urgency had arisen but could say no more until they met in person.

Negotiating the Old City's narrow streets proved challenging. Lola was forced to elbow her way against two relentless streams of humanity. The first headed to the Carnaval celebration at Castillo de San Salvador de la Punta. The old fortress offered food, music, dancing and children's games on this Sunday three days before Ash Wednesday when Havana would publicly capitulate to the constraints of Lent. The second torrent— protestors—surged toward Parque Central and the adjacent Capitolio. The government continued to delay paying the salaries of teachers and agricultural workers.

Lola considered whether Fernando had misled her, had planned a surprise for her birthday, which occurred this day, March second. But why would he rouse her from sleep barely after noon? Moreover, she hadn't mentioned her birth date to Fernando or even Elena. Such a detail might inadvertently be passed on and help lead American or Cuban authorities to Albert—if anyone was still looking for Albert. No, Fernando had summoned her regarding a different matter. That her birthday would pass unnoticed left her dispirited.

Half an hour after setting out—the walk normally took fewer than ten minutes—Lola arrived at Fernando's door. Foregoing kisses, he pulled Lola into the apartment's small entry with its gold-framed mirror and color lithograph of a costumed singer, breasts bare, legs exposed to the thighs. It advertised Club Gardenia. Beneath the lithograph sat two suitcases and a small cardboard carton. Fernando led Lola into the living room with its Art Deco furniture—inexpensive copies to be sure. They would invigorate Papa and Mama's apartment had they Fernando's impeccable taste.

A man slight of build slumped in a chair upholstered in daffodil yellow. He wore a gray suit, white shirt and tie the blue of a night sky from which the luster had been eradicated. Dark hair streaked with gray receded towards the back of a freckled scalp. A hint of sparse stubble marked his cheeks. He reached inside his jacket, withdrew a white lace handkerchief and dabbed at reddened eyes. "Thank you for coming," he said in the voice of a vaguely familiar woman.

Fernando motioned Lola to the adjacent loveseat and sat by her. "You remember Victoria," he said.

Lola recalled the woman who'd welcomed them into the basement room that hosted the Noche Buena party attacked by hooligans. She could not believe that this nondescript, debilitated man was that elegant, vivacious woman. Yet Alberto Torres and Lola Flores were one and the same. *Two* and the same.

Fernando gestured to the brass coffee table. A bottle of rum and three glasses sat on its oval, pale green onyx top. One glass remained empty.

Lola poured a drink.

Fernando sighed. "Victoria lost her job."

Victoria again dabbed her eyes.

"I am sorry," said Lola. "But why—"

Fernando patted Victoria on the knee. "Victoria worked as a bookkeeper at El Encanto."

Lola well knew of the largest, most elegant department store in all Havana.

"As a woman," Fernando said.

"Eight years," Victoria whispered.

Lola nodded in sympathy. So many Cubans were losing their jobs. The lucky ones only suffered reduced wages.

Fernando's eyes signaled that Lola misunderstood. Victoria—it was safer not to mention her male name even among the three of them—had been a valued employee. But El Encanto had not cast her adrift due to dwindling business.

Crimson splotches erupted across Victoria's cheeks. "They found out," she said, half sobbing. As to the men's suit she wore, it was dangerous for her to appear in women's clothing.

A coward with no name, Fernando explained, telephoned her supervisor. The supervisor spoke to the store manager, who did not believe what he had been told. The calls continued. Then someone mailed to the manager an old photograph of Victoria as the man society insisted she be.

"I refused to deny myself," said Victoria. "Anyway, it would have done no good."

Fernando squeezed Victoria's hand.

Lola fought back tears.

"The store withheld the pay they owed Victoria," said Fernando. Making matters worse, someone notified her landlady. Victoria barely managed to pack a few of her things and rush here."

"There should be a law," Lola said.

"What is it you always say?" he responded. "From your lips to God's ears?" He went behind Victoria's chair and placed his hands on the distraught woman's shoulders. "Victoria can stay here for a few days, but what if this coward—how Americans say, stoolpigeon—knows about *me*?" He kissed Victoria on the top of her head.

Lola realized that Fernando and Victoria once had been lovers. "Cannot our mutual friend protect you and also Victoria?" She withheld Frida's name.

"The matter is delicate." The powerful people with whom their friend was associated preferred to avoid scandal even if their photographs and unflattering stories most often appeared in the foreign press. "Victoria has no choice but to drop out of sight and create a new identity."

"And to find another job," said Victoria.

Fernando returned to the loveseat. "Cariña, I ask only that before this new week is over, Victoria stay with you. Just for a few days."

"But the apartment is so small. And you know it is not mine." She thought better of mentioning Elena's name. Victoria might let it slip to another member of the Noche Buena group, one of whom could be the informer. She also lamented that the bright lights of Club Gardenia failed to free her from a world of dark secrets.

Victoria placed her palms together as if praying. "Only for a few days."

Lola's search for a comforting response only brought up questions. Had she a right to involve Elena, who'd already placed herself in jeopardy? If she asked and received *no* in return, could she fault Elena? And if she were in Elena's position, what would be her own response?

The climb up to Elena's apartment left Lola exhausted. After unlocking the door, fatigue gave way to shock. Elena lay slumped over the mahogany table. Sweat stained the back of her dress. Lola shook her.

Elena struggled to sit up. Her left arm hung lifeless. The left corner of her mouth drooped as did her left eyelid.

Following her mother's practice, Lola pressed the back of her hand against Elena's forehead, as if the only matter of concern was a fever.

Elena attempted to smile then collapsed.

# MARCH 1930

# MAN PLANS, GOD LAUGHS

The arched French windows of Frida's third-floor apartment overlooked the waterfront. The scene provided Lola yet another opportunity for self-reflection. That morning, dressed inconspicuously as Lola Torres, she'd attended Elena's Funeral Mass. Rather than create suspicions, she endured the self-debasement of consuming the wafer and wine of Holy Communion. Walking home from Colon Cemetery, she petitioned the God of Israel for forgiveness. The God of Israel left the matter unsettled. Now, following a sleepless night, her emotions drained from playing her role as Elena's only remaining relative in Cuba, she longed to lie down. Apprehension kept her on her toes.

Awaiting her audience with Frida, Lola gazed at the freighters bobbing in the harbor. Fewer arrived each week as demand for the island's sugar crop diminished. This in turn increased the Depression's toll on ordinary Cubans.

She closed her eyes and looked inward. Elena's death entailed not only sorrow but guilt. She'd become so dependent on her Cuban "aunt" that she'd failed to see, or refused to acknowledge, the telltale signs of Elena's illness. More, even after finding a job at Club Gardenia, she'd offered Elena nothing but promises. Now, she could never fulfill them. At the same time, Elena's death rendered the memory of Moisés Finkelstein akin to a ship embarked for its home port and vanished beneath the horizon. Would she dismiss Elena's memory as quickly? How could she not?

Lola accepted the necessity of Elena's memory fading into obscurity. Compassion threatened to put a chink in her emotional armor. First and foremost, she had a duty to Lola Flores. This required continuously reinforcing that armor until the world underwent a fundamental change—not likely—or Lola Flores became so successful that the world relented and accepted her as she was. She would never become another Victoria.

Lola recognized that the rigid shell into which she vowed to confine herself threatened to blur the few happy memories to which she clung of Mama, Papa and Tosia. Even those of Sylvia. But building the future of which she'd so long dreamt required demolishing a tortured past. At the same time, she saw no way to unbind herself from the tormenting fusion of flesh and spirit that was Albert.

Turning back to the living room, Lola opened her eyes and studied one of the many symbols of Frida's prosperity—a stunning mahogany breakfront. Along with fine china and crystal, it displayed two ornate silver candlesticks mounted on heavy, rectangular bases. They reminded Lola of the pair that sat idly on the sideboard in Mama and Papa's dining room save for random Friday nights when Albert lit them, partly in observance, partly as a matter of undeclared spite.

Frida emerged from the kitchen carrying a silver tray laden with a silver teapot, two sets of china cups and saucers, and a small silver bowl filled with sugar cubes. After placing the tray on a coffee table topped with white, gold-streaked marble, she sat on a ruby-red sofa and patted the bare cushion next to her.

Lola joined her.

Frida held up a silver cigarette box, its cloisonné top ornamented with butterflies bearing wings of red, pink, yellow and blue.

Lola declined.

"Pastries maybe you would like?" Frida asked. "I have treats from a wonderful bakery on Calle Damas. Or maybe mandelbrot like from the old country?"

"Tea will be fine. A girl has to watch her figure."

Disregarding Lola, Frida went to the kitchen and returned with a silver dish heaped with mandelbrot. "From my own oven. Light and crispy like they make in Warsaw on Krochmalna Street."

Thinking it prudent to please her hostess, Lola accepted one and took a bite. "Delicious," she said.

Frida's smile registered a Jewish mother's delight, although the closest she'd come to motherhood was two abortions. "So, nu?" she asked.

"I wanted to thank you," said Lola. "You gave me an opportunity when the Maestro—"

Frida snorted then placed a hand on Lola's knee. "When I heard you at that excuse for a piano in the Jewish Market, I knew. Maybe I was taking a chance, but no chutzpah, no greatness."

"Chutzpah you seem to have in abundance."

Frida grinned. "A woman sees an opportunity, she grabs with both hands. As to the Maestro, I had you audition so he would think he had control over the orchestra. That he had power." Her grin dissolved. "I know what men need."

Lola perceived the conversation taking a darker turn.

"And Lola Flores?" Frida went on. "I sense that with men you have little experience."

Lola glanced at Frida's hand on her knee.

Frida withdrew her hand and nestled it cat-like in her lap. "A woman of little experience— A virgin— In Warsaw, that would be the expectation."

Lola anticipated Frida's next remark.

"I suspect, woman of mystery, from Warsaw your family came."

Lola played the innocent. "Why do you say that?"

"Your Yiddish."

Lola clasped her hands.

Then there was Lola's Spanish. She must have come to the island as a small child.

Lola counted Frida's assumption a small victory.

Still, Frida heard another accent. "Faint but adding to the mystery."

Lola took another bite of mandelbrot.

Frida returned her hand to Lola's knee. "We all have secrets, no? Before you ask me for what you came, maybe some of mine I should tell you."

"That is not necessary."

"But it *is*. Women can depend only on each other, and that requires trust. For us, life is not milk and honey. And a woman in Havana alone—"

"Must a woman have a man?"

Frida laughed. She'd been married—once. Shmuel was a man of ordinary appearance but flaunted a keen sense of purpose and destiny. They arrived in Havana a month before the start of the Great War having required a sudden change of scenery. A cousin who'd arrived on the island two years earlier offered Shmuel a job selling sewing machines he repaired in a tiny shop. Shmuel balked. In Warsaw, a job he'd never needed. Money he had, although always he lost it drinking and gambling. Warsaw was home to more than rabbis, businessmen, shopkeepers and hardworking laborers. Jews also could be gangsters. Like Shmuel. But in Warsaw, Shmuel swam in circles, a small fish in a big pond endlessly evading big fish with insatiable appetites. One big fish in particular. Havana offered safety and given the smaller pond, the opportunity to become a big fish. This required a ruthlessness Shmuel lacked. "The police found his body on the docks. Out the window, you can see where."

Although Lola thought herself now hardened to death, Frida was taking her beyond the Pale. "And what did you do?"

"What any decent-looking young woman does when she has no prospects."

Lola pressed her hand to her mouth.

"Please! You think Jewish women didn't sell their bodies in Warsaw?" Frida saved every peso. In time, money enabled her to cultivate friendships. The right friends extended their admiration and became investors. She bought a house and filled it with beautiful girls. "Some not so beautiful but what you might call interesting." She developed a well-to-do clientele. She bought a second house. When Club Gardenia faced ruin, she bought it. The weak economy hurt only the poor. Wealthy habaneros and tourists from America spent enough money to let her turn a tidy profit. Her apartment? She owned the building. "So then, to everyone in Havana, Lola Flores remains a woman of mystery. To Frida, no."

Lola's eyes widened.

Frida leaned close. To climb out of the gutter—to rise far above it—a woman had to become familiar with more than people's bodies. Frida Herskovits probed souls like a doctor examined bones in one of those x-rays. "I saw that Fernando was different when he first came to me. Did I care? No. He had talent and a passion for the work that would help make Club Gardenia successful. That Sunday at the Jewish Market? I alone saw you as you are."

Lola wanted to stand but found her legs unresponsive.

"You think you are unique? Every now and then a girl like you comes to me. I find a place for her. Many men and not a few women enjoy experiences beyond what society considers proper." Frida stroked Lola's cheek. "I have had and been had by every kind of man and woman created in whatever image of himself God could imagine. Farshtay?"

Lola nodded but remained unclear regarding Frida's intentions.

Frida again withdrew her hand. Her sighted eye glinted with a coldness that gave the impression of life to her other of German glass with its gold-flecked iris. "Now business."

Lola had come to make a request. Certainly not a demand. She had a duty to settle Elena's medical and funeral bills. Appealing to the Jewish relief society was out of the question. She needed a loan.

"And the family?"

"None." Lola left unmentioned Maribel and the letter she had Fernando post after the funeral to an address in East Harlem to avoid a grieving sister coming to Havana. As to Hector, his whereabouts were unknown.

"Have you considered seeking assistance from Colonel Gallegos?" Frida asked.

"He is a married man."

"And this is Cuba. The Colonel can be very generous." She moved closer. "We all have needs."

*Dark clouds gather above Manhattan's U-shaped Polo Grounds. Threaten the exposed lower deck. Eight-year-old Albert glances at Papa. He, Uncle Mendel, cousins Isaac, Julius and Gerald all wave half-eaten hot dogs.*

*The Giants' lead-off batter ambles towards home plate. The crowd cheers. Thirsts for first blood. Papa joins in. No longer Yankev but Jack.*

*Albert wishes he was at the hotel in the Catskills. Mama, his sisters, Aunt Agnieska, cousins Dora and Frieda are there fleeing August's sticky heat.*

*The Boston Braves' pitcher awaits a sign from his catcher.*

*Clouds coalesce. Gun-barrel-gray to mourning-black. Colors worn by wives and mothers deprived of husbands and sons. This month, the Great War marks four years trampling life out of Europe. America's doughboys entered sixteen months earlier. Thunder rumbles. The pitcher looks up. A downpour follows. The umpire waves. Players desert the field. Fans rush up the aisles.*

*Sheltered under the second deck, Papa and Uncle Mendel confer. They've abandoned business on a Saturday. New York bans Sunday baseball. A plan to save the day emerges. The Museum of Natural History. Dinner out. Isaac, at thirteen the oldest boy and recent bar mitzvah, pleads for Chinatown. Approved unanimously. Almost. Albert abstains.*

*Soaked but boisterous, the Sobels reach Mendel's 1917 Franklin Series 5 parked close by on 155th Street.*

*Albert remains morose.*

*Don't you worry, says Papa. They'll go to another game.*

*"I want to go home," Albert responds. Hates baseball. Hates all sports. Wants to practice piano.*

*Isaac reaches across the back seat. Jabs the heel of his hand into Albert's shoulder. Uncle Mendel scolds. Albert remains resolute. Papa claps his cheeks. "A musician, he can provide for a wife and children?"*

*Albert opens the car door.*

*Papa calms himself. Why always Albert upsets him? Such narishkeit! Albert loves the piano? Fine. Why not also baseball? Why always wants to be alone? Suggests a detour.*

*Uncle Mendel and the cousins groan. For show. Losing a few minutes from their special Saturday? A small price to pay for ridding themselves of Albert.*

*"Maribel is probably out," Papa announces. The maid gets off after lunch each Saturday. Usually leaves. Returns Sunday evening. Albert can stay by himself. "Dinner, you can scrape from the icebox," Papa says. "Food I ain't bringing."*

*Delivered to the front of the building, Albert makes no effort to wave goodbye. Ignores the doorman's quizzical expression. Takes the elevator. In the foyer, removes soaked shoes. Soaked socks. Hears a soft cry. A moan. Tiptoes towards Maribel's room. Hesitates. Opens the door.*

*Maribel, in bed, buries her head under a white sheet. Conceals her body intertwined with that of another woman.*

"Take a bit of advice from a woman who has lived long enough to learn its value," said Frida. "Vos nutst koved az men hot nit tsu esn?" What use is honor if you have nothing to eat?

"My mother used to say, if you sleep with dogs, you get up with fleas."

"They say," Frida countered, "if you're rich, you're handsome and smart—also you can sing." She held up her right index finger boasting a gold ring set with an amethyst. "Also, neither do you worry from fleas."

"I have my music," Lola said. But would her music, without the right friends, be enough?

Frida acknowledged Lola's ambition, talent and youth. "But you think just like that, you will rise to the top like cream in a bottle of milk? Man plans, God laughs." She squeezed Lola's thigh.

Lola, fearing God's laughter would be boisterous and portend the smashing of her dreams if she refused, followed Frida to the bedroom.

# OCTOBER 1930
# EL BARRIO CHINO

B oisterous applause rang in Lola's ears as, trailed by Fernando, she entered the lavish dressing room constructed after she moved in with Frida. The dinner show crowd had provided the illusion of a full house, although scattered empty tables indicated the growing distress of even the well-to-do. That afternoon, President Machado suspended constitutional guarantees following the previous day's confrontation with students at the University of Havana whom he denounced as following orders from Moscow. Prior to the show, Colonel Gallegos, Lola's self-professed most ardent admirer, telephoned to apologize for not attending. The increasing number of demonstrations kept him virtually locked in his office. However, he had good news. Lola would receive a special visitor.

As Fernando helped her out of her gown, Lola's post-show elation gave way to reality. Frida, on doctor's orders, remained home with a heavy cold bordering on pneumonia. Hospitals were not to be trusted, and while a new drug named penicillin was in the offing, it was unproven and, at any rate, unavailable in Cuba.

Lola remained further troubled that sunset had marked the beginning of Yom Kippur, the Day of Atonement. In New York, this had been the only day of the year the Sobel family attended synagogue—a disagreeable but socially required obligation. Sylvia lackadaisically took part in the congregation's responses. Only Albert found uplift in the mournful music sung by the cantor and choir during the evening Kol Nidre service and throughout the next day. Now, Lola's spirits plunged. At Frida's insistence, she'd absented herself from synagogue, cut herself off from her one childhood experience, beyond music, worthy of fond remembrance.

Raised voices sounded in the hallway.

"Not another fight, I hope," said Fernando. "People drink too much."

"Drinking is our business," said Lola, no longer the wide-eyed innocent. Anticipating her visitor, she slipped into a silver robe and matching slippers. After pouring a Scotch, she settled on the expensive green divan purchased by Frida and elevated her feet on a matching footstool. The white and purple mariposas on her dressing table caught her eye. Frida had a different arrangement delivered each afternoon.

Restless, Lola picked up a pack of Lucky Strikes. Her mind replayed the advertising slogan from American radio: "Reach for a Lucky instead of a sweet." She drew a flame from the gold lighter Colonel Gallegos had presented her, identical to the one given President Machado.

Someone knocked.

Fernando went to the door and accepted a dozen roses—half red, half white. "From you know who."

Flowers from diverse admirers were common, but only the Colonel sent them every night and always the same. Did señora Gallegos know? Or care? Yet following his impulsive kiss on New Year's Eve, the Colonel hadn't touched her. She found the situation confusing. Did she want him to seduce her? Then again, he knew of her involvement with Frida who, despite the many kindnesses she extended, had the power to destroy her. Still, Lola found their sex satisfying. Their lovemaking obviously was not conventional, but what did *conventional* mean? Going to bed with Manuel Gallegos might prove awkward. Or thrilling.

Outside the dressing room, a familiar voice bellowed, "Son of a whore!" Another commotion followed.

Fernando went into the hallway then returned. "Gott in Himmel!" he said. Although they were alone, he covered his mouth having revealed one of the Yiddish phrases he'd picked up from Lola along with much American English. "The Maestro," he said. "I have never seen him so upset, cariña."

Knuckles pounded on the door.

Fernando opened it, received a business card and announced, "Colonel Gallegos' special visitor."

Lola stood.

A man in a tuxedo entered. Like the Colonel's, his black hair, brushed back from his high forehead, glistened with pomade. A pencil mustache stretched above a smile that lit his broad face and attested to a polished charm. Behind him stood a short, narrow-faced man with slim shoulders. Like Siegel and Lansky, the smaller man seemed familiar.

The man in the tuxedo bowed. "Xavier Cugat at your service." Born in Spain, raised in Havana and having made his mark in New York as a teen-age violinist, Cugat spoke Spanish with an American accent. He kissed Lola's hand then gestured towards his companion. "My manager, Leon Greenspan."

Greenspan offered a tight-lipped smile revealing an element of awkwardness.

Lola turned back to Cugat. "Your reputation as a brilliant musician has preceded you, señor." His violin once accompanied the great Caruso. She thought it prudent not to remind him that he'd stolen Club Gardenia's piano player, earning the Maestro's undying enmity. Also, that Cugat had earned a measure of gratitude from her since his theft—the word seemed harsh; musicians weren't property—had paved the way for Lola Flores' career. "I understand that you are doing quite well in Los Angeles."

Cugat's eyebrows, by nature slanted down towards the bridge of his nose, ascended. "America is the land of opportunity. With talking pictures the new rage, Hollywood offers musicians attractive prospects."

"May I offer you a drink?" Lola asked.

Fernando held up the bottle of Scotch.

"And *you*, señor Greenspan?" she added.

"Leon does not speak Spanish," said Cugat. "But on behalf of both of us, thank you, no." He gestured towards Fernando. "And this would be Fernando Fallon?"

"Yes," said Lola. "I am indebted to Fernando."

Cugat nodded. "Forgive me, señorita. I must be brief. Another pressing appointment demands my attention this evening, and tomorrow I must return to Los Angeles, although Leon will remain here." He looked at Greenspan then back to Lola. "You speak English?"

"Yes."

"Permit me to say then that from what I have just heard, your music is almost on a level with my own. But neither you nor I will rise to our deserved heights unless we, as they say, test our wings."

"And what would that involve?"

Cugat eyed a gold wristwatch encrusted with diamonds. "I would consider it a great favor if, after your shows tomorrow night, you would have dinner with Leon."

Lola nodded. "If Mr. Fallon can accompany me."

Cugat smiled. "You will not be disappointed."

A coughing fit forced Frida to sit up in bed.

Lola placed a pillow behind her.

Frida closed her eyes. "If you must engage in such foolishness today, ask God to forgive my sins."

Lola, who'd awakened early the next morning and set tea on her patient's nightstand, touched the back of her hand to Frida's forehead. "You are still warm."

Frida muttered something and drifted off.

Lola brushed the left sleeve of the black suit coat Fernando purchased for Alberto and altered to provide style and comfort without drawing undue attention. Maintaining the Yom Kippur tradition of self-affliction, cloth suspenders replaced a leather belt, hemp sandals leather shoes.

Alberto then donned a dark Fedora. As Alberto, Lola was free to attend synagogue unnoticed and unmolested. The Siamese twins of the soul tiptoed downstairs.

In the morning sunshine, shopkeepers and café proprietors with clouded faces swept the narrow sidewalks. They appeared resigned to another day of few customers. Alberto/Lola empathized but, on this day, could do nothing to alleviate the merchants' woes. They strolled on, compelled for reasons they could not wholly understand to appear in the synagogue where they and Fernando had mourned Moisés Finkelstein and daven with kavanah—pray with true intention—on this holiest day of the year.

Approaching the shul, Lola spotted a short, narrow-shouldered man struggling to communicate with a synagogue official. Alberto spun on his heels. Lola provoked him with vexing questions: Will God write us out of the Book of Life? Is there really a God? Are we endangering our souls? Neither found satisfactory answers but agreed they faced less danger foregoing exposure to God's judgement than to the scrutiny of Leon Greenspan.

Following the late show, Lola and Fernando sat with Greenspan in a restaurant in Barrio Chino, Latin America's largest Chinatown. Other than a nearby all-night bodega, the barrio's shops and theaters were dark.

"Jews, we're crazy for Chinese food," Greenspan said. "And mah-jongg. The women. It's like gin rummy only with tiles instead of cards."

"That sounds very interesting," said Lola. Mama was a devotee.

Greenspan patted his stomach. "You wouldn't know, but yesterday was a Jewish holiday. Not so much a holiday but a day to do without." Jews went to synagogue. He himself stopped in for an hour at the cost of a pretty penny. "They sell tickets." Jews fasted. The old-timers. "Meshuganeh. Means crazy." Even having had breakfast, lunch following his short time in the shul and a big dinner at Club Gardenia, he was starving.

The waiter set down menus in Chinese and Spanish.

Fernando selected several dishes to be shared.

"I'll have a beer," said Greenspan. "And look, I'm not a guy who beats around the bush. Let's do business."

"Certainly," said Lola.

Fernando nodded.

Cugat—everyone called him Coogie—was doing very well in Los Angeles, but Los Angeles wasn't New York. Coogie was ready to go back to the Big Apple and make a big splash. "You know what I mean, the Big Apple?"

"To be truly important," said Lola, "something must take place in New York."

Greenspan and Coogie wanted to get the city excited before his return. Big money could still be made in the Big Apple. Many New Yorkers had no idea that the rest of the city experienced hard times. To assure Coogie's triumph, Greenspan would make sure New York's top newspapers columnists—Walter Winchell, Ed Sullivan, Nick Kenny—had plenty to write about. "They make stars, they bury 'em. But we gotta give 'em something big." His eyes darted from Lola to Fernando and back. "We hit New York after a smash tour of Europe."

Europeans liked Latin music. Those who didn't soon would. "And there ain't no Prohibition there which, for certain friends of mine, offers great business opportunities." Sure, Europe also got hit by the Depression, but money was there. The Xavier Cugat Orchestra would play major nightclubs in the Continent's capitals. "Before that, late December, early January, the band's gonna rehearse in Miami. Then, like how major league baseball teams play their way north from spring training, it'll go to Chicago, Detroit, Cleveland and Philadelphia." Again he turned to Fernando. "You know baseball?"

"Yes. We play baseball here in Cuba." Fernando smiled. "Not me, personally."

Late January, the band would sail from New York to Hamburg and take the train to Berlin. April, they'd finish in Copenhagen. After returning to New York, they'd play three shows at the Roxy, a six thousand-seat movie theater. "Jesus, it's almost Madison Square Garden." Attendees would hear Xavier Cugat and see a Hollywood film for one price.

Lola let Greenspan keep talking so that he might reveal some hidden intention or a weakness she could exploit.

Less patient, Fernando asked, "And Lola?"

"What? I asked you here because I missed chow mein?" Coogie's vocalist, his wife Carmen Castillo, had throat problems. "Doctors ordered six months rest. Lola plays piano and sings." He took a long swig of beer—Mayabe, a local favorite. "For that kind of break, she should pay *us*." Naturally, Carmen would rejoin the band at some point, and Coogie would hire another piano player. But Lola Flores would return to Havana as an international star. "Everybody wins."

Lola hesitated to respond. The opportunity to play Europe thrilled her, but what would happen in New York? She'd played with a number of musicians there. Would she be found out? On the other hand, her playing had matured, grown richer. Her appearance, thanks to Fernando, bore no resemblance to that of the Lola—she'd never provided a last name—who appeared in those small clubs. Besides, the musicians with whom she'd played would never condescend to see a commercial star like Cugat, even with a movie thrown in.

The greater threat of exposure resided with her family. But Albert was dead to Papa and Mama. Tosia, too. She'd undoubtedly hurt Sylvia, but what choice did she have? Lola Flores would appear in New York's newspapers only as Xavier Cugat's Cuban discovery. Albert being unearthed was less probable than Herbert Hoover winning re-election as president in 'thirty-two. Given the worsening Depression, Hoover's chances ranged from slim to nonexistent.

The waiter arrived with their order. Lola passed on the shrimp and pork, prohibited by Jewish law. She offered a more acceptable rationale. "I'm a vegetarian. It is better for my voice."

Fernando calculated that the matter might be more complicated than Greenspan let on. "Your offer is very kind but unexpected. We will need time to think about it."

Greenspan filled his plate. "You two chew it over. But I head back to L.A. tomorrow. Call me by Tuesday or you'll blow the best opportunity you'll ever have right out your asses."

The next afternoon, Lola strolled with Fernando along the Malecón. Waves hurtling against the gray seawall created explosions of white foam. Her pink skirt fluttered in the breeze. The matching ribbon on her straw hat resembled the flapping wings of a flamingo struggling to take flight.

Stretched out beneath the blue sky, the broad promenade lay almost deserted. Half the restaurants and cafés displayed CLOSED signs. Habaneros dismissed by the city's factories, docks, offices, shops and markets showed little desire to reveal their lack of employment. The few locals finding inspiration at the seaside walked with the restrained cadence of mourners. A smattering of tourists took photographs with Kodak Brownies.

"You remain unsure?" Fernando asked.

"The offer from Cugat is interesting, yes."

Fernando did not wish to exert undue influence but pointed out that Cugat would pay Lola more than Frida if less than what she was worth. More important, Europe would fall at the feet of Lola Flores. "Have you ever been to Europe? Except to be born?"

"A few years ago. We visited the parents of my mother in Warsaw. I went, of course, as Albert."

"It might be difficult, but perhaps we can arrange a visit."

"My grandfather died in 'twenty-eight and my grandmother three months later."

Fernando scanned the sea. If Lola chose to accompany Cugat, perhaps after playing New York they should return to Europe. Paris, for example, might offer a better life to people like them. Havana, he feared, would always be dangerous. "You recall Noche Buena?"

Lola still had bad dreams.

"Do not think me mad," said Fernando, "but have you ever wondered if Frida was responsible?"

"You cannot be serious."

"But I am." Perhaps Frida sought to remind them that they withheld no secrets from her, that they depended on Frida Herskovits not only for their livelihoods but their very lives. "Someday, however, people like Frida will no longer hold power over us."

Lola hoped Fernando was right but could not imagine that day being in her lifetime.

Fernando disagreed. "Remember what I told you about that Danish man? The one who lives openly as a woman?" She had undergone the first of several operations in Berlin to make her a woman in every way. "I have written to her doctor."

Lola wondered if such surgery might someday enable Lola Flores to present the world proof of her womanhood. "I would like to meet this brave woman," she said. She raised her face to the sun. "But to tour with Cugat—"

"Whatever you owed Frida, you have repaid. Frida and the Maestro will find a replacement—not brilliant like Lola Flores but suitable." And if they returned to Havana—*if*—Frida would welcome her. She hardly could turn her back on a new international star bound to fill Club Gardenia every evening while rival clubs begged for customers.

They arrived at an open café, sat beneath a red-and-yellow striped umbrella and lunched on fish, salad, bread and coffee. After, Lola ordered rum.

"Tell me, cariña," said Fernando. "Is Club Gardenia all you want from life?"

Lola drained her glass.

Frida finished the chicken soup, Lola's attempt to emulate Mama's before leaving for Club Gardenia. Color returned to Frida's cheeks. She patted the edge of the bed.

Lola sat.

"This tour with Cugat," Frida said in Yiddish, the matter too important to be entrusted to Spanish. "Do you not love me?"

Lola tucked another pillow behind Frida.

"Have I not found ways to please you?" Frida asked.

"You have," said Lola. She did not equate love with pleasure, but pleasure she'd experienced in full. Lola had never imagined all the ways a woman could satisfy her, but sexual gratification, she'd come to understand, required only desire and a willingness to explore possibilities.

"Why?" Frida asked. "Why would you go to Europe with the man who almost ruined Club Gardenia? What have I done that you should express such ingratitude?" She squeezed Lola's wrist. "You must know, I can keep you here."

The next day, Lola took a taxi to the gate of Barrio Chino. Wearing a nondescript brown wig—she had acquired a small collection to help disguise her appearance—dark glasses and a shapeless flower-print housedress her mother would have condemned as a shmata, she walked past the restaurant in which she and Fernando had met with Leon Greenspan. At Calle San Martin, Manuel Gallegos stepped out from the doorway of a bakery, its window displaying pork bao, almond biscuits, mooncakes and banana rolls. They walked to a nearby bar identified by a small sign as El Papagayo Verde.

Inside, murky light revealed tacky paintings, sculptures and taxidermy paying homage to the establishment's namesake green parrot. An unseen Victrola played Alejandro García Caturla's symphonic *Tres danzas cubanas*. At the bar, three of eight stools propped up men with heads bent, thoughts unshared. Of a dozen tables and booths, only two hosted patrons.

The bartender, his face revealing Chinese ancestry combined with African—Cuba had permitted entry to Chinese men but few women—straightened his white apron, its broad pocket stuffed with a white rag. He gestured towards a high-backed wooden booth along the far wall.

Lola and Gallegos sat across the table.

The bartender brought a bottle of rum.

"¡Salud!" Gallegos toasted.

Lola barely caught herself about to respond L'chaim! "You are kind to discuss this matter," she said.

"A man in my position attends to many interests." An influential business associate had put Cugat in touch with him. This associate had expectations. "Yet Frida Herskovits takes exception to your touring Europe and boasts powerful friends—Jews like her."

"Friends more powerful than yours?"

Before Gallegos could answer, a burly man with a creased face, the sleeves of his faded blue shirt rolled up over impressive biceps, staggered towards them. Like the bartender, he evidenced mixed blood. He smiled. His yellowed teeth betrayed numerous gaps. "Pretty woman," he said, not put off by Lola's wig and dress, "we do not very often see such beauty here."

"Go about your business," said Gallegos.

The man extended his arms towards Lola. "I think you would like to dance with me."

Lola recoiled.

"I will repeat myself only once," said Gallegos. His voice carried across the room. "Go about your business."

The man placed his large, scarred hands—several of the fingers bent—over his heart. "Oh, how you frighten me, señor. You in your fancy suit. On the docks, if you had a job—if *I* still had a job—an asshole like you would get it right up the asshole!"

The bartender, a hand in his apron pocket, approached.

"This gentleman was just leaving," said Gallegos.

The man reached for Lola.

The bartender's left hand grasped the man by the neck while his right pressed the muzzle of a short-barreled revolver against the man's temple.

A stain spread across the man's trousers. Shoulders slumped, he retreated and left.

"Thank you, Efrain," said Gallegos.

"As always, señor."

Lola emptied her glass and felt herself ready to empty her bladder.

Gallegos patted her hand. "We were discussing Lola Flores becoming a great star in Europe. Despite the difficulties involved, nothing would please me more."

Seated at her dressing table before the dinner show, Lola embraced the telephone receiver.

Fernando hovered over her, taking care not to disturb one of Lola's now-fabled flower hats.

"Thank you, Mr. Greenspan," she said. "I will be honored to tour Europe with Mr. Cugat."

"So," said Fernando. "Frida gives you her blessing?"

Inside Colonel Gallegos' office, Lola perched on the edge of a pale-blue, Spanish Revival loveseat. Throughout the wing of the Presidential Palace housing the Sección de Expertos, serious men carried on serious work while ordinary habaneros spent Sunday morning praying, sleeping or, for those with means, dining out. Gallegos sat behind a nineteenth-century, ormolu-gilded French desk. Light poured through the windows. Lola had pictured the Colonel interrogating Communists in a basement shut off from the sun by walls of drab gray rather than brilliant rose.

"You are comfortable?" Gallegos asked.

Lola's eyes drifted past him to a mahogany credenza displaying porcelain miniatures painted with an intense palette: two mounted horsemen, a soldier in a three-cornered hat shouldering a musket, four village women dancing, young lovers holding hands.

"Ah, you also admire Meissen," said Gallegos. "German craftsmanship at its finest, no?" The pieces were well over a hundred years old and safe enough here, although he secured the much larger balance of his collection elsewhere.

Lola thought of the tchotchkes Mama purchased at Woolworth's and McCrory's and exhibited in her living-room shrine to America: tin models of the Statue of Liberty, the Brooklyn Bridge, a yellow taxi with a black-and-white checker pattern running its length and a rectangular coin bank portraying Macys on Herald Square. Several plates hung on one wall displaying images of New York Harbor, the winged Bethesda Fountain in Central Park known as the Angel of the Waters and the New York Public Library on Fifth Avenue, as majestic as Havana's Presidential Palace.

Gallegos went to the door and locked it. Returning to his desk, he deposited the key in his right trouser pocket. "Our conversation must remain private."

Lola leaned forward. "I will need a passport."

Gallegos rested his palms on the desk's green leather surface. "I am puzzled. A passport may be obtained by any loyal citizen of Cuba."

"I leave in two months."

He acknowledged the glacial pace of Cuba's bureaucracy. "Take your birth certificate to the passport office. I will have them expedite the matter."

"I also will need a birth certificate."

Gallegos fingered the collar on his coat. "You cannot procure this document on your own?"

Lola made no reply.

He looked away. The request for a simple favor had taken an unexpected turn. A deep breath signaled his decision. "A new birth certificate will resemble that from a town whose city hall burned down some years ago, its records destroyed. Your passport will be processed in a few days."

"I will require the same for Fernando."

Gallegos stood and stepped around the desk. "You understand that Frida has not yet withdrawn her objection to your accompanying señor Cugat. Perhaps she would look more favorably on your leaving if Fernando remained in Havana."

Lola shook her head. "Is Fernando to serve as a hostage?" And who would look after her among strange people in unfamiliar places, anticipate unexpected dangers?

Gallegos' tongue flicked out of his mouth then withdrew. "Do not underestimate the complexity of the situation. Assuming that you tour Europe and return, certain people may nonetheless feel unsettled. Put upon. Offended." He would have to call on his position and the powers of persuasion that accompanied it to convince them that granting him authority in this matter would provide for their mutual advantage. "Then, our futures, yours and mine, will be interwoven." He stepped towards Lola.

Lola leaned back.

He rested a hand on her shoulder. "Given the jeopardy into which you now place my career, I welcome a token of your appreciation."

She placed a hand over her chest. "You will always occupy a special place in my heart."

Gallegos grasped Lola's left elbow, forced her to her feet and encircled her with his arms. His hands pressed into the small of her back. His breath, redolent of morning coffee and pastries, penetrated her nostrils.

Lola's eyes glanced towards the locked door. Gallegos' office, for all its unanticipated furnishings, served as the cell she'd imagined. Flight was impossible. She could cry out, but to what purpose? The floor was filled with men, all his subordinates, none likely to respond. The only women— including his secretary—toiled in a room down the hall. She might as well be flotsam out at sea drifting towards the Straits of Florida. Resist? At best, the tide would return her broken body to the harbor and wrap it around the piling of a disused pier. Still, every muscle in her body tensed.

"I cannot reject what I feel for you," Gallegos said. "Nor will I any longer deny myself."

Lola weighed her options and decided. She would no longer hide behind her carefully constructed façade. She would confront the Colonel with the truth and pray that his disgust might move him to dismiss rather than savage her.

Before she could speak, he brushed his lips over hers. "Do not think I am unaware of all the ways a man can take his pleasure with one of Frida's extraordinary courtesans."

Lola found herself rendered immobile and mute as Gallegos removed his coat, unfastened the buttons on his fly, turned her around and bent her over the loveseat. She vowed that while she could not thwart Manuel's triumph of the flesh, she would see her humiliation redressed.

The next morning, Lola awoke to the aroma of coffee. She went to the kitchen. Pain accompanied each footstep.

Frida stood at the stove, four white eggs at her right hand.

"Why are you out of bed?" Lola asked.

"The Malach HaMovis, I should make it easy for him to find me?" she answered, her voice robust. And if the Angel of Death *could* find her, he would be running a fool's errand. That afternoon, Frida had important business before seeing Lola at the club.

"Wonderful news," Lola said. She masked her concern that Frida's unexpected recovery would mar the arrangement she'd made with Colonel Gallegos. Manuel, he insisted. As to breakfast, she only wanted coffee.

"Your strength you have to keep up," said Frida. She turned off the gas. "Yesterday morning, you left me alone."

"I needed air. This is a difficult time for me."

"Only for *you*?"

"I promised I will return."

"You are too young and inexperienced to understand." Frida's other businesses were suffering. Men now defied their instincts and turned for sex to their wives. Her real-estate holdings required upkeep. Depression or no, she needed capital to pay for workers and materials. Also, a new singer would require new gowns. You faced reality or it slapped you in the face. "Only Lola Flores can keep the clientele of Club Gardenia from shrinking further. At that, I may have to cut back to one show a night. But that might represent an admission that the club is losing popularity. Business may drop even more." She sat at the small kitchen table. "You think Manuel Gallegos will help you leave Cuba? That he *can*?"

Lola bit her cheeks.

Frida rolled her eyes. "I know you had dinner with that landsman Greenspan in Barrio Chino."

"Colonel Gallegos—Manuel—swore to me his protection."

"Manuel, is it? Better for you if he offered to make good my losses."

"What will you do? Kill me?"

Frida's good eye cast Lola a dismissive stare. "You should be so lucky." Should Lola set foot on a ship to Miami, Frida would expose her. Lola would arrive in the States only to be deported. "But the government of Cuba will bar your return. You will be a real wandering Jew."

"Manuel would never—"

"Manuel will retreat to his work knowing that his father-in-law will be displeased should someone inform him of his enchantment with you." As to arrangements he believed he'd made with the Americans Lansky and Siegel, Manuel deluded himself. "We Jews take care of each other."

"And where does that leave me?"

An unearthly light shone in Frida's good eye. "So then, no more foolishness. I will see you at the club tonight after I meet with poor, misguided Manuelito. Rest assured, the matter will be settled."

Lola, made up and gowned, reached for a tissue on her dressing room vanity. She hoped Fernando would think she was coming down with a cold, which was as far from the truth as Havana from New York—or Warsaw. She had no desire to reveal that she was upset. Doubly so because she'd concealed from Fernando that Frida was probably meeting with Manuel at this moment, that having kept such a secret from Fernando, she had slighted their friendship, which had made them emotional intimates.

She rationalized that Fernando would be troubled to know that Frida and Manuel were bargaining, perhaps exchanging threats veiled and explicit, to determine her future—and his—without their consent. Unless Manuel confused her surrender in his office with consent. Unless, given not only his physical strength but also her ambition, it was.

A between-shows drink in hand, Lola lit an ivory-tipped Marlboro, advertised in all the leading magazines as a woman's cigarette.

Fernando fussed with her hat. "Cariña, your voice," he scolded.

"My voice has never been better."

"I still have not seen Frida at her table. Perhaps she has taken ill again. Shall I telephone?"

Lola considered that Frida might well have suffered a relapse. Her recovery seemed almost miraculous and Lola—like Albert—had no faith in miracles. Concluding that a relapse was the case, Lola's spirits rose. Frida and Manuel had not met. Or they'd spoken on the telephone at a calming distance, recognized their common interests and reached an agreement. The threats that shook her to the core would end.

The stage manager knocked.

Lola took her position in the wings.

Despite the modest audience, the band played with gusto. The Maestro's trumpet sounded almost as rich and warm as Lola's voice.

Frida's table remained empty.

Following the show, Lola waited in her dressing room for Fernando to free her from the restraints of her gown. She poured another drink.

Fernando burst through the doorway. His cheeks conjured the ghost-white complexion of his Irish grandfather. "Frida!" he moaned.

"She answered the telephone? She is in bed?"

"No. Barrio Chino. An alley. They found her body."

# FEBRUARY 1931

## LILI ELBE

A tomb-like silence enveloped the Palm Tree Room in Haus Vaterland, the multi-story entertainment complex on Potsdamer Platz. The overflow audience seemed to hold its collective breath as Lola sang Moisés Simons' "El Manisero"—The Peanut Vendor. When she finished, the audience exploded with delight. Their cheering intimated the howitzers that shelled Allied lines during the disastrous Great War. One of Cuba's most treasured songs now touched hearts in a Berlin that gave the appearance of healing.

As the crowd quieted, Lola played the introduction to a love song written during rehearsals in Miami. Based on the biblical Ruth's petition to accompany her mother-in-law Naomi back to Bethlehem, it made no mention of God or Israel. In a departure from the show's other numbers, the piano served as her sole accompaniment. The adagio rhythm reinforced the intense, almost brooding desire in Lola's lyrical plea:

> *Where you go, I will go.*
> *Where you live, I will live.*
> *Where you die, I will die.*
> *Two hearts. One heart.*

The last fading notes gave way to shouts of Zugabe! Encore! Lola glanced at Cugat, received his approval then repeated the song. The audience demonstrated the same gusto.

Cugat summoned Lola to his side.

Smiling, Lola bowed but sensed herself trembling. She'd reached a new and terrifying awareness. Over the four months since Frida's murder—Fernando learned that her throat had been slashed—Lola had made Manuel's secret hers. Now, she feared she'd emptied her soul of what measure of virtue she'd brought to Havana.

Albert continued the reproach. She had cauterized her feelings for anyone in her past who threatened her future. Frida Herskovits hardly represented the worst of her transgressions since she hadn't wielded the knife. She'd all but erased Papa and Mama from her memory along with Tosia and, for the most part, Sylvia. That, too, constituted a form of murder. God would judge them both.

Lola shuddered. If only she could purge Albert of his naïveté, which denied him the opportunity to put his soul at rest. Worse, imperiled her success. Her survival. *Their* survival. His lack of worldliness left her one final choice. But what would happen to her if she rid herself of him?

Baltic gusts knifed through the late-afternoon darkness. Snow hurtled across tree-lined Unter den Linden. Tree trunks swayed. Branches, leafless and slick with ice, trembled, as did Lola and Fernando. Determined to see the sites on foot—the New York winters of her childhood had launched similar assaults, yet people went about their business—they lowered their heads. Twenty paces from the shelter of the domed City Palace on the Spree River, home of German emperors following unification, she conceded it would have been wiser to take a streetcar. Better, hail a taxi. Two more performances lay ahead that night.

Fernando could not imagine enduring similar discomfort in Frankfort, Zurich, Paris, Brussels, Amsterdam and Copenhagen. When spring officially arrived in six weeks, even the latter two cities would not warm to anything close to a Cuban's satisfaction. New York in April offered no promise of relief.

Lola, adapted to Cuba's warmth, prodded Fernando to go on. Would they ever enjoy such an opportunity again?

Fernando matched her step for step, He took grudging comfort that their destination required walking only halfway towards the boulevard's western terminus—the Brandenburg Gate topped by the Quadriga, a chariot pulled by four horses.

Despite their haste, they could not avoid noticing many large red banners with white disks that enclosed crooked black crosses, the symbol of the National Socialist party. Every block or so, they encountered marching men in brown overcoats and boots, their movements more belligerent than precise, mouths extruding a metallic vapor, ruddy faces as hard as the facades of the city's stone and brick buildings.

Lola slowed to peer into the window of a store selling exquisite objects of silver—goblets, tea and coffee sets, serving trays, candlesticks—some ornate, others sleekly modern. She wished they had time to go in and marvel at household objects fit for display at the Metropolitan Museum of Art. And, of course, to warm up. They turned to continue their journey.

Two brown-coated men approached. One, whose fleshy pink jowls bordered on grotesque, raised his right arm. "Heil Hitler!" he barked.

Lola and Fernando made no effort to return the salute. They were Cubans.

The jowly man stepped forward and grabbed Fernando's shoulder. He balled his massive right hand into a fist.

Lola gasped.

The man's companion, although smaller, pulled him back. "Please excuse us," he said in German. "My friend meant no harm."

Lola comprehended his remark since German was close enough to Yiddish for her to pick up a great deal of conversation among Berliners. Still, she refrained from making a simple response. Her Yiddish accent would expose her and imperil Fernando.

The smaller man led his intimidating compatriot back to the group with which they'd marched.

Lola's shivering increased. She grasped the arm of the equally shaken Fernando. She'd read about the National Socialists and their leader Hitler, who loathed Jews, blamed them for Germany's defeat in the Great War. "These men. Are they soldiers?" she asked.

"Stormtroopers," said Fernando. "Hitler's private army." He related that the previous September, the National Socialists won the second most seats in the Reichstag—the German parliament. That night, they broke windows in Jewish shops all over Germany.

The wind swung about and pummeled them from the west. The stripped tree branches shook furiously. Their clatter resembled a chorus of death rattles. Lola and Fernando clamped gloved hands on their hats and pushed on.

They reached their goal at Friedrichstrasse, blocks from the Reichstag. Inside the Café Kranzler, Fernando held up three bone-chilled fingers. "Drei," he said to the maître d', putting to use his guidebook German. "I am Herr Fallon," he continued in English. "We are expecting a guest." He pointed towards the back of the room where they might enjoy a reasonable degree of privacy.

Patrons in the half-filled café spoke in hushed tones reflecting concerns about rising unemployment and the menace Lola and Fernando had just encountered. They arrived at a booth in a corner formed by golden-honey walls. Mirrors climbed to the white molding bordering the ceiling. Lola settled on a banquette upholstered in chocolate-brown leather. Fernando sat opposite on a dark wooden chair with a rounded back and matching leather seat.

A waiter in a white shirt, black vest and white apron descending below his knees presented menus.

"I believe," Lola informed Fernando, "he will take our orders when our third party arrives."

"This place will not be inexpensive," said Fernando.

"But it is the *right* place for a special occasion," Lola said.

A moment later, a woman in a dark-gray coat with a fox collar approached their booth.

Fernando helped their guest off with her coat.

With the eye of a painter, the woman appraised his dark hair and Latin complexion, so much in contrast to those of the winter-pale Germans and hers.

Lola found the woman, closer to her mother's age, far more attractive than she had expected. She exhibited a slim figure. Her eyes sparkled. Deep-red lipstick highlighting full lips drew attention from her broad chin.

The woman sat next to Lola. "So delighted to meet you," she said in English. Her accent reflected her Danish origins.

"Allow me to make a formal introduction," Fernando said in his ever-improving English, the one language they shared. "Lili, this is Lola Flores. Lola, this is Lili Elbe with whom I have corresponded these past few months and spoke with yesterday on the telephone."

Lola nodded.

"Do you think it a coincidence that our names sound so much alike?" Lili Elbe asked.

"Perhaps so," said Lola.

Lili smiled, although her eyes betrayed a measure of physical discomfort. "I look forward to your performance this evening. The *Berliner Tageblatt* acclaims you a great success."

"You are most kind," said Lola.

"If I may confide in you, stopping in Berlin defied doctor's orders." She glanced at Fernando. "But Fernando's touching letters required me to see you, since I am on my way from Paris to Dresden where I shall undergo further surgery."

The waiter returned.

Lili ordered in German. Coffee, of course. And while her doctors might disapprove, several Kranzler's specialties: Berliners, a form of jelly doughnut; Linzer Augen, cookie halves filled with jam; and a Prinz Regententorte—Bavarian seven-layer sponge cake with chocolate buttercream and a chocolate glaze topped with apricot jam. "Also, this must be my treat, as the paintings of Andreas Wegener—my former self— are selling so well in Copenhagen."

The waiter gone, Fernando leaned forward. "Dear Lili, I have burned all your letters."

"I have done the same with your correspondence," said Lili. Safety was a greater concern than ever, but Lola and Fernando should not be troubled if anyone here recognized her. They would think Lili only enjoying the company of fellow artists. "As to the Nazis, they dare not create a disturbance inside or out of such a venerable establishment as Kranzler's. Even *they* cannot be capable of such sacrilege."

Lola took comfort in Lili's assertion. Who were the Nazis but another of Germany's many political parties, although this one included the most rabid of anti-Semites?

"Sooner or later," said Lili, "Germans will get fed up and give the Nazis the boot. But we have more important matters to discuss."

"Indeed," said Lola. "Fernando relates that you will have a uterus implanted. And also have made a vagina."

The pain revealed in Lili's eyes became more pronounced. "You come to the point," she said. "One expects that more from Americans than Cubans." She took a deep breath. "I have undergone several operations. Also, injections for what are called hormones. These are chemicals that make men and women each what they are." Only a few people understood such science, which involved much experimentation. Having received great support from her former wife Gerda along with King Christian, who annulled their marriage, and the Danish people, she was anxious to complete the procedures. Already, her voice had risen. She had hips and breasts. "In that regard, I believe you are more fortunate than I was." She grasped Lola's hands in hers, larger than hers but delicate. "Perhaps there is a physician in New York who can perform this surgery for you."

"After arriving in New York, we must sail to Havana," Fernando said.

"And will you stay in Cuba permanently?" Lili asked. "Might New York be a better place for Lola to advance her career?" She could enquire of her German doctor whether there might be a physician in New York helping women like them to become who they really were.

Lola fiddled with her napkin. New York offered wonderful opportunities and living there would represent a sort of poetic justice, but she could not discount the increased likelihood of discovery. On the other hand, over a year had passed since she'd fled to Havana. Her former persona of just-Lola had undergone a major transformation.

Then there was Manuel. He expected her return to the island and for good reason. He held the same power to expose Lola Flores as had Frida although doing so personally would run counter to his interests. More likely, he would avenge his honor by sending someone to New York—or calling on a contact there—to kill her. Also, she could never link him to Frida's murder. And if he *did* grant his permission to leave Cuba, finding it judicious to take seriously the vows he'd exchanged with his wife and avoid a confrontation with her family? Lola would be free to undergo the dangerous procedures that left Lili weakened but still enthused. "You demonstrate such courage, Lili."

"Not so much courage as love. I wish to bear a child for my wonderful Claude, an art dealer in Paris and the dearest man in the world. I have just come from seeing him."

"Are you not already a true woman? Must we bear children to avoid suspicion or antagonism when others considered women from birth can remain childless?"

"Yes, we are both true women. May I share another confidence?"

"Of course," Lola said.

"What has been most difficult—and yet entirely necessary—has been the death of Andreas, my former self."

The waiter approached with their coffee and pastries.

"I understand," said Lola, "that you wish to live with Claude as Lili rather than Andreas. As to my relationship with Alberto, I find it far more complicated than I expected." She wanted to separate from Albert, of course, but could she really inflict such violence on his leave-taking? His excised penis—so small it had made him the butt of countless cruel jokes yet a monstrous hurdle to overcome—would serve as an offering like an ox or sheep slaughtered in the Temple in Jerusalem. Yet God surely had created Albert/Lola in his image despite most people's smug assumptions.

Lili acknowledged that these surgeries and all they represented were so new as to be difficult to grasp. To be sure, the possibilities were encouraging. "But change, even in service to the bidding of one's heart, can leave one unsettled."

"May I ask you, Lili," said Fernando, "to provide us with the address of the clinic in Dresden?"

"I shall send a note to your hotel."

Lola, her pastries untouched, said, "I have my own confession to make. I often find it difficult to believe that good will prevail."

Lili patted Lola's hand. "Do you remember the Old Testament story of Pharaoh chasing the Israelites to the edge of the Red Sea? When the worst seemed inevitable, God parted the waters."

Lola chose not to respond that following their deliverance, the Israelites demanded a golden calf to worship and wandered in the wilderness for forty years.

# APRIL 1931

# THE HAVANA SPECIAL REDUX

As the Havana Special headed south from Charleston, Lola experienced another spell of agitation. On the table sat a yellow Western Union telegram from Miguel, delivered to her Times Square hotel the day the Cugat orchestra arrived in New York. Its message remained cryptic.

Lola refilled her tumbler with Scotch and surveyed her bedroom compartment. A single like Fernando's, it resembled the one in which she'd been assaulted during her escape from New York. That she had agreed to repeat the rail journey to Key West signified the desperation that brought her down to earth after such a glorious tour of Europe. She and Fernando had intended to return to Havana by sea, avoiding Lola's reliving the conductor's attack, which she'd never disclosed, but the shipping lines had reduced their schedules. Fewer Americans vacationed in sultry Cuba. The first liner bound for Havana wouldn't sail for a week.

Determined to avoid the train, Lola proposed that they remain in Manhattan during the interim. Fernando had seen only a handful of the sights. He objected. Adding an extended hotel stay plus meals to their passage would reduce their limited resources. Lola's tour income had been greatly diminished by Leon Greenspan making considerable deductions for miscellaneous expenses. *Normal stuff that always pops up, which maybe Lola's contract didn't lay out in so many words. Not worth complaining, if you got my drift.*

Lola assented to taking the train. Objecting risked being interrogated by Fernando, who possessed unnerving insight and the tenacity of a New York police detective. She'd known one. She'd also be traveling under Fernando's protective wing. At Penn Station, she summoned the strength to board the train in what appeared to be good spirits. In bed, she wept until sunrise.

The flat, green South Carolina landscape hurtling by and Fernando napping, Lola diverted her attention from the telegram by skimming the Sunday *New York Times*. Mayor Jimmy Walker denied corruption charges. Navy warships were rushing to Honduras. Spain's King Alfonso, a refugee, was heading to London having been booted out of Paris. She closed her eyes and let her thoughts drift.

Cugat's engagement at the Roxy had proved as successful as the tour of Europe. True to Leon Greenspan's assurances—if he was a crook, he at least was well-connected—Walter Winchell, Ed Sullivan and Nick Kenny lavished praise on Cugat in their columns. Most important, they hailed Lola Flores as Cuba's newest musical sensation.

Her reflections shifted back to Frida's funeral. The shiksa Lola Flores sat upstairs in the synagogue's women's section occupied by two Jewish matrons along with Club Gardenia's female dancers and seamstresses. Frida's madams and working girls extended the courtesy of staying away. Downstairs, Fernando joined Eduardo Ruiz, the band, male choristers and staff. Several rows in front, three elderly members of the congregation augmented by paid mourners formed the minyan of ten Jewish men required to recite Kaddish. Manuel appeared after the service started and looked up at her. His expression of public sorrow failed to mask his private resolve that he would tolerate no one's interference in matters of business as well as politics, least of all hers. As the service concluded, Lola recited Kaddish in her heart as if to deny her complicity in Frida's death. She left doubting that she'd swayed the heavenly court.

The day following Shiva—the seven-day mourning period—Frida's attorney revealed that for all her business acumen, his client had accumulated debts that required liquidation of her assets. Her interest in Club Gardenia—a minority interest—would pass to its investors. Frida's will made no provisions for Lola.

The train rolling on, Lola reviewed the plans she and Fernando had made in Europe. Cuba's economy and politics continued to deteriorate, but money still could be made by those who controlled the entertainers. For now, Lola Flores would leverage her newfound celebrity and Fernando manage her career. He would add to their income by designing costumes and stage sets. When the economy found firmer footing, they would open a club of their own.

Lola picked up the telegram. Its three words remained vexing: ARRANGEMENTS MADE HAVANA.

# JUNE 1931

# SUITE 848

The elevator in the Hotel Nacional rose. Lola's spirits sank. Only hours remained before the opening of the Nacional's showroom, and doubts assailed her.

The elevator operator, a wiry, copper-faced man in a green uniform with gold braid on both shoulders, eased the car to a halt at the top floor, opened the gate and smiled. "Have a wonderful show tonight, señorita Flores."

Lola barely managed, "Thank you, Luis."

Entering Suite 848, her attention leaped from the panoramic view of the Bay to Manuel sprawled on one of the living room's white sofas. The violet belt of his purple satin robe rode above a stomach revealing the victory of affluent middle age over a once-athletic figure. Manuel had competed in the modern pentathlon at the 1920 Olympic Games in Antwerp. Swedes took the three medals and fourth place, but Manuel drew the attention of a wealthy Cuban seeking to match his daughter with an accomplished man of pure European blood.

"Should you not be resting?" asked Manuel.

"Should you not be in your office or spying around the city?" Lola responded.

He sat up. "So, you ignore the tranquility that has embraced Havana this past week." The Sección de Expertos had learned much from Italy's Benito Mussolini, all the ways he terrified the adversaries he subdued in North Africa. Those who would betray Cuba now cowered before the clenched fist.

"Perhaps these traitors are only catching their breath."

Manuel scowled. He preferred that Lola focus on music rather than state security. He could say with certainty that the Communists and the students had lost their courage. He held up the index finger of his right hand like a scolding parent. "You failed to answer my question."

"Always the interrogator," Lola said. She sat on the sofa opposite and lit a cigarette. "Yesterday, I asked Carlos to revise several arrangements. This afternoon, we rehearsed longer than I anticipated. The show tonight must be nothing less than perfect." She kicked off her shoes.

"Your feet—" said Manuel. "They are those of a woman."

She wondered if he meant his comment to be flattering or demeaning.

Manuel poured each a Scotch, although in public he made a show of drinking rum. "Tonight, all of Cuba—at least, those who are important—will worship at those feet."

"And you?"

"Of course."

"And Ysabel?"

His wife would stay home while he entertained business associates.

"A patriot *and* a businessman," Lola retorted.

He held out his arms. "My business provides you with all this."

Lola could not deny the appealing arrangements Manuel had made, although he'd not consulted her. She lived in the city's newest, most impressive hotel, built by Americans and inhabited mostly by Yanquis, a term she freely employed. Atop Taganana Hill, the rocky cliff rising from the Malecón, the hotel bordered the affluent Vedado neighborhood. Its red-tile-roof crowned a statement of elegance made by Moorish, Roman and Art Deco motifs. Its elongated lobby ran between rows of graceful arches, a wood-beamed ceiling overhead. Illuminated at night, the Nacional's two towers served as beacons along the island's northern coast.

Still, Lola chafed at being a kept woman. But what choice had she? She and Fernando faced an uncertain reality without Manuel's patronage. Worse, should Manuel become sufficiently desperate or deranged, he could expose her and send her career toppling.

"Let us not quarrel," she said. In the brief time since she'd returned to Havana, they'd come to resemble a long-married couple—Papa and Mama? Each pointed out the other's faults like a child picking at a scab until it bled. Not that they saw each other with marital frequency.

Preoccupied with work, Manuel visited once or twice a week. Sometimes, she discovered him in her bedroom when she woke. He would return to the office when Fernando, settled in a modest apartment near the one he'd formerly occupied, visited to discuss details of the show, or when she wrote music at the baby grand piano or went downstairs to rehearse with the band. At other times, he appeared for dinner and spent the night. Ysabel conceded his periodic need to "sleep at the office." That fiction created a certain tranquility, if as deceptively calm as the eye of a hurricane.

"You are nervous," Manuel said. "That is normal."

Lola emptied her glass. Her nerves were fine, she protested. "I am concerned. Eduardo Ruiz was an outstanding musician. Cugat even better. I will accept nothing less than to rise above them both. *Far* above."

"You *will*. It is *Lola Flores* who will open the showroom at the Nacional tonight. Why? Because *I* convinced very important people that Lola Flores, fresh from her triumph in Europe, must be the Nacional's premier performer. Manuel Gallegos-Lucchese has friends."

These included President Machado who, in return for expediting construction and liquor permits, secured a small, undisclosed share in the Nacional for himself and another for Manuel. The Nacional quickly became the preferred destination for wealthy Americans, who would always possess the means with which to pamper themselves. To uphold this status, order would be maintained. The Nacional's silent partners included Americans, who guaranteed excellent relations with staff, suppliers and everyone else crucial to smooth operations. Eventually, Manuel would leverage this and other business dealings to sever his financial dependence on his father-in-law.

Lola conceded that Manuel had laid the groundwork for what promised to be a bright future. Even before the ink dried on her contract, the hotel's publicist dubbed her "The Cuban Firecracker." The nickname burst across Havana.

What unsettled her was the bankrolling of the Lola Flores Orchestra. By the time she received Manuel's telegram, he had enlisted several unnamed investors in what was to be her enterprise. Their capital enabled Lola to hire Havana's finest musicians along with Carlos Sánchez, an arranger worthy of her talents as a composer and songwriter. They also designated Fernando, who would continue to design Lola's stunning gowns and spectacular hats, as the band's manager of record. In time, they would permit Fernando to book Lola into other clubs around the island in which the investors held interests. He would even sign Cuban record and film contracts the investors negotiated. Or dictated. Naturally, the investors' generosity would be rewarded with the first share of the band's revenues.

Manuel dismissed Lola's concerns. Her backers would open doors to major clubs and hotels in Cuba, and soon in the States, through which she could not hope to enter on her own. This made her share in the band infinitely more valuable than if her own meager funds provided her one hundred percent interest. Still, she fretted that her one-third share left her in the position of little more than chattel.

Lola poured another Scotch.

Manuel stood, stretched then settled next to her. "May I ask you something?"

"You require my permission?"

He brushed his lips across her neck.

Despite the restraints he imposed on her, Lola took pleasure in Manuel's finding her desirable. Their sex was good, far gentler than that of their first encounter, which she acknowledged as rape. She suffered bouts of guilt but not for accepting what he'd done to her. She hadn't accepted that at all. Frida's murder continued to upset here.

Manuel made indirect references to her when Lola expressed thoughts he took as too independent. Each left unsaid that Lola understood the circumstances of Frida's death and that Manuel would never compromise himself by mentioning his role outright. Lola's silence served her own interests. She accepted a measure of self-loathing as the cost of doing business. In time, the scales of justice would seek balance. Manuel would suffer his punishment while she bore with fortitude any judgment God rendered against her. Success—survival—demanded a price. She would pay it.

Lola's fingers flew across the keyboard as the band reprised its opening number to begin the show's finale. Female dancers swayed their hips in costumes revealing even for Havana. Fernando insisted that they practically bare their breasts. Male dancers clasped their hands over their hearts then leaped towards the women and embraced them as they whirled in a Latin waltz. Lola segued to the concluding lyrics of the song she wrote after meeting Lili Elbe:

> *What is a woman?*
> *Strong arms.*
> *A faithful heart.*
> *A soul as deep as the sea.*
> *Woman! Woman! Woman!*

Following a standing ovation and two encores, Lola returned to her dressing room—twice the size of that at Club Gardenia. Flowers sprouted from tables and filled every open space on the floor, creating the ambience of a conservatory.

"Cariña," said Fernando, "you were wonderful!"

Lola beckoned him forward to help her out of her gown. "Hurry," she said. "The night is not over."

Armed men saluted as Lola approached the door to Suite 848. Inside, waiters poured champagne and served hors d'oeuvres. Lola accepted praise from President Machado and his wife. Steps away, one of the Nacional's American developers and the president of the hotel's management company roared in self-congratulatory laughter. Fernando engaged several high-ranking government officials and their wives—or mistresses.

Gathered at a living room window, three men ignored the showgirls accompanying them and gazed out into the darkness.

Manuel, with measured steps calculated to avoid surprise, approached the oldest, seemingly near his own age. The man's dark wavy hair, olive skin and drooping right eyelid added a sense of menace to his unsmiling face. Manuel bowed. After receiving a discreet nod, Manuel escorted the man to Lola.

The other two men followed a deferential step behind.

President Machado took his wife's hand and led her away.

Lola understood the man with Manuel to be one of the Nacional's investors but recognized only the men who appeared to be his subordinates.

Manuel glanced at the olive-skinned man with a deference never conveyed towards the president. "Permit me to present Lola Flores," he said. "Lola, we are pleased to have as our honored guest señor Charles Luciano from New York. You have previously met señores Lansky and Siegel."

From the New York newspapers, Lola knew Luciano had been a protege of Arnold Rothstein, the biggest Jewish gangster of them all, murdered several years earlier, presumably over a gambling debt. With America's Prohibition floundering, Luciano, Lansky and Siegel, who'd made fortunes smuggling and distributing liquor, targeted Cuba for new business opportunities. Only now did she realize that *they* had been the true owners of Club Gardenia. Clearly, they'd overruled Frida and loaned her to Cugat to establish Lola Flores as an international star prior to her opening the showroom at the Nacional. She wondered how much of the Nacional they owned.

Luciano kissed Lola on each cheek. Lansky did the same.

Siegel preferred Lola's lips.

"You're a regular songbird," said Luciano, his voice accented by his youth in New York after coming to America from Sicily at age nine. "I caught your show with Cugat at the Roxy. My money, it's on you."

"Thank you, señor Luciano," said Lola. She'd entered a world unlike any she'd expected but one promising the opportunities she craved. "Had I known you were there, I would have invited you to my dressing room."

Luciano winked. "I'm sure you would have."

"Sometimes, it is wise to keep what they call a low profile," Lola returned.

Luciano turned to Lansky and Siegel. "Smart cookie."

A waiter approached with a platter of ceviche served in shot glasses.

"What's this?" asked Siegel.

"Fish," Manuel answered. "Raw. With spices."

Siegel grimaced.

"It has been cured in lime juice," said Lola. "Almost the same as cooking it."

Luciano waved the tray away.

"Not that I don't feel like eating," said Siegel.

"You can *always* eat," said Lansky.

"I can have the kitchen prepare something," said Manuel.

Siegel shook his head. "Let's go out for Chinx. What I hear, Havana has the largest Chinatown in Latin America. There's this restaurant, it's open practically all night. As good as New York, although that I gotta see."

Lola's heart pounded.

"Whaddaya say," said Siegel, "we grab el Presidente and his wife and head over there?"

"You're sure that's smart?" Lansky said. "Going out with Machado, what with all this unrest?"

"Shit, we're invested here, aren't we?" Siegel shot back.

Manuel placed his right hand over his heart and turned to Luciano. "I assure you, we would never have welcomed you to Havana if any difficulties were not short-lived."

Siegel tapped his suit jacket beneath his left shoulder. "Short-*lived*? You bet your ass!"

"I will call downstairs," Manuel said. "You gentlemen, señorita Flores and I will ride in the presidential limousine. It is not the famous armored Cadillac of señor Al Capone but quite sufficient to the task. Señor Fallon will escort your lovely ladies in a limousine following us."

"Get the girls," Luciano instructed Siegel. He turned to Lansky. "Round up Machado and his wife." He placed his hand on Lola's left cheek and stared into her eyes. "Know what you are? A beautiful flower opening up to the world."

*Albert locks the bathroom door while the family and Maribel gather in the living room. Tosia has tuned the radio to WJZ. Newark. Papa studies the Tribune. Mama knits. On the floor, Tosia and Maribel leaf through* Woman's Home Companion. *Sylvia drums her fingers. Awaits Albert. Feels closer to him. Tosia, the eldest, bosses her around. Seems unhappy with everyone.*

*The Vincent Lopez band begins its theme song, "Nola."*

*Sylvia calls out.*

*Albert looks forward to the show each week. Often transposes to the piano or violin tunes played on the program. But he's preoccupied. Peers into the mirror. Squints. Opens his eyes. Squints again. Opens again. Unbuttons his shirt. Reveals the white sleeveless undershirt caressing his skin. A Christmas gift from Maribel six months earlier. She does the laundry. No one else has seen it.*

*Albert runs a finger over the white lace at the neck. The tiny bow. He soon will outgrow it. His twelve-year-old body is changing.*

*Sylvia calls out again.*

*"What? What?" Papa bellows.*

*Albert studies what protrudes from beneath the cotton fabric. Remembers a verse from Genesis. Adam and Eve. Male and female He created them. Presses his fingertips against small but budding breasts.*

A police car led the motorcade through the Nacional's gated entry followed by a black sedan with four members of the secret police cradling Tommy guns. Trailing them came the presidential limousine, the second limousine with Fernando and another police car. The vehicles halted. Through windows curtained but opened for air, Lola heard a man's voice amplified by a megaphone: "Down with Machado! Long live the Cuban people!"

A hundred voices repeated his call.

Lola wondered why Manuel had dismissed the risk of protestors. The newspapers and radio had announced the president's planned attendance at her opening. Could Machado really depend on Manuel? Could *she*?

The protesters grew louder.

Lola struggled to free herself from the image of the fountain at Plaza Vieja and the lifeless body of Moisés Finkelstein.

Manuel parted a curtain.

An egg splatted against the driver's side of the windshield.

"¡Dios mío!" cried Evelina Machado.

Luciano, Lansky and Siegel matched her response with variations of "Motherfuckin' sonsabitches!"

Manuel's face contorted with confusion.

Lola cringed.

A hail of eggs struck the limousine.

A gunshot cracked.

The limousine's right-front headlight went out.

Lola dreaded being shot and taken to a hospital. Better that she should die. Although disgraced, she would be spared having to endure the revulsion and scorn produced by ignorance.

Police and security men ran from their vehicles, weapons drawn.

A secret policeman motioned the driver of the presidential limousine to back up and follow the retreat of the second limousine.

Manuel, tightlipped, remained in his seat.

The man with the megaphone bellowed, "¡Viva Cuba! ¡Viva libertad!"

The police and security men fired into the crowd.

Elvira Machado sobbed.

The limousine jerked to a stop at the hotel entry.

Siegel drew his gun and reached for the door. "I'm an American," he barked at Manuel. "I don't have to take this shit."

Luciano looked at Lansky, who pulled Siegel back.

Another fusillade shattered the night.

Lola listened for the man with the megaphone. She heard nothing.

Manuel exited the limousine and returned a moment later. "The situation is under control."

A lone shot rang out in the distance.

Manuel smiled. "No doubt justice for one of the traitors."

"Hopefully, that'll teach 'em a lesson," said Luciano. "Help keep Cuba safe for honest businessmen."

Beyond the hotel's grounds, crying and weeping filled the darkness.

Lola heard Moisés' voice scolding, "What did I tell you?" Her lips barely moved as she responded, "Mind your own business."

Manuel hurried the group into the hotel's lobby.

Siegel made a fist. "I'm president, I kill 'em all!" Again, he withdrew his gun. "Shit, I'll go back out there right now and finish off any of those Red bastards still drawing a breath."

Lansky gripped his arm. "Leave it to Colonel Gallegos' boys, Benny. Not worth the cost of the bullets."

"Always thinking like a fuckin accountant," Siegel said. Years of friendship tempered the edge in a voice that would have left most men shaken.

Luciano glanced at Siegel.

Siegel holstered his gun.

Manuel placed a hand on Machado's shoulder. "We will return you to the Presidential Palace as soon as I have overseen completion of the business at hand."

A moment later, Fernando escorted Lola to the elevator. "Were you frightened, cariña?" he whispered. "I believe I will need to have my trousers cleaned."

Lola saw no point in disclosing that the incident had raised serious questions about the situation in Cuba. And about Manuel Gallegos.

# SEPTEMBER 1931
# THE BOOK OF LIFE

For the third and final time during the evening service, the cantor sang "Kol Nidre," requesting the Jewish people's release from all vows made foolishly or under duress. Wrapped in a tallis purchased at the Jewish Market, Albert closed his eyes and lost himself in reflection. He had prodded Lola to go with him to Fernando's apartment, urged her to change into the man's suit of restrained cut and cost kept for him there and overcome her last objections to entering the shul. Yom Kippur fell on a Sunday evening with no show scheduled at the Nacional. Further, matters of state security would keep Manuel at his office day and night through the week ahead. Surely, God had sent signs.

As the cantor's baritone ascended to heaven, Albert opened his eyes and stared at the eternal light above the ark that contained two hand-written Torah scrolls. All evening, he'd accompanied Lola through a spiritual hall of mirrors, clinging to the ancient faith with a renewed fervor he could not explain while she maintained grave doubts that the kept woman of a murderer and thus a willing conspirator could, despite prayer and confession, atone for her sins. Albert renewed his prayer that when the gates of repentance closed after sundown the following day, he and Lola—singly and as one—would be sealed in the Book of Life.

At the service's conclusion, the synagogue's front doors opened out to darkness. Women descended from the balcony and exited into an alley. Men grown somber during hours of repentance and now fasting spilled out onto the narrow sidewalk and into the street.

Alberto exchanged Yiddish wishes for health and prosperity and set out with Lola for Fernando's apartment. Having gone no more than a block, he froze. Sirens wailed. Police whistles shrieked. Men shouted. Voices responded marked by anger, shock, fear.

He changed course to skirt the commotion. With each step, he wondered if, like some habaneros, he'd grown indifferent to the continuing unrest and the government's violent responses, concerned only with his own safety. Lola's safety. *Their* safety since Lola pushed Alberto away with one hand while holding him close with the other.

The month before, Manuel's efforts fruitless, Carlos Mendieta and former president Mario García Menocal led a coup attempt in Fernando's home province of Pinar del Río. In a first for the nation, President Machado ordered airplanes to attack them. Four days later, Mendieta and Menocal surrendered. Less than a week after, forty revolutionaries seized a police station in Gibara at the eastern end of the island. The army made quick work of them. But what could Alberto Torres do to bring Cuba the justice for which he also had prayed? He was only a poor Jew—and at that, an illusion.

Lola Flores represented a different matter. On this night, she expressed remorse but continued to play the dissatisfied Faustus, albeit in woman's form, seeking not a knowledge of magic but public acclaim and its attendant riches through a soul-surrendering bargain with Manuel Gallegos' Mephistopheles. While not the Devil—if such a being existed— Manuel served Ben Siegel and Meyer Lansky. They in turn ministered to Charlie Luciano, a very dark angel. Atonement seemed far-fetched.

The next morning, Lola again walked to Fernando's apartment. Unable to stifle a series of yawns—the morning service would start well before her customary awakening—she dressed in Alberto's suit.

"Are you certain you wish to go?" Fernando asked.

"Of course," Lola answered. She made no mention of her sense of desperation—one more small but not trivial sin.

Fernando offered to accompany her.

She declined.

Fernando retreated to his thoughts then announced, "There is something I should have told you as soon as you came through the door."

Lola spun Alberto's fedora in her hands. "Which is—?"

"Last night, a friend called. Not a Jew. He knows nothing about you. But it seems that all over Havana there is news. *Bad* news."

Lola loosened the knot in Alberto's tie as if her/his/their neck had been draped with a noose. She considered asking for a drink—on Yom Kippur, unthinkable.

"The police," said Fernando. "Last night. Those Jews, the ones who hate religion—"

Lola grasped his reference to the Kultur Farain—the Unión Cultural Hebrea. Left-wingers, they'd led strikes against Jewish industrialists in the late 'twenties. Each Yom Kippur Eve, they held a ball to thumb their noses at their observant brethren.

The police, Fernando informed her, had burned their library with its collection of Yiddish books. They'd also dragged fifty people to jail.

Lola's jaw went slack. She now understood the commotion she and Alberto had heard following Kol Nidre.

"Some in the government hate the Jews," Fernando said. "But this?"

Lola looked towards the door as if anticipating footsteps on the stairs.

"Also," said Fernando, "I have heard about a new organization. Very secret. They call it ABC. Who these people are I do not know, but they also wish to bring down President Machado."

"Should I tell Manuel?"

"God forbid, cariña! He will want to know who told you. If you mention my name, he will think that I am one of them."

"Are you?"

Fernando shook his head.

"But this frightens you."

He nodded.

Lola put on Alberto's hat. "And also, me."

That evening, Lola remained unsettled as the elevator took her down to the showroom. Seated at the piano for the dinner show, her spirits rose. The unrest afflicting Cuba lay beyond her control, but she held sway over her performance, exhibited a skill and flair no other hands, no other voice on the island could duplicate. During those few hours when audiences forgot their worries with music, drinks and laughter, her anxiety gave way to elation.

At the show's end, she left the bandstand in triumph. Her mood lasted no longer than a rising champagne bubble. Before Fernando could help her out of her gown, she lit a cigarette and poured a Scotch. She could not help brooding about the way Charlie Luciano, abetted by Ben Siegel and Meyer Lansky, held complete power over her career and the relationship Manuel had forced upon her, often fierce, sometimes tender, always distressing. In disturbing moments of clarity, she acknowledged that it was she who'd composed the music that created the singular backdrop of her life, danced willingly with partners who could further her ambitions. At those times she conceded the inevitable. Someday, perhaps when she least expected, the piper would exact payment.

Fernando tried to cheer her. "You were wonderful tonight, cariña."

"You say that every night."

"Because I know how upset you are."

Lola looked at him quizzically then remembered his mention to her the attack on the Kultur Farain. "I have an obligation to my audience."

He unzipped the back of her gown.

"That group you told me about this morning—"

Fernando scratched his chin. "ABC."

"*Are* you a member?"

"God forbid. Whatever group of revolutionaries might topple the government, Cubans will suffer. Except for the ruling class. They will change their loyalties the way you and the dancers change costumes during each show."

Lola put on a dress to make a sufficiently glamorous impression on her way upstairs where she intended to immediately drop into bed.

Fernando lowered himself onto the sofa and patted the seat.

Lola sat next to him.

"I have received a telegram."

Lola raised a hand to her cheek.

"Lili Elbe."

Lola paled.

"A little over a week ago. In Dresden. The operation. Complications."

"Who will live and who will die," Lola whispered, repeating part of the Yom Kippur liturgy. "Lili should have been written into the Book of Life. Why did God fail her?"

121

"The God you believe in only when it suits your purpose?"

She emptied her glass then kissed him on the cheek. "Do not be concerned. I will write and seal *myself* into the Book of Life. And *you*. Whatever that may require."

# MARCH 1933

# BLACKOUT

The electricity out again, the Nacional's elevators were down. Whether for minutes or hours, the hotel staff couldn't say. Fortunately, eight floors above the lobby, a skylight above the stairway permitted enough rainy afternoon light to guide anyone wishing to ascend.

One hand on the bannister, Lola craned her neck, took a breath then started the climb. Her footfalls echoed on the marble steps.

She stopped at the fourth floor, her legs heavy, her feet yearning for a soak in bath salts. Silence met her above and below. Other guests returning from sightseeing or shopping had accepted the manager's offer of free drinks in the bar as they awaited a resolution to the electrical outage.

The capital, like all of Cuba, had experienced increased turmoil as opposition to the Machado government mounted daily. Laborers engaged in slow-downs and strikes to protest delays in being paid. Although Cubans and visiting Americans expressed little interest, Lola's attention had been drawn to Germany where a fire broke out in the Reichstag days earlier, only four weeks after President Hindenburg named Hitler as chancellor. Seeking scapegoats, Nazi stormtroopers unleashed a violent campaign against Communists and trade unionists. Manuel lauded the Nazi response.

Lola again launched herself upward. She hoped that a touch of optimism would boost her towards the stairway's pinnacle. The American Congress had proposed a Twenty-First Amendment to repeal Prohibition. Meanwhile, Americans buoyed by the recent inauguration of Franklin Delano Roosevelt were coming to the island in growing numbers. They disregarded Cuban politics as they did Germany's, as long as rum, whiskey, champagne and fine wine continued to flow, and gambling and beautiful women remained available.

At the sixth floor, Lola stopped again. She regretted declining the bell captain's offer to send a boy along to carry her shopping bag. She lowered her head then raised it. At twenty-three, she surely was young enough to scale the stairs under her own power. Besides, the several records and sheet music she'd purchased hardly represented a burden. At least, they hadn't in the lobby. Enduring stabbing pains in her calves, Lola mounted the next flight of steps.

At the seventh floor, she glanced down to see how far she'd come. She also looked within. After two years headlining at the Nacional, her photo appeared in all the island's newspapers and magazines, as well as in American and Canadian travel articles. When she went out, which she did rarely, habaneros asked for autographs. A record released after the New Year sold well in Cuba and attracted notice in the States. Still, she seethed with discontent.

Her career seemed to have peaked well short of what she considered its summit. She gave her all to each audience and welcomed nightly ovations but performing in Havana had grown stale. She focused more attention on writing music, both afternoons and following shows when Manuel worked late or stayed home. Her songs blended Cuban musical forms with Brazilian samba, Argentine tango and American jazz. She loved Louis Armstrong, Bix Beiderbecke, Count Basie, Earl Hines, the Dorsey brothers.

Cuba had become a lovely outpost in a vast ocean linking massive continents. Reputations were not established here or even in Europe. One made a name in America.

The Nacional symbolized the limitations Cuba imposed. It stood all of eight floors. New York's recently opened Empire State Building towered one hundred and two stories above Fifth Avenue. When would her so-called partners, eager to expand their business, send her out into the larger world? She believed with all her heart that in America, the land of opportunity she had fled and now longed for, Lola Flores would reach the heights of which she'd dreamed, for which she'd borne so many dangers.

Or was she deluding herself? The leap north—opportunity and success were different matters—presented all performers with the risk of failure.

Reaching the eighth floor, Lola bent over to catch her breath. Then she set out down the hall, passed the stilled elevator and unlocked her door.

Finding her way in the dim light, she placed her shopping bag on the dining table and went to the bathroom. Returning to the living room, she tried the lights. They flickered on.

Perhaps an unknown power had sent a sign.

Several hours later, a room-service waiter laid out a white tablecloth, linen napkins, fine china, silverware with handles displaying the figure of a woman in a native headdress and crystal glasses. After lighting two white candles, he summoned Lola and Manuel, who accepted the proffered white Burgundy. The waiter served a pre-show supper of red snapper escabeche and salad with avocado, newly in season. Before leaving, he set out a bowl of Valencia oranges, the year's last, as a figure-flattering dessert.

Manuel stared into his wine.

"Has something happened?" Lola asked.

"The lights went out earlier."

"Yes, but now they are on."

Manuel's expression remained dark. "How long are these outages to continue?" His fist hammered the table.

Lola pressed her back into her chair.

"Forgive me," he said.

She regained her composure as always, despite Manuel's outbursts becoming more frequent and intense. "Something else concerns you?"

Manuel searched her eyes to ferret out the reaction she might display to what he had to say. His own disclosed uncertainty. "Meyer Lansky telephoned from New York."

Lola intuited that Lansky's message was one she'd long awaited and about which, despite her ambition, she remained ambivalent. She made no reply.

"Señor Lansky wishes for you and the band to play the States. He has someone organizing a tour of sixteen cities from the middle of May to the end of June."

"Señor Lansky spoke with *you*? About *me*?"

"Prohibition is ending. Our friends are moving more of their interests into legitimate businesses." Lansky now spoke on behalf of Charlie

Luciano and believed that Lola Flores would fill the nightclubs, hotels and dancehalls in which they and Ben Siegel were investing.

Put out that she'd been circumvented, Lola turned the tables and interrogated Manuel. "And *you*? What do *you* wish me to do? What do *you* think is best?"

Manuel took Lola's hand. "Serious men proposing serious matters demand serious consideration. With all that is happening in Havana, we will need our friends in New York."

Lola yanked her hand away. How dare Meyer Lansky relate Charlie Luciano's plans to Manuel behind her back? "And if I will not go?"

"Where would you be if you tried to do these things yourself?"

"One of the most powerful men in Cuba surrenders his manhood by making his woman a common whore to please these Yanqui gangsters?"

Manuel displayed his fist.

The lights went out.

In the candlelight, flickering shadows cast Manuel with the chilling aura of a dybbuk—a demon of ancient Jewish lore—determined to possess Lola's body and subjugate her will. "Mi amor," he said in a voice intimating the serpent in the Garden of Eden, "without their assistance, you will find the doors barred to every showroom you wish to play."

I would not be so certain."

"I know *this*. Señor Lansky gives neither of us a choice."

# MAY 1933

## "WHADDAYA THINK OF
## THE BIG APPLE?"

Flashbulbs popped like revolvers as Lola greeted the press at Pier 51 in Lower Manhattan. She wore a blue-green full-length dress with a square neckline. Buttons descended the left side towards a pleated hem above her ankles.

Reporters barraged Lola with questions. The tour would start at New York's Roseland Ballroom before heading west to Los Angeles then back east to Miami. They dismissed her appearances west of the Hudson.

"Whaddaya think of the Big Apple?"

She'd just come off the ship but remembered the city fondly from performing at the Roxy with Xavier Cugat.

"How does New York compare with Havana?"

Every musician wished to perform here. "I love New York."

"Catchy little phrase, but what's doin' with all them revolutionaries down in Cuba?"

She was a musician, not a politician.

"How'd you learn to speak English so good?"

Many Cubans spoke English. Cuba and the United States had a special relationship.

"Cute accent."

Lola continued fielding questions while her thoughts lay elsewhere. In 1912, the Sobels had landed in America just across the Hudson from where she stood. Now, Papa and Mama, Tosia and Sylvia conducted their lives without Albert. Without *her*. Of course, Lola Flores meant nothing to them. But did Albert live on in their memories? Despite Lola's best efforts, they remained in hers.

Fernando tipped the bellman, who'd finished hanging up Lola's dresses in the bedroom of her suite at the Waldorf Towers. Then he poured drinks at the living room bar.

The doorbell rang.

Fernando shrugged and opened the door.

Ben Siegel stepped forward and took off his hat. He held a black leather folder under his left arm. "Nice to see ya. Both of ya. We thought we'd pay our respects."

"We?" Lola asked from the sofa.

"Betcha didn't know we're neighbors. Me and Esta—Esta's my wife— we bought an apartment here two years ago."

Lola couldn't imagine Ben Siegel being married.

"But I'm not talkin' about Esta," said Siegel. "Or Meyer. Right now, he's got other fish to fry." He snapped his fingers.

Leon Greenspan entered the room.

Fernando closed the door and stood by Lola.

"No hard feelings?" Greenspan asked Fernando. He and the band would stay at an inexpensive hotel near Times Square, blocks from Roseland. "We got a budget, right?"

Siegel winked. The simple descent of an eyelid hinted at a mix of mirth and malice. He gripped the folder and gestured with it towards two armchairs across the coffee table. "Mind?"

"Please," said Lola.

Seated, Siegel placed the folder in his lap and pointed to Fernando's drink.

"Scotch," said Fernando.

"Not rum?" Siegel asked. He chuckled. "I'll take one." He turned to Greenspan. "You, Leib?"

Greenspan gave a thumbs-up. "By the way," he said, "Leib's my Jewish name. Means *lion*. After a while, my parents changed it to Leon. American, right?"

Fernando poured their drinks then sat by Lola.

Siegel raised his glass. "L'chaim! It's a Jewish toast. Means 'to life.'"

"L'haim!" Lola returned, pronouncing the "ch" as 'h' since the sound made at the back of the palate was foreign to Spanish, as well as other western languages.

Siegel laughed. "Like Charlie says, you're a sharp dame. Anyway, I know what you're thinking."

"Like *I* always know what *Ben's* thinking," said Greenspan. "Me and him, we go way back. With Meyer, too. And Al."

"Al?" Lola asked.

"What? You never heard of Al Capone?"

Lola wondered just how deeply she'd gotten involved with America's gangsters, although she could hardly claim ignorance. Albert knew a great deal about them. "Of course," she said in a whisper. "Chicago."

"Capone, he's from Brooklyn," Siegel said.

"Ben can tell stories," said Greenspan.

"They'd send me up the river," Siegel said. He held up the folder. "Charlie thinks you can be a real moneymaker, and he oughtta know." He hoisted his glass. The remainder of his whiskey vanished. "Charlie makes a lot of money with women."

"And you wish from me what?" Lola asked.

"Direct, to the point," Siegel said to Greenspan. "Also holds up when things go south, like that night at the Nacional."

Lola wished Siegel hadn't recalled the attack on their motorcade. At least nothing like that would happen in New York.

Siegel motioned to Fernando for a refill. "Anyways, we're making a little adjustment to your contract."

"An adjustment?" Lola asked.

"From now on, Leib manages the band."

Lola's carefully penciled eyebrows shot up.

"Here, Cuba, everywhere," Siegel continued. "Also makes the deals for records, radio, whatever." He looked at Greenspan. "Not to worry. He keeps his hands out of the till."

Greenspan's Adam's apple bobbed.

"Is this not irregular?" Lola asked.

Siegel offered a jack-o-lantern grin. "What I say, that's regular. Fernando here. He's out. But he's *in*."

"I fail to understand," said Lola.

129

"Dames," Greenspan said.

Siegel stared at Greenspan, who lowered his eyes. "Fernando stays on the payroll as your personal assistant. Does your gowns, those crazy hats. Looks after you. Like always, right? Gets paid good." He opened the leather folder and withdrew three copies of a typewritten contract.

Lola recalled signing her contract with Frida Herskovits and where that led.

Greenspan produced a pen. It's mottled jade green body suggested the marble that covered the walls in bank lobbies.

Lola expressed neither delight nor dissatisfaction. She did not doubt that Ben Siegel and Meyer Lansky could deliver on their promises to move her career forward in return for her helping them and Charlie Luciano advance their new, legitimate business interests. She understood as well that Siegel and Lansky would find any number of ways to enrich themselves at her expense. But as with the former arrangement, about which Manuel had been correct, she'd still come out ahead. She accepted the pen.

"So you know," said Greenspan, "I got one of the most important guys in town comin' to tomorrow night's opening."

The next morning's *Daily Mirror* displayed Lola's photo and a write-up by Walter Winchell: "Heading out for a night on the town this fine evening? Roseland is the place to see and hear Lola Flores, 'The Cuban Firecracker.' George White and Jake Shubert, if you're looking for a star for another big hit on the Great White Way, this goes double for you."

Glowing, Lola called room service for coffee and a soft-boiled egg. "Also, please, I would like to try what is a bagel and what you have that goes with it." After eating, she put on a stylish but not pretentious dress and an everyday wig topped by a wide-brimmed hat in robins-egg blue. Sunglasses in place, she walked up Park Avenue confident she would be beyond even Mama's recognition—although that always had been the case.

Anticipating a later outing to shop Fifth Avenue with Fernando, Lola intended only a short stroll to observe a familiar city with new eyes. Captivated by the sunshine and a gentle breeze, she crossed 57th Street and walked up to 66th where she examined the brickwork 7th Regiment Armory with its crenelated entry tower and corner rooflines.

Her heart overpowering her head, she continued up to 69th, turned right and crossed Lexington Avenue, Third then Second. She stopped in front of the apartment building in which she'd lived less than four years earlier and tried to compose a mental family portrait but struggled to visualize Papa, Mama, Tosia and Sylvia as they might appear now. Tosia and Sylvia would have undergone significant changes. Tosia might even live elsewhere with a husband. As to Papa and Mama, who knew how the Depression was treating them?

Beneath the building's green-canopied entry, a glass door opened. A uniformed doorman—Johnny, she remembered—stepped out and touched his right hand to the bill of his cap. She studied the familiar Irish face—watery blue eyes, long, slender nose, red-splotched, parchment-delicate cheeks.

"Lookin' for an apartment, Miss?" he asked, revealing no hint of recognition.

"No, señor. I was just— I was looking and imagining," Lola said, maintaining her accent.

The affability drained from the doorman's face. He crossed his arms in front of his chest and spread his feet to signify that an Irish doorman was as tough as an Irish cop. Any attempt to enter the building would prove hopeless. "Just to make things clear, the landlord don't take the Spanish."

Seeking to avoid a disturbance, Lola made no effort to explain herself. Neither Johnny nor most people grasped the idea that people unlike themselves might possess the same moral rectitude. She retreated to Second Avenue and walked south towards the Waldorf. At 55th Street, she changed course. After turning east, she stopped in front of the synagogue her parents had joined as a matter of duty.

*Like a stage, the bimah rises above the seated congregation. Albert settles behind the reading table. Androgynous in his blue serge suit. Acknowledges his family. Papa and Uncle Mendel's business associates. Students from the Talmud-Torah. The synagogue regulars who appear Saturday mornings. Devour food and schnapps after the bar-mitzvah.*

*Albert chants the opening blessing to his haftarah. Baruch Atah Adonoi, Eloheinu Melech Ha-Oylam— Tone sweet and resonant. Chants the haftarah.*

*From I Kings. Masters the complex musical cantillation. Exhibits an expansive vocal range.*

*The congregation murmurs its praise. Rabbi Weiss kvells. Cantor Fateman beams.*

*Albert hopes all acclaim will be directed to him. Not Papa. No assistance. Not Mama. No religious education. Not Tosia. Ignorant. Not Sylvia, who at least has been encouraging.*

*His voice drifts upward. Suggests the smoke of offerings at the Temple. First and Second. Pleasing to the Lord.*

*Sees himself as a sacrifice. Like Isaac. No choice but to appear on the bimah this day. Undergo a son's rite of passage. Demonstrate what good Jews Papa and Mama are. Justify a celebration flaunting prosperity. Real or illusory.*

*At first, Albert had protested. Hypocrisy. Then something unexpected. Enjoyed his studies. Found comfort. Related what he'd learned at the dinner table. Suffered when Papa spurned his zeal. "Soon you'll be done with this nonsense."*

*Completes his haftarah. Chants the long closing blessing. Clears his throat. Now for the ritual speech. Refer to the week's Torah portion. Cite the golden calf. Condemn the Israelites for dismissing miracles wrought in Egypt by the unseen God. Forgetting the lightning and thunder at Sinai. Turning their back on the Ten Commandments. On a reality they could not imagine. Refused to consider.*

*"Today I am a man." Smiles. "Although not necessarily."*

Thirty minutes after the band's opening show at Roseland drew thunderous applause and much whistling, a limousine headed north on Central Park West for a night on the town. Lola and Fernando rode with Ben Siegel, Leon Greenspan and Walter Winchell.

Greenspan turned to Lola. "You want muscle on your side? Forget Ben. The pen's mightier and all that. Walter's syndicated. Forty million readers from here to the Coast."

"*Fifty,*" said Winchell.

"Sunday nights, he's on the radio. Gives the scoop to millions of Mr. and Mrs. USA-types."

"*Twenty* million," Winchell said.

"My apologies for interrupting," said Fernando, "but we are going where?"

Siegel turned to Lola. "Ever hear of the Cotton Club?"

"Of course," Lola said. "Duke Ellington plays there. Cab Calloway. Jimmy Lunceford."

"They ain't Spanish," said Siegel, "but I'll give the niggers their due. They got rhythm."

Lola, fearful of antagonizing Siegel, made no reply.

Siegel pointed at Winchell. "This guy. His pal Owney Madden bought the Cotton Club to sell beer during Prohibition. Turned it into a classy joint. Whites only. A real American success story. But Walter's got dirt on everybody. Madden lets out he's thinking, what if Walter's got shit on *him*?" He drew a finger across his throat. "Walter hightails it to California."

"An Irishman's the wrong kind of pal for a landsman," Greenspan said.

"Landsman," said Siegel. "A Jew. Charlie Luciano's a wop, but Jews and Italians understand each other. Charlie does a favor and wipes Walter's slate clean with Madden. Naturally, Walter has to play ball, use his column to ease some of the pressure City Hall, Albany and the feds are putting on Charlie Lucky."

Winchell raised a middle finger.

Siegel laughed.

Winchell withdrew a small pad and pencil from his coat pocket. "So, business. You like American music, Lola?"

"Very much, señor Winchell."

"I like *your* music. I remember you with Cugat at the Roxy two years ago. You like America?"

Lola offered her standard response. She'd always wanted to perform in the States, the land of the free and the home of the brave. Babe Ruth. Clara Bow. Jazz!

"Jesus, you talk like a real American," said Winchell. "These days, we've got all these Bund members holding rallies for Hitler and unions run by Reds. But don't get me wrong. I'm all for FDR. It's just, real patriots, they're hard to find. "Anyway, where'd you grew up? How'd you get into music?"

As the limo neared Harlem, Lola recited the biography she'd created complete with the fire that destroyed all the records in her hometown. Her parents had died years earlier. Sadly, she had no sister or brother.

Winchell made copious notes.

Lola thought herself a good actress. Perhaps someday she'd make movies in Hollywood.

Winchell closed his notebook, stuck his pencil behind his ear and rested his hand on Lola's arm. "Let me lay something out for you, kid. People who can push you up in the world? Show your appreciation. Present company included, they can drop you into the toilet."

# AUGUST 1933

# MR. WELLES HAS HIS WAY

Agitated ranks of habaneros surged past the window where Lola and Fernando occupied a table in the Hotel Plaza's near-empty ground-floor café. Six weeks after returning from America, the situation in Cuba stood at a tipping point. That morning, before Lola and Fernando met in the Old City to purchase fabric for new dresses, the radio announced that President Machado had reached agreement with the Communists to leave office. The date of the president's departure had yet to be established.

Men and women, victory close but still uncertain, trooped towards the nearby Presidential Palace. They chanted, sang and waved signs declaring MACHADO, LEAVE NOW! and TIME FOR A NEW CUBA! If Machado expected continued patience, he'd made a fatal mistake. Many Cubans long had been out of work. Others had joined the general strike called that morning by the Communists and the ABC. The latter, with its reputation for violence, expressed grave doubt about Machado's intentions. The president at first had resisted the new American representative to Cuba, Sumner Welles, who urged his resignation for the sake of peace. Perhaps Machado, believing he had offered sufficient accommodation to the protestors and Washington, was reneging on his promise.

"Whatever happens," said Fernando, "I fear Cuba will always be under the heel of the Americans."

Lola agreed. America's concerns involved its business interests in everything from the sugar industry to tourism. A new government might punish the functionaries who worked for Machado, including Manuel. It could easily set a match to the "Cuban Firecracker."

The voices in the street grew more strident.

Lola took out another cigarette.

Fernando scowled.

Lola lit it. Her nerves required soothing. The American tour had taken its toll with all the train travel, media interviews and Leon Greenspan's mismanagement. Unable to sleep well, she'd fainted after a show in Kansas City and again ten days later in Dallas.

"Cariña," Fernando said, "perhaps we should go before something happens. We can find a taxi nearby."

Lola raised an eyebrow and blew smoke past his head.

"Ah yes," Fernando replied. "The general strike. I can walk you back to the Nacional."

In the distance, sirens and whistles wailed. Gunshots, now all too familiar, exploded from the vicinity of the Presidential Palace. Shouts and screams followed.

Outside the window, marchers elbowed each other aside attempting to reverse course. Many stumbled. Some fell. Frightened compatriots trampled them.

A woman in a pink-and-white striped shirtwaist toppled forward, landed on her face and clambered to her knees only to get knocked down again. Summoning a will that touched Lola's heart, the woman struggled to her feet. Blood covered her face. She threaded her way through the onrush and stumbled to the café's entrance.

Lola ran to the doorway, pulled her inside and barked instructions to a waiter.

Fernando pulled out a chair.

The woman, a hand pressed against her forehead, collapsed into it.

The waiter returned with napkins and water.

Fernando suggested summoning the hotel doctor.

Lola shook her head. "What if the doctor betrays her to the police?"

Fernando went to the kitchen in pursuit of a sharp knife.

Lola attempted to lower the woman's hand.

The woman resisted.

"I must clean the wound," Lola said. "Then we must get you home."

The woman sobbed then yielded.

Lola held a damp napkin to the woman's forehead. "You are fortunate. It looked far worse than it is."

Fernando handed Lola a makeshift bandage.

The woman attempted to smile. She appeared to be Lola's age. Her black hair and dark skin attested to a different heritage, but Lola thought they shared the same spirit.

Outside, the snarled flow of panic-stricken demonstrators began to thin. In turn, the cracking of pistols and rifles subsided. Cries and moans now filled the street.

Lola again recalled the image of Plaza Vieja, the wailing as Moisés Finkelstein lay dying. She could do nothing then. Now, she could.

Fernando leaned in. "Should we take this woman—"

"Graciela," said the woman. "Please do not think me rude if I do not tell you my family name or ask yours."

"Should we take Graciela to a hospital?" Fernando asked.

"No!" Graciela pleaded.

Lola's eyes made clear that the secret police would look for marchers in all the hospitals. Besides, the wound was not serious.

"I live nearby," Graciela said.

They would take her home, Lola informed Graciela. "First, you must regain your strength with something to eat and drink. Soon, all the police in the neighborhood will reassemble at the Presidential Palace. We will leave then."

An hour later, a downpour had cooled off the now-deserted street. A mixture of water and blood encircled glistening cobbles and formed small, reddish pools where the stones had been removed. The sun peeked through the clouds.

Lola helped Graciela stand.

Fernando paid the waiter, doubling the tip for his silence, and took Lola's shopping bags.

Lola gave Graciela her hat to conceal her bandage.

They walked east along San Juan de Dios. Several blocks on, three soldiers appeared. Two young privates, one thin, the other stout, carried rifles. A swarthy sergeant with a pointed chin wore a pistol on his hip. His features implied ancestry from Africa and China as well as Spain.

Fernando shifted the shopping bags to his left hand and raised his right to his hat. Acknowledging the soldiers instead of looking away might demonstrate the innocence of a man and two women who, despite the disquieting unrest, had ventured out on a modest shopping spree.

"Halt!" the sergeant ordered.

Fernando maneuvered himself in front of the women.

The sergeant shoved him aside.

"There is no need for that," said Lola.

The thin private stared.

The sergeant pointed to Graciela's bloodstained blouse. "Your hat. Remove it."

Graciela refused.

The stout private flung the hat into the street.

"An accident while we were shopping," said Lola.

The thin private turned to the sergeant. "I think the señorita tells the truth. We should let them pass."

The sergeant glared. "What did you say—*private?*"

The thin private pointed to Lola. "This lady—"

The sergeant looked down, fumbled with his holster and withdrew his pistol.

Fernando and Graciela stepped back.

Lola held her ground.

"I believe," said the sergeant to Lola, "you may have something you wish to tell me."

Despite her show of bravado, Lola envisioned herself confined in a jail cell, one far from resembling Manuel's office. She would endure a physical examination that would destroy her career—if she survived the assault that followed. Seeing no choice but to display strength, she stood as erect as a palace guard. "Are you going to shoot me?"

"Sargento, please," said the thin private. "I know who this lady is. This is Lola Flores!"

"¡Dios mío!" the stout private whispered.

The sergeant bit his lips then holstered the pistol. "Your pardon, señorita Flores." He raised his hand to his hat brim. "Permit me to suggest that you be very careful about the people with whom you associate."

Eight days later, Gerardo Machado refusing to leave office, Havana continued to simmer with discontent. Lola's audiences at the Nacional revealed their apprehension by consuming record quantities of liquor. Manuel spent most nights at the Presidential Palace surrounded by heavily armed troops. Bodyguards accompanied him on the few occasions when he returned home or motored to the Nacional to sleep with Lola as he'd done the evening before.

At daybreak he went to the office. Late in the afternoon, he returned.

"You seem breathless," Lola said. "The elevator again?"

Manuel collapsed on the sofa. "Machado is gone." Hours earlier, the president had met with the army general staff at Camp Columbia. They presented an ultimatum. He flew to the Bahamas. "The ABC fired on his plane but failed to hit it."

Lola poured drinks. "Who will be the new president?"

"General Herrera accepted the position, but Sumner Welles was not happy. We will have an interim president—Manuel de Céspedes."

Lola handed Manuel his drink. "And you?"

His chest still heaving, Manuel sipped slowly. The matter was unresolved. He felt badly for Machado, who had been kind to him, and certainly for Elvira, but he was a practical man. He'd prepared his staff to satisfy the generals and keep Havana calm to safeguard their own positions.

"Then why are you not at the office?" Lola asked.

"Given the situation, it is best that I go about the city to determine for myself the mood of the people."

Lola sat and lit a cigarette. "And the mood of *this* habanera?"

That is why he'd come. These difficult times had taught him what was really important. "Despite the Church, I will find a way to divorce Ysabel."

That Manuel and Ysabel had long grown apart was common knowledge, but no one expected him to risk the consequences of leaving his wife. A Cuban man could have a wife and keep a mistress without censure. "What then?"

"I will marry *you*."

Lola looked away. Marrying Manuel was out of the question. She would have to surrender her status as an independent woman. Also, she did not love him.

He clutched her shoulder. "Have you not waited for this?"

Lola broke free. "I am flattered, Manuel. But what of the cost to you? And really, a husband for *me*? I simply cannot."

Manuel flung his glass across the room and burst from the suite.

# SEPTEMBER–OCTOBER 1933
# REVOLT OF THE SERGEANTS

The taxi carrying Lola and Leon Greenspan along Calle Agromonte inched forward among blaring horns and shrill curses. It reached the Museo Nacional de Bellas Artes, just past the Hotel Plaza where Lola and Fernando had encountered the young woman, Graciela. The driver braked. Yet another convoy transporting soldiers brandishing rifles and machine guns blocked their route.

Over the three weeks since Manuel stormed out of Suite 848, Havana had mirrored the tension of his and Lola's relationship. Students, union members and Communists protested daily. Government forces dispersed them following bloody clashes but could not halt the growing anarchy. On this early Monday afternoon, the army's presence far outstripped any previous show of force.

Lola turned to Greenspan. "Pay the driver. From here, we will walk. The place you wish to go is only a block further."

At El Floridita, a restaurant and bar popular with both habaneros and Americans, the host led "señorita Flores and her friend" to a table. The commotion inside, fueled by alcohol and politics, echoed that of the snarled traffic.

"Maybe you don't know," said Greenspan, "but this is where they invented the daiquiri."

Lola smiled to indicate her appreciation for information contained in every Havana guidebook.

Greenspan ordered the requisite daiquiris then lit Lola's cigarette.

Lola had been hearing a good deal from Fernando that she smoked too much. She dismissed his concerns. Cuban men indulged in the island's cigars. Next to a cigar, a cigarette was a cub compared with a lion. Women also had the right to enjoy life's simple pleasures.

"L'haim!" said Lola when the daiquiris arrived. She found it prudent to sustain the mispronunciation.

Greenspan laughed. "Kid, you're one of a kind."

Lola sucked on a pink straw matching her lipstick.

Greenspan leaned forward both to be heard and signal his desire for confidentiality. "So here's the scoop. Charlie and the boys are thinking, maybe you'll come to the States before the end of the year. Stay a while."

Lola offered a wan smile to hide her uneasiness. Would Manuel defy Charlie Luciano and prevent her from leaving again? If he failed, would he be so enraged that he'd reveal her ruse even if it cost him his reputation?

Greenspan misread her distress. "Not to worry. Fernando goes, too."

Lola smiled more deeply to keep him in the dark. "Why now?"

Greenspan took her hand and squeezed. She should know he was a serious man. On the square. "This new president, Céspedes? Charlie and the boys didn't like him. Neither do the people who called the shots in Washington. But if the Reds kicked Céspedes out, what then?" Things in Cuba could get worse. Besides, the situation in America had changed. Prohibition was kaput. FDR might actually be lifting the country out of the Depression. Charlie, Meyer and Ben weren't going to sit on their asses—pardon his French—waiting for Cuba to figure itself out. They were buying or taking over clubs, hotels and restaurants in New York and other places. These legitimate businesses would be profitable but also perfect for concealing income from other interests. "Long story short, Lola Flores plays the circuit, brings in the big spenders, makes everything look legit."

Lola ran her finger along the rim of her glass then mashed her cigarette into an ashtray.

"What?" asked Greenspan. "I just asked you to jump into the harbor without a bathing suit as a publicity stunt?"

Lola now was certain Manuel would do all he could to keep her from leaving. As she struggled to answer Greenspan, a man with dark hair and a thick, dark mustache made his way towards them. Six feet and broad-shouldered, he displayed impressive physical power and a nimble grace born of uncommon confidence.

"Lola Flores!" he greeted her in American English.

Greenspan looked up, his face blank.

"Leon," said Lola, "this is Ernest Hemingway. Papa, Leon Greenspan."

Greenspan laughed. "You're a little young to be Lola's papa, huh?"

Hemingway grabbed the lone empty chair in sight and pulled it up to the table.

"Papa is a writer," said Lola. "Novels. Stories, too. I read him in English."

"What're you reading now?" Hemingway asked.

"*Julius Caesar.*"

Hemingway chuckled.

"You live in Havana?" Greenspan asked.

"Visiting. We have a boat. When we dock here, we stay at a hotel. Close by."

"Sounds great," said Greenspan. "But señorita Flores and I have business to discuss." He waved his hand like a man, having just unbuckled his belt, dismissing a waiter's proffer of another dessert.

Hemingway stayed seated. Drinking in El Floridita, he explained, was *his* business. So was Cuba. Someday, he'd write a great novel about the island. Maybe fishing. Or a woman like Lola Flores. He tapped Lola's chin with his fist. "In a way, we're like two peas in a pod."

Lola grinned. They shared a stronger bond than Papa knew. She too created fiction, only without a typewriter.

"Talk about drinking," Hemingway said, "it's a damn good time for a daiquiri. Maybe two. Maybe more."

"Has something happened?" Lola asked.

Hemingway motioned to the waiter then turned back. "You haven't heard?"

The following Sunday, Alberto having reminded her that Rosh Hashanah was two weeks off, Lola found herself caught in the expanding web of political turmoil stretched across the island. She and Manuel, each dressed inconspicuously, stood in the back of the restless crowd outside the heavily guarded Presidential Palace. Manuel had insisted that Lola, her face all but concealed by a wide-brimmed hat and dark glasses, accompany him. A seemingly married couple would draw less attention as he observed the mob.

The so-called Sergeants' Revolt, led by Fulgencio Batista, an unknown stenographer-sergeant self-promoted to colonel, had deposed but not arrested the army's chief of staff, General Julio Sanguily. Suffering a stomach ulcer, Sanguily had retreated with several hundred well-armed generals and senior officers to the Hotel Nacional, now practically a fortress. Batista then ousted President Carlos Manuel Céspedes. In moments, Cuba's new president, Ramón Grau San Martín, would appear on a small balcony to address a jittery nation.

Fortunately, Batista kept Manuel and the Sección de Expertos on duty. But Manuel, unable to predict which way the wind would blow next, saw an opportunity to shelter himself from any future gale. Prior to the overthrow, he'd left Ysabel and moved into Suite 848. His continued residence at the Nacional legitimized, Manuel would ingratiate himself with Batista as a double agent. Claiming to disdain Cuba's new and lowborn ruling clique, he would offer Sanguily misleading information regarding the usurpers' intentions. Gaining the general's confidence, he would pass on to Batista false plans supposedly made by Sanguily in concert with the American representative Sumner Welles, who had just moved his residence to the Nacional. Should matters come to a head, Manuel would have ingratiated himself to both sides.

The crowd stirred. Lola's heart raced. She wondered whether violence might break out and, despite the relative safety of their position, sweep them along with it. Of one thing she was certain. Manuel's ill-conceived game of double deceit posed a singularly bad risk for both of them.

In the showroom, Lola bolted to her feet. The piano bench toppled and hit the stage with the crack of a lion-tamer's whip. Ten minutes into a pre-show rehearsal the afternoon preceding Kol Nidre, the band had fumbled a new number. "The fourth bar," she shrieked. "A major seventh!" The timbre of her voice resonated with fatigue overlaid by foreboding.

While the musicians stared at their instruments, Fernando approached with the empathetic deliberation of a parent seeking to calm an overwrought child. "Cariña," he said, "this is a difficult time for us *all*."

Difficult for Fernando, Lola thought, but doubly so for her. Nearly three weeks into the Grau presidency, Cuba had sunk into turmoil. Defying Batista, Grau proclaimed a social revolution. Leftists hailed the new president while Sumner Welles conveyed to Batista Washington's disappointment. The old guard, including the generals occupying much of the Nacional, itched for a fight. Lola took no position on affairs of state. Not that she lacked affection for Cuba. She loved the country but directed her affection to the people rather than the government. Neither Batista nor the generals appealed to her. Whoever emerged the victor would pillage the island.

The unsettled situation had left Manuel increasingly disagreeable. Lola suggested he claim ill health and retreat to the countryside. That, he countered, would lure an assassin's bullet. He could return to his wife, she proposed, and make a public show of asking forgiveness. Surely no one could question his seeking to uphold the laws of God and the Church. He refused to dishonor himself. Besides, he was too committed to his course of action. Leaving the Nacional would forfeit his value to Batista. Likewise, he could not permit Lola to move out, eliminating the rationale for his residency at the hotel and stoking the generals' suspicions.

Lola became increasingly distressed as Manuel played both sides in a game of political chess. Heaping lie upon lie, he erected a house of cards growing higher each day and bound to collapse not only on him but also on her.

Lola also abandoned hope that Charlie Luciano would come to her rescue. Charlie, through Meyer and Ben—they were on a first-name basis now—expressed reservations about the Batista-controlled government but sent no summons for her to return to New York. How was she to keep her feet on the ground when everything was up in the air?

Fernando approached the stage. "Cariña, you must rest."

Lola collapsed into his arms.

Fernando swiveled his head towards the band, signaling the rehearsal's termination.

Lola sobbed.

He took her to the elevator.

She insisted that she go upstairs accompanied only by Luis, the elevator operator.

Although reluctant, Fernando complied.

Opening the door to Suite 848, Lola heard voices. Manuel sat with two men. One wore a well-tailored gray suit, the other an open-necked white shirt and slacks the color of black coffee. Two others in shirtsleeves, pistols slung on hips, stood near the wall.

"I— We did not expect you," said Manuel.

The man in the suit set down a glass of rum and stood. His thin-lipped mouth topped by a clipped gray mustache implied someone who kept important secrets and demanded reciprocity. Preempting Manuel, he introduced himself. "Señorita Flores, I'm Sumner Welles, President Roosevelt's special envoy to Cuba."

Lola took his offered hand.

Welles glanced at the man in the other chair who struggled to stay erect. His round face displayed a pallor approaching the white of the milk in his glass. His clenched jaw registered discomfort. "Let me introduce you," said Welles, "to General Julio Sanguily Echarte."

"¡Mucho gusto!" Lola said.

Sanguily nodded.

Welles opened a silver cigarette case.

Lola accepted a cigarette and joined Manuel on the sofa. Obviously, the men planned some sort of intrigue. Lola found it difficult to believe that they trusted each other.

"We were discussing the current situation with Colonel Gallegos," Welles said. "I assume you are aware of Cuba's uneasiness."

Lola could not believe Sumner Welles would insult her. Was anyone in Cuba *not* aware? And would anyone use the word *uneasiness*? Did he not see the cruelty in avoiding the obvious—that Cuba lurched towards a new wave of violence, lost lives, shattered hopes? "Yes, Mr. Welles," she said, avoiding a response that might lead to unpleasantness and even danger. "I know a few things." She knew, of course, that Sanguily and Welles refused to recognize the legitimacy of the Sergeants' Revolt and Fulgencio Batista's covert leadership, and that the Nacional bristled with weapons to counter a possible government assault.

But Welles had no idea about all she knew. Manuel had disclosed that Batista's newly appointed officers were inexperienced. The hotel was cut off but offered the generals a sound defensive position on the small cliff above the Malecón. An expanse of lawn on all sides left Batista's troops exposed to deadly fire. Moreover, because Welles and many Americans lived at the Nacional, a military confrontation initiated by Batista risked provoking Washington's deep displeasure. Still, it seemed inevitable that one or both sides would make a major miscalculation born of overconfidence.

"Cuba will benefit by your being here," Lola said.

Welles chuckled. "I've been told you're a clever young lady."

Lola wondered what he'd say to Alberto.

Manuel stood. "You may trust Lola, Mr. Welles. Batista repels her."

Welles turned to Lola. "Nonetheless, señorita, I must ask that for now, you return downstairs with one of our associates. Leaving the hotel obviously is out of the question."

One of the armed men approached Lola.

Lola stood. Additional concerns troubled her. What role was Welles playing here in Havana? Had Manuel thrown in with Sanguily and America? Or was Manuel loyal to no one—herself included?

Three days later, the sound of puttering in the kitchen roused Lola from the first deep sleep she'd enjoyed in weeks. She looked at the clock on her nightstand. It indicated just past eight. She reached out to the other side of the bed. Once again, it was empty.

Manuel had confided that Batista saw no benefit in challenging Sanguily. He would wait the generals out while the new Cuban ambassador to Washington went over Sumner Welles' head to Roosevelt's secretary of state Cordell Hull. Still, the generals entrenched in the Nacional remained on high alert and he, maintaining his double game, with them. After returning from his office where he took frequent naps, Manuel played his role like an actor in a film and met with Sanguily's top advisors until late in the evening. After, he roamed the building—sometimes with others, sometimes alone—to inspect its defenses before retreating to the bar, open through the night.

Lola dropped her head to her pillow and drifted off.

A moment later, Manuel entered with a tray containing half a grapefruit, bread and jam, and coffee. "I thought it would be best if you rose now. I must leave soon. A small matter requires my immediate attention."

"What could be so important that I must have breakfast at this hour?"

Receiving no answer, she sat up and raised the coffee to her lips. "You might as well open the drapes."

"That would not be wise," Manuel responded.

Lola looked towards the window.

"Batista has positioned soldiers on the Malecón and along the streets surrounding the hotel," said Manuel. At first light, he and several of the generals had surveyed the situation. They estimated the number of Batista's men at two thousand. He was laying siege.

Lola put the coffee down, nearly spilling on the tray. "Siege?" she asked.

"Batista will not let anyone, guests included, in or out."

"But certainly, *you* are free to come and go."

Manuel shook his head. Just before the troops assembled in the darkness, an associate in the Presidential Palace—perhaps the last man in Cuba he trusted—sent him a message. Batista had been informed of his double game.

"How can Batista think," asked Lola, "that he can lock up everyone in Havana's most important hotel, including Americans, and escape serious consequences?"

"The soldiers outside are no illusion," said Manuel. There would be no audience for her shows tonight except for guests of the hotel. No food or liquor would be delivered. No newspapers. "Especially not newspapers. Not until Sanguily and the generals agree to surrender."

"And you?" she asked.

"And me."

"What will you do?"

"I must throw in my lot with Sanguily. We will wait until this mixed-blood stenographer realizes that the people of Cuba, and America, will never permit him to stay in power."

Lola reached towards her nightstand.

Manuel lit her cigarette then inspected his manicured fingernails like an ancient diviner studying the entrails of a bird.

Her eyes mocked the formidable security official defeated at his own game.

Their silence disconcerted her more than a scream.

Manuel turned towards the window and stared.

Like a condemned prisoner resigned to the noose or the bullet, Lola exchanged fear and disgust for an air of nonchalance and stubbed out her cigarette. "If this is the way things are to be, I shall go back to sleep."

As she lay down, a burst of machine gun fire battered the bedroom's exterior wall. Several rounds shattered the window. Shards of glass shredded the drapes.

Manuel rushed into the bedroom and pulled Lola to the floor.

She sprawled on a rug offering a warm counterpoint to the cool tile beneath it. The breakfast tray's contents scattered around her, she covered her head with her hands. Fearing injury that would leave her incapable of playing the piano, she reached up, pulled a pillow on top of her head and tucked her hands beneath her body.

Her cavalier attitude abandoned, Lola considered the likelihood that her life, along with Manuel's, would end here. Yet death would fail to free her from harm's reach. Lola Flores' body—and Albert's—would be exposed to soldiers or someone preparing her for burial. Albert whispered that she need not worry. "In the World to Come, we will enjoy an existence free from the restrictions of earthly life."

Lola rejected his optimism as cruel fantasy. Since when did Albert believe in the World to Come? Clearly, everyone died, but what mattered was the memory others held of you. The discovery of Albert would destroy the legacy of Lola Flores, her only opportunity to enjoy life after death. Those who'd once cheered her would condemn her as unnatural, her music as sinful. Only Fernando, safe in his apartment, would mourn her. And where would she be buried? A Catholic cemetery? A potter's field without a gravestone? Her neshama, her soul in constant struggle with Albert's—if either or both had one—could never bear that. If she survived, she would find a way to make Jewish funeral arrangements wherever she might be.

A continuous pock-pock-pock lacking any sense of rhythm marked the generals returning fire from the floors below.

The army answered. Hundreds of rounds peppered the Nacional's walls.

Manuel rose to one knee. "I must join the others. You will be safe here."

"You call this safe?"

"You must trust me." When he began his subterfuge, he informed Batista that none of Sanguily's generals resided on the seventh and eighth floors. Batista praised him for providing that intelligence. The officers would order their soldiers to concentrate fire on the floors below. This would safeguard civilians, of course, but primarily conserve scarce ammunition.

A burst of three rounds penetrated the wall on the other side of the window.

Manuel sprinted to the bedroom door.

The bedside light went out.

Lola remained on the floor. The rug grew damp.

As the morning wore on, gunfire alternated with periods of silence. The latter grew longer. Lola remembered reading that one Christmas during the war, French and German troops put down their weapons to play soccer. Had Sumner Welles negotiated brief truces with Batista to enable each side to tend to its wounded before continuing hostilities?

At noon, Lola took advantage of what appeared to be a ceasefire to wash, dress and go to the kitchen for bread, cheese and a bottle of wine. Leaving all but the wine untouched, she took a chair and Aldous Huxley's *Brave New World* into the relative safety of the hallway. She found two dozen guests assembled there.

The women verged on tears or sobbed outright.

The men feigned stoicism. Their eyes revealed fear.

Footsteps sounded on the stairs. A guest from England announced that during the last lull, he'd descended to the lobby. It had suffered considerable damage. Near the main entry, he'd glimpsed the bodies of three soldiers and a dead defender.

A woman in a red-and-white-striped blouse and white slacks with a broad blue belt approached Lola. She whispered in Lola's ear then returned to her husband, a heavyset man dabbing his forehead with a white handkerchief.

Lola went back to her suite and returned with a guitar.

"Play anything," the woman called out with a heavy New York accent.

Lola gave no thought to trying out one of several songs she was writing and began singing one of her mother's favorites, a tune by Irving Berlin. She even imitated the faux-Yiddish accent of the star who made the song famous, Fanny Brice.

*Everyone was singing, dancing, springing*
*At a wedding yesterday.*
*Yiddle on his fiddle played some ragtime*
*And when Sadie heard him play . . .*

The guests applauded.

Lola sat, her face unresponsive. What had she been thinking by playing Irving Berlin and mimicking Fanny Brice? Had she been thinking at all? Was she still capable of thinking?

"You must have learned that in New York," said the woman who'd requested a song. "And the Yiddish accent. Almost like you came from the old country. Right, Julius?"

Her husband patted his handkerchief on the back of his neck. "She's still a shiksa."

Maintaining ignorance of the reference to her as a non-Jewish woman, Lola attempted to recover her wits by tuning the guitar. She'd performed twice in New York and never raised suspicions. Now, she'd let herself drift across the boundaries of her several identities in complete disregard to discovery. Satisfied with the guitar's tuning, she let her fingers skip over the strings until they led to one of her new songs.

Despite periodic muffled gunshots, the guests listened to their unanticipated concert with rapt attention.

Two hours later, Lola rested the guitar on her lap and closed her eyes. She'd done all she could to lift the guests' spirits even if her own remained numbed.

The woman from New York burst into tears.

Lola hugged her.

The woman's sobs turned to whimpers then subsided. "God bless you," she said.

At six, the illumination provided by the skylight had dimmed. Guests could barely see each other at arm's length. Hotel staff emerged from the stairway and set out electric hurricane lanterns.

Shortly after, Manuel, clutching a rifle, ascended the stairs and announced that darkness had, by agreement, halted the fighting.

The guests returned to their rooms.

In the living room of Suite 848, Manuel lit not one lantern but two.

Lola collapsed onto the sofa.

Manuel poured drinks but remained on his feet. His hair disheveled, his shirt sweat-stained, he renewed his grip on the rifle, posturing like a Roman conqueror satiated with victory but yet to enjoy its spoils. "We have defended the Nacional!" His voice rang with pride. "Two of our men have been killed and several wounded, but we have exterminated as many as thirty of Batista's vermin."

Lola willed herself to rise on an elbow and emptied her glass. "Will the army leave now?"

"Batista has withdrawn many of his men. These so-called soldiers and their so-called officers have no stomach for war. Their veins run with impure blood like the Jews, who suck the strength from this nation."

As many times before, Lola wondered if Manuel suspected she was a Jew but through perceived magnanimity made her an exception. Or perhaps her circumcision, difficult to detect given her anatomy, had escaped him.

"When we restore order," he continued, "Cuba will heed a new voice of dignity and order like those of Il Duce and señor Hitler in Germany."

Not caring to be one of "the good Jews," Lola considered reaching for Manuel's rifle but realized she could not wrest it from him.

"Tonight," he said, "we will guard the hotel in four-hour shifts. I must report downstairs at eleven."

Outside the hotel, a thick mist softened the single crack of a rifle.

Exceptional stillness marked Lola's waking shortly after dawn. Sunlight filtered into the bedroom, diffused by sheets Manuel had placed over the tattered drapes. His side of the bed again remained empty. Lola listened for his presence elsewhere. Only her own shallow breathing reached her ears. Despite the calm, she dropped to her hands and knees to crawl to the bathroom. Disgusted with her timidity, she regained her feet. Exhausted afterward, she returned to bed.

At ten-thirty, she opened her eyes and listened for renewed turmoil. She discovered a tranquility she'd believed lost forever. Had bloodshed dismayed the army? Or had Sanguily and Welles signed an armistice with Batista and Grau?

Filled with a tenuous optimism, she put on a robe and slippers. In the kitchen, electricity remained unavailable, but her match produced a flame on the gas stove. She put on coffee, sliced a plantain for frying and cut away the spoiled parts of a Swiss cheese. In the oven, she warmed the remains of a loaf of bread and a half-eaten guava pastry. Several minutes later, breakfast consumed with unanticipated gusto, she stood to clear the dining table.

An explosion knocked her to the floor. Lamps toppled. What remained of the glass in previously shattered windows hurtled across the living room.

Lola crept under the table.

A second explosion rattled the walls. Chunks of ceiling rained down. Again, she wet herself.

A third explosion followed then a fourth. Both assaulted the hotel's lower floors.

Folly overwhelming fear, Lola left the shelter of the table and staggered across the living room. Glass crunched under her feet. She peered out a window.

In the bay, two Cuban navy ships trained their guns on the Nacional.

Following the surrender, a frail Sanguily, his generals and other senior officers, all with hands on heads, were marched off the hotel's grounds towards a fleet of army trucks. Observing from beneath the Nacional's covered entry, Lola grew curious and set out to follow.

A sergeant blocked her advance.

She turned and startled. A dozen defeated officers, hands bound behind their backs, took places along the grassy, palm-lined median running down the center of the hotel's lengthy driveway. On the order of a major, they knelt in a single, straight rank as if taking part in a macabre military review.

A soldier with a rifle approached behind each prisoner.

Lola spotted Manuel among the captives. His resigned calm contrasted with her sudden sense of exhilaration. She was about to witness divine justice, redress delayed but not denied for the humiliation Manuel had forced upon her. The low buzz of a conversation distracted her. She turned to see two senior officers of Batista's victorious army engaged with a smiling Sumner Welles. Lola caught Welles' eye.

He looked away.

She turned back to Manuel.

The major raised his pistol.

Each soldier placed the muzzle of his rifle inches behind the head of the prisoner before him.

As sunlight glinted on the weapons' barrels, Lola's mood darkened. Was divine judgment really to be executed this way? Or was she about to observe—to exult in—the savagery exercised by victors convinced that they themselves would endure such barbarism in defeat? She refused to believe that she'd become as cynical and pitiless as Manuel and Batista. Albert asked, "Are you sure?"

The next day, Lola sat in Fernando's small dining room as his houseguest while an army of workmen on orders of Fulgencio Batista refurbished the Nacional and hopefully Cuba's image. Leaving her salad untouched, she reached for the bottle of Scotch on the table and refilled her glass. It wasn't yet two o'clock, and it might have been her third. Possibly her fourth.

The telephone rang.

Fernando went to the apartment's entry and sat on the small chair next to the mahogany telephone table. After an exchange of pleasantries, he called, "For you. From America. Leon Greenspan."

Lola emptied her glass and retraced Fernando's steps.

"Thank God you're all right," said Greenspan. "The papers, the radio— They're sketchy on details. So anyway, you *are* okay, huh? I want to hear it from you."

"Yes."

"You sure? They say Manuel—"

"I am sure."

"Good. I mean, this is bad, right? But it's good. *Better* than good. Meyer, Ben and Charlie? All of us, we were scared shitless. Scout's honor. Anyway, Charlie spoke to some people in Havana. They gave assurances. I mean, the situation with the generals is done, right?"

Lola stared at the wall.

"So anyway," said Greenspan, "forget what I told you before about maybe coming to New York. At least not anytime soon. Things have changed, right? You stay put in Havana. But don't worry. We have big plans for Lola Flores."

"Of course, you have," Lola said. "But you will have to change them."

# NEW YORK

# APRIL 1935

# "I WILL DO *ANYTHING*, MISS BURKE!"

Lola fidgeted on the bar stool in Sardi's where the late-lunch Theater District crowd came to drink as much as to eat. She wished her backside contained just a little more heft, well aware that most women groaned about theirs displaying too much. She also recognized that her nervousness had nothing to do with her tuchus.

Fernando patted her shoulder. He and Leon Greenspan sat beside her, joined by Heshy Kaplan, a short, squat emissary of Ben Siegel. Scanning *The Wall Street Journal* in his rumpled gray suit, Kaplan gave the impression of an easygoing older brother content with his life as a loyal subordinate. The bulge under his coat revealed a willingness to engage in violence, but his placid, almost bovine, face suggested he would do so without malicious intent.

A glass of champagne in hand—this was a special occasion—Lola scanned the walls filled with caricatures of Broadway, radio and film stars. If lunch went well, she would give Vincent Sardi good reason to add her to his collection.

The restaurant's host approached.

Lola, Fernando and Kaplan stood. Greenspan, having downed two Scotches, not necessarily the day's first, slipped off his stool. Kaplan caught him.

The host, deadpan, led them to a private dining room.

A carefully coifed matron at a white-clothed table studied a crystal vase. Its half-dozen canary-yellow roses matched her jacket. The stems and leaves complemented her green jade necklace.

Lola was thrilled to meet Billie Burke, who'd starred on Broadway then in silent films, returned to Broadway and in 1932 resumed her screen career in talkies. Lola saw no reason why she couldn't be as big as Billie Burke. Bigger.

To Billie Burke's right stood a smooth-cheeked man little older than Lola. His eyeglasses featured circular gold rims and thick lenses more appropriate to a university professor than a man with clout on rough-and-tumble Broadway. His double-breasted blue blazer featured two columns of three gold buttons. A maroon ascot with white polka dots draped his neck. His breast pocket displayed a matching handkerchief. "Miss Flores," he said, "Miss Burke and I are so delighted to meet you."

Before Lola could express her own excitement, Greenspan collapsed into a seat and asked, "So who are *you?*"

Billie Burke's pencil-thin eyebrows arched towards her hairline.

"Why, I'm Arthur Devlin, Miss Burke's assistant," the man said. "And you must be Leon Greenspan. We spoke on the telephone a week ago and again yesterday."

Billie Burke extended her hand to Lola.

Lola gushed, "I will do *anything*, Miss Burke!"

Billie Burke revealed the hint of a smile. "Determined girl." She nodded for Lola to sit.

Greenspan looked at Devlin and pointed his thumb at Fernando. "This here's Fallon. Irish he ain't. Runs errands for Miss Flores. Just so you know who you're dealing with."

Devlin nodded towards Kaplan. "I'm afraid I haven't made the acquaintance of this other gentleman."

"Heshy Kaplan," said Greenspan. "A friend of Ben Siegel and Meyer Lansky. We're *all* friends if you get my drift."

"So much for pleasantries, Mr. Greenspan," said Billie Burke. "As my late husband Florenz used to say, pleasantries are no substitute for the hard work that creates art and turns it into commerce."

"I wish I had known Mr. Ziegfeld," said Lola. She had ceased addressing people as señor and señora and urged Fernando to do the same. His English fluency had blossomed over their eighteen months in New York after Ben Siegel relented on behalf of Charlie Luciano and welcomed her to the Big Apple. Fitting in was critical.

Billie Burke patted Lola's hand. "Before lunch—"

"And drinks," said Greenspan. "Where the fucking waiter?"

"A drink, of course," said Devlin, "But first let me tell you about *The Ziegfeld Follies of 1936*." The show would open at the Winter Garden in January. Billie Burke was producing with the Shubert brothers, Lee and Jake. Ira Gershwin was writing lyrics for Vernon Duke's music. They'd already signed Bob Hope, Eve Arden and Helen O'Connell. "And our star will be Fanny Brice."

Lola had fantasized about performing with Fanny Brice, whose records Mama adored. This involved risk, which Lola dismissed. Mama and Papa went to the movies and occasionally the Yiddish Theater on Second Avenue, which by the 1920s had become Americanized, but never—Fanny Brice or no—to Broadway shows, which were truly American. Even if they attended the new *Follies*, they'd never anticipate seeing Albert, let alone recognize him in the guise of Lola Flores. Not after all this time and the clean break she'd made with her past. Since returning to New York, Lola had refused to re-visit the old apartment building or the synagogue, despite Albert's encouragement. Occupying a place in a world of specters and spirits, Albert hovered over her. If he glossed over his pain, Lola stood condemned to carry hers—theirs—to the grave.

"The new *Follies*," said Billie Burke, "will be perfect for the Broadway debut of our up-and-coming star, Lola Flores."

Lola did not doubt that despite Ben Siegel's pull and Walter Winchell's constant plugs, she'd earned the opportunity. She'd filled mob-owned clubs throughout the New York area and headlined at the Roosevelt Grill, the Hotel New Yorker's Terrace Room, the Madhattan Room at the Hotel Pennsylvania and the Glen Island Casino. She'd even helped open the new Paramount Theater on Broadway.

And she'd gone out on the road, a task more daunting than glamorous. The travel fatigued her, and Leon often engaged in pointless disputes with venue bookers and managers. A month earlier, he'd quarreled with the iconic Eddie Cantor less than an hour before she appeared on his radio show. Granted, she and Fernando were living pleasantly in Manhattan, but band expenses were considerable, and she always returned to New York exhausted. The *Follies* would provide stability and steady pay but most of all the chance to achieve success on the highest level in the city where she was, in truth, a native. She considered it a shame—an outrage—that the

Big Apple would never really know the woman who swept it off its feet, but she'd rather reach for the stars here as Lola Flores than remain an earthbound refugee in Havana.

"If I may ask, Mr. Devlin," said Fernando, "exactly what do you and Miss Burke have in mind for Lola?"

Greenspan pushed his chair back.

Kaplan placed a thick hand on Greenspan's shoulder.

Billie Burke took a beat pause. "We're going to stage a big Latin number. Towards the end, Fanny will engage in a brief sketch with our Latin singer." She turned to Lola. "I heard you on the Cantor show. You have a natural comedic flair."

Lola never thought of herself as funny in Cuba, but in New York, freed from violence, discovered that she indeed could play the comedienne. Perhaps comedy related closely to tragedy as represented by the twin masks in ancient Greek theater.

A waiter brought menus.

"Jesus, where the hell you been?" said Greenspan. "Scotch rocks. Chop chop!"

Fernando rested his hand on Lola's wrist.

She shook it off. "Scotch also for me."

Billie Burke and Devlin ordered Bloody Marys.

"Tea," said Kaplan. "Sugar, please."

Fernando pointed to his own empty water glass.

Greenspan turned to Devlin. "How many numbers does Lola get? Because Fanny Brice— Everyone knows she's over the hill."

Billie Burke stared at Lola.

"I assure you," said Devlin, "that our Latin number will shine New York's brightest spotlight on whichever singer we cast."

Greenspan pounded the table. Glasses, plates and silverware rattled.

Billie Burke, eyes narrowed, lips tightly pressed, gazed at the roses then back at Greenspan. "Frankly, that was not the response Arthur and I expected."

Kaplan shook his head. "Please excuse Leon, Miss Burke. He takes his clients' careers serious. He's the one who got Xavier Cugat into the Waldorf."

"It's a pity," said Devlin, "that Mr. Greenspan no longer represents Mr. Cugat."

"Miss Burke, Mr. Devlin," Kaplan said, "you've been very kind." He squeezed Greenspan's neck like a ventriloquist manipulating his dummy. "Isn't that right, Leon?"

Greenspan nodded.

The waiter returned.

Billie Burke held up her hand. "Our guests will be adjourning to the bar."

Leaving Sardi's in a huff, Greenspan insisted they get lunch at Jack Dempsey's joint on Eighth Avenue across from Madison Square Garden.

Lola had no appetite but, while furious, was in no position to refuse the man Ben Siegel designated to manage her career—if she had a career left.

As the taxi navigated Midtown traffic, Greenspan commented, "Beach weather soon. Remember Coney Island, Hesh?"

"Memories, right?" Kaplan countered.

"Coney Island's okay," said Greenspan. "But California? You can go to the beach Christmas and New Year's. Like Miami Beach or Havana but without the humidity."

"I got a cousin in San Francisco," Kaplan said. "According to him, the water's so cold, even in the summer you can't go in past your ankles. *Especially* in the summer."

"And the women!" Greenspan said.

Lola yanked his hand off her thigh.

*Albert hurries from the lake. Rushes into the changing room. Hopes to towel off and dress before the other boys arrive. Two weeks at Camp Lehman, the 92$^{nd}$ Street YMHA's summer camp, approach their end. He wishes he could stay. Since his bar mitzvah a year earlier, Papa and Mama scold incessantly. Tosia hurls taunts. Only Sylvia sympathizes. Maribel remains his confidante.*

*Still, camp leaves him uncomfortable. The boys tease. Mock. Scorn. He conceals himself when he changes clothes. Sticks his nose in a book during free time. Prefers arts and crafts to sports. Lacks interest in girls.*

*One small measure of respect they begrudge him. He's the group's strongest swimmer. Papa took him to the pool at the Y's annex when he was five.*

*Followed the Talmud's instructions. Circumcise your son. Prepare him for a trade. Teach him to swim.*

*Unbeknownst to Papa, Albert regularly tests his mettle in the East River. Sometimes enters the defiled water opposite nearby Roosevelt Island. Often journeys south to Pike Slip beneath the Manhattan Bridge. Overcomes the choppy, often-frigid water. Navigates the areas posing grave danger.*

*Albert recovers his dry clothes. Retreats to the far corner. Removes his wet trunks and shirt. Freezes.*

*Three boys approach. Silent as the breeze blowing across the lake. One spins him around.*

*Albert tries to cover himself.*

*The other two seize his arms. "See," says the first camper. "His schmeckel's like a baby's. Can't tell if he had a bris. Ain't got no hair. But tits. He got tits."*

*"I'm a boy," Albert says. A lie. They leave him no choice.*

*"Maybe," says a second camper. "A fairy."*

*Albert wriggles in their grasp. Fails to break free.*

*The first camper touches Albert's breast. "He's a girl. That's why it's okay us coppin' a feel. Us not bein' fairies." He takes his penis out of his trunks.*

*Albert shuts his eyes. Hears the boy moan.*

Greenspan stumbled out of the taxi. "Don't be disappointed," he said, "but Dempsey's only here nights." He threw a left-right combination at a ghost unable to hit back.

Lola, who once accompanied Manuel to a fight in Havana, thought his punches feeble.

Greenspan tapped his fists. "Nobody fucks with Leon Greenspan. Am I right, Hesh?"

Kaplan smiled. "Let's eat, already."

After lunch—Lola picked at tuna salad—she and Fernando waited at the bar with Kaplan while Greenspan went to the "little boy's."

"May I confide in you, Mr. Kaplan?" Fernando asked.

"Heshy, please. I'm just an ordinary schmo. And I know what you're gonna say. Leib can be a real schmuck. But Ben, Meyer and Mr. Luciano? *Them*, you wanna show respect."

"Of course, Heshy. Thank you. What I was thinking—"

Lola cut Fernando off. "I thought it would be better to say nothing at lunch, Heshy, but for a long time, Leon has been causing problems. I feel I can trust you, so I reveal to you that it was Fernando who contacted Eddie Cantor's people, so *they* could call Leon and book me on the show."

Heshy tapped Fernando on the chest. "You got balls."

Lola fought back tears. After all her struggles, Billie Burke and Arthur Devlin would derail her Broadway career by casting another Latin singer and telling all the important people they knew about their brief and unpleasant encounter with Lola Flores. Even her club dates might disappear.

Heshy took a mint from a large glass bowl and carefully undid its cellophane wrapping. "Leib and booze, they don't get along. The sauce cost him Cugat. And his wife. That's why she still lives in L.A. His mistress, too."

"Can you say something to Mr. Siegel or Mr. Lansky?" Lola asked. "Perhaps even to Mr. Luciano?"

"Benny, Meyer and Mr. Luciano got their hands full."

Lola's face fell.

Heshy grinned. "My wife and me, we loved you on Eddie Cantor. As far as the *Follies* goes? You'll get the job."

"Heshy," said Fernando, "can Mr. Siegel really tell people like Miss Burke and Mr. Devlin who they should cast?"

Heshy stuffed mints into both jacket pockets. "One thing you never want to do is sell Benny short. Leib? He's been screwin' up. Benny's not happy about it, but there's something you got to understand."

People thought Ben Siegel lacked a soft spot in his heart for anything or anyone. Not so. One long-ago summer evening the gang—Meyer organized them as teenagers to stand up to the Irish and Italians on the Lower East Side—went to a party in Brooklyn. They allowed Leib to tag along. his mother being close to Ben's. Membership in the Bugs and Meyer Mob? Out of the question. As kids on expeditions to candy stores to steal Butterfinger bars and copies of *Artists and Models*, only one boy got caught regularly. Leib. He also ran from fistfights. When escape proved impossible, he suffered bloody defeats. But that night, as they passed around a bottle of bootleg hooch in the middle of the street, a car approached at breakneck speed. Leib tripped over his own feet and bumped into Benny, knocking him out of the way. The car grazed Leib. Unhurt, he bawled all the way to his apartment.

"After that," said Heshy, "anyone messes with Leib, they have to deal with Benny. We found the car. Turned it into junk." He unwrapped another mint. "A word to the wise. Lola Flores has Ben Siegel in her corner. Leave it at that."

Lola appreciated Heshy's trying to cheer her up after the disaster with Billie Burke. She wished he'd succeeded.

The next morning, the phone rang in Lola's apartment two floors above Fernando's and thirty blocks south of where she'd grown up off Second Avenue. She put down her cigarette and took a breath to steady herself. She would take the bad news with grace and so avoid a scene that would further blacken her name up and down Broadway—as if that mattered now—and bring down the wrath of Ben Siegel. Her hand shaking, she picked up the receiver. "Yes?" she said.

"Arthur Devlin here. Out of courtesy, Miss Flores, I thought I'd call you before I spoke with Mr. Greenspan."

Lola shuddered. Arthur Devlin was about to deliver the coup de grace, his voice evidencing no more compassion than the unnamed soldier who brought a gruesome end to Manuel Gallegos.

"So then," said Devlin, "welcome to *The Ziegfeld Follies of 1936.*"

# JANUARY 1936

# OPENING NIGHT

A hand patted Lola's behind as the final curtain descended. "You were aces, kid," said Bob Hope, who'd had a previous Broadway hit. In the wings, Fanny Brice gave Lola a knip, pinching the flesh of Lola's left cheek between her thumb and index finger. "Oy! A Cuban *me*, only prettier."

Lola returned to her dressing room packed with bouquets and members of the press.

Fernando uncorked champagne.

Walter Winchell grabbed Lola's glass, gulped it down and blew a kiss. "Thanks for the interview," he said.

"But I did not say anything," said Lola.

"No need," Winchell said, halfway out the door. "Gotta phone in my story."

Other reporters shot questions at Lola then departed in Winchell's wake. They, too, had deadlines.

Lola showered and slipped into a sleeveless navy evening gown. A silver, rose-shaped bow covered her modest cleavage.

Fernando helped her into a black cashmere coat accented by a fox collar.

Outside the stage door, opening-night fans spilled onto Seventh Avenue. Flashbulbs illuminated the breath-induced mist hovering above them. Standing in front of a purple velvet rope, three New York policeman glowered.

Lola noticed a broad-shouldered man who might once have played football channeling a path through the crowd. A woman with bright red hair and sharp elbows followed. She reminded Lola of a younger, prettier

Frida Herskovits. The woman thrust out a *Follies' Playbill* and a pen. "I'm
Blanche," she said. She nodded towards the man who'd led the way. "My
husband Morris. Could you autograph this for our daughter Kay? She's
three. When she's older, we can show her we saw Lola Flores the night she
became a star."

As Lola autographed the program, she wondered what Mama and
Papa—and Tosia and Sylvia—would say about Lola Flores. What she
would do if, no matter how unlikely, she spotted them in the crowd.
Would she beckon them forward? Whisper an invitation to her apartment
where she could bare her soul? Would they embrace her? Embrace Albert?
Despite her new life and continuing attempts to erase the family from her
memory, she missed them. Every child wanted her family's support and
praise, prized most when they were withheld. Having been rejected, how
could she hope to draw them close now? Convince them that the Broadway
star Lola Flores was Albert Sobel as he—she—was meant to be? Could she
really expect her celebrity status to convince Papa and Mama to accept her
at the price of casting the family's reputation into the gutter? Returning
the *Playbill*, Lola rebuked herself for letting ghosts overrun her defenses.
At the same time, she wondered if exiling Papa and Mama from her heart
represented a cruel self-deception. Worse, a form of suicide.

Ben Siegel rose to his feet in the Stork Club's windowless private dining
room. Accessible only to those occupying the highest level of celebrity or
notoriety, it offered its clientele the liberty to make a show of entering
and departing from the main restaurant or slipping in and out through
a narrow alley undetected. Exercising his usual precaution, Siegel had
positioned himself at the room's rear, the wall shielding his back, the lone
door opposite in full view. Proud to host an intimate post-opening supper
feting Broadway's newest star, he grinned at Lola, seated on his right, then
bent down to peck her on the cheek. Were he not merely four years older,
he might have been perceived as the father of the bride.

Lola returned his chaste kiss. If at times she found herself uneasy about
consorting with gangsters, she was nobody's fool. Ben Siegel exercised
a powerful influence on her career while providing the comfort of his
protection.

The guests—men in tuxedos, women in evening gowns—tendered

smiles of approval and admiration to curry favor with Siegel and avoid his mercurial temper.

Siegel held up a glass of champagne.

The guests stood.

Lola remained seated, the object of what she hoped would be many toasts saluting a series of triumphs, each more impressive than the last.

Siegel turned to his left and, continuing clockwise, saluted each guest: Leon Greenspan, who a moment earlier raised a small fuss by insisting that as Lola's manager, he occupy the seat on the left of his childhood friend. Leon's companion, a six-foot blonde with an impressive bust and a fierce resolve to abandon the life of a veterinarian's assistant in rural Minnesota for the theater or, to escape the ravages of winter altogether, Hollywood. Meyer Lansky, interrupting a business deal in Chicago. The showgirls he and Siegel brought along—two each. Heshy Kaplan, attending solo, the babysitter having canceled at the last minute. A prominent judge on the payroll of a major crime family allied with Charlie Luciano. A union president who approved or doomed construction projects throughout the five boroughs, all of which provided Charlie Lucky a piece of the action. And a red-faced Irish leader of Tammany Hall, Manhattan's Democratic political club which took its lumps following the election of FDR but eyed recapturing power. The three latter men, being family oriented, squired attractive young women they introduced as their nieces. Siegel ended his survey of the room with a nod to Fernando.

"You'd think Charlie would have shown," Greenspan said, his voice laden with alcohol-fueled irritation.

Siegel scowled. In no more than the time required to open a fist, his face regained its celebratory glow. He extended his glass towards Lola. "I'm gonna say something about Broadway's newest star."

Greenspan hoisted his glass. "A star, fuck yeah! Know why? Because Leon Greenspan *makes* stars." He winked. "Not to mention Swedish goddesses." He turned to the blonde. "Or did you say you were Norwegian?"

Red-faced, Siegel took a step away from Greenspan as if to dissociate himself from such crude remarks.

Greenspan's chin dropped to his chest.

Again composed, Siegel looked at Lola. "May Lola Flores be on everyone's lips and in everyone's hearts. And I gotta add that every day since she returned here from Havana, this dame gets better lookin'." He looked down at his champagne. "Must be the water."

The guests laughed but not so heartily that Siegel would think they made Lola, rather than New York's water supply, the object of their amusement.

Lola and Fernando knew better. Her enhanced appearance involved a matter more daring than water, along with diet and cosmetics. After arriving in Manhattan, Fernando responded to a letter from Lili Elbe and contacted Dr. Gerstner, who'd studied in Germany with Lili's senior physician. Dr. Gerstner could not perform surgery on Lola. None of the forty-eight states permitted it. But he headed a clinic offering men and women with what he termed "conflicting anatomies" medical care in strictest confidence. For the few individuals bold or desperate enough, he provided hormone treatments still in the development stage.

Lola agreed to see Dr. Gerstner for several mild ailments but expressed no desire to undergo such treatments. Fernando did. After putting himself in Dr. Gerstner's hands, his mustache thickened, his beard coarsened and his voice deepened with no apparent impact on his health.

Weighing potential complications against the risks to which her body exposed her and the stress she endured daily, Lola began an ongoing series of hormone treatments. Her small breasts increased a cup size, her hips displayed more pronounced curves, her backside exhibited a roundedness a performer selling glamor as well as talent could flaunt. Daily vocal exercises left her tone and range unimpaired.

Siegel raised his glass higher. "To Lola Flores."

Glasses clinked. Guests drank.

Lola beamed.

Greenspan dropped back into his seat and called, "Speech! Speech!" He thrust his glass towards Lola. Its remains spilled into her lap.

Lola twisted in her chair and knocked her own glass to the floor.

As Siegel bent down to retrieve it, a muffled voice outside the door said, "Sorry, gentlemen. Private party inside."

The response took the form of a loud *crack* and the door bursting open.

The guests dove under the table.

Lola toppled backward.

Siegel shot to his feet and fired a .38 from each hand.

Heshy, with his lone gun, followed suit.

Cries and whimpers rose then descended into silence.

Smoke from heated muzzles drifted towards the ceiling.

Siegel spat. "Okay, folks. Show's over."

The guests held their places.

"Dammit," Siegel roared, "I said it's *over*!"

The guests emerged, some near-catatonic.

The blonde former veterinarian's assistant retched into a snow-white napkin.

Heshy went to the door. With the toe of his right shoe, he probed the bodies of two gunmen collapsed atop the dead waiter who sought to deter them.

"Shit!" Siegel bellowed.

All eyes shifted to Leon Greenspan, face down on the table. A red stain surrounded his head. Clumps of brain protruded from his skull.

"Nothing to worry about," Siegel said, as if he'd just won a teddy bear at Coney Island knocking down metal ducks with a popgun. "They'll clean this shit up. Meanwhile, Heshy'll make some calls. No one says nothin'. No one *knows* nothin'."

Heshy led the dumbfounded guests over the fallen men towards the door to the alley.

Siegel, not seeing Lola, turned. He found her on the floor.

Fernando cradled her head in his hands. "She has *not* been shot! She has *not* been shot! She has *not* been shot!"

Siegel lowered himself to one knee.

Lola opened her eyes. Two blurred Ben Siegels appeared.

"Jesus!" said Siegel. "Her eyes. The pupils. Big as dimes."

"I believe Lola hit her head against the wall," Fernando said.

Lola attempted to speak.

Siegel pressed a trigger finger against her lips then stroked her cheek. "Everything's hunky-dory," he whispered. He motioned Fernando to help lift her into a chair.

Lola noticed Greenspan and gasped.

Siegel patted her shoulder. "A shame, but Leib always was a putz." He placed his hand under her chin. "But *you*. If you hadn't dropped your glass—" His lips brushed her forehead. "It's official. Lola Flores is Ben Siegel's new good-luck charm."

Fernando handed Lola a glass of water.

"Heshy'll have a car get us outta here," Siegel said. "We'll get Lola to a doctor. I got a guy."

Lola had enough presence of mind to shake her head.

"Lola *has* a doctor," Fernando said.

"You nuts?" Siegel asked. "He asks questions—"

"I assure you," said Fernando, "Lola's doctor is— What is the word? Discreet."

Siegel's eyes narrowed.

"Lola slipped," said Fernando. "She bumped her head. Nothing more need be said. I beg you, Mr. Siegel. Let Lola see her own doctor."

"Please," Lola murmured.

Siegel scratched his chin. "Anyone else, fuck no. Lola Flores?" He went to the doorway. His chest heaved. "Motherfuckers!" He fired a single shot into the temple of each of the would-be assassins then grabbed a half-filled glass of champagne from the table and drained it. "Wasting," he said, "is a sin."

# FEBRUARY 1936

# SYLVIA

Three days later, Lola collapsed onto her living room sofa, enveloped in the black dress she wore hours earlier to Leon Greenspan's funeral in Brooklyn. One hand held a glass of Scotch, the other a cigarette. She gave thanks that Broadway theaters went dark Sundays. With luck, she'd get a decent night's sleep. A lot of luck.

Fernando crossed his legs in the armchair he favored when keeping Lola company, which he now did often. He joked that they might as well be married. Leaving Lola to her silence, he dwelled on what he had embraced as his primary role—advancing Lola's career. Having secured Ben Siegel's indulgence, he'd circumvented Leon Greenspan over the past months to negotiate a record contract and radio appearances. But New York's harsh winters provoked him to consider other possibilities. California beckoned with its twin lures of the silver screen and year-round golden sunsets. Patient and pragmatic but not prone to letting attractive prospects slip past, Fernando allowed himself to hold that vision in abeyance pending the right opportunity—and Ben's approval.

Lola glanced at Fernando. How could he restrict himself to tea or club soda after the attempt on Ben's life, which cost Leon Greenspan his and could have ended *theirs*. As to his frequent observations that she drank too much, nonsense! Who didn't deserve a measure of comfort when confronted by life's fragility? Not that Leon's death depressed her. She grieved publicly to accommodate the press and with Ben. The God who may or may not have borne responsibility for Leon's misfortune expected no less. She kept private her elation. Leon's death, like Manuel's, granted her a significant measure of freedom, if within bounds set by Ben Siegel.

Fernando agreed. She did not doubt that Ben, with copious blood on his own hands, would understand, not that she would ever open her heart to him.

Yet a small incident at graveside left her bewildered.

To assure Leon's burial taking place as soon as possible in accordance with Jewish law, his widow—they'd been separated but not divorced—and the children made the 24-hour flight from Los Angeles. When the male mourners, including Ben, tossed shovelfuls of dirt on Leon's grave before joining with the rabbi to fumble through Kaddish, the widow betrayed no emotion. Afterward, she announced she would neither host a meal nor sit Shiva. Tomorrow, she and the children would take the train back to the Coast.

But the new widow was not the source of Lola's upset.

Fernando interrupted her recollection. He required a break from her gloominess. He was going to the candy store for a Hershey bar.

"Pick up a Sunday *News* if one is left," she said. "And a pack of Raleighs." She'd again switched brands, this time to collect the coupons on the back redeemable for stockings, glassware, even a multi-purpose jackknife.

Fernando bundled himself in his topcoat, wrapped a scarf around his neck, put on his hat and went out.

Lola found her solitude unnerving. She tossed her half-smoked cigarette into an ashtray crowded with similar remains. An artist might pass it off as a miniature cemetery desecrated by toppled headstones. She dismissed playing the piano or putting on a record. Her mood would debase the music. She picked up Dashiell Hammett's *The Maltese Falcon.* She'd read half the novel prior to opening night but hadn't advanced a page since. Not that she wasn't intrigued. In San Francisco, a city she found charming, someone murdered a private detective named Miles Archer. His partner Sam Spade despised Archer but as a matter of honor determined to find the killer. She opened the book then put it down. Despite the new advantage she enjoyed, murder no longer seemed a fitting entertainment.

Lola lit another cigarette. She couldn't shake the suspicion that she was at fault for the violence that took lives intertwined with her own. That these unnatural deaths represented God's—or the universe's—response to sins committed by Lola Flores. Or Albert Sobel. Or both.

Her thoughts swerved back to the incident with Ben.

Brazenly, she'd violated tradition at the graveside and stood next to Ben, the lone woman in a knot of rough-hewn if well-dressed men. At least she'd remained silent as Ben and all his associates but Heshy floundering with the Hebrew. At some point, she shivered. Ben draped his arm around her. The gesture prompted Lola to see Ben in a new light. Gone was the underworld figure whose photos titillated newspaper readers, the brutal thug whose fists and guns thrust forward her career no less than they ended those of his rivals. Here was a man who embraced his passion and ambition without shame—a swashbuckler handsome and dapper—and yet, in his way, chivalrous.

Had Ben, in such an unlikely place, signaled that he wanted to sleep with her? Beyond the crude remark made in Yiddish to Meyer Lansky when they first met in Havana, he'd never intimated such desire. For that matter, he'd never intimated anything. Ben Siegel demonstrated little capacity for subtlety. Yet following that first meeting, he treated her like a sister. A princess. But what if he *did* want to sleep with her? Her body hadn't deterred Manuel. But Ben Siegel?

More perplexing, after Frida and Manuel, did *she* want to sleep with *him*? With any man? With anyone? She was almost glad that the conflicting sexual urges she experienced in Cuba deserted her in Manhattan.

Until, possibly, now.

Fernando held up the front page of Sunday's *News* with its massive headline: DEWEY BUSTS BROTHELS. New York State District Attorney Thomas E. Dewey had sent police to two hundred houses of prostitution in Manhattan and Brooklyn. Unlike after past raids organized by city officials for show, Dewey insisted that the women and their madams would stay in jail until they identified the mob figures they worked for. His objective: bring down Lucky Luciano.

"Will this be bad for Ben?" Lola asked. "For *us*?"

Fernando shook his head. "Ben will know what to do. You and I, cariña? We are guilty of nothing. And Mr. Luciano has kept his distance from us since Havana, although he is, how they say in boxing, in our corner." Dewey, Fernando explained, targeted Luciano with politics in mind. A conviction would earn him great acclaim and enable a run for governor and even president, although not this November. "President Roosevelt will easily win a second term."

"Perhaps I will vote for FDR," Lola said.

Fernando's stare reminded her that she could not risk doing so as Albert Sobel and had no right to do so as Lola Flores. She lived in New York at the sufferance of the United States, a guest whose position remained anything but secure. Many in Congress wanted few foreign nationals to enter or remain in the United States, even Cubans. Roosevelt went along. A well-known entertainer like Lola Flores could be deported on a whim. Although she and Fernando enjoyed the protection of a congressman in Charlie Luciano's pocket, the stitching on that pocket could unravel.

"At any rate," said Lola, "Mr. Dewey must be a regular Sam Spade."

"Who or what is that?"

Lola stubbed out her cigarette. "That, my dear Fernando, is what *you* are about to become."

On Tuesday afternoon, several hours before they would go to the Winter Garden, Fernando again sat in Lola's living room.

Lola poured a drink.

Fernando held out a small notebook. "Does this make me look like one of those private eyeballs?"

"Private *eyes*," Lola said.

"Yes. And in only two days, I have become a regular Sam Spade."

Lola raised an eyebrow.

Fernando made a show of opening the notebook. At Lola's insistence, he'd gone to the Sobels' old apartment building on East 69th Street. A five-dollar bill elicited a grin from the same Irish doorman Lola approached three years earlier and a vow of cooperation. Fernando, forced by life to become an accomplished actor, announced that he was the brother of Maribel Torres, the Sobels' maid. He had just arrived from Havana in search of his sister. The doorman found his memory clouded. Another five cleared it. Maribel left the Sobels in 1931. *The day after the feds sentenced Al Capone to eleven years in prison*, the doorman said. Given hard times, the Sobels could no longer afford a housekeeper. *Where'd she go? No idea.*

"And the family?"

*Moved just before FDR booted Hoover out of the White House.* If the doorman remembered right, the Bronx.

Fernando tracked the family to a building on Jerome Avenue then found their telephone number. "Sylvia answered. I told her I was Maribel's younger brother Hector, that our family had not heard from her in a very long time."

"And?"

"She looks forward to speaking with us."

The following Sunday morning, Lola and Fernando left their apartment building in Murray Hill and walked west. A February sun teased shivering New Yorkers that spring was not all that far off. Lola dismissed such folly.

They approached an alley out of character with the neighborhood but now an all too familiar sight. Near its entrance, a fire burned in a 55-gallon drum. Inside, cobbled-together shacks offered a semblance of home to men, women and children in dire straits. Wisps of smoke ascended from makeshift chimneys protruding from roofs at odd angles. The inhabitants considered themselves luckier than people forced to seek refuge in churches and armories, they in turn more fortunate than those sleeping on sidewalk heating vents or huddled together beneath windswept bridges.

Lola stopped and studied a nearby shack.

A broken pane of glass in a small window scavenged from a demolished or fire-gutted apartment building revealed a pair of eyes.

She entered the alley.

Fernando followed and gripped her shoulder. "Cariña, this place— And we must meet your sister."

Lola approached the shack. A makeshift door pieced together with lumber scraps posed little obstacle to intruders, none to wind and cold.

A small, upturned nose pressed against the glass's remains.

Lola gestured towards a handle, another piece of salvage.

The door opened the width of Lola's hand. A child peered out.

Lola held out a ten-dollar bill.

"Cariña," said Fernando, "have you any idea—"

A small hand, dirt encrusting jagged fingernails, snatched the bill. The face disappeared. The door slammed shut.

Lola stepped back and took Fernando's arm. Exiting the alley, she kept her eyes on the sidewalk. The gesture marked not surveillance but guilt. Why did she and Fernando live so well and others not? She'd just given away ten dollars and suffered no sense of loss. For all the alley's residents knew, their visitors could have been King Edward VIII of England and his American fiancée Wallis Simpson, although she and Fernando bore no resemblance to them and dressed in worn clothes bought at second-hand shops to avoid arousing Sylvia's suspicions. To better play the role of Maribel's sister, Lola also wore an old wig. A darker makeup base covered her face, neck and hands. Fernando, caught up in deception's theatrical spirit, tore a button from his suit jacket and left the thread dangling.

At Seventh Avenue, they turned right, entered a Chock full o' Nuts and settled in a booth.

Ten minutes later, Sylvia entered.

Lola stood, gripping the table to restrain herself from dashing towards her younger sister.

Fernando helped Sylvia off with her coat.

Lola observed how Sylvia, at twenty-three, had become a beautiful young woman with soft, dark curls, full lips and an impressive bust.

Sylvia sat. "Oh, my God," she said. Her eyes expressed joy and sadness. "Maribel's brother Hector. And Alejandra."

Lola had instructed Fernando that she'd need yet another name to avoid Sylvia's connecting Lola with either Albert or the Lola Flores of *The Ziegfeld Follies*.

"I am so pleased to meet you, Alejandra," Sylvia said. "It makes me sad that Maribel never mentioned you."

"I was born after Maribel left Havana. Hector and I came to New York to find her."

Fernando smiled. "I am thinking I may stay."

Lola scolded Fernando with her eyes. Would Sylvia expect to see him again? Develop some sort of relationship and not find out who he really was?

Sylvia failed to pick up Lola's annoyance. "Can you really stay, Fernando? It's so hard to enter the United States these days. For Jews like us, very hard—unless they're famous."

Fernando sympathized. For Cubans, fortunately, it was easier. They hoped to find Maribel soon.

Sylvia sighed. "I wish I knew where she was. She left the family after Papa and Uncle Mendel's business collapsed and lived with people she knew in a run-down tenement. At first, she telephoned every week. She tried to sound cheerful, but I could tell she was blue. She couldn't find a steady job."

"Have you her address?" Fernando asked. "Perhaps a telephone number?"

It seemed to Lola that Fernando had taken Sam Spade to heart.

Sylvia shook her head. The people Maribel lived with couldn't afford a phone, so she called from pay phones. "I guess she was ashamed to visit us on 69ᵗʰ Street. When we moved to the Bronx, she called less often. Then we lost touch."

A waitress approached.

"Just coffee," Sylvia said. "I'm watching my figure."

Lola smiled.

Fernando ordered three coffees.

"Do you miss Maribel?" Lola asked.

Sylvia's eyes glistened. "And Albert, of course."

Lola placed a hand on Sylvia's. "I am so sorry, Sylvia," she said, drawing out her sister's name, letting its sweetness roll over her tongue the way Albert always let the last piece of chocolate babka linger in his mouth. "But please. Tell us about yourself."

Sylvia still lived with Mama and Papa and worked as a secretary at an insurance company. She had to give a false name to get the job since they didn't hire Jews. But that was for now. "I'm taking night classes in accounting at NYU. I don't know if I'll get a degree, but I hope to land a better job. My boyfriend goes there, too."

"And who is this boy?" Lola asked as if she was Mama.

"Danny. Seligman. We knew each other in high school. I'm not sure if it's serious. It could be. How do you really know?"

"And your sister?"

"Tosia married a lawyer. Eugene Birnbaum. Gene's involved in politics. Very ambitious. They live near us on Summit Avenue. They have a son named Lawrence. Larry. He's three. And a baby daughter. Carole." Sylvia took a handkerchief from her purse and blew her nose. "Did you know we all had an older brother?"

*Sixteen-year-old Albert roams Warsaw's snaking, summer-baked streets. A tourist in the city of his birth. Of Chopin's childhood and young manhood. Exotic sites. The Vistula River, producing a tepid breeze. Baroque Wilanow Palace. The columned Grand Theater. St. Anne's Church where in 1794, revolutionaries hanged Bishop Jósef Kossakowski. Signs in Polish identify shops, restaurants, cafés. Albert reads only those in Yiddish.*

*At noon, he returns to the apartment of Zayde Zalman and Bubbe Elke. Grandpa and Grandma. Mama's parents. Attempts to engage them in Yiddish. In New York, Papa refuses to speak the mama loschen. The mother tongue. Prohibits Mama. Tosia and Sylvia know only English. Not so Albert. Aunt Agnieska taught him. Papa objected. "This is America!" Objection overruled.*

*Here, Yiddish takes Albert just so far. Zayde and Bubbe shower Tosia and Sylvia with affection. So do aunts, uncles and cousins. All hold Albert at a distance.*

*After lunch, Zayde naps. Stomach cancer. Bubbe watches over him.*

*The Sobels ride the streetcar to the cemetery. Stand at the graves of Papa's parents. Zayde Chaim. Bubbe Kaila. Papa sighs. Mama wails.*

*They turn to Solomon. Shlomo before Papa and Mama chose to remember him in English. Their first child. Eternally three years old.*

*Albert wonders. Does Solomon rest in peace? Does heaven exist? Or is Solomon simply gone? Fingers Chopin's "Marche Funèbre" on his thighs. Seeks tears. Fails to summon them. He never knew Solomon. Neither did Sylvia. Tosia was too young to remember. His sisters dab at their eyes. Papa sniffles. Mama sobs. When she stops, each places a pebble on Solomon's headstone. Proof he is not forgotten.*

*They return to Zayde and Bubbe. Drink tea. Stuff themselves with chocolate kokosh.*

*Zayde observes Albert as if examining jewelry in his store. The high pitch of his voice. The hairless upper lip. The sway of his hips when he walks. Questions Papa. "This is the Albert, he'll run your business someday? A business, it takes a man. You should pray God gives you another son. A real son."*

*Albert chuckles to himself. He and Zayde finally agree on something. Looks to Papa. Papa will defend him. Must defend him.*

*Papa's silence matches Solomon's.*

Lola fought against tearing up. She'd given no thought to Tosia having a family of her own just as the obvious had escaped her—Sylvia was a woman in her own right. "And your parents?"

Papa and Mama were scraping by. The Sobel family enterprise, like countless other businesses—particularly with owners heavily invested in stocks on margin—had gone under. "Papa works in the Garment District for a company making women's overcoats." Humiliated, but of necessity, he joined the International Ladies' Garment Workers' Union. Mama cleaned at the Automat on Eighth Avenue. The Depression left its mark in other unexpected ways. Papa and Mama attended lectures sponsored by the neighborhood Democratic club. Sylvia offered the hint of a smile. "Seeing Maribel again, I'd feel so much better."

Lola took Sylvia's face in her hands and looked into her eyes.

Sylvia stiffened.

Lola's palms held fast. She refused to surrender the softness and warmth of Sylvia's cheeks, more intoxicating than whiskey or rum. At the same time, she castigated herself. What foolishness—what insanity—had overwhelmed her? She'd crossed a boundary near sacrosanct, come down from the stage to reveal her costume and makeup as illusions. The life she'd knit over the past seven years would unravel. Even if inadvertently, Sylvia was bound to betray her. And if Sylvia *could* keep her secret? What right had Lola to burden her with Albert's ghost? Still, Lola could no more resist opening herself to Sylvia than the tide could defy the pull of the moon. She opened her arms.

Sylvia fell into her embrace.

# MAY 1936

# ONE CURTAIN DROPS

A spotlight followed Fanny Brice as she tottered down the orchestra's center aisle.

Lola, seated at the *Follies'* ebony Steinway grand, vamped the bridge to a whimsical song written with the venerable Ira Gershwin and Vernon Duke.

Brice appeared a loving caricature of a Jewish mother in a shapeless robins-egg blue housedress patterned with white flowers and highlighted by an oversize white lace collar. The raised hem exposed nylons rolled down over the tops of pumpkin-orange high-button shoes. A white yarmulke-size hat perched on her head. From it drooped an oversized daisy, its center egg-yolk yellow. Her costume created a striking contrast with Lola's red-sequined gown, the bodice clinging like a second skin, and new hat, two feet high and composed of silk flowers in red, white and blue.

Brice continued towards the stage. Her head swiveled right and left. Wide eyes and a gaping mouth conveyed the bewilderment of a woman estranged from her natural environment. Approaching a ramp leading over the orchestra pit, she stumbled as if she'd just downed a glass—likely two—of Shabbos wine.

The audience chuckled.

Lola vamped.

Brice hesitated, scratched her gray wig, looked over her shoulder, squinted up at the theater's ornate ceiling then lowered her head. Her shoulders heaved as she contemplated her fate on the edge of the abyss. Turning towards the audience, she placed her hand over her heart.

The audience cheered her on.

Encouraged, she pivoted back to the ramp, took a hesitant step forward then darted across.

Applause rewarded her efforts.

Again, her shoulders rose and fell. Might she ever recover from the perils of such an adventure?

The audience cheered more loudly.

Emboldened, she emitted a sigh of relief and moved forward to wander among the Latin dancers positioned downstage.

Lola's hands almost faltered on the keyboard. Brice had passed her mark and failed to deliver her line.

Brice recovered, performed a mock-military about-face and approached a blonde chorine, at six feet half-a-foot taller.

The chorine seemed confused.

Brice mugged as she beckoned the chorine with an extended arm and wagging finger. "Yoo hoo! Miss!" she called. The words fluttered away as silent as a butterfly. She cleared her throat and repeated her call. The exaggerated volume of her voice simulated the ignition of a bulldozer.

The audience laughed with gusto.

"Vould you be so kind," Brice asked in her familiar faux-Yiddish accent, "is this maybe the place vere a lady, she should get the train she should go up the Grand Concourse?"

The audience howled.

Brice began to sway. The wine had taken full effect.

The startled chorine forgot her line, which shot out from the wings to compete with the increasing volume of laughter.

Without waiting for the chorine to repeat it, Brice patted the girl's cheek, whirled and crossed the stage to one of the male dancers. A step away, she lurched forward.

The dancer caught her under both arms.

The audience again responded with laughter.

Lola wondered if Fanny had decided to improvise, break the monotony of a scene repeated eight times a week.

Brice ran her hand along the dancer's arm. "Oy, such muscles! And so handsome! But he don't *look* Jewish!"

The audience roared.

Lola felt awed that Fanny could take such control of a show and lead an audience wherever she wished.

Brice clapped her hands to her cheeks then skipped towards Lola like an elderly version of her famed Baby Snooks character.

Lola relished another opportunity to sing briefly with the one-and-only Fanny Brice—a routine that never grew routine—before plunging into her big Latin number.

Halfway to the piano, Brice collapsed.

An hour after Billie Burke informed the cast and crew that Fanny Brice was ill, Lola and Fernando sat stone-faced at a corner table at Sardi's. Fanny wouldn't just be taking a few days off. She'd worked herself to the bone and couldn't continue. Without her star presence—and despite Bob Hope's protest that the rest of the cast hardly was chopped liver—the *Follies* would close.

A waiter brought bowls of pasta with vegetables.

Lola tapped her glass, emptied of her second Scotch since leaving the theater.

Fernando held a finger up to the waiter. "Miss Flores will pass on that drink."

"The hell I will!" Lola shot back.

The waiter offered Lola a deferential nod.

Fernando gritted his teeth. "Cariña, there is nothing to worry about."

"Except money," Lola said. "This show was supposed to run through the end of the year."

"We have money."

"Really?"

"Enough. Besides, Eddie Cantor would love to have you back."

"And then?"

"There are other radio shows."

"And then?"

"We can put together a new band. Things may be a bit unsettled, but surely Ben will help."

Lola lit a cigarette. "It feels like starting over."

Fernando gestured towards the wall above them hosting Lola's caricature.

The waiter set down Lola's drink.

Fernando moved it away.

Lola ignored the glass and used her fork to nudge the vegetables on her pasta as if she was prepping a photo shoot for *Ladies' Home Journal* or *McCall's.*

"You must eat," Fernando said.

"And *you* have become a real Jewish mother."

As Fernando held a finger to his lips, a voice called out, "Well look who's here." Walter Winchell tossed his hat on the red-leather banquette and squeezed next to Lola. Spotting her untouched drink, he glanced from Lola to Fernando then gulped half. "Sorry about Fanny and the show. What's next for Lola Flores?"

"Many wonderful things," Fernando assured him.

"Even with your contacts in New York shrinking?" Winchell asked. "Too bad they arrested Charlie Luciano down in Arkansas last month. Word is he's never getting out."

Lola gave Winchell what might have passed for the evil eye. She'd no need to be reminded of bad news, even if Meyer and Ben still stood behind her.

"You thinking maybe Hollywood?" Winchell asked. "What with Ben Siegel and his pal Heshy Kaplan spending so much time there lately, you could get some introductions. If the law doesn't catch up with them first."

Lola yanked the glass away from Winchell.

He waggled a finger. "The sauce'll kill a career almost as fast as I can."

Fernando took the glass from Lola.

"You know what you two need?" said Winchell. "A little cheering up. Meet new people. People who could be helpful."

"And how do you propose we do this?" Lola asked.

"As it happens, a socialite who loves getting her name in my column is hosting a little shindig Wednesday night. I'll be there. So will a VIP I just spoke with—one worth saying hello to." He turned to Fernando. "You have a tux?"

Fernando nodded.

Winchell had no need to ask if Lola Flores had evening gowns. "Anyway, since you two probably don't have plans, I'll get you cleared."

"Cleared?" Lola asked.

"What's the New Testament say? Many are called but few are chosen."

"I did not know you read the Bible," Lola said.

"Not *my* Bible, but this is America."

"And who," Fernando asked, "is this important person we are to meet?"

Winchell shook his head. "Mum's the word."

"Just wanted to let you know I'm heading back to the Coast tomorrow," Ben Siegel said on the phone. "Me and Heshy."

"Did you mention that to Walter Winchell?" Lola said.

"No. Why?"

"It is not important. It is just that you have been spending so much time in California."

"You got a problem with that?"

Lola couldn't tell if he was being sinister or jovial. Much of what Ben said exhibited the timing, accompanied by his Brooklyn accent, of an old-style vaudeville comic. "Of course not, Ben," she answered. She feared the tone of her voice betrayed her. She'd become disheartened with his frequent, often lengthy, jaunts to Los Angeles. Ben Siegel was her protector, the man who not only took an interest in her career but also pushed it along. She'd grown dependent on him despite his apparent lack of romantic interest.

"Look, kid," he said, "it's not that I don't wanna stay in New York, especially after this bad break with Fanny Brice and you bein' out of a job. For the moment, anyway. But certain people here—"

Lola knew that despite his fearsome reputation—perhaps because of it—Ben had enemies.

"Besides, there's loads of opportunity in California," he said. "Whadda they call it? The Golden West?"

That California might offer a bright future, Lola agreed. New York, however, would always be the heart and soul of America.

"But what the hell, I'll get you my phone number. Anything you need, you dial the long-distance operator."

"Yes, Ben, I can do that," said Lola. She wished life was that simple.

The following Wednesday evening, a taxi delivered Lola and Fernando to the towering Park Avenue apartment building to which Walter Winchell had directed them. "Must be nice, how they call it—puttin' on the Ritz," said the driver. His voice reflected the weariness of a man who considered himself lucky to drive someone else's hack twelve hours a day to barely make the rent on a fifth-floor walkup with a bathroom down the hall.

Fernando paid and opened the door for Lola.

A man in baggy striped trousers and a checkered coat ripped at the left shoulder darted towards them. He thrust out his right hand. "Help a guy get a cup o' joe? Maybe a piece o' pie?" His face registered equal measures of hope and despair.

The papers and the radio—*Time*, as well—reported that the New Deal was taking hold, the economy recovering even if unemployment remained high. She scoffed at statistics. When would relief come to this man, who might once have supported a family, been a proverbial pillar of his community, played music that touched souls? She didn't need Albert to remind her what the Rabbis taught: Before heralding the coming of the Messiah, the prophet Elijah would appear as a beggar. Lola opened her purse.

The building's doorman, gold epaulets and shoulder braid on his uniform weightier than those of a Tsarist general, charged from his post.

The man spun on the remains of his heels and ran off empty-handed.

"And don't come back, you goddam bum!" the doorman shouted. "I'll call the cops—if I don't lay inta ya myself!" He turned and smiled. Sorry, ma'am. Sir. Even on Park Avenue if you know what I mean." He led them towards the building's entry, opened the door and saluted. "You got a good heart, ma'am, but really, it just brings 'em back."

The doorman's treatment of the beggar—the man—troubled Lola. Here she'd arrived in a taxi wearing a gown designed by Fernando—burgundy with lace cape sleeves, fitted waist, skirt flared from the knees and plunging V-back. The night chilly, a matching wrap. Fernando, making an odd display of empathy for the downtrodden, sported a tuxedo purchased from a second-hand store. The original owner had worn it only once. But beautiful clothing easily concealed a tattered soul. Given the way she attracted death, the ill-dressed man may well have been a better human being.

In the lobby, the doorman ran his finger along a typewritten list.

Satisfied, he directed them across the white-and-gold marble floor to a uniformed elevator operator of seemingly lesser but still impressive rank.

The elevator stopped at the 28th floor and opened onto a vestibule with a high ceiling befitting a palace. Opposite stood massive oak doors guarded by a burly man in a dark vested suit. He, too, examined a typewritten list.

Walter Winchell greeted them in the foyer, larger than Lola's living room. Oak-paneled walls displayed paintings by Copley, Fragonard, Gainsborough, West. A glass case exhibited an American flag with a circular pattern of thirteen stars, white stripes yellowed, edges frayed. Their feet sank into a thick oriental carpet of red, purple, blue and gold.

Winchell led them to a larger room. A pianist from the New York Philharmonic played the fourth movement of Rimsky-Korsakov's *Scheherazade*. Lola scanned the guests. The men wore tuxedos. The women flaunted couturier gowns and necks ringed by diamonds and emeralds. Each guest wore a gold crown and held a gold mask mounted on a gold stick.

A dwarf outfitted like a Turkish sultan approached. He juggled three gold balls, bowed and moved on. Young men dressed as court eunuchs carried gold trays filled with champagne in flutes of Waterford crystal. Harem women in abbreviated tops and flowing slacks offered caviar, foie gras and pastry-wrapped lobster.

Fernando leaned into Winchell. "This looks like a costume party, except that the guests do not wear costumes."

Winchell winked. "That's what they pay the help for."

Lola pointed towards the bar.

Fernando tugged her away.

"Lady's choice," Winchell said. He procured a drink for Lola then made introductions to their hosts—a prominent banker and his wife, whose birthday celebration three weeks later would welcome four hundred close friends to their estate on Long Island's Gold Coast. Tonight's guests included more bankers, real estate developers, corporate executives and attorneys with the city's most prestigious firms. Politicians—with exceptions—were verboten. The men's smiles revealed a desire to further their acquaintance with a star of the unfortunately defunct *Ziegfeld Follies*. The women's eyes expressed distaste for the presence of a performer.

Initial pleasantries concluded, Winchell directed Lola and Fernando's attention to a fortune teller in a purple robe and white turban studded with faux rubies. Seated at a small round table, she read the palm of a man unmasked, his broad face familiar. "Hoover," Winchell said. "The ex-president."

"Is he the man who wants to meet Lola?" Fernando asked.

"I'll make introductions later," said Winchell. "Lola's here to talk with someone more important." He plucked Lola's drink from her hand, left it with a eunuch then led them down a long hallway. He stopped at a door displaying a brass eagle identical to that on the great seal of the United States.

Lola thought something amiss. Instead of holding an olive branch in its right talon and arrows in its left, the eagle clutched arrows in both.

Another hulking man, his eyes ice blue, reminded Lola of the uniformed men in Berlin. He knocked then opened the door several inches. "Mr. Winchell," he called.

"Come in," a voice returned.

Behind a large oak desk sat a man with a round face, dark eyebrows and curved jaw. His small mouth sloped down from left to right. It implied the same preoccupation with secrets displayed in Havana by Sumner Welles.

"The *other* Hoover," said Winchell.

"Pleased to meet you, Miss Flores," said the man who had summoned her. He made no effort to extend his hand.

Lola recognized J. Edgar Hoover, head of the FBI, but thought his appearance anything but menacing. The press widely hailed Hoover for killing or capturing some of the nation's most notorious criminals, dubbed by one journalist the "hick outlaws," including Machine Gun Kelly, John Dillinger and Baby Face Nelson. Lola had read lesser-known stories that Hoover had been absent from each of those events. The Bureau's publicity flacks knew their business. "How do you do?" she said, at sea as to why the fabled Mr. Hoover wished to meet her unless he was a fan of Broadway. If so, why all this secrecy?

Hoover glanced over his right shoulder at a dark-haired man with a thin face and square jaw. The man's tuxedo included a violet cummerbund matching Hoover's and the same American-flag lapel pin. "My deputy, Clyde Tolson."

Tolson nodded.

Hoover motioned Lola and Fernando forward to a pair of green-leather armchairs.

"Talk about guys named Hoover," said Winchell. "You can bet Edgar's record tops our visiting ex-president's."

Hoover smiled, exhibiting a charm that caught Lola off guard. "Walter's too kind. We do important work, but we're not in the papers nearly as often as we should be despite what Walter thinks—and what I assume are his best efforts."

"I do my best," said Winchell.

"Generating recognition of the Bureau's accomplishments during such troubling times," said Tolson, "couldn't be more important to the nation."

Hoover nodded.

Lola caught Fernando studying Hoover and Tolson. Did he suspect that their relationship might be more than professional? Fernando's ability to identify people usually condemned as unacceptable struck her as uncanny. But then, at Club Gardenia, he'd sized her up at first glance.

"I must say," said Hoover, "I love your gown." He turned to Fernando. "No doubt one of yours, Mr. Fallon."

The small talk struck Lola as a ruse. But what had she and Fernando done wrong? They'd entered the country with valid Cuban passports. Had they overstayed their visas? Did their visas have expiration dates? The arrangements had been made through Ben Siegel, so she assumed them to be correct. Of course, an American citizen had every right to leave and enter the country, but that privilege belonged to Albert whose passport she retained. She could use it in an emergency if it hadn't expired. Now that she thought about it, it probably had. If she and Fernando had violated some law or other, why were they being hauled in front of J. Edgar Hoover? And why here?

Hoover folded his hands in his lap. "I must tell you that two months earlier, Clyde and I attended *The Ziegfeld Follies of 1936*. We loved the show. So sorry about Miss Brice."

"Thank you," said Lola, hiding a small sigh of relief. So it *was* about Broadway.

Hoover's eyes narrowed. "Now to get down to brass tacks."

Lola looked at Fernando, whose eyes reflected her fear that something was amiss.

"Walter Winchell," said Hoover, "is a good friend and a damn loyal American. People like him are hard to find these days, and the country needs them more than ever. You may not realize it—most people don't—but this nation is under attack. I don't mean war. Not yet anyway."

"May I have a drink?" Lola asked.

Hoover cracked his knuckles.

"A cigarette?"

Tolson reached into his jacket and withdrew a pack of Lucky Strikes. Hoover picked up a crystal lighter from the desktop.

"Mr. Hoover," said Lola, "I do not understand."

"Understand what?"

"Why Mr. Fallon and I are here."

"Of course not. A lady like yourself shouldn't have to be involved with people like Clyde and me."

Lola confessed to remaining confused.

"I'll enlighten you." The previous March, as she knew if she read the papers or listened to the radio, Germany reoccupied the Rhineland in violation of the Treaty of Versailles. No question, Hitler had his eye on all of Europe. So did Russia's Stalin. To place the continent under Nazi rule, Hitler had to find ways—some of them subtle—to influence America to keep its distance and buy time to determine how Uncle Sam might respond if it didn't. "As we speak, German corporations are making inroads all over Latin America. Their executives include Nazi spies. Am I right, Clyde?"

"On the nose, Chief."

Winchell held up a fist. "Those goddam Nazi bastards with their goddam Nuremberg Laws. They'll be coming for *us* before you know it."

Hoover chuckled. "Loyal Jews like you, Walter, will remain safe if I have anything to do with it. And I have a *lot* to do with it."

To assure that Hitler couldn't attack the United States from a base in the Western Hemisphere, Hoover had his eye on Cuba. Instability on the island would play right into Nazi hands. Germany could not be allowed to make inroads in Havana. "The situation's murky, and I like clarity. Order. Now, it seems, General Batista, the power behind the government, is about to replace President Agripino."

Tolson placed his hand on Hoover's shoulder. "Batista's not the problem. He has a good relationship with your friends Meyer Lansky and Ben Siegel."

"I am not sure I would use the word *friends*," Lola said. Regarding Ben, she also suffered confusion.

Hoover patted Tolson's hand while training his eyes on Lola. "No need to be coy, Miss Flores. Lansky and Siegel's business dealings might be suspect but like Walter, they're real Americans. Lansky's been helping the FBI, although Clyde and I aren't at liberty to explain. Anyway, if the Bureau gets its hands dirty every now and then, it's for the good of the country."

Lola waved her cigarette. "Mr. Hoover—"

Tolson cut her off. "The Bureau needs information on Kraut sympathizers in the Cuban government. Also, about Cuban businessmen fond of Herr Hitler. The kind of people who pose a threat to American interests."

Lola pressed her hands together. If the FBI wanted such information, all well and good. But she and Fernando had spent the last two and a half years in New York. "I am afraid I am in no position to assist you."

"But you *are*," said Hoover. "That's why you're going to Havana next week."

Lola blanched.

Fernando stood. "With all due respect, sir, that will be impossible. We are making plans to play nightclubs in New York, perhaps go on tour, possibly do a weekly radio show." That such plans were formless, a hodgepodge of "what ifs," Fernando kept to himself. Neither did he divulge Lola's antipathy for Batista, although he imagined that Hoover knew about her relationship with Manuel and his execution.

Hoover's palms slammed the desk.

Fernando sat.

"If I may speak for the Chief," said Tolson, his expression boyish and calm, "every foreigner enters and remains in the United States at the pleasure of our government."

Lola ground her cigarette into a crystal ashtray.

"That said, no purpose will be served if Lola Flores and the Bureau are at odds with each other." Given the circumstances, returning to Havana would be very much to Lola's benefit. Although Ben Siegel was occupied with other interests, Meyer Lansky would secure Lola a nightclub booking in Havana at a fee Marlene Dietrich would envy.

"How long am I to stay in Cuba?" Lola asked.

"Until no later than the end of the year," said Hoover.

"That is a long time. We are quite fond of New York."

"And I imagine you'd like to be able to come back."

Lola considered her options. Refusal would lead to deportation. Ben and Meyer would desert her. The deals they'd likely made with Hoover offered far more profitable opportunities than an interest in a nightclub performer who once played Broadway. She and Fernando would be left to scramble for work in the Cuban hinterlands. Or Lola Flores could disappear, reassume her identity as Albert. Aside from leaving Fernando in the lurch, she had no taste for retreat. Surrender. Albert remained part of her but living as him would be impossible. No one had the right to wrench the soul from her body. "What assurance have Fernando and I that you will let us back into the country?"

Hoover stood and held his arms out. "Aren't we all on the same team? Lola Flores conquered Broadway. Only in America, right? Havana's just for a few months. A perfect way to show your gratitude. All we ask is that you meet people, get them talking."

"That is all?" Lola asked.

And write weekly reports for one of the Bureau's people at the Embassy. Small tidbits create big pictures. "You might even hear something important."

Lola looked down, lost in thought.

Hoover retook his seat. His fingertips beat a heavy, bellicose rhythm on the desk. Then his drumming ceased. "What the hell is it, Miss Flores, that you want?"

Winchell stepped forward. "Edgar, I may be speaking out of school—" He turned to Lola. "You name it, the Bureau can deliver. Even if they have to take matters to the highest level. Edgar has dirt on everyone—right up to the White House."

Lola needed no convincing about Hoover's playing that card. Yet he hadn't played it tonight, having nothing on her or Fernando. Attempting to make something of her relationships with Frida Herskovits and Manuel

Gallegos would lead nowhere. The affairs were public knowledge in Cuba and hardly a departure from the carryings on of Broadway and Hollywood celebrities whom Americans treated as a privileged class. On the other hand, Hoover had the power to boot them out of the country and keep them out—no questions asked. Let no one believe that Lola Flores lived with her head in the clouds. Her hands were tied. She saw no choice but to give Hoover what he wanted.

Of course, she would be adamant regarding what she expected in return.

# JULY 1936

# ANOTHER CURTAIN RISES

D amas y caballeros," the emcee sang out. On this first evening of July, as over the past four weeks, his voice trilled with excitement. "Hotel Nacional welcomes our beloved island's beloved daughter, the conqueror of Broadway—"

Behind the curtain at the rear of the stage, Lola emptied a glass of Scotch and held it out to her maid.

"The Cuban Firecracker now also a Yankee Doodle Dandy—"

The sold-out audience laughed, joined by Fernando seated at his customary table opposite the piano.

Lola took a breath to clear her head.

*"Lola Flores!"*

A spotlight shone. The curtain parted. The showroom shook with applause.

Making yet another grand entrance, Lola approached the piano with tiny, unsure steps reminiscent of one of Fanny Brice's comic routines. The applause heightened, suggesting that some in the audience had seen the recent *Follies* or read about its closing performance and thought Lola to be offering Fanny Brice a lighthearted tribute.

Lola knew better. While Havana's press held up her performances as the model of a triumphant return, her arrival in the capital caused her spirits to plummet. She was, of course, grateful to Meyer, whose influence in Cuba continued to increase. And Ben had kept his promise to stay in touch from Los Angeles. Certainly, she was treated as a star. The Nacional paid her travel expenses and a generous salary. Sympathetic to what she'd endured during the battle three years before, management provided her an apartment in a new luxury building nearby and one for Fernando.

But most nights, she tossed and turned before drifting off to a sleep tormented by apparitions. The spirits of Moisés, Frida, Manuel and Leon hurled accusations echoing the Ghost in *Hamlet* proclaiming, "Murder most foul." Lola denounced herself, assumed some responsibility for their deaths. She found relief only in whiskey and rum.

The applause waned.

Lola lowered herself to the piano bench and composed herself.

The audience hushed with expectation.

She nodded to the band then set her hands dancing across the keyboard.

The audience cheered.

Lola missed a note but played on, the audience none the wiser. Since opening night, her playing at times was erratic. Complex chords and key changes resisted her. Havana's supportive Walter Winchells, enthusiastic but lacking musical training, let pass the errors. The musicians exchanged sly glances. With increasing frequency, Fernando inquired about her mood and general health.

Then there were the weekly reports she was forced to write, a chore even more tedious than she'd imagined. Hoover expected her to fill a minimum of one page with concise, illuminating observations. Having none, she found ways, as did Shakespeare, to make the simplest of statements complex. As instructed, she addressed these pointless reports to Ambassador Caffery, since Sumner Welles had left Havana in December 1933 when the two countries temporarily halted relations. Caffery, a name without a face, never responded.

Following several such reports, Lola received a call from the Bureau's man at the Embassy. She doubted the name he gave—Michael Phillips. Whoever he was, he reproached her efforts with the authority and conviction of a government operative wielding the weight of Washington officialdom. She was cheating the Bureau and the United States of America given handwriting too large and contributions correspondingly small. Her chats with government officials and businessmen—most Cuban and American—revealed nothing. How could the Bureau offer its support here in Havana if she failed to uphold her end of the bargain?

Lola took umbrage. She *had* passed on the remark of an executive from

IBM expressing "restrained admiration" for Hitler and Mussolini, "who know what it takes to create a good climate for business."

Phillips dismissed the observation as immaterial given the enormous amount of business IBM did in Germany.

Lola protested. She was doing her best. She'd held a lengthy conversation with a German businessman from Berlin, although he had emigrated to Cuba after Hitler took power. *That dreadful man! In the War, I fought for the Fatherland. They awarded me an Iron Cross second class. But I am a Jew.* She could only relate to Phillips what she assumed he already knew. The Cuban government, for all its faults, seemed uninterested in meaningful economic ties with Germany.

Phillips instructed Lola to double her efforts. After each night's performance, she should have supper with, or attend a gathering of, prominent people. Surely, she was showered with invitations. She must charm the men into speaking freely and encourage their wives, who often heard secrets from their husbands, to gossip.

A dozen dancers entered from the wings, drawing the room's spotlights. Semi-obscured, Lola reached to her left where a glass of Scotch had been placed on the piano bench. Playing with her right hand, she drank. A discordant note rang out. The dancers stumbled into each other.

The audience laughed, assuming more humor in the style of Fanny Brice.

Lola's spotlight returned. She switched to playing scales.

The dancers shrugged and milled about like drunk celebrants during Carnaval.

Laughter increased. A madcap element of Broadway had come to Havana.

Lola's heart pounded like the band's twin congas.

On July Fourth, Lola put a face to her FBI contact. A uniformed marine escorted her and Fernando into the flag-lined entry of the American Embassy. She shivered in the miraculous air conditioning. Americans loved the heat generated by tropical people but not their weather. She covered her shoulders with a light jacket.

A large man in a cream-colored sport shirt printed with palm trees stepped forward. His sandy hair and ham-pink cheeks attested to an all-American Iowa farm boy attempting, but failing, to go native. Lola wondered if such a man could ever really understand Cuba.

"It's me," he said. "Mike Phillips." He turned to Fernando. "No need to tell me who *you* are, Mr. Fallon. Or should I say, *señor* Fallon?" He extended a massive hand.

They shook. Fernando winced.

Phillips turned back to Lola. Geniality displaced the tone of censure with which he'd addressed her on the phone. "I thought it was time to say hello in the flesh. That and ask a favor if you don't mind. Considering all you're doing for us."

Lola turned up her jacket collar. "And you would have me do what, *Mister* Phillips?"

Phillips nodded at Fernando, took Lola by the arm and led them to a high-ceilinged ballroom with a red-tile floor. Guests stood in small clusters below a gray-blue haze of cigar smoke. The far wall displayed the Great Seal of the United States. Before it, music stands and a grand piano awaited while Lola's band smoked in the shade of an inner courtyard. Seated on a stool, an Embassy employee sang Stephen Foster's "Camptown Races," accompanying himself on a banjo.

Phillips pointed to a man in a white suit. "Ambassador Caffery. The fellow in the gray suit with eyebrows like Groucho Marx— Have you ever met Groucho? That's President Gómez. And Mrs. Gómez." There was no Mrs. Caffery, although word had it that the Ambassador was planning to marry. "I'll introduce you around. But first, Lola— May I call you Lola? Call me Mike. Anyway, Lola, we're thrilled you agreed to sing here at our little celebration."

A bronze-cheeked Cuban waiter in a starched white jacket presented a tray of crystal glasses.

"Lemonade," said Phillips.

Lola sighed.

Phillips chuckled. "The Ambassador prefers holding off on spirits until evening. Me, I enjoy a rum cocktail with lunch. Better, two." He held out a Timex Mickey Mouse wristwatch with a black leather band. "Anyway, it's three-thirty, see? You're scheduled to perform from four-forty-five to five-fifteen. Dinner's at six. That's early for Cubans, but it'll enable us to conclude at a reasonable hour—for Americans—with fireworks. We've got a destroyer just offshore that's going to set them off."

Lola remembered the Cuban ships that bombarded the Nacional.

"So, that favor," said Phillips. "We have time— How do you say it in show biz? Before you go on. A special guest would like to meet you privately."

Lola cocked her head. Submitting to Walter Winchell's request in New York had landed her back on the island in a situation only a novelist like Hemingway might have conceived.

"You want to know who, right?" Phillips said. "You'll see. Meanwhile, we'll let señor Fallon scoop up all those oysters and shrimp out there." He pushed Fernando in the direction of the buffet.

Lola had no idea who wanted to meet her unless Hoover had flown down and wanted to exercise his fondness for secrecy. But he already had Phillips and the Ambassador to question her. And scold. Besides, Phillips realized that she knew nothing. Or so she thought. Clearly, the FBI was in the driver's seat. Assuming any attempt to leave the Embassy prematurely would be blocked, she nodded her assent.

Phillips led her to a small reception room and knocked. "Lola Flores, sir."

"Please, show señorita Flores in," a man returned in English with a thick Cuban-Spanish accent.

"I'll be right down the hall," Phillips told Lola sotto voce.

Lola went inside, froze and drew her jacket over her chest.

A dark man in the uniform of the Cuban army rose from a cherrywood armchair, its back and seat upholstered in fabric matching the blue in the American flag. He motioned her closer.

Lola wanted to bolt from the room but feared the consequences. "¡Mucho gusto, General!"

"I am flattered that you recognize me," said Fulgencio Batista. He stepped towards Lola and grasped her wrists. His hands, although small and delicate, were strong enough to keep her from breaking free.

Repulsion overcame her. Those hands, even more than hers, had spilled the blood of Manuel Gallegos. Certainly, Manuel had violated her and constricted her life like the fabled African python that crushed its prey before devouring it, but the little sergeant had had no right to play judge and executioner.

Batista pulled Lola towards him and grazed her cheeks with his.

The mixed scent of cologne and rum soured Lola's nostrils.

Satisfied with his display of dominance, Batista dropped his hands and granted her release. "I believe we have met before."

"A woman had been injured near the Presidential Palace. You were then a sergeant." She rejected any notion of letting him claim legitimacy for the position of power he'd usurped from Cuba's elected—if ineffective—president. "How quickly you rose to colonel."

"The reawakening of a nation demands that patriots rise to the occasion." He fingered the star on his collar. "I am a simple servant of my people."

The farcical blend of humility and pomposity transformed Lola's apprehension into anger. Did this little man—he'd been a stenographer!—think he was Teddy Roosevelt or Black Jack Pershing? She'd more than held her own with J. Edgar Hoover, to whom even the President of the United States gave heed. Batista was nothing less than a thief. He would loot Cuba with American approval as long as he served America's interests. "And I," she said, "am a simple musician."

He placed his hands on her cheeks. He did not reveal whether he felt the heat that rose in them. "You are too modest, señorita. Now that Cuba and America have entered a new era of goodwill, your music and your beauty—"

"I do not consider beauty one of my assets."

Batista placed his right hand over his heart. It nudged the medals on his chest.

Lola could not imagine why they had been awarded since Cuba had not been at war for decades. Most likely, Batista bestowed them on himself. No, that was splitting hairs. Even before America cast its long shadow over the island, Cuba had been at war with itself.

"Such modesty!" said Batista. "Every song by Lola Flores, every note assures America that Cuba is its friend."

Lola wondered if he would offer her a seat. And a drink.

He stood immobile, his eyes locked on hers.

"My music expresses what is in my heart. In my soul."

Batista took her right hand in both of his.

She found them cold.

"I am sorry if I have not made myself clear," he said.

Lola thought otherwise. Batista's eyes and all-too-visible smirk clearly betrayed his intentions. She withdrew her hand and scanned the room for a decorative knife or a heavy ashtray to serve as a weapon with which she might defend herself. Yet how could this self-declared general assault her in the American Embassy? Had he reached a prior agreement with the Ambassador through which Lola Flores would serve as some sort of international currency?

Batista ran his fingers across his medals. "With your permission, I will speak as one patriot to another. When you return to New York—"

Whatever Batista had in mind, Lola resolved to put him off. "Which appears to be many months from now."

He charged ahead. "When you return to that great city, Americans will flock to hear Lola Flores. In turn, *you* will listen to what Americans say about Cuba. Then you will provide us observations of Yanqui attitudes— the *real* American people, particularly those in positions of importance— we cannot get from their newspapers and radio broadcasts. Until then, of course, you can listen to what Americans here in Havana are saying."

"You ask me to be a spy?"

Batista arched an eyebrow.

Lola balled her newly freed hand into a fist. How could she have failed to pick up on the undercurrents of their conversation? He suspected her of working for Hoover. The Cuban Firecracker was a traitor and thus subject to any and all penalties the state, personified by Fulgencio Batista, might impose. "I have a show to perform," she said. She turned towards the door.

Batista grabbed her right shoulder. "Señorita, the Yanquis are friends of Cuba. However, to maintain that relationship to our advantage, we must know what they think about us. What they *really* think."

Lola again attempted to free herself.

Batista tightened his grip. "Your friends Mr. Lansky and Mr. Siegel have important interests here. Interests that depend on my cooperation. Would you displease them?"

Lola acknowledged to herself what she'd long attempted to deny— what Hoover held over her head in New York. Ben and Meyer viewed her as just another asset and a minor one at that. If they felt their business threatened, they'd abandon her in a heartbeat.

"Clearly, some decisions cannot be rushed," said Batista. "In three days, I will send a car to bring you to the Presidential Palace." He let his hand slide from her shoulder, thrust it inside her jacket and brushed it across her breasts.

An hour before her call at the Nacional, Lola sat at her dining table picking over reheated black beans and rice, her free hand cradling an empty glass. Her thoughts wandered to corned beef and pastrami sandwiches when Papa took the family to Katz's on the Lower East Side or Reuben's on Madison Avenue, one of the few family outings she enjoyed. Albert enjoyed. How life had changed. Whether for the better, she'd begun to doubt. She'd established herself as Lola Flores, the woman she was, and achieved a good deal of celebrity.

For the second time, Lola filled her glass with Scotch, disregarding Fernando, who increasingly pestered her about her drinking to the point at which they occasionally engaged in a row. What she drank and how much, she insisted, was *her* business. She still drew big crowds to the Nacional. After shows, escorted by Fernando to oversee her safety, she went to restaurants or late-night clubs with Cuban businessmen, socialites and celebrities, along with their foreign counterparts. She held her liquor. What more did he want?

Regrettably for Phillips and Hoover, she learned nothing about German designs on Cuba. Several times she met Hemingway for drinks at La Floridita. Displaying a well-rehearsed naivete—she fancied herself an accomplished actress—she asked what he knew. He joked that she must be working for J. Edgar Hoover. She laughed. He laughed. But Papa was nobody's fool. She entertained the odd thought that perhaps *he* worked for Hoover.

Finding her stay in Havana tedious, Lola toyed with the idea of leaving. But how would she explain her sudden exit to Ben and Meyer?

Fernando's key rattled in the lock. He entered with a dozen pink roses and flashed a smile as broad as Havana Bay.

Lola raised her glass.

Acknowledging the fruitlessness of his expectations, he placed the roses on the table.

"It is not my birthday," she said.

He kissed her on both cheeks. "No, cariña. But you are about to feel reborn."

Early the next afternoon, an army captain led Lola and Fernando up the grand staircase of the Presidential Palace for an audience with Fulgencio Batista. The General's office stood in disturbing proximity to that in which Manuel had raped her. Although shaken, she followed the captain with a steady step, head held high. Men like Batista despised weakness. She would project an unexpected strength that would leave the little sergeant unsettled.

Batista, his hands clasped behind him, stood peering out a window only meters from the balcony on which Ramón Grau San Martín, the first of the presidents he had foisted on the nation, addressed Cubans three years earlier.

She had witnessed the speech alongside Manuel. Despite the crowd's enthusiasm, an invisible hand had pressed down on the scale that balanced hope and despair, giving far more weight to the government's interests than the needs of its people. Now, she saw no reason to believe that anything had changed except her will to resist.

Batista wiggled his fingers.

Lola and Fernando stepped forward.

The captain withdrew.

Batista turned. "I hope, señorita Flores," he said without offering them seats, "that you have considered my request. Perhaps the presence of señor Fallon signals that you see the matter in a new light."

"I am a loyal Cuban," said Lola, "but I cannot do as you ask."

Batista's eyes darkened. "Last night, you told the Hotel Nacional that you will leave Havana at the end of this month. You failed to inform *me*."

"An important matter came up," Fernando said. "Entirely unexpected."

"I am addressing señorita Flores."

"For the sake of my career," said Lola, "I must return to New York. *The Ziegfeld Follies of 1936* will reopen."

"The fourteenth of September," said Fernando. Fannie Brice had

201

recovered and would again star but with a whole new cast—except for the return of Lola Flores, who'd been offered a larger role.

"Do señor Lansky and señor Siegel know of this?" Batista asked.

"With your permission, General," said Fernando, "señor Siegel called me yesterday from Los Angeles. It was he who encouraged the producers to bring señorita Flores back to Broadway."

"And you really think the Americans will let you return?"

Lola found in Batista's question confirmation that he knew her real purpose in Havana. "I have the Embassy's assurances," she said. Phillips had called to express Hoover's deep disappointment but assured her he had reached an understanding with their mutual friends and released her from her obligations.

Batista rested his hand over his medals. "That Cuba occupies such a small place in your heart causes me great sadness. I hope your departure will not suffer a long delay."

Lola grasped Fernando's hand.

Batista adjusted the knot on his tie as if they were exchanging pleasantries at a cocktail party. "I am advised of questions regarding your passports. A disregard for proper procedures. Matters involving certain records—"

"I am sure you will find our passports in order."

Batista examined his fingernails to convey that their dilemma was out of his hands. "I am afraid you must remain in Cuba." He raised his index finger. "Unless—"

Lola took a cigarette from her purse to demonstrate a measured nonchalance. How much abuse did the little sergeant expect her to take? "Really, General. If you wish to confiscate our Cuban passports, feel free to do so. But I do not believe that Cuba wishes to be embarrassed by an international incident that will reduce tourism and trade."

Batista's brow furrowed. "I have no idea what you are talking about. Nor do I think that *you* do. Cuba has every right to issue—or withdraw—its passports."

Lola blew smoke towards Batista. She considered that a gentler, more ladylike form of grabbing his testicles and squeezing. "I agree. But the U.S. Embassy will attest that señor Fallon and I are American citizens holding American passports."

Batista turned his back on them.

Lola glanced at Fernando. She had grabbed and squeezed. and not at all gently.

Batista spun around. His face expressed not torment but vindictiveness. "Do not think, señorita, that you will ever be allowed to return to Cuba. Or if somehow you do, you will ever be safe." Reptilian eyes exposed the depth of his rancor. "Even if I am gone from the island, powerful friends will avenge this insult. Lansky and Siegel? Even *they* will be powerless to protect you."

# OCTOBER 1936

# REUNION

A week into the Follies' return engagement, Lola experienced a near-debilitating fatigue. Dr. Gerstner ran tests. They proved inconclusive. The fatigue continued. She summoned her deepest reserves of will to perform.

Granted a reprieve from her lethargy on an Indian-summer Tuesday evening, Lola suggested to Fernando a post-show stroll from the Winter Garden to their apartment building.

Fernando agreed. Fresh air could only promote Lola's wellbeing.

Entering Times Square, they contended with boisterous crowds of New York night owls and out-of-towners. Lola, her mood elevated, overlooked laughter a little too loud and the occasional bump of a shoulder, accepting the collective display of manic gaiety as an attempt to defy the lingering Depression not unlike whistling in a graveyard.

Arm in arm, she and Fernando headed east. At Sixth Avenue, the city quieted. At Fifth, they turned south then east again along 34th Street. Further on, a tunnel would be dug beneath the East River to connect Midtown with bucolic Queens and the World's Fair planned for 1939. Only the intermittent squealing of tires and honking of horns disturbed the unusual tranquility.

A wispy breeze nuzzled Lola's cheek, a softer version of Fanny Brice's ritual post-curtain knip. When the opening-night curtain dropped, Fanny proclaimed to the entire cast, "Oy, if Lola Flores was Jewish, Fanny Brice would be playing Trenton and Baltimore. Who in New York would want to see an old broad like me when they got here a young Lola Florewitz?" Lola beamed. Fanny's compliment reflected the leap she'd taken after

Billie Burke assembled a new cast and ordered material written for the performers' distinct skills and personalities, hers included. Of course, the audience clamored to see the French-American Josephine Baker and after she left, Gypsy Rose Lee, the burlesque queen who put the *tease* in striptease. But Lola Flores emerged as a star in her own right, the Cuban Firecracker transposed into a talented comedienne.

Coping with her unnamed infirmity, Lola demonstrated a renewed capacity for self-discipline. She limited herself to a single drink each afternoon and arrived at the theater fully in control. Onstage slip-ups vanished. She rewarded herself with a single post-show Scotch in her dressing room. Sometimes a second. A drink picked up her spirits— when it didn't shove her down in the dumps. On occasion, she went to a midnight supper, club or party—always with Fernando at her side. She attempted to limit herself to a single nightcap.

Still, Fanny's dubbing her Lola Florewitz left her uneasy. Had the Cuban Firecracker, like a snake, merely shed one skin for another? Was she now hiding behind yet another identity? How many more would she put on before their collective weight crushed her?

Lola bore her distress in silence. Why trouble Fernando? As concerned as he was about her, he saw himself on top of the world—or at least climbing daily towards its pinnacle. He'd proved himself an effective business manager. He'd also created a personal life, establishing friendships and romantic relationships with others also forced to cloak their identities and accept confinement to the shadows.

Fernando urged Lola to do the same. Wasn't she also a creature of flesh and blood, a woman with needs? She demurred. Fernando could remain hidden from public view with relative ease. Celebrity made invisibility for Lola Flores difficult if not impossible. More, although she did not confide this to him, she hesitated to engage in physical intimacy, fearful of again experiencing pain and shame, even if those she slept with were like her. Fernando thought her reasoning illogical. She disagreed. Nothing could be more logical than refraining from anything that felt uncomfortable or threatening. He dropped the matter.

Although they strolled at a moderate pace, Lola's heart fluttered. Her breathing demanded a measure of effort. She attributed the sudden onset of symptoms to guilt. After returning to New York, Albert had re-asserted himself. He proposed they go to synagogue on Yom Kippur, a day to be ignored at her—*their*—peril. She refused. He insisted. She continued to refuse. He continued to insist. His relentlessness wore her down.

They arrived late, a black fedora pulled low over Albert's face, a ticket in hand for the last row of the men's section. Standing, sitting, bowing and swaying with Albert, praying and chanting the familiar Hebrew with him, Lola empathized with the specter for whom occasional religious observance represented the only life she allowed him.

As Albert beat his chest in contrition, Lola sensed the gates of repentance closing in front of her, locking her out. She'd transgressed the Law, denied the body—if imperfect—God had given her. Dressed as a women. *Lived* as a woman. Grieved her family then heightened their pain by compelling Albert to commit a form of suicide. Lola Flores, no less than Manuel, Batista and, yes, Ben, was a murderer.

Still, if there were such a thing as a heavenly court, she would defend herself, seek God's vaunted mercy. Albert Sobel had become Lola Flores of his own free will. How could God object? Why would He want Albert to deny her true self? Deny the world her talent?

As to that talent, she had no way of knowing whether Lola Flores would be remembered and *if* she were remembered, how. Poor Lili Elbe pointed to the likely outcome. Lili painted a brilliant self-portrait of pluck and mettle only to be forgotten beyond a small circle of friends and admirers. Had the wider world known of her, Lola had no doubt it would have dismissed her art and condemned Lili as a man obsessed with self-mutilation, a sham, an embodiment of evil.

Lola felt her lungs collapsing. The holiest day of the year, devoted to atonement and forgiveness, left her despairing on the very edge of life itself.

*Anne Feldman and Dottie Sachs spin Albert around in Anne's bedroom. Laugh. Applaud. Fellow high-school seniors, they are Albert's best friends. Only friends. Co-conspirators.*

*Anne's parents are off to dinner. Then to* The Ziegfeld Follies of 1927 *with Eddie Cantor. Post-theater drinks. Home well after midnight. This being Friday, Anne's twin brother Sid will sleep at a friend's. Anne and Dottie have Albert all to themselves.*

*Albert is not like other boys. Although not a girl. How can a boy be a girl?*

*A kindred spirit. Thrills them at the piano. Mirrors their tastes in popular music. Books, no. He's a deep reader. Movies, yes. Shares their devotion to the memory of Rudolf Valentino.*

*They've planned an adventure. A journey across town to the all-boys DeWitt Clinton High School. A pre-Thanksgiving dance. New boys! The boys they know prefer conversation about the Yankees winning the World Series two months earlier. And Benny Friedman, the Jewish All-American quarterback at Michigan. Plays professionally for his hometown Cleveland Bulldogs. But this is not really about boys. It's about playing a big joke. Albert appearing in public. As a girl.*

*Albert poses. Dress, shoes, wig provided by Maribel. Secreted out of his apartment in an overnight bag. A story that he will sleep over at Sid Feldman's. Papa and Mama thrilled. Albert has a male friend. Why hasn't he mentioned Sid before? To forestall discovery, Albert will return home later in the evening. Say that Sid's coming down with something.*

*Anne and Dottie ooh and ah. Albert looks in the mirror. Relishes release from his imprisonment. Thinks about a name. Obviously not Cinderella. Not Lola. Maribel calls him Lola. A Jewish Lola? Suspicious. Perhaps Lillian. Yes.*

*The three classmates grasp hands. Go downstairs. Hail a taxi. Giggle through crosstown traffic. Enter the crowded Clinton gymnasium. Nod to teachers and chaperones. Draw the casual glances ritually accorded new arrivals.*

*A Victrola plays "My Blue Heaven." The band led by Paul Whiteman. "King of Jazz." They dance together. Gene Austin sings "Has Anybody Seen My Gal?" A boy beckons Anne. Dottie and Lillian signal approval. Another takes Dottie's arm. "Baby Face" sung by Whispering Jack Smith brings a third. Albert/Lola/Lillian considers the risk. Claims the onset of a cold. The boy smiles. A gentleman.*

*An hour later, Anne, Dottie and Lillian slip away in triumph. Defy the perils of Hell's Kitchen and walk to 57th Street. Hail a taxi. Emerge at a familiar East Side coffee shop. Tumble into a booth. Down mammoth slices of apple pie. Endless cups of coffee. Talk. Talk more. Call it a night.*

*Lillian changes in Anne's building. Emerges as Albert. Accepts animated congratulations. Says a reluctant goodnight.*

*Heading home, Albert experiences a sense of confirmation. He is Lillian. Lola. The girl he knows himself—herself—to be.*

*Crossing 71ˢᵗ Street, a guillotine-sharp gust of cold air slices across his neck.*

Approaching their building, Lola observed a man loitering against a parked car. A glowing orange dot revealed a cigarette but nothing else. She assumed that the doorman had wandered from his post to stretch his legs. Several steps on, she noticed that the man lacked both the doorman's hat and paunch.

The man stepped towards them.

Lola tugged on Fernando's arm.

Fernando pulled her close.

"Please, señorita Flores, I hope I have not frightened you," the man said in Cuban Spanish. Although his words were clear, his lips, embracing the remains of the cigarette, barely moved.

Lola wondered how the man knew who she was. Perhaps he recognized her broad-brimmed hat. More appropriate to protect her from the sun than a moon playing peekaboo behind ranks of dark clouds, she wore it to achieve a small measure of anonymity. Then again, fans always saw her wearing such a hat when she left the theater and often in newspaper and magazine photos. They'd become almost as recognizable as her celebrated flower hats. She tried to place the man. Even in the semi-darkness, a drawn face and shapeless suit revealed a physique less slim than gaunt. The only bright aspect to his appearance consisted of a yellow scarf around his neck. She drew a blank.

Fernando stepped in front of Lola. "Just who do you think you are?" he said, hinting that being taller and heavier, he would give no second thought to coming to blows.

The man tossed the remains of his cigarette towards the curb. "I know who *I* am," he said. "More important, I know who Lola Flores is."

Fernando puffed out his chest. "Millions of people know Lola Flores."

"And no one is more pleased about that than *me*."

Lola gasped. Her response purged any pretense of denial.

The man offered a tight-lipped grin then held out his hand to Fernando. "As Lola knows, I am called Hector Torres."

Fernando had been told that Elena's brother had visited briefly, met Lola and disappeared. He ignored Hector's hand.

Displaying neither disappointment nor offense, Hector turned to Lola.

"Permit me to say how proud I am of all you have accomplished these past seven years. I remember the Lola Torres I met in Havana. As to dear Elena—" He made the sign of the cross. "I only found out about her death a year later." He ran his hand across the scarf. "But here we are, and I must say that it took some time to find you, my cousin. Well, cousin in a manner of speaking."

Lola wondered what Hector might be suggesting about the family relationship explained to him by Elena.

Hector stepped closer and lowered his voice. "But should we be speaking of such matters here?"

Fernando led a short, silent trek to an all-night diner.

Over coffee in a booth removed from the half-dozen other customers occupied with their own late-night circumstances, Hector related his story. Two years earlier, after traveling throughout Latin America and all the while cold-shouldered by Lady Luck, he arrived in New York. He scoured the Cuban community and found Maribel.

"How is she?" Lola asked. "And where?"

Hector held up his right hand.

Lola pursed her lips in expectation.

When he found Maribel, he asked after their distant cousin Lola. She had charmed him. Leaving aside any further details of his conversation with Maribel, Hector announced that sadly, only a month later, he was left alone in the world. Their beloved Maribel had perished in a tenement fire.

The blood rushed from Lola's cheeks.

Fernando clasped her arm.

She struggled for words.

Hector expressed what might have been her thoughts. "Why does God do such things? What can be His purpose?"

Lola took a handkerchief from her purse but found her tears stopped up. Death had become all too familiar.

Casting aside theology, Hector described scrambling through each day in New York. Occasionally, he earned a few dollars making music. More often, he survived "this way and that, New York affording prospects to an enterprising gentleman." Always, he looked to the future. Then something extraordinary happened. Two weeks earlier, a friend played a record by

Lola Flores. Her music reminded him of meeting his distant cousin Lola in Havana years before.

Lola lit a cigarette.

Hector held out his hand seeking one for himself—a small token of her affection.

She ignored him and returned the gold case to her bag.

Hector displayed a frown of resignation.

Lola ignored it. "You never heard me play the piano in Havana," she said. "Elena did not have one."

Hector demolished her last hope of ridding herself of him. The Sunday following their meeting, he went to the Jewish Market to sell several items that had come into his possession. "Difficult times force a man to survive as best he can." As expected, he disposed of the goods for far less than they wore worth. "The Jews always cheat you." Then he heard someone playing a piano. The music touched his soul. He stood at the edge of the crowd and saw his cousin. She played with prodigious skill and passion. "As much as I wished to, I did not dare say hello and attract attention." He scratched his neck beneath the scarf. "I *did* glimpse a red-haired woman standing near you. She seemed as enraptured as myself."

Lola thought back to the day she met Frida. Had she fleetingly noticed Hector but failed to recognize him? Chosen to ignore him? The years that had passed seemed like decades, yet old wounds continued to fester. A cough signaled her defeat.

Fernando rested his hand on her back. "Cariña, what have I said about smoking?"

Lola dismissed him with a wave of her hand. "How did you find me?" she asked.

Hector smiled. As before, he spoke with lips that seemed sewn together. "Lola Flores stars in *The Ziegfeld Follies of 1936*. Each night, she receives the cheers of her audience. I, like most people, struggle to put bread on the table—if I possessed a table." He drew on the little money he had to buy a balcony ticket. "Lola Flores and Lola Torres were the same woman." After, he waited until the crowd mobbing the stage door dispersed then followed Lola and Fernando home. He bought another balcony ticket for this evening's performance. "Marvelous, like the first." As Lola took her curtain call, he left for their building, determined to wait for her arrival.

"I will call the police," said Lola.

Hector bowed his head low enough to demonstrate sincerity without conveying servility. "If I have caused alarm or given offense, please accept my apology. But the world rewards only those who seize an opportunity when one presents itself."

"You could have sent Lola word at the theater," said Fernando.

Hector held up his cup in the general direction of the counter, which opened onto the kitchen.

The diner's lone waitress, strands of damp gray-blond hair clinging to her cheeks, nodded.

Hector turned back to Lola. "Meeting at the theater could have proved awkward. What if you refused me? The police might have mistaken my intentions to discuss a serious matter of business."

Fernando leaned across the table and pressed a finger into Hector's chest. "What kind of business, and why would Lola be interested?" He sat back as the waitress refilled Hector's cup then bounded forward again.

Hector poured cream and added three lumps of sugar. Exuding satisfaction, he raised his cup. "To the future."

"The future?" Lola asked. "Whose future? What future?"

"A future that does not repeat the past," Hector said.

Fernando shook his head. "You speak in riddles."

Hector clasped his hands in front of his chest. "Do not misunderstand. Recently, I located a Cuban compatriot here in New York. A man who has found success but whose name need not be mentioned. I proposed that I might be of some assistance regarding his business dealings."

Lola glowered then lit another cigarette.

"Several days ago," said Hector, "my compatriot offered me an interest in a new venture. Something that could make us both rich."

"Nonsense," said Fernando.

Hector raised his right hand. "In the name of the Holy Virgin! What both of you must understand is that in America, great possibilities await everyone. But entering into a business partnership requires a man to demonstrate his commitment."

"Commitment?" Lola asked.

"Investment. Capital. Cash."

"And this is why you came to me?"

Hector offered a broader smile. It revealed yellowed teeth marred by half-a-dozen-gaps. "Ten thousand dollars which, because I am as patient as I am serious, I will require in one week."

Lola stubbed out her cigarette in a tin ashtray.

Fernando snorted and stood.

Hector grasped Fernando's wrist. "Please, hear me out. For the sake of Lola and yourself."

Fernando sat.

"Elena and Maribel—poor, sweet Maribel—would help me raise the money if they did not now sit at the right hand of Jesus. Still, they remain present in my heart. Only last night, Maribel came to me in a dream."

Neither Lola nor Fernando responded.

"She said, 'Dear brother, I have done so much for Lola and never asked to be repaid. Not a penny. Now she is famous. I know she will honor my memory by helping you in any way she can.'" He reached into his coat pocket and withdrew a scrap of ruled white paper torn from a child's notebook. "Call this number tomorrow. Leave *your* number. I will get back to you." He placed the paper on the table.

Lola lit another cigarette. "When you spoke with Maribel—" She cut off the question. She knew what Maribel had told Hector. His repeating it would not do her justice.

Lola, the telephone receiver at her ear, tried to stifle a yawn. She'd gotten only two hours sleep. Her other hand clutched an empty glass. Hector's sudden appearance and brash demand the night before had given her every reason to consume her allotted afternoon drink earlier than usual then follow it with a second. All the Scotch did was leave her head with the sensation of being smothered in cotton batting.

She'd made the long-distance call without telling Fernando, wishing to avoid yet another squabble. Over the past weeks, they'd argued with increasing frequency about her drinking and what it could do to her career. He kept his voice and manner subdued in wanton betrayal of his Latin heritage as if to mock the fury she could not suppress. As to Hector, they had failed to reach agreement.

"I have told you everything," Lola said to the man she hoped would serve as her champion, whose power extended far beyond any that

Fernando could summon, whose strength and influence had so far helped her safeguard her identity—even from him—and her life. "Please Ben, what should I do?"

Ben Siegel made no attempt to disguise his own yawn. "Sorry. On the Coast here? It's only noon. Anyway, first thing, stay calm."

"But you will speak with Hector?"

"Things can be smoothed out, sure."

"A word from a man such as yourself—"

"Men like him, they make mistakes. He'll see the light. Anyway, he gave you how long to pay him off?"

"A week?"

"And how much?"

"Ten thousand dollars."

"Well, you got the shekels."

Taken aback, Lola poured another Scotch. Ben obviously knew that at Fernando's insistence, the Nacional had wired her salary to a New York bank account and how generously Billie Burke paid her for the *Follies'* autumn run. Then there were fees for radio shows on which she'd appeared and royalties from records. She'd become—she hesitated to think it lest she attract the evil eye—a star. Yes, she had the money.

"You can't believe how many Hollywood people let all their dough slip through their fingers. It's criminal."

Given what Lola knew of the plight faced by some film stars and others on Broadway, her annoyance with Fernando and his fussing about her—their—finances faded.

"Anyway," said Ben, "whatever it is this Hector knows and you wanna keep from me, I don't take it personal."

"Thank you, Ben."

"And don't worry I'll ever ask. Everybody's got something they don't want even their best friend to know. Not that there ain't ways to find out anything about anyone."

"I am sure there are, Ben. You are very kind. But what do you advise me to do?"

"String Hector along a few days. Just so he don't jump the gun and do something dumber. You can do that?"

"Yes."

"You don't want him thinking something ain't kosher."

"No, Ben."

"What you'll do is show this guy some good faith with a small down payment."

"And how much will that be?"

"Five hundred."

"What if he wants more?"

She should tell him her money was tied up. Five hundred was what she could get her hands on now. "Remember, he gave you a week. You're holding up your end of the deal. He's gotta hold up his."

"He will go along with this?"

Ben assured her that the down payment would make Hector fool himself into believing he was in control.

"And then?"

"You tell him your business manager—not Fernando, *another* guy— is gonna give him the rest. He's out of town, but he'll be back soon. Meanwhile, Heshy'll fly to New York."

"Heshy?"

"Things how they are, I can't leave L.A. Besides, you know Heshy. The most easy-going guy in the world. Mister Reasonable. Someone makes a fuss, Heshy calms the waters."

"And Hector will leave my life?"

Ben chuckled.

Seated at her living room piano a moment after sunrise, Lola reached for coffee rather than Scotch. Despite Fernando's concession to Ben and making the initial payment to Hector, and Heshy Kaplan's comforting arrival in New York, she'd again found sleep elusive. No longer able to read or even listen to the radio, she lay in silence and prayed for relief. A moment later, the kernel of a song made an unannounced entrance, burrowed itself into her mind and refused her efforts to evict it with the tenacity of a bedbug in a flophouse mattress. Relenting, she took pencil and notebook from her nightstand drawer and gave inspiration free rein. Twenty minutes later, she completed lyrics and the notation of a basic melody. Her mood lighter, she drifted off only to awake at first light impatient to start the day. For the first time in months, she felt fully alive.

The song, penciled on manuscript paper propped on the music rack in front of her, would be different from anything her fans had heard. While employing a strong Latin rhythm, it would speak to every American, cheer the down-and-out seeking jobs with the Works Progress Administration or lining up at soup kitchens. The more fortunate, subject to the troubles endured by rich and poor alike, would find hope. Lola imagined impressive sales of records and sheet music. After all, unlike the Depression's unofficial theme song, "Brother Can You Spare a Dime," this number approached America's ongoing struggles with optimism and humor. Playing chords, she sang with gusto:

> *Ay, ay, ay!*
> *Ay, ay, ay!*
> *Ay, ay, ay!*
> *Ay, ay, ay!*
>
> *The skies are gray.*
> *It is dark all day.*
>
> *Ay, ay, ay!*
> *Ay, ay, ay!*
>
> *There's a hole in my shoe,*
> *And the rent is due.*
>
> *Ay, ay, ay!*
> *Ay, ay, ay!*
>
> *I would have to steal*
> *For a decent meal.*
>
> *Ay, ay, ay!*
> *Ay, ay, ay!*
> *Ay, ay, ay!*
> *Ay, ay, ay!*

*Oh, why*
*Has this happened to me?*
*The sky keeps falling*
*As everyone can see.*
*I walk the streets*
*With an empty purse.*
*Can it, could it,*
*Might it get*
*Worse?*

*Ay, ay, ay, ay, ay!*

*When I am hot,*
*My man is not.*

*Ay, ay, ay!*
*Ay, ay, ay!*

*His heart grows cold,*
*And I grow old.*

*Ay, ay, ay!*
*Ay, ay, ay!*

*Still, all the while,*
*I will keep my smile.*

*Ay, ay, ay!*
*Ay, ay, ay!*

*At the end of my rope,*
*I will not give up hope.*

*Ay, ay, ay!*
*Ay, ay, ay!*

*If today brings sorrow,*
*There's a sunny tomorrow.*

*Ay, ay, ay!*
*Ay, ay, ay!*
*Ay, ay, ay, ay, ay!*

She'd keep the song under wraps for now, fine-tune the lyrics and melody, come up with a proper arrangement. But "Ay, Ay, Ay!" already was a success. It had sent her malaise packing.

That night, Lola and Fernando strolled down Seventh Avenue to a midnight supper hosted by Walter Winchell. He'd invited a dozen Broadway notables to a "small soiree" at which he'd squire Josephine Baker, the Negro singer who'd headlined the Folies Bergère in Paris and preceded Gypsy Rose Lee in the *Follies'* autumn reincarnation.

At 47th Street, Fernando slowed as a newsstand proprietor finished displaying copies of the early-edition *News* and *Mirror*.

"We shouldn't keep everyone waiting," said Lola.

Fernando stopped.

Lola looked up and clamped a hand over her mouth.

The *News* headlined: KIDS DISCOVER BODY. The *Mirror* offered: STRANGLED MAN FOUND AT BROOKLYN PIER. Both displayed similar photos of the victim, whose gaping mouth lacked several teeth. A soiled scarf remained tied around Hector's neck.

# NOVEMBER 1936

# "FIND DR. GERSTNER AT ONCE"

The near-empty bottle of Dewar's hurtled towards Fernando's nose.
He swayed left as if dancing on a conga line.

The whirling projectile grazed his right ear then burst against the dressing room wall behind him.

Fernando took a white handkerchief from his jacket pocket and waved it in surrender. Experiencing a small measure of discomfort, he patted the back of his neck. The formerly pristine silk cloth displayed two tiny fragments of glass set gem-like against diminutive bloodstains.

Edna, Lola's maid, scurried to the closet in the far corner and secured a broom, dustpan, mop and pail.

"It can wait," Fernando said. He nodded towards the door.

Edna retreated without protest.

"Thanksgiving is only one week off, cariña," Fernando said. He held out the handkerchief. "Is this the gratitude I have earned?"

Lola raised her middle finger then finished shimmying into the purple gown she would wear in her opening scene.

Fernando tossed the soiled handkerchief onto the coffee table in front of the sofa. "Do not pretend that Hector's death has been the sole cause of your drinking again and—" He explored the back of his neck with a finger. "Ill-mannered behavior."

"Ill-mannered, my tuchus!" Lola shot back.

Fernando held a finger to his lips. "This drinking, it began long ago. I blame myself for hoping that you would recover your senses."

"Go to hell!" Lola snarled. She tapped her foot.

Fernando zipped her up.

She braced herself against the wall and slipped down six inches before righting herself.

Fernando refused to let the matter drop. "It is almost as if I cannot remember when you were *not*— What is the word? Sulking."

"Sulking?"

"But you have never acted like *this*."

"You have never *insulted* me like this."

The toe of his right shoe nudged aside a jagged piece of glass. "I spoke only the truth." Not that he lacked faith that Lola could be made whole. Make *herself* whole. Thanks to Jesús, the God of the Israelites and whatever other deities might exist, total disaster had not befallen them since the *Follies'* reopening. To be sure, Lola stumbled several times a week—a near pratfall crossing the stage, a forgotten cue, a missed note. Each time, she caught herself. Always, she won over the audience, as if it recognized its frailties in her and saw no other choice than to forgive. But what really protected Lola, he believed, was the prodigious will that had enabled her to reach Havana years earlier, make a new life, prosper and survive. A will that enabled her to conquer Broadway while keeping the scandal-loving press at bay. A will that now, insisting on its invulnerability, made light of the dangers lurking behind the smiles, laughter, applause and adulation, dismissed the knife in the back waiting to pitch Lola Flores into the gutter as Manuel Gallegos had done to Frida Herskovits. No longer could he turn a blind eye. Lola—the two of them—stood not so much at a crossroads as at a precipice. "Cariña, you cannot perform in this condition."

Lola reached for her empty glass then looked about for another bottle.

Three taps on the door interrupted her. "Five minutes, Miss Flores," the stage manager sang out. "Everything okay?"

"We are fine," said Fernando.

The stage manager went on his way.

"We are *not* fine," Lola barked.

Fernando clasped his hands as if in prayer. "At last, we find ourselves in agreement. But to be precise, *you* are not fine."

Lola cocked her arm. Before she could fling the glass at Fernando, her knees buckled. She toppled to the floor, the glass unbroken. A guttural cry emulated the sound her gown made as its seams ripped. She clutched her right elbow.

219

Fernando went to the bathroom, returned with a small towel and filled it with ice from the bucket on the coffee table next to which Lola lay prostrate. He thanked the god of small miracles that she hadn't hit her head on the marble top. As she sobbed, he pried her fingers loose from her injured elbow and applied the improvised ice pack.

Lola sensed the dressing room fading to black like the theater prior to the overture. Then darkness gave way to light. As if seated in one of Manhattan's movie palaces, she viewed a newsreel of the mind, a screen on each wall so that she could not turn away. Moisés Finklestein lay prostrate at the edge of the fountain in the Plaza Vieja soaked in his own blood. Frida's corpse sprawled in an alley in Barrio Chino. Manuel's upper body again and again propelled forward onto the lawn of the Hotel Nacional. Leon Greenspan's brains spilled across a starched white tablecloth at the Stork Club. The tabloids' front pages displayed Hector's death agony.

A voice, its adolescent tone familiar and jarring, assailed her. "Who binds these lost souls?" Before she could respond, it delivered its indictment: "Lola Flores." The image of a face flickered before her. Albert, his now-ageless spirit as restless as that of Hamlet's father, flaunted a twisted grin.

She protested yet again. Lola Flores had accomplished what they'd both sought. She'd never intended that blood be shed in the process. Albert had no right to keep tormenting her. "No right," she cried out. "No right."

Fernando slapped her.

She opened her eyes.

"Wiggle your fingers," he ordered.

She sobbed.

Fernando gestured towards the door. Miracles abounding, no one had heard her fall. He placed a finger on her lips.

Lola's sobs ebbed to whimpers.

He lifted her onto the sofa.

She reclined as if attending a traditional Passover Seder.

"Keep the ice against your elbow," he said.

Lola startled. Fernando's voice projected a strength, a force, a determination brooking no opposition. Had he become a Cuban version of Ben? She held the ice in place.

Fernando left the dressing room and returned a moment later. "Can you bend your arm?"

Lola shook her head.

"Try!" he urged.

She attempted to flex her arm and moaned.

"We will take care of this," he said. "However, I have informed the stage manager that you will not perform tonight."

A surge of adrenalin drove Lola upright. "The house doctor cannot examine me," she cried.

"Of course not," said Fernando.

Lola fell back.

Fernando sat beside her.

"Tomorrow then," she said. "Audiences have paid to see Lola Flores."

"And Fanny and Rose and everyone else," said Fernando. He coaxed her to her feet, placed her left hand on his shoulder for support and unfastened what remained of her zipper. Then he eased the tattered gown down over her hips. "Not tomorrow night, either. Not for the run of the show which, anyway, has only a month remaining."

Lola attempted to kick Fernando but mustered only sufficient energy to nudge his shin with hers.

Undaunted, Fernando slipped the gown out from under her feet. "We—you—have no choice. Do you think Billie and the cast know nothing about your drinking? The mistakes?"

"*Everyone* makes mistakes."

"Not on Broadway. Not in the *Follies*. If not for Fanny, Billie would have released you weeks ago."

"But what will people think?"

Fernando removed the dress she'd worn to the theater from its hanger and slipped it over her head. "Walter will take care of that. He will write that you are ill. Exhausted, as was Fanny during the show's first run. And your relationship with Ben and Meyer is no secret. Everyone in the business will play along." He eased her back down on the sofa and placed her everyday shoes on her feet. After securing the makeshift ice pack to her elbow, he reached into his coat pocket for a black leather-bound address book and picked up the telephone receiver.

"What are you doing?" Lola asked.

The rotor whirred as he dialed.

"Who—" Lola sputtered. Drained, she again closed her eyes. The ice had eased the worst of the pain in her elbow, but the newsreel inside her head was replaced by Joe Louis and Max Schmeling pummeling each other for the heavyweight title.

"This is Fernando Fallon," Fernando said into the phone. "Find Dr. Gerstner at once."

Lola made out a voice on the other end of the line. It sounded like the buzzing of a bee.

"Yes," Fernando replied. "It *is* a matter of life and death."

The next morning, Fernando sat in Lola's living room sipping coffee and nibbling a bagel, cream cheese and lox. Leafing through the morning *Mirror*, he appeared the picture of a man at his ease.

Lola, dressed in a forest-green suit, lay on the sofa. Her right arm rested in a sling. Her coffee remained untouched. "Guttenyu, it might as well be the middle of the night," she muttered.

Fernando looked up. Of late, Lola often spoke like the New Yorker she once was. He found this amusing in private. A slip in public might earn laughter but also prompt dangerous questions.

Now, her muted voice and slurred words indicated that the pills he'd given her, added to the sedatives Dr. Gerstner provided the night before, had taken full effect. She'd be as docile as he supposed a newborn to be. As to her elbow, Dr. Gerstner believed it sprained, not broken. His associate, Dr. Sherman, would take precautionary X-rays.

Seeking to keep Lola calm, Fernando acknowledged her concern about the hour with a touch of flattery. "Hardly the middle of the night but early for a famous Broadway star like Lola Flores."

Her response proved unintelligible.

He glanced down at the *Mirror* then back to Lola. She would need to be kept tractable—Dr. Gerstner taught him that word—but sufficiently alert. He updated her on the news. "Did you know, cariña, that the main span of the Golden Gate Bridge joining San Francisco to Marin County on its north will be completed today?"

Lola offered no comment.

Fernando searched for another article to spark her interest without causing upset. He passed over stories concerning Europe, where each day

Hitler seemed closer to leading Germany to war. He found nothing. "Are you sure you do not want something to eat?"

Lola grunted.

He checked his watch. It was almost ten.

"Why must we take a car to the hospital and not a taxi?" Lola asked, returning to her Cuban English. "And how long can an X-ray possibly take?"

"Taxi drivers talk, cariña. Walter says they supply him half his information. This driver will be discreet."

The apartment's intercom buzzed.

Lola dozed.

Fernando buzzed back and opened the door, next to which sat two suitcases. A moment later, he greeted a middle-aged woman in a long gray skirt, matching jacket and white blouse with a large ruffle. Her black shoes could charitably be described as sensible. She was followed by a fortyish man in a dark blue suit. The hair at the sides of his head was trimmed to a stubble. His ears protruded at near right angles.

Without waiting for Fernando's cue, the woman shook Lola's shoulder. "Dear, we're here."

"You pack her bags?" the man asked.

Fernando nodded towards the suitcases.

The woman rested the palm of her right hand on Lola's cheek.

Lola's eyes fluttered open. "Sylvia?"

"No, dear," said the woman.

"Who are you?" Lola asked. "I am supposed to go to the doctor for an X-ray."

The woman helped Lola to her feet. "Of course, dear. You'll be X-rayed this afternoon."

The man hefted Lola's bags.

Experiencing a panic-induced moment of clarity, Lola asked, "This afternoon? Fernando said it is now morning."

Fernando patted her hand. "It is morning of course, cariña."

"Where are you taking me?" Lola asked.

"To a good place," Fernando said.

Lola attempted to shake free.

The man put down Lola's bags and stepped forward.

An upward tilt of the woman's chin motioned him back.

The man hinted at a scowl and picked up the bags.

With a practiced gentleness, the woman tightened her grip on Lola's arm.

"We are going to see Dr. Sherman," said Fernando. "Dr. Sherman is an associate of Dr. Gerstner. He will care for you."

"Is he a Park Avenue doctor?" Lola asked as they walked towards the door. "Are we going to Park Avenue? Why do we need so many people to go a few blocks?"

"We are going to Connecticut, cariña. To a place where you can get well."

"Connecticut? How long will I be in Connecticut?"

Fernando looked away.

# MAY/JUNE 1939
# CHOICES

The light from a table lamp with a fringed shade guided Lola as she paced the apartment's modest living room. At three-thirty in the morning, even Manhattanites were tucked in, although some had just gone to bed. Others would rise before the sun. Under the covers half an hour earlier, Lola had caught a news report on the radio. An ocean liner, the MS *St. Louis*, sailing from Hamburg with over 900 passengers, most of them Jewish refugees, had dropped anchor in the outer reaches of Havana Harbor. The Cuban government denied the ship use of the usual docking facilities. Only twenty-eight passengers—twenty-two of them Jews—were allowed to disembark. Lola feared the fate awaiting the rest.

The news disturbing, she determined to stroll in endless circles for however long it took to lure sleep. Over the more than two years since she'd returned—*been returned*—to New York from Connecticut, she'd taken to marching around the apartment at all hours, lap after lap like a marathon runner confined to a miniature indoor track.

The prospect of sleep remaining bleak, Lola fondled the half-smoked pack of Chesterfields in the pocket of her robe. She'd chosen to leave untouched the sleeping pills in her nightstand drawer prescribed by Dr. Gerstner. They worked but only after a fashion. Even one left her lethargic and out of sorts when she awoke, usually late in the afternoon. At first, she embraced abandoning the early-to-bed, early-to-rise routine imposed by the clinic, but as she explored her narrowed career choices, the pills condemned her to committing the great American sin of wasting time. Her punishment would fit her crimes, leaving her life forever frozen in the winter of its discontent with no prospect for a glorious summer while its waning balance crept in its petty pace towards a fateful day of reckoning.

Cigarettes refused her a choice. How else was she to calm her nerves? On her first day in Connecticut, Dr. Sherman, who chain-smoked Philip Morris, ordered her to give them up. Easy for him to say. Cigarettes were unavailable to patients. Even if the staff accepted bribes—no chance, since each was as strait-laced as the evangelist preacher Billy Sunday—the nurse who accompanied her on the ride from New York forced her to surrender the money in her purse. Lola went cold turkey. In three weeks, the food mediocre, she put on eight pounds. She added seven more over the remainder of her four-month stay.

When Fernando took her back to New York, he consoled her that she hardly could be called zaftig. Moreover, the added weight, heralding renewed health, had added to her bustline, flattered the figure of a woman her age.

A woman of her age?

Every morning, Fernando involved with one enterprise or another, she telephoned the candy store a block away. They delivered newspapers, magazines, chewing gum—and cigarettes.

Fernando objected, nagged, occasionally fumed. More than once, he threatened to sue the candy store owner.

Lola, resentful of his practically having her jailed in Connecticut, insisted that her stay at the clinic had served its purpose. She was quite capable of running her own life. Wasn't that why he kidnapped her in the first place? And hadn't Dr. Sherman advised that only by making choices—good ones, naturally—could she return to a full life and hopefully renewed success? So yes, she chose to keep smoking. She also decided to chew Wrigley's Juicy Fruit. The gum would extend the intervals between cigarettes. That surely created a healthy compromise.

Fernando capitulated. What choice did he have unless he spent twenty-four hours a day every day at her apartment?

Lola's weight fell. Her mood, unfortunately, resisted a corresponding upswing.

She turned back to liquor. Insomnia, she reasoned, posed as big a risk to her health as anything else. When walking the apartment failed, she sipped Scotch on the rocks. Surely, ice diluted the effects of alcohol. If drowsiness evaded her, she poured a second glass. A third usually sent her to bed—unless she required a fourth.

For what could have been the fifth, tenth, twentieth or hundredth time, Lola passed the Zenith radio Fernando gave her for her twenty-ninth birthday two months earlier. The occasion had left her shaken. How could she be exiting her twenties? The beginning of the end approached. The gift itself was lovely but incomplete. She'd expressed a desire for one of those elegant new radio-bars—a cabinet that unfolded to reveal cocktail and shot glasses, mixing and seltzer bottles, even a lighted mirror. Below the bar, two doors provided access to knobs for tuning a radio to AM, the new FM stations and short-wave.

Fernando had picked out a walnut floor-model radio—stylish but lacking any connection to alcohol.

Lola preferred the birthday gift she'd received two years before—her freedom. Dr. Sherman, after consulting with Dr. Gerstner, pronounced her fit to return to New York, although he advised that her nerves remained fragile.

Back home, she confined herself to her apartment, content with her records and books. Shakespeare's comedies proved delightful, but the current world viewed through the *Daily Mirror* and *New York Times* along with *Life*, *Look* and even *Mademoiselle* proved depressing. Civil war bloodied Spain. Germany banned Jews from all professions. Lola could not imagine why so many chose to remain. Emotionally spent, she left the papers and magazines unread except for Walter Winchell's column, which reconnected her with the city. The marquees of Broadway glowed despite her absence.

Doctor Sherman via telephone and Dr. Gerstner during house calls urged her to break free from her self-imposed captivity. Four months after her release, she relented. On a muggy mid-July day reminiscent of Havana, she and Fernando strolled once around the block like mourners completing the sequestration of Shiva. Two weeks later, concealed by a hat and sunglasses, she shopped the A&P. Following Yom Kippur, on which her attempt to fast after a late dinner ended with an early, half-finished lunch and Albert's displeasure, she and Fernando attended Rodgers and Hart's *Babes in Arms* at the Shubert Theatre. They sat in the orchestra's back row. At intermission, Lola insisted they leave. A month later, they dined at a neighborhood chop house. Lola—lighter than when she entered the clinic, her face haggard, delicate crow's feet etched around her eyes—went unrecognized. Her veal went untouched.

Following that outing, she left the apartment no more than weekly.

Music offered a measure of relief. Following Fernando's persistent urging, she summoned the strength to record "Ay, Ay, Ay!" Sitting at the piano in a studio, surrounded by talented musicians, some of whom remembered her, Lola's spirits soared. After listening to the record, they plunged. She'd waited too long. The oppressive weight of the Depression had somewhat lightened while her hands had grown heavy. She'd put all her hopes into a flop.

Americans proved her wrong. Finding "Ay, Ay, Ay!" witty and encouraging, they bought enough records and sheet music for *Your Hit Parade* to air the song, although performed—as all the show's numbers—by a salaried vocalist.

At Ben Siegel's behest, several nightclub owners offered dates. Lola turned them down. Singing in a recording studio was one thing. Appearing before an audience again? Someday maybe but not now. Ben accepted her refusals with an affability reserved for no one else.

Fernando conceived of other ways to capitalize on the success of "Ay, Ay, Ay!" He approached the managers of several popular vocalists and sold them on having Lola write new songs for their stars, complete with arrangements. Lola's first effort ascended *Billboard* magazine's music hit parade. Two more achieved similar results. Bandleaders like Ziggy Elman and Glen Gray approached Fernando to have Lola arrange some of their tunes.

Lola worked when she chose and earned a healthy income despite insisting on an unusual proviso before undertaking a project. Clients could speak freely with Fernando but were required to communicate with her only in writing. She renewed her reputation as a brilliant musician while establishing a new one as a recluse.

One afternoon in mid-November 1938, Lola, Fernando at her side, entertained her first guests. Still, her mood remained subdued. Days earlier, Nazis across Germany burned hundreds of synagogues, ransacked more than seven thousand Jewish businesses and left many dead. After a fortifying drink, she welcomed Walter Winchell, who faithfully reported her new achievements, along with Fanny Brice, two weeks divorced from the impresario Billy Rose. Fanny brought chocolate babka from Katz's deli. "You perform like a Jew, you should eat like a Jew. You're too thin, anyway."

At Christmastime, Ben visited. He pressed Lola to come to California. Sure, it was different, but a great different. What was she doing now? "Bupkes compared with what a babe with talent can do in Hollywood. Even without talent. And there ain't no snow."

Accompanied by a beautiful redhead—Esta and the girls remained in Los Angeles—Ben took Lola and Fernando to a seafood restaurant in Far Rockaway. Queens, forget Long Island, was where the world stopped. They could dine unrecognized. Ben didn't need to explain that when business brought him back to New York, the smart thing was to lay low. "But I hadda see you. No offense, you're like my kid sister. Imagine, a Jewish guy from Brooklyn lookin' out for a doll from Havana, and it ain't physical."

Filing away her memories, Lola lit a cigarette, poured a drink and turned off the lamp. Guilt accompanied her dejection. By most measures, she'd reconstructed a good life. But while she spoke regularly with a member of Dr. Sherman's staff—a psychologist with the clipped, upper-crust speech of the actor Edward Everett Horton, who she knew was born in Brooklyn—she could not shake the gloom that overwhelmed her.

The bottle of Scotch little more than a silhouette on the table next to her, she refilled her glass. What better companions than liquor and darkness? Light was a charlatan. It deceived people that better days awaited.

Cumbersome thoughts tumbling over each other like acrobats, sleep remained elusive. She considered prayer, rejected it, relented. The attempt proved futile.

She remembered the pills.

The next afternoon, Dr. Gerstner sent Lola home with a stern warning. "Thank God, Fernando found you when he did—and you apparently took only one pill. Sleeping pills and alcohol—especially in your condition. The next time— There simply *cannot* be a next time."

Fernando put his foot down. "Cariña, you—we—have only one choice."

Two days later, Fernando and Lola went to City Hall. He could no longer care for her from a separate apartment. *You have your moods, cariña. And I know you are drinking again.* He proposed—commanded—a solution. A man and woman unrelated or unmarried could not rent an apartment together in a building like theirs without provoking unwanted gossip or outright antagonism. Cubans considered lacking basic American decency, they might find themselves in a scandal even Walter might have trouble controlling. God forbid Ben should step in. As it was, several of the building's residents still opposed to *that Soviet dupe Roosevelt* arched an eyebrow whenever they encountered their Latin neighbors.

In the city clerk's office, they presented Cuban birth certificates, American passports and the results of blood tests by Dr. Gerstner declaring that neither had syphilis or rubella.

The clerk noted the name Lola Flores without comment.

The following Tuesday morning, Lola and Fernando returned. Lola wished Sylvia could serve as the required witness but conceded that her presence could lead to a disastrous slip of the tongue. The clerk summoned a secretary.

That afternoon, men hired through the super moved Lola's clothing and furnishings, along with Fernando's things, including his armchair, into a two-bedroom apartment made available by their marriage certificate.

The next day, Walter Winchell would announce their marriage in his column. He would not report that the newlyweds had no intention of consummating their union.

The movers, their job finished, accepted handsome tips from Fernando. "Nice guest room you got there," said one as Fernando prepared to open a celebratory bottle of ginger ale. "Make a nice nursery."

# MARCH 1940

# THIRTY!

Lola slipped on a yellow apron decorated with pink, blue and white flowers. It resembled one Mama used to wear. Or did it?

She'd begun to question her memory but knew that she'd put a brisket in the oven. Fernando hungered for Jewish cooking and even provided Lola several Jewish cookbooks. Now, the brisket demanded her attention. A hearty dinner would lessen the bitter chill of a lingering New York winter. They increasingly grumbled about the cold and with good reason. Over the past weeks of dropping temperatures, the building's steam heat came on only at fleeting intervals and never for long. Despite two sweaters, wool slacks, calf-length socks and fur-lined bedroom slippers, Lola shivered.

The open oven door released a burst of heat. Lola rocked back, recovered her wits and sniffed. Was she turning into Mama? She added water to the pan to keep it from burning. Something outside the kitchen window caught her attention. She thought New York was enduring another snowfall, but the twilight sky was clear. Not snowflakes but flurries of gray ash hovered in ever-shifting whorls. Someone had knocked the lids off the massive metal cans on the sidewalk. The residue produced by the building's incinerator prematurely darkened the remains of the day.

A premonition of doom seized Lola. It intimated a calamity too horrible to comprehend, one advancing without resistance. She tossed her gum into the trash and lit a cigarette. Still unsettled, Lola sang the child-like song Dr. Sherman taught her:

*It's a beautiful day.*
*It's a beautiful day.*

> *I will make my way,*
> *Come what may.*

Whether in response to the cigarette or the song, her anxiety lessened. She scolded herself. How could she feel blue on such a special day? Then again, how could she not?

Today she was thirty!

In the living room, still aproned, Lola turned on the radio, collapsed onto the sofa and covered herself with an afghan. Her resolve to hold the world at bay had eroded. Someone had to bear witness. Her jaw clenched, she listened to Edward R. Murrow report with solemnity from London. The plight of Warsaw— especially its Jews—under Nazi occupation proved more dismal each day. She sighed with relief that her grandparents hadn't lived to see such degradation. To be degraded. Gratitude warped into guilt. To the best of her knowledge, six aunts and uncles, along with assorted cousins, remained in Poland. What would happen to them? The *Times* had detailed a recent diplomatic mission to Germany by U.S. Undersecretary of State Sumner Welles. Just reading his name made her tremble. The visit produced nothing. The war in Europe went on. Would America keep its distance forever?

Her emotions drained, Lola struggled to her feet, turned off the radio and placed "Ay, Ay, Ay!" on the Victrola. Embracing the lighthearted music, she danced in a trance-like fashion, her feet rooted to the carpet, her hips barely swaying. Following the bridge, she stood motionless then raised her chin and sniffed.

Lola hoped she hadn't set the oven's heat too high given its eccentricities. The super claimed the stove was fine, his wife had no trouble with theirs. Lola sniffed again. The brisket was fine. She would serve it to Fernando as a triumph.

"Happy birthday to me," Lola sang softly then stopped. A voice in her head whispered—its faintness drawing more attention than a scream—that thirty was an age to lament. Her youth was gone. She'd been banished from the spotlight, branded a has-been. Less-talented singers took advantage of her writing to record hits and appear in New York's smartest supper clubs. Performers lacking her musical and comedic gifts strutted Broadway's stages. Audiences wondered, "Whatever happened to Lola Flores?" Oh, but she knew.

Lola Flores had a brisket in the oven. Gott in Himmel, she'd become a hausfrau.

She stumbled towards the kitchen just as the song ended. The record spun on, the speaker emitting the scratching sound of needle on shellac. She went to the sink, kneeled and opened a cabinet stuffed with cleaning materials. Reaching in past her elbow, she withdrew a pint bottle of whisky.

A light snow fell as Fernando walked home from Rockefeller Center, warmed by a fur-lined hat and not one but two accomplishments. He'd just played the major role of a Spanish Royalist for a radio drama to be aired on NBC's Red network. And prior to going into the studio, he'd reached an agreement for Lola to write a song for a young Cuban bandleader, Desi Arnaz. Appearing at the Imperial Theater in *Too Many Girls*, Desi was enthused about what a Lola Flores tune could do for his career. *After the show closes in May, I'm going to Hollywood to appear in the movie version of "Girls." A hit record when I arrive in Los Angeles will get people to take me more seriously. Desi Arnaz can't just be known as that "Babaloo" guy. It's just a novelty song. And only a Cuban can truly share the passion of another Cuban, right?*

A block from the apartment building, Fernando sighted a fire engine, red lights flashing. He attempted to run, but after only a dozen steps found his footing treacherous, his breathing labored. Approaching the building's entry, he saw the doorman whirling his arms like a third-base coach exhorting his runner to dig deeper and beat a fielder's throw home. He stumbled into the lobby.

Lola sat on a sofa. A blanket draped her shoulders. A fireman stood behind her.

Fernando took Lola's hand.

The fireman asked, "She the missus?"

Fernando nodded.

"So anyways," said the fireman, "seems somethin' in the oven caused a little fire. Not that big a deal in the scheme of things. I seen a lot worse. But the kitchen, it'll need airing out. Repainting. Some other work. You'll wanna check into a hotel."

Fernando sat by Lola. "Cariña, what happened?"

Lola pulled the blanket tight.

The fireman stepped forward. "Looks like the little lady fell sleep in the living room. Neighbor called. We had to break down the door. Anyways, another couple of minutes and I can take youse upstairs to secure your valuables, pack a suitcase, get the lady a heavy coat. A warm hat, too. Gonna get even colder tonight."

"This is terrible," said Fernando. His reservoir of optimism filled to overflowing had been depleted.

"No," Lola responded. The single word—the one syllable—projected a will so resolute that resistance would prove futile. During the interval between her rescue and Fernando's arrival, she'd recognized the fire not as a misfortune but as a godsend. Even as Fernando sat long-faced, his perspective on the future clouded, Lola experienced a clear and compelling vision of a paradise like that granted to Adam and Eve before their insubordination and expulsion. There, wholeness would be restored to her shattered soul—and perhaps to Albert's.

# LOS ANGELES

# JUNE 1940

# HOLLYWOODLAND

B en Siegel lead-footed the gas pedal, sending the canary-yellow Cadillac convertible, its top down, racing west along Hollywood Boulevard. Lola, her back pressed against the seat, placed one hand on her hat, its brim fluttering. The other examined the bow tied beneath her chin. She savored the golden mid-afternoon sunshine that constituted one of the few attributes of Los Angeles free from illusion.

At Fairfax Avenue, Ben took a sharp left. Oncoming cars braked and swerved. Tread marks streaked the asphalt.

Lola, wearing the pink sundress she'd slipped into that morning before the Super Chief pulled into Union Station, braced herself against the passenger door.

Approaching Santa Monica Boulevard, Ben accelerated, roared through a red light then made a hard right. The Caddy's whitewalls squealed.

A siren answered them.

Ben slowed and pulled over.

Lola's hands shook.

Ben chuckled.

A thick-necked policeman with a permanent sunburn exited the patrol car and ambled towards them. His pronounced swagger emphasized the authority granted by his badge. "You and the missus expectin' the stork any minute?" he asked. His accent suggested origins in Minnesota or Wisconsin. Although he could have made the trek west from Iowa like so many other Angelenos. "Maybe goin' to a fire? Somethin' like that?" He eyeballed the Caddy. "License, please."

"My license?" Ben asked. "A man needs a license to drive a car in California?"

The policeman rested a brawny hand on his nightstick.

Ben grinned at Lola.

Lola wondered if the Southern California weather had seduced Ben into abandoning all caution. Did people from more hostile climates really lose their senses in what some called Lotusland? Would *she*?

Ben turned back to the policeman and raised his hands like a rustler in a western corralled by a heroic lawman. "Just jokin'," he said. "You got a sense of humor, don't ya?"

The red in the policeman's face deepened. His compressed lips and narrowed eyes displayed a distinct lack of mirth.

With an exaggerated deliberateness suggesting that neither an impending birth nor a fire would ever prompt him to drive with undue haste, Ben withdrew his wallet from his jacket pocket and held out his license.

The policeman's head snapped back. His cheeks paled. Everyone in the L.A.P.D. knew Ben Siegel, who'd brought a reputation for ruthlessness from New York along with the mob's orders to take control of its gambling and other illicit enterprises. They knew as well that neither the mob nor Ben Siegel himself could control his temper. Word had circulated through the department that the past November, Siegel, along with several colleagues, shot to death Harry Greenberg—on the lam from the New York mob—outside Greenberg's Los Angeles apartment. "Big Greenie" had been Siegel's childhood friend.

Lola had seen that story in the New York papers but remained ignorant of the details—if anyone knew the details let alone could make a legal case. With Ben Siegel, truth blended into legend, although she'd witnessed a terrible truth that night at the Stork Club when he shot two men. But that was in self-defense. Even the Rabbis allowed killing under those circumstances. Then again, she'd struggled to come to grips with Ben's delivering to each would-be assassin the coup de grace. Yes, they were already dead but still, how was she to make sense of yet another display of brutality? Most likely, the memory of that brief but bloody confrontation, heaped onto all the other savageries preceding it, Hector's murder included, had festered throughout that dreadful year of 1936 until it pushed her over the edge and up to Connecticut.

Now, here she was on the far side of the continent, again placing herself under the wing of the man many people called, though never to his face, Bugsy. During her most charitable moments, she considered him something of an angel sent by God, one willing to get his hands dirty. Perhaps because she was the only one of his undertakings that was legal, he devoted himself to helping her reach her deserved place in the world. More, Ben always acted the gentleman in her presence, their relationship as chaste as it was helpful. Of course, there were other reasons to stay close to him. Could she—could anyone—walk away from Ben Siegel and not risk paying a terrible price? And what if she found her association with him as thrilling as it was frightening?

"Jesus, Mr. Siegel," said the policeman. "I'm sorry. Jesus, honest." He tipped his cap.

Lola, her cheeks pallid, released an audible breath.

"Really miss, I didn't mean nothin'. You have a good day. A wonderful day. God bless." He shuffled back to his patrol car, his head shaking.

Ben snickered then inched the Caddy forward.

Lola wondered whether he did so in deference to her or to mock the policeman.

As they drove west, Lola scanned the earth-hugging shops, restaurants, drug stores, bungalows and garden apartments punctuated by palm trees and dominated by a vast blue sky. Despite Ben's earlier maneuvers behind the wheel, California's scale and pace struck her as the polar opposite of Manhattan's.

"You see the Pacific when you played out here?" Ben asked.

"I confess that I did not." Rehearsals, the press and sleep had consumed her.

Ben laughed. "There's a first time for everything."

No doubt the ocean was lovely, but why the rush? She and Fernando had arrived in Los Angeles only hours earlier. They were met by Heshy Kaplan and another of Ben's lieutenants, Mickey Cohen, a former boxer once involved with Ben and Meyer's associates in Chicago. A suite awaited them at the Spanish-style Roosevelt Hotel on Hollywood Boulevard. It included a piano and offered a view of the famous HOLLYWOODLAND sign up in the hills. Ben had secured the suite at a weekly rate unimaginably low.

Their bags still packed, they celebrated with champagne. As they nibbled on salad, fruit, bagels and pastries sent up from the kitchen with the hotel's compliments, Ben extolled the wonders of Southern California. "San Francisco? You might as well be livin' at the North Pole." Then he announced big news. He'd contacted an agent, who'd take Lola on. She was scheduled to meet the producer of a low-budget comedy shooting after July Fourth. "What they call a look-see. They already signed a dame to play the part, but you never know."

As anxious as she was elated, Lola wondered if Papa and Mama experienced the same reservations when the family reached New York. She also wondered why they remained in her thoughts. She'd long determined that her survival depended in great part on cauterizing her family memories and their accompanying false hopes of acceptance. After all, Papa and Mama practically decreed Albert dead to them before he departed their lives and so rejected Lola. Yet during times of uncertainty, the ethereal memories of Mama and Papa came to her unbidden. Even after they rejected her, did she still require their comforting presence?

Clinging to the flaw she feared could undo her, she vaguely recollected Papa hoisting Anshel above the railing of a nameless ship to see the Statue of Liberty and uttering words just beyond her recall. Finding herself in permanent residence on the other end of the continent and preoccupied with a distant memory defiantly incomplete left her confused.

When Ben suggested a drive—just the two of them—she feared that her face revealed her confusion as clearly as the marquee of Grauman's Chinese Theater across from the Roosevelt displayed movie titles.

They continued in silence. Nearing downtown Santa Monica, Ben turned left on Lincoln Boulevard, a section of California 1, which ran up and down most of the state along or near the coastline. At California Avenue, he made a right towards the ocean. "Out there," he said. "Just past the three-mile mark. We had gambling ships. The Feds cracked down. They don't like anyone havin' fun except what *they* think's good for 'em."

Before them rose a giant roller coaster dominating the Venice Amusement Pier, one of a string of amusement parks jutting out over the Pacific along the endless beach. Spurning the pier's image of gaiety, Lola's thoughts turned to a beach thousands of miles away. Two days earlier, the last of 75,000 French troops followed in the wake of the British army and retreated to England from Dunkirk. If America entered the war, no longer a remote possibility despite the vehement opposition of Charles Lindbergh and the America Firsters, would California escape its ravages? Would she and Fernando lose their place of refuge?

Ben pulled into a parking lot.

A young man—blonde and tan—ran towards them. "Got it, Mr. Siegel," he said with a broad smile. His white teeth sparkled as if he appeared in ads for Ipana or Colgate's dental cream. Lola couldn't recall seeing anyone that cheerful in New York.

Ben tossed him the keys.

Lola unfastened the ribbon beneath her chin.

They entered the amusement zone. Twelve hundred feet long and five hundred wide, the pier offered dining, dancing, games of chance and thrill rides.

Ben took a deep breath. "That smell."

"The ocean?"

"Money." He took her to the roller coaster's ticket window. "The Giant Dipper," he said. "Eighty-five feet high. Thirty-three hundred long. Takes maybe two minutes to ride."

"You certainly know a lot of interesting details," she said.

"In my business, you want to know things."

Lola remembered going to Coney Island with girlfriends in the summer of 1927, an outing concealed from her parents. They rode the Cyclone, which had just opened, getting off weak-kneed but exhilarated.

"They got a carousel here if that's more your speed," Ben said.

Lola hesitated to answer.

"It's your call, but here's the thing. You ride the carousel, all you do is go around in circles. Like if you stayed back in New York. You bein' from Cuba, maybe you can't see it, but New York? That's yesterday. California's the end of the rainbow. Hell, that's why you came out here, right? But that ain't all. Las Vegas, that's a town in Nevada, next state east. Railroad stop in the middle of the desert. They built the Boulder Dam near there. Anyway, just you wait." He pointed up to the arching track that represented the Giant Dipper's highest point. "You want to be somebody, you gotta go new places, handle the ups and downs. Maybe you toss your cookies now and then but so what? Who doesn't?" His eyes searched hers.

Lola reached for the ribbon on her hat and tied a double bow.

Two weeks later, the early evening sky flourishing its last streaks of purple and pink above the intersection of Hollywood and Vine, Lola and Fernando entered the Brown Derby. Manhattanites at heart—how far away Havana seemed—they'd walked from the Roosevelt, although Fernando was taking driving lessons from Heshy Kaplan.

At one end of a leather-upholstered booth sat Desi Arnaz. A striking redhead accompanied him. The table displayed four drinks, a slice of lime perched on the rim of each glass.

"I ordered Cuba Libres," said Desi. "Anyway, everyone who is anyone in Hollywood comes to the Brown Derby for lunch or dinner."

"I have heard the food is, how you would say, unexceptional," Fernando said.

"The food?" said Desi. "Amigo, the food is not important. It's about seeing and being seen. Same as New York."

The redhead's crimson fingernails tapped a faux Morse Code distress signal on her bread-and-butter plate.

Desi clapped his hands to his cheeks. "Ay, ay, ay!" He nodded to the redhead. "So let me introduce you to Lucille Ball. She's shooting *Too Many Girls* with me a few blocks away at RKO."

The corners of Lucille's mouth, her lips the crimson of her nails, remained unmoved.

"Lucille," said Desi, "this is the wonderful Cuban couple I told you about. Lola and Fernando." Before Lola could speak, he raised his glass. "To Lola Flores, who wrote me a new hit song and who's gonna be one of Hollywood's brightest stars."

Lucille glowered. "You're not thinking of getting in the way of *my* career, are you?"

Lola, taken aback, shook her head.

Lucille nodded. "Good answer. You stick to singing and comedy like on Broadway, and there'll be room in Hollywood for both of us." She leaned towards Lola. "But if you have other ideas, watch out, sister. I've been busting my ass in B-movies and on the radio way too long."

"But Lucille," said Fernando, "you are a *star*."

Lucille offered a feeble smile. "Tell that to the movers and shakers in this town so my agent can triple my fee. And *that* won't get it up to where it should be." She lifted her glass towards Lola's.

A familiar voice called out, "Hold that pose. Wish I had a photographer here." A flashbulb went off. "Oh, I do." Walter Winchell, his hat pushed back on his head, nudged Fernando closer to Lola and squeezed into the booth.

Lucille's eyes narrowed. "Jesus, Walter, can't you ever leave anyone alone?"

Winchell raised an eyebrow. "Lucille Ball and Lola Flores—you both look great, and you, too, Desi—together at the Brown Derby? You mind the publicity?"

"Thank you, Walter," Lola said. "We certainly do not."

"At least I got *one* of you properly trained." He turned to Fernando. "Señor Fallon's another story, 'cause somebody's gotta do the dirty work behind the scenes."

Fernando attempted to smile.

"Thanks for the lesson in charm," said Lucille. "And what are you doing so far from New York?"

"My readers like me to dish dirt from Hollywood every now and then."

"Walter," Fernando cut in, "is Lola's drink in that photo?"

Winchell reached for Lola's Cuba Libre then snapped his fingers at the photographer. "The negative on that. Destroy it. Can't have alcohol in a shot with Lola Flores. As far as Mr. and Mrs. United States know, she's a teetotaler." He drank from Lola's glass. "Don't get me wrong, Fernando. Lola Flores is one of my favorite people. My readers'll want to know she's getting back into the spotlight. Or should I say going under the Klieg lights?"

"We will also put together a new band," said Fernando.

Desi leaned forward. "Maybe I can sit in for a few shows."

Winchell ignored Desi and spoke to Lola. "A word to the wise, kid. California sunshine can burn."

"Walter," said Lola, "you make Hollywood sound dangerous."

Lucille rested a hand on Lola's arm. "Walter's just warning you that even with the right friends, most actresses get ahead in this business by figuring out who they have to fuck."

"Such language!" Walter shot back with mock amazement.

Lucille pointed a finger at Walter's nose. "New York's not the only place where kids grow up rough and tumble. For a good-looking girl, life's not easy anywhere."

Lola looked down into her lap.

*Two weeks past Albert's eighteenth birthday. Three months before graduation. Albert plays Chopin. Attempts to please István Heller. A Jew from Budapest. Former concert star. Determined to give the world its next Heller. Equally devoted to his terrier-like Affenpinscher. Béla.*

*Heller listens from the kitchen. Takes a kettle from the stove. Returns to the living room. Shelves lined with books. Shakespeare, Dickens, Goethe, Heine, Hugo, Flaubert. In English, German, French. A great musician must read to develop his soul. Places a silver tea set on a small table. Sips Pálinka. Traditional fruit brandy. Reddens. Bellows, "Nem, nem, nem!" Continues sotto voce. "You are attempting to play a Chopin etude, not one of those horrid jazz or Latin songs you are humming when you enter my apartment. For Chopin, you must listen to the deep beauty of the melody and not just play the notes."*

*Albert adjusts his technique.*

*Heller downs more Pálinka. Again rebukes Albert. "You must let the melody wander. It must not be a slave to your left hand. When a note decays, you cannot pound on the next like some ironworker building one of those beastly skyscrapers."*

*Albert wishes he was anywhere else. Preferably one of the clubs where he plays music he really loves.*

*Heller scolds. "You must match the volume of the previous note to connect all the notes as if the piece is being sung. Yield to your passion."*

*Albert repeats the passage.*

*Heller clutches Albert's shoulders. "Passion," he hisses into his right ear.*

*Albert's hands stumble on the keyboard.*

*Heller yanks him up from the piano bench. Leads him to a chair. Bends him over. Holds his head down.*

*Albert's cheeks flush. Does Heller think he's a naughty child? That he can spank him? Humiliate him? Attempts to stand.*

*Heller pushes him down.*

*Albert again tries to rise. Again fails. Finds himself immobile.*

*Heller unbuckles Albert's belt. Unbuttons Albert's fly.*

*Albert's trousers tumble. Undershorts drop. He attempts to cry out. Bleats like a lamb.*

"Those Shirley Temple images the studios put out?" said Walter. He shook his head. "Hollywood's a nasty town."

"New York isn't?" asked Lucille.

"New York *is*," Winchell said. "Only, the Big Apple doesn't pretend otherwise."

Lucille scowled. "That's where the difference ends. They're both run by bankers, and you know what *they* did to this country."

Winchell placed his hand over his heart. "Miss Ball, you're not one of those Hollywood Reds, are you? Career moving along nicely thanks to all the freedom Uncle Sam sees that you enjoy—life, liberty and all that—but secretly in love with Joe Stalin?"

Desi rolled his shoulders. "Walter, this is getting a little out of hand."

Lucille patted Desi's arm. "That treaty Stalin signed with Hitler last year? If I was a Communist, Walter, I'd have left the party two seconds after I got the news."

"If?" said Winchell. He signaled a waiter for another Cuba Libre. "A word from a pal. Any connection you ever had to the Party could come back to bite you."

A new drink appeared.

"The way the French surrendered Paris last week," Winchell said, "a man needs a little extra fortification."

Lola mourned the fall of Paris, of course, but who spoke for Warsaw? The Nazis were cramming Jews into a ghetto.

Winchell raised his glass and proposed a toast. "To Lucille Ball and Lola Flores. Two dolls as American as apple pie. Each, of course, in her own way."

"Walter," said Lucille, "you've had one too many."

"You think? Well, here's what *I* think. Mr. and Mrs. United States'll want one thing above all from Tinseltown when Roosevelt gets us into that war in Europe, which he *will*."

"And what's that?" Lucille asked.

"Old-fashioned, flag-waving patriotism. You can wave that flag, right Lucille?"

Lucille hoisted her middle finger.

"Now, Lola Flores here." Winchell motioned the photographer closer. "She had her chance to prove she's a patriot, as a mutual friend will testify. He wasn't all that happy about the way things turned out. But happy endings, they're for the movies."

# JULY 1940

## ESMERELDA O'BRIEN

Lola's key light came on in the small studio where, Ben as good as his word, she would perform her first screen test only weeks after arriving in Hollywood. Costumed in a powder-blue waitress uniform accented by a white apron, she took her mark in front of a small counter displaying a coffee pot, several white mugs and a wire rack containing three faux pies from the studio's prop department.

The cameraman nodded to the director, who glanced back at the film's producer, Bradford Townes, a slim man in his early forties with brown, wavy hair and the conspicuous absence of a tan. Townes's camel-hair sport coat and plaid slacks implied he was about to meet someone for afternoon drinks, probably at the Chateau Marmont above Sunset Boulevard. Hollywood personages went there to defy the Hays Code, which not only censored films but sought to restrain actors and others in the business from behavior it classified as immoral, and which proved all too common. Next to Townes and a decade older stood Lola's agent, Irving Shapiro, natty in a dark gray suit befitting a studio executive, which he'd once been. Doris Edelman, the script reader Shapiro had lured from Metro, accompanied him. Several years older than Lola, she countered her boss's solemnity with tangerine slacks and a forest green blouse. The outfit suggested a color-saturated palm tree. The left side of her chest displayed a round porcelain pin illustrating a geisha clad in a blue-and-gold kimono. She wore her raven hair swept to the left.

"Mr. Fallon?" the cameraman called. He tapped his forehead.

Fernando made several small adjustments to Lola's wig.

The director brought Lola's attention towards an assistant on the other side of the camera. "Tom's reading the lines of your husband Joey, but you look and speak right to camera. And remember what I told you earlier. This isn't Broadway. Don't play to the back row. Everyone in a movie theater can hear you even when you whisper."

"Even when you pass gas," Doris Edelman called out. "The Hays people won't let you say fart."

The tension eased from Lola's shoulders.

The assistant held up several pages from the script of *A Long Way from Brooklyn*. Shooting had been scheduled to begin three days earlier but was suspended after Walter Winchell, back in New York, scooped Hollywood's "unholy trio" of Hedda Hopper, Louella Parsons and Sheila Graham. The actress playing the role for which Lola would test had undergone an abortion two months earlier in Tijuana. A contract player with only minor roles on her résumé, she lacked even minimal leverage. The studio dumped her.

Doris Edelman caught a lingering revelation of uncertainty in Lola's eyes and flashed a thumb's up.

Lola appreciated the vote of confidence. The movie called for only a three-week shooting schedule and paid a modest fee, but *A Long Way from Brooklyn* offered a perfect vehicle for her Hollywood debut. Moreover, thanks to Irving's long relationship with Ben Siegel, the stylist's guild accepted Fernando as a union member, so he could deal with Lola's wardrobe, wigs and make-up.

The script, hardly challenging, suited Lola's talents. She would play Esmerelda O'Brien, a Cuban-born housewife. She and her Irish-American husband, a good-hearted gangster—Lola thought of Heshy Kaplan—flee New York after a rival falsely accuses Joey of ratting on the mob. They open a diner in a small Iowa town. Naturally, the couple struggles to fit in. Meanwhile, the lingering Depression threatens to torpedo their fresh start. Then, as Joey repents the mess he's made of his life and vows to go straight, Esmerelda adds Cuban touches to the corn-fed menu. The diner's business picks up. At the end of the fourth reel, Joey and Esmerelda save the town from two toughs sent from the big city. The locals embrace them as their own.

Another crew member brought down the top of a clapperboard.

The director called, "Action."

Once again, Lola felt herself reborn.

# OCTOBER 1940

# BUT WHAT DID LOLA FLORES WANT?

Having changed gowns from candy-apple red to sequined silver, Lola bounded onto the stage at the Cocoanut Grove. She was ready for the second half of her opening-night show. The first had gone well, although it took three numbers to calm her nerves. It had been a long time since she'd performed in front of an audience, and the past two weeks had distressed her with yet another crisis of the soul. Albert had reappeared and pled with her to accompany him to Yom Kippur services. She refused. The studio had rushed *A Long Way from Brooklyn* into theaters. Fernando could provide Albert with a decent suit and hat, but Lola Flores' image splashed across one-sheets and billboards exposed her to the kind of mass scrutiny felons received on post-office *Wanted* notices. Albert kvetched for days before retreating.

Lola played the introduction to "Ay, Ay, Ay!" The full house erupted with vigorous applause. The audience's embrace added another magical element to the club's fairytale setting—an Arabian Nights ambiance conveyed by arches inspired by a sultan's palace, ornate hanging lamps, palm trees and a curved bandstand tented by a canopy of burgundy and gold.

Ecstatic, Lola blew a kiss towards a long, white-clothed table bordering the dance floor. At its center, amidst flowers and champagne glasses, Ben Siegel held court. His girlfriend Virginia Hill—he remained married to Esta—sat at his right along with the dashing movie star George Raft. Then came Betty Grable, just moved over to Fox, Irving and Adele Shapiro, and Fernando. To Ben's left sat another dapper Hollywood star, Cary Grant, squiring RKO's latest starlet—Lola couldn't remember her name—but seemingly uninterested in her. The young hopeful chatted with Desi

Arnaz, who would soon sit in with the band on congas. Seated further on were Lucille Ball—one eye on Lola, one on Desi—Bradford Townes and Doris Edelman.

Scattered among the Hollywood luminaries and downtown business leaders, Hedda Hopper, Louella Parsons and Sheila Graham occupied tables far enough apart to satisfy egos as mammoth as any of the stars their columns created and destroyed. In a far corner, a stringer for Walter Winchell scribbled in a notebook as did local reporters. Heshy Kaplan, Mickey Cohen and half-a-dozen broad-shouldered men in dark suits monitored the crowd.

After finishing her classic novelty hit, Lola began Sindo Garay's "The Afternoon." The song celebrated a woman who inspired the kind of love Lola conceded she would never know.

> *The light burns in your eyes*
> *And if you open them, it will dawn.*
> *When you close them it seems*
> *The afternoon is dying.*

Ben stood and swayed to the music. His guests followed, inspiring the rest of the audience to join them. As Lola played and sang, her towering hat of flowers rocked gently. Another of Fernando's engineering marvels, it drew gasps and cheers when Lola first appeared. At ringside, Bob Hope, who'd hosted the Academy Awards at the Cocoanut Grove the previous February and stopped by Lola's dressing room before the show, pressed his hand to his heart.

After the show, Ben and his entourage, along with several audience members of sufficient eminence to pass muster with Heshy and Mickey, crammed into Lola's dressing room. Doris elbowed her way through the crowd. She wore a white blouse, a Japanese pendant with two cranes, their bills touching, and a fitted silver jacket with wide lapels and three large buttons. Her dark, flowing skirt proved to be slacks. She kissed Lola on both cheeks. "Remember," she whispered, "we have an appointment tomorrow afternoon."

The taxi cruised west on Melrose, crossed Fairfax, turned left a few blocks on and pulled up to a small bungalow, its stucco and trim painted an indifferent beige. A black Oldsmobile occupied the carport.

Lola stared. The house came nowhere close to matching her expectation.

"There a problem, miss?" the driver asked. He was either ignorant of the identity of his carefully disguised fare or too used to driving film stars to invade their privacy.

Lola handed him the slip of paper on which she'd printed Doris's address.

"This is it," he said.

Lola paid then walked up the cracked concrete pathway. It bisected a small front yard spread with crushed rock the color of the moon and just as devoid of greenery. She wished she'd asked the taxi to remain. The driver obviously had been mistaken. Hoping she could use the residents' phone to call another cab, she climbed three concrete steps to the bare porch. The door opened. Lola did a double take worthy of an actor in the silent era.

Doris greeted her in an outfit that might have served as a costume in the previous year's Hollywood hit, *The Wizard of Oz*: shimmering cornflower blue blouse, peach slacks and silver slippers with ruby bows.

Lola grappled with doubt. She'd selected a peach day-dress with a modest neckline and short sleeves, just the thing for a matron wishing to go about her day unnoticed. Doris's ensemble made her feel dowdy.

Entering the living room, Lola wondered if she'd departed reality not for the Emerald City but for Wonderland and followed Alice down the rabbit hole. The brick-red walls practically vibrated. On either side of a white marble-topped coffee table stood matching loveseats, one upholstered in turquoise, the other in cobalt blue. To her left, an antique Japanese screen displayed a pulsating red-orange sun against a backdrop of gold. The wall to her right exhibited a watercolor of an ethereal white house next to a blue pond surrounded by cherry trees with pink blossoms in full bloom. Next to it hung two framed fans. Each displayed a Japanese woman, black hair piled high and fastened with gold pins. The profiled women gazed at each other, their expressions filled with desire.

Doris went to the fireplace, faced with bronze-colored tiles, and pointed to a foot-high porcelain cat embellished in red, blue, gold and green, its right paw raised. "For good luck," she said. "In this town, you need all the luck you can get."

Lola noted a print above the fireplace, something altogether different—Picasso's *Nude Woman with a Necklace*. On the mantel and returning to the room's Japanese theme, an oak stand displayed a curved knife with an eight-inch blade, black-and-gilt handle and matching scabbard. Lola drew closer. The polished steel mirrored her eyes. They displayed uneasiness.

"That's a kaiken," Doris said. "Handy if someone tries to break in, although I suppose a gun would be better. You can shoot a gun from a distance. Except guns scare me. As you can figure, I went to Japan a few years back. Me and a girlfriend. Everything they do there is art." She placed a hand on Lola's right shoulder. "Please, sit."

Lola chose the blue sofa and took off her sunhat.

Doris pointed to Lola's head. "My mother wears a wig but for different reasons. We're Jewish, but she's from the old school. Holds onto things. My father's gone, she won't leave the house in Boyle Heights." She raised her hand to her right cheek. "Jesus, I'm running on. Tea?"

Lola shifted her weight, feeling awkward for no apparent reason other than that she owed Doris a great deal. Over the past three months, Doris had guided her through the new world of Hollywood. Several times during shooting *A Long Way from Brooklyn*, she drove to the studio from this very house, where she did most of her work, to offer her support. After the movie wrapped, Doris turned Irving away from the schlock scripts other agents would have pursued to make a quick buck. She also encouraged Lola and Fernando as they assembled the new band.

"Something stronger?" Doris asked.

Despite the transformative kitchen fire in New York and Walter Winchell elevating her to a sham moral high ground, Lola had never gone teetotal. But this didn't seem like the right time. "Tea would be lovely," she said.

Doris went to the kitchen.

Lola lit a cigarette then stubbed it out in a porcelain ashtray enameled with pink and violet camellias. It would be rude to smoke without her hostess's permission.

Doris returned with a white tea set hand-painted with red plum blossoms. "So, let's cut to the chase which, you should know, is the best part of any western. Irving says a couple of studios want to sign you."

Lola remained deadpan, as if a smile would expose her as overeager, a real Hollywood greenhorn which, despite her one movie role, she was. But Doris's good news called for a response. "That is wonderful," she said.

"Maybe. Maybe not," said Doris. "If you'd have stepped off the bus from Peoria or Cedar Rapids, the ink on your contract would be long dry. You'd be thrilled to get a paycheck while they trained you then put you to work. Maybe they'd lend you to another studio. For a pretty penny, of course. Maybe you *wouldn't* work. The studios call the shots. That's the way the system works. With exceptions."

"Exceptions?"

Cary Grant called his own shots and got a ton per picture, Doris explained as she poured tea, now properly brewed. But how many Cary Grants were there? "Anyway, *A Long Way from Brooklyn* may have been a B-flick, but what's important is what *Daily Variety* said about Lola Flores. The studios smell money like a shark smells blood."

Lola loosed a smile. "Then Irving should get me a very *good* contract."

Doris stuck out her lower lip then withdrew it. With what passed for a good contract, Lola might make enough money to keep up her wardrobe—if she confined her shopping to May Company—but only until the studio brought in another fresh face. "The turnover—" The key to building a career was landing the right roles in the right productions. What that required represented a story folks back in Peoria and Cedar Rapids never saw on the silver screen. "Let's be honest. You're no kid. But that won't matter. Practically every studio executive, producer and director in this town's still gonna want to yank your panties down around your ankles, which I assume you've figured out. I mean, coming from Broadway."

Lola understood but couldn't help cringing.

"And don't count on Ben Siegel. Sure, he pulls the levers behind the Screen Extras Guild and the studios pay him off to avoid them striking, the stagehands, the Teamsters—"

Lola shook her head then raised her hand to keep her wig from slipping. She knew all about Ben but thought his business interests, about which he never spoke, lay outside Hollywood.

Doris stared in astonishment, not at Lola's wig but in response to an innocence she hadn't expected. Everyone knew Ben Siegel was involved in more than gambling and women, not only muscling in on the unions but also shaking down many of the industry's top stars. "How do you think he can afford that mansion in Holmby Hills?"

Lola, aping Ben and in a display of loyalty to him, balled her right hand into a fist.

Doris placed a hand on top of it. "Look, all I'm saying is, I know Ben Siegel's been good to you. He thinks you're special, and he's not the only one." But the situation wasn't all that simple, as Irving would confirm. The not-so-gentlemanly gentlemen who ran the studios had *their* connections, and those connections went all the way to the top where even Ben Siegel had to watch his step. "Besides, I hear he's skating on thin ice, legal-wise. So, when some producer—"

"Bradford Townes never—"

"Bradford Townes is a homosexual. I'm sure you know what that is."

"Yes. Of course."

Doris squeezed Lola's fist with the gentleness of a housewife assessing the ripeness of a peach. "Me? I say, live and let live. Some of my best friends if you know what I mean. There's nothing wrong with people hitting the sack with whoever they want. But Hollywood's a helluva lot tougher town in that regard than New York."

Lola fixed her gaze on a vase filled with chrysanthemums.

Doris withdrew her hand. "Am I shocking you?"

Lola shook her head.

"Well, for whatever it's worth, here's where I spill my guts." Doris had been married once. The bastard started cheating right after their honeymoon on Catalina Island. The sex? Maybe Lola had heard the old joke: When sex is good, it's great. When it's bad, it's still good. "Don't believe it. Men don't have the tenderness a woman wants." She rested her hand on Lola's knee. "What a woman *needs*."

Lola's heart raced. Clearly, Doris wanted her. But what did Lola Flores want? She found Doris attractive, but what of it? The prospect of another physical relationship, even if entered freely, left her apprehensive. Frida and Manuel had wanted her and accepted her as she was. Would Doris turn away from Lola's body? Or had she already seen through her ruse? Either way, there was no escaping practical matters. Could she and Doris—she and anyone—keep their involvement concealed despite her show-marriage to Fernando? And when the affair ended—if she understood anything, it was that Hollywood poisoned relationships—would Doris, out of frustration or spite, reveal Lola's possession of the last vestige of Albert Sobel? Lola looked towards the fans with the two Japanese women. An artist had determined that each would spend the rest of her existence gazing endlessly at the object of her desire, never touching, never being touched. But a woman of flesh and blood had every right to determine her own fate. She placed her hand on Doris's.

Doris pulled hers away.

Stunned, Lola drew back. "I am sorry," she said.

Doris shook her head to assert Lola's guiltlessness. "It's just that I've had my heart broken more times than I care to count." Single women? After a few months, they always seemed to find someone else. Married women? Sooner or later, they had second thoughts, feared losing the husband, the children, the house. "You end up staring at four walls again. They may be beautiful walls—"

Lola found herself lurching between laughter and tears. Doris cared enough to reveal her own true self, to expose her vulnerability, something Frida and Manuel never had done. More, Doris understood that two women being attracted to each other and free to act on that attraction were perfectly normal. Doris Edelman and Lola Flores might be unusual, but what could be more normal than a human being's longing for intimacy with someone whose soul touched hers? Lola smiled.

Doris stroked Lola's cheek.

That touch, tender and resolute, evoked two memories. Lola recalled the first time she'd flown. High above the earth, she held her hand over the window and hid an entire city far below. The simple, childlike gesture reminded her that she possessed significant power over her life subject only to exercising her will. Then there were the photos *Life* ran in 1937 of the ill-fated German airship Hindenburg. Almost the length of the Titanic, its tail fins displaying the dreadful swastika, the Zeppelin hovered above the airfield at Lakehurst, New Jersey. Although the event had concluded, as witnessed by fixed black-and-white images on coated paper, Lola couldn't help raising her hand to her mouth not only in sympathy with the passengers onboard but as if her display of compassion somehow held the power to halt the inevitable. Rendering her good intentions hopeless, the magazine documented the Hindenburg's final moments as it burst into flames and plunged earthward.

A tear descended from the corner of Doris's left eye.

Lola lifted her hand and wiped it away.

# DECEMBER 1940

# MORNING SUNSHINE, AFTERNOON RAIN

Fernando, seated at the small dining table, looked up from *The Hollywood Reporter*, open alongside *Daily Variety*, the *Examiner* and the *Los Angeles Times*. His creamy yellow sport shirt and pale blue slacks would be entirely appropriate when he left to spend the remainder of the day at the small office he rented on Vine Street. He lifted a carafe and poured Lola coffee.

Lola kissed the top of his head then stretched her arms as if trying to touch the living room ceiling. The way she felt this morning, perhaps the sky. Christmas season was in full swing, although in Los Angeles the lights and music seemed far less necessary for lifting moods than in New York. Chanukah remained weeks off, the first night falling on Christmas Eve. She and Fernando would light candles. Dropping her arms, she extracted a pack of Sweet Caporals from the pocket of her pink satin robe. Buoyed by the sunshine filling the suite at the Roosevelt, she turned the pack in her hand then dropped it back into her pocket.

Fernando waited until Lola added cream and sugar to her coffee then said, "I do not wish to nag."

Lola frowned. Why did Fernando constantly attempt to burst her bubble, despite the weather stretched thin? Not that he could. Not if she refused to let him.

"Please be assured I will not repeat myself," he said.

"Until you do," she shot back.

"You are playing with fire," he said. He held his right thumb and index finger together and ran them across his lips.

Lola slowly stirred then sipped her coffee to give herself time to sort matters out. She thought they'd resolved their disagreement the previous evening. "This is narishkeit."

"Foolishness? Really?"

Lola grimaced. What did Fernando have to be concerned about? Her smoking? Her voice sounded as powerful as ever, full of color from light to sultry. Her drinking? Given all she'd been through, it could only be classified as moderate. She saw nothing wrong with an occasional social drink. Or two. Three at most. Excluding rare exceptions when a fourth might be perfectly fitting. She'd learned her lesson, retained the memory—if vaguely—of the night she teetered through the *Follies*. More than one night. But that was before Connecticut. Yes, she fell off the wagon afterward, but she took control of herself, learned to contain her moods. As Ben said, New York embodied the past. California offered everyone a fresh start. She'd toed the mark through every scene of *A Long Way from Brooklyn* and sailed through her shows at the Cocoanut Grove.

As far as marriage to Fernando went, the press and public saw only a normal couple. A *usual* couple. All the while, they remained free from the complications that confronted a typical husband and wife. Their finances were sound. They even planned to buy a house. Something modest nearby. Fernando also wanted to buy land. He advised her that shrewd investors were gobbling up all the San Fernando Valley that remained available. Someday, when Los Angeles outgrew the confines of the Basin, they'd cash in.

Her career? The run at the Cocoanut Grove proved such a success, Fernando fielded offers from major clubs up and down the West Coast for January and February. On the horizon was a new movie.

Let no one take Lola Flores for ungrateful. Fernando had become the picture of an enterprising businessman, managing two additional bands, one fronted by a former side man with Glenn Miller. And while Irving dealt with the studios, Fernando booked Lola Flores on all the top radio shows produced in Los Angeles.

Still, when she'd returned home the previous evening from a rare night off, Fernando expressed annoyance. Peevishness. The situation with Doris left him unsettled. This was new to him. Well, it was new to *her*. After years burdened by confusion, reluctance and frustration, she'd embraced a physical passion breathless, sweaty, ecstatic.

As Irving raced his custom-painted bronze Chrysler New Yorker up Pacific Coast Highway north of Santa Monica, Lola braced herself in the front passenger seat. Doris had suggested she sit with her in the rear, but Irving nixed that thought.

"Someone sees Lola Flores with a woman and thinks I'm their driver, then what? They take a picture of you two, sell it to one of the papers and the studios wonder if they've got another Garbo and Dietrich on their hands. The L-word if you know what I mean, and I know you do. Only, those dames still had big names then. Real clout. And don't look for Ben Siegel to play the cavalry riding to the rescue. Not now."

Behind Lola, Doris hummed Tommy Dorsey and Frank Sinatra's "Our Love Affair."

Lola studied the Pacific. Even in early December, it shone a brilliant blue. Undulating breakers frothed against the endless beach. Gulls soared and swooped over bobbing whitecaps. She imagined them fearless RAF Hurricanes and Spitfires dogging the Luftwaffe's Messerschmitts during the Battle of Britain. But even the Golden West endured a winter of sorts. Above the horizon, dark clouds mustered.

Irving pointed to a sign jutting skyward. It guided motorists to Carl's Sea Air Lodge, a popular restaurant, gas station and motel tucked beneath the palisades.

"Really," Doris said to Lola, "you should learn to drive. I'd have driven myself, but Irving insisted. Men having to be men and all."

"It's what we do," said Irving.

"Really?" Doris shot back. "This is nineteen-forty, for God's sake."

Irving remained unruffled. "Sorry Fernando couldn't join us," he said. "I'll phone him later. A courtesy."

"There is a problem?" Lola asked.

"How could there be a problem?" he returned. "But you eat in town at a place like Musso & Frank, everyone knows your business before they bring you your cheesecake." He coasted into a parking spot.

Inside, their booth, like all the others, offered a postcard view. Lola sat. Irving and Doris flanked her.

Irving ordered dry martinis.

Doris stroked Lola's thigh.

Lola contained her excitement. She wished she could bring herself to making a public display of their romance.

"Read the paper?" Irving asked. "The Royal Air Force bombed Dusseldorf and Turin."

Lola and Doris nodded with satisfaction.

The waiter brought their cocktails.

Irving proposed a toast. "To *Belle of the Tropics.*"

A week earlier, MGM had greenlighted production on a Busby Berkeley-style musical set in Havana. Moreover, Irving won Lola her name above the title, unheard of for an actress making her second film. Shooting would begin in March. He smiled at Doris then looked to Lola. "This is all on the Q.T., but the studio's got its eye on your co-star."

Lola stared at Irving.

"I'll give you a hint," he said. "A few weeks ago, he eloped with a beautiful redhead."

Doris smiled.

Lola's eyes went wide. "Desi?"

Irving clinked his glass against Lola's then Doris's.

The martini set off a tremor in Lola almost as powerful as the explosion she felt each time she and Doris made love.

Doris's smile collapsed. "We all love Desi, but that's not why you brought us all the way out here."

Lola looked at Doris as if she'd spoken a foreign language.

Irving turned contemplative.

"What you want to tell us, Irving," said Doris, "is that the studio *wants* to sign Desi—"

"It does."

"But—"

"A bump in the road."

"Bullshit. They're putting *Belle* on hold."

"This bump," Lola said. "It must be a very big one."

Doris scowled. "The studio and the banks are nervous, aren't they Irving? And it's not about Italy invading Greece or what the Japanese are doing in China and Manchuria."

Irving signaled the waiter for another round.

Doris pointed at Irving. "I thought you'd shoot straight with us."

"Fuck!" Irving said. "You heard."

Doris lowered her hand. "I work from home, not a tomb."

Lola looked from Doris to Irving. She had no idea what they were talking about. How long would it take to get her finger on the pulse of Hollywood?

Irving shook his head. "The war in Europe and Asia. And all the talk about America getting involved, our boys getting dropped into the thick of it. Uncertainty makes the banks skittish."

"Who are *you?*" said Doris. "Some radio commentator like H.V. Kaltenborn? Get to the fucking point."

Lola blanched. There could, she realized, be only *one* point. The studio had uncovered her affair with Doris.

The waiter placed fresh cocktails on the table.

"It's Ben," Irving said. "It hurts to say it, because my family and his go back to Brooklyn before my folks moved us out here. I'm a lot older, but we're cousins. Second, actually. Could be third. Anyway, mishpuchah."

"Family," Doris translated.

Lola wanted to scream, *I know what mishpuchah means. I know more about the two of you than you could ever imagine.* She raised the fresh martini to her lips and held it there while she thought things through. The secret she and Doris worked so hard to keep appeared to be safe. Yet Ben, who'd done so much to advance her career, might end up destroying it.

Irving wiped his nose. "In August, when they arrested Ben for killing Harry Greenberg? It was all over the papers."

Lola shook her head. "But the district attorney dropped the case."

"Insufficient evidence," Irving said, "but plenty for the studios to worry about." In California, Ben kept his nose clean—at least in public. Palled around with Louis Mayer and Jack Warner, guys who said what pictures got made and who worked. Guys who knew exactly what Ben was and how to keep their names and photos out of the papers. Then Ben got hit with the Greenberg murder rap. The story was too big to cover up. The people who ran Hollywood saw risks that would hit them where it hurt—at the box office. The way John and Jane Doe would see it, anyone associated with gangsters was damaged goods. "They say even bad publicity is good.

Bullshit. The industry's reputation could take a nosedive like some fighter plane shot down over the English Channel."

Doris shook her head. "I thought you had bigger cojones." She turned to Lola. "You know what *that* means."

Lola feigned a look of modesty intended for Irving, although she wanted to say, *yes. In Yiddish its baitsim. Balls.*

"As far as Ben goes," Doris said, "the heat's on for now, sure, but Louis Mayer and Jack Warner, they've got cojones in spades. They'll let things settle down then get back to business." This was your classic tempest in a teapot. No studio would ever pass up a chance to make money, and a lot of people saw Lola Flores as one of Hollywood's newest meal tickets. Shooting on *Belle* would only be delayed until April or May. "June the latest."

"From your lips to God's ears," said Irving. He stood. "If you ladies will excuse me for a minute."

Lola's eyes followed Irving as he started for the men's room then scanned the restaurant.

"Looking for someone?" Doris asked.

"No, of course not. Irving invited us to lunch here for the privacy. Who would I—?"

"Ben Siegel?"

"Ben?"

"I see the way you look at him. Hear how you talk about him. He's a good-looking guy."

"Doris!"

"Or maybe you're looking for someone else. Someone new."

Lola gripped Doris's arm. "Doris, this is crazy."

"Or maybe *I'm* crazy. Falling for Lola Flores. Ben Siegel's pet. A woman—"

Lola shook her head.

Doris pressed her lips against Lola's ear. "Your secret's safe with me," she whispered. "You know how I like that little thing of yours. And what you do to me. If word got out, it wouldn't be only *you* finished in this town."

Lola stood.

Doris, her cheeks red, yanked her down. "Oh, God," she whimpered. "I just became unglued, didn't I?"

Lola draped her arm around Doris' shoulders.

"Just don't—" Doris stammered. "Don't look at anyone but *me.*"

# NOVEMBER 1941

# THE CLINK

The cell door slid open.

"Somebody should oil that fuckin' thing," Ben said.

"Sorry, Mr. Siegel," said the guard. "We'll have it taken care of, sir." Leaving the door open, he retreated down the hall.

Jerry Giesler, Ben's lawyer, took off his hat. A stocky native of Iowa with a receding hairline and black-framed glasses, he wore an elegant navy three-piece suit attesting to his many and very public triumphs. Akin to guiding someone to the witness stand, he pressed his free hand lightly against Lola's back.

Lola stepped forward.

"If I didn't know it was you," Ben said to her, "I wouldn't know it was you."

Playing yet another role, Lola had accompanied Giesler to the Hall of Justice in full costume: brunette wig streaked with gray and covered with a scarf of pallid greens and blues, librarian's eyeglasses with round, gray metal frames and shapeless brown coat draping a shapeless brown dress. Nondescript black flats with thick soles and a featureless black handbag completed the outfit. She carried identification procured by Giesler in the name of Martina Delgado.

No one looked at it.

Ben closed the purple curtain hung inside the cell's barred front. "They got me off in a corner by myself, but you can never play it too safe. Am I right, Jerry?"

Giesler nodded.

Ben smiled. He'd made himself at home, having surrendered five weeks earlier after the State of California again sought to prosecute him for the Harry Greenberg hit.

"So? Waddaya think?" Ben asked Lola.

"You are making the best of a difficult situation," Lola said, trying to keep Ben on an even keel. She felt anything but steady on her feet. Now or in a moment, Ben would ask her another, more crucial question: Why had she waited so long to see him? She'd rehearsed her answer, although it left her anything but confident about his reaction. Still, she'd deliver her lines as if she was on the set. *I have been so busy winding up shooting* Belle of the Tropics *before the studio rushes it to theaters for a Christmas-season opening. And they made me meet all these owners of independent theaters and speak with the press. No rest for the weary.* All that was true, but she feared his disappointment and the anger it could trigger.

Ben continued to smile.

Lola's stomach did cartwheels.

Giesler's anger offered timely relief. "Ben Siegel being locked up constitutes a travesty of justice. Especially with tomorrow being Thanksgiving."

Lola pursed her lips and blinked her eyes in a show of empathy.

Giesler offered a handkerchief.

She shook her head.

Giesler waved his hat in dismissal of the district attorney's efforts. "Ben's only been *accused* of murder, and you know what happened last time."

Ben laughed. "Jerry ain't a member of the tribe, if you get my drift, but wow. Back in 'thirty-one, he defends this guy, Alexander Pantages. The guy who owned all the theaters in the West."

"And Canada," added Giesler.

"It's Pantages' second trial. Rape. First trial, the guy lands a fifty-year sentence."

"He had a different attorney," said Giesler.

"Jerry gets the woman on the stand, he destroys her. Pantages walks."

Lola struggled to avoid revealing even the slightest expression suggesting she was sympathetic to the victim, which she was, and contemptuous of Jerry Giesler, which she couldn't afford to be. "But until your trial, you must stay in this awful place."

Ben shrugged. He might well have been pampering himself at the Beverly Wilshire or out in Santa Monica at the Georgian. He gestured towards his queen-size bed covered by a pale blue chenille spread. An oval throw rug in shades of caramel and brown covered a portion of the concrete floor and provided a home for a pair of oxblood leather slippers. A few feet away stood an easy chair adjacent to an end table topped by a brass lamp. A console table held a coffee pot, electric burner and radio beneath the cell's lone window, which overlooked downtown Los Angeles. Ben's hand darted to a small dining table nestled against the left wall—like the cell's two other concrete walls, chipped and cracked but newly whitewashed. "The Biltmore sends up my meals. Tomorrow, I figure on a pretty good spread." He placed the two matching dining chairs across from the easy chair but remained standing.

Lola sat, followed by Giesler.

Ben pointed towards the curtain. "Warms the place up, huh? Anyway, they let me out to see my dentist in Beverly Hills. I need a lot of work. At least, that's what *he* says. And I get visitors. Not just you. Esta, she don't come, but Virginia, she does. Also a few other ladies. But let's talk about Lola Flores. You showed real guts coming here."

Lola felt like a prisoner awarded a reprieve. Still, if the visit didn't end up stirring Ben's wrath, it risked incurring the anger of the studio, not to mention Fernando, Irving and worst of all, Doris. Doris would rage, given her continuing bouts of jealousy, each followed a day or two later by tearful remorse and passionate lovemaking that left them both elated and shaken.

Despite the risks, she knew she had no choice, although her visit to Ben involved less guilt than guile. Studio heads and producers were notoriously fickle. Her career was on the upswing, but it could nosedive as fast as a big shot lashing out when she resisted his advances. In that regard, Lola knew what Ben had left unsaid. Even from a jail cell, he could keep doors in Hollywood open to her. Or order them shut. She would preempt Ben's temper from igniting. "I owe you so much, Ben. I would never desert you."

"Nothing to worry about," he said. "Everyone knows how Jerry got this same charge dropped last year. Dockweiler, the D.A.? You bet your ass he'll drop the charges again once the trial starts."

Giesler stroked the brim of his fedora. "If we even go to trial."

Ben took Lola's hand. His eyes suggested neither anger nor amusement but an unfamiliar solemnity. "So?"

Lola's throat tightened.

"You gonna ask?"

Had he read her mind? But then, the conversation seemed only to follow its natural course. Her only practical stratagem was to play the innocent. "Ask what, Ben?"

He appeared to go along with it. "If I did it. Killed Big Greenie."

"I never thought—"

"C'mon. You *gotta* be wondering."

Lola had no way of knowing if Ben had killed Harry Greenberg, but she well knew he was capable of murder. She'd seen him shoot those two men in New York. And while he never regaled her with stories of his gangland activities, he understood that she knew who and what he was, and never pretended to be otherwise. Maybe she should have been ashamed of being here, of pledging her loyalty to a murderer, even if he hadn't done in Harry Greenberg. But she could never dismiss all that Ben had done for her, never forget where she would be without him. Society might condemn him as a vicious criminal, but she saw another side to him. Ben Siegel was and always would always be her Prince Charming. If the standard-bearers of American morals found that objectionable, let them look to their own lives—the family and friends whose misdeeds they overlooked, the errors and offenses they committed that would never stand up to the scrutiny of the commandments. Life was anything but simple, and only the simple-minded were quick to judge.

Ben laughed. "Looks like you're the only one in L.A. who don't have some action on the State of California versus Benjamin Siegel." He chucked her lightly under the chin. "I appreciate it, you coming to see me. You done what they call a mitzvah. A good deed. I won't forget."

Lola looked down at her feet. Would she be wearing old-woman's shoes like this in ten years? Twenty? Next year?

# DECEMBER 1941

# CHATEAU MARMONT

The waiter in the cramped, dimly lit Bar Marmont approached the booth in which Lola, Fernando, Doris and the Shapiros huddled. Irving waved him off. The last thing they needed was another bottle of champagne, he said. Two in the morning seemed a lot later than it used to. It was time to wind down the celebration.

That evening, *Belle of the Tropics* premiered at the Egyptian Theater despite the Japanese attack on Pearl Harbor five days earlier. The only component missing from the black-tie-and-evening-gown opening's formulaic gaiety was searchlights. Angelenos had begun covering their windows with blackout curtains and drapes, but the studio less feared guiding enemy bombers to the heart of America's motion picture industry than creating the image of Hollywood as unpatriotic. Press releases saluted the studio's enthusiastic response to FDR's call for Americans to carry on with their lives even as the nation prepared to strike back at Japan and go to war against its Axis partners Germany and Italy. *Belle of the Tropics* would open with filmland's brightest stars illuminating the festivities solely with their glamorous presence in defiance of marauders from the far side of the Pacific. Left unmentioned was the holiday season's considerable potential for box-office with entertainment more needed than ever.

A limousine took Lola and Fernando to the event. Doris arrived with the Shapiros. She made no effort to mask her displeasure at not accompanying the film's star.

Lola strutted the red carpet down the Egyptian's elongated courtyard, fans bunched on either side contained by red velvet ropes and jaded policemen. Her Persian-green gown and matching wrap shimmered.

Halfway to the theater's columned entry, she modeled one of the production's outrageous flower hats. Still photographers and newsreel cameramen flashed broad smiles as she struck poses ranging from voluptuous to comic.

When the movie concluded, Lola and Desi Arnaz appeared on stage to spirited applause.

Outside the Egyptian, a chill breeze blew across Hollywood Boulevard and wound its way into the Egyptian's courtyard. A studio minion placed a fox stole complete with tails over Lola's shoulders.

As she signed autographs, Lola felt as if she was ascending high above the crowd, free of gravity's restraints. Another Peter Pan. No, Tinker Bell. The weight of her achievement forced her to descend and anchored her in reality. Lola Flores stood on the threshold of Hollywood's pantheon, a star to be honored, loved and venerated, but always at the mercy of someone she might foolishly allow to get too close, offer a peek behind the curtain. How eloquently Shakespeare wrote of Julius Caesar's betrayal. Surely, some Brutus in a well-tailored suit or elegant dress skulked in the shadows, bided time before raising the dagger of blackmail or, in the name of morality, making a public declaration that Lola Flores was a depraved illusion, her deception an affront to everything that was right and good. The world, which preached loving one's neighbor and doing unto others, would receive the revelation with anything but empathy and compassion. The wounds it inflicted would be lethal, if not to her body, then to her soul. And all because people's vision was so narrow, their blind spots so wide. The Allies' chances to defeat the Axis were far greater than those of her emerging victorious doing battle with the self-righteous. This night's triumph sought to deceive her that Lola Flores' future was limitless. If she looked towards tomorrow free from delusion, she would find that the end was near.

Half an hour later a sobered Lola, feigning joy and accompanied by her entourage, met Desi and Lucille for a late supper at Ciro's. They were joined by Francis X. Riordan, who'd produced and directed, along with the film's co-stars and a flock of studio executives.

In the powder room, Lucille confided, *God, I wish I had your ability to carry off zany comedy.*

When the partiers dispersed after midnight, Doris insisted on drinks at Chateau Marmont, the white-walled hotel overlooking Sunset Boulevard and inspired by a chateau in France's Loire Valley.

Irving's Rolex now showing ten after two, he rose, joined by his wife. After requisite kisses, the Shapiros ambled towards the hotel's entrance to hand the valet the ticket for their car.

Fernando turned to Lola. "We also should go, cariña."

"*You* go," Doris said to Fernando. "Go back to that lovely Spanish-style house on Doheny. *You*." She kissed Lola on the cheek. "Not *her*."

"You are drunk," said Fernando.

"Could be. But not *too*. See, I have a surprise for Hollywood's newest star. I rented us a suite here. Us being Lola and me. It even has a kitchen 'cause they built this place as an apartment building. And I arranged it so we don't have to check out till tomorrow afternoon."

"You cannot be serious," said Fernando.

Doris crossed her eyes and turned her lips up into a smile. The contortion suggested Fanny Brice's Baby Snooks leaping out from the darkness in a carnival's house of horrors.

Fernando stared his disapproval then addressed Lola. "*Cariña*, you *must* come home with me."

Doris's expression shifted to disbelief. "The two of you, you've been in Hollywood what? A year? No, it's more." She tapped the side of her head to exhort them to think about where they were. Nobody at Chateau Marmont would snitch. The staff? Mute like Swiss bankers. The celebrities who carried on here? They knew better than to gossip and give the bloodhounds of the press something meaty to chew on. Back in 'thirty-three, Jean Harlow was screwing Clark Gable here right after marrying that cinematographer. Sure, insiders heard rumors, but the matter stayed under wraps. "And Scott Fitzgerald." She turned to Lola. "I hope you don't mind me bringing up Fitzgerald, since he had such a strained relationship with Ernest Hemingway, and it's too bad Hemingway doesn't keep in touch with you, but I loved *The Great Gatsby*, and there's *The Last Tycoon*. That's the unfinished novel they just published after Fitzgerald died near here a year ago. A lot of Hollywood bigshots are fuming, but fuck 'em. They have it coming. Anyway, Fitzgerald wrote here. Drunk every day. His readers—at least the people who used to read him—never heard a word. And that's just the tip of the iceberg."

Lola shook her head. "I understand what you are saying, but Fernando is right. I cannot do this."

Doris kissed Lola on the lips. "You can if you love me."

Shortly after noon the next day, Doris held up a glass in the kitchen of their suite at the Marmont. "Screwdriver. Hair of the dog and all that."

Lola took it. She needed it. A bit woozy, she felt nowhere near as good as she thought she looked in a pair of shimmering butterscotch silk pajamas, the top with a lace-bordered collar and pockets. Doris had them and a matching set in ruby red delivered the previous afternoon from a shop in Beverly Hills. She'd also dropped off practical items—changes of clothes and cloth bags for their gowns and dress shoes.

"Coffee's fresh," said Doris, standing at the small counter. After emptying half her own glass, she spread cream cheese on a bagel. The blade of the small silver knife was barely longer than her thumb and flared out towards a rounded tip the size of a nickel and almost as dull. "I'm starving," she said. "I had cream cheese and lox sent up. Pickled herring, too. I don't know how many Cubans like Jewish food the way you do, but it can't be many." She held the knife aloft. "Wait, I got it. You're a Marrano! Your ancestors in Spain converted to Catholicism but kept doing Jewish stuff in secret." She shrugged. "But they wouldn't know from bagels, would they?"

Lola cast Doris an expression of feigned ignorance.

Doris held the knife up. "You know, that little thing of yours looks circumcised."

"I cannot imagine what you are talking about," said Lola. "You drank quite a lot last night."

"Look who's calling the kettle— Not that it affected you and me in the sack." Doris spread cream cheese on another bagel. "Anyway, I had the newspapers sent up. Long story short, the trades and the regular rags all loved *Belle*." She nodded towards the living room.

Lola brought back the *Examiner*. "Since you have, how they say, tipped me off, I will read the reviews later. But here—" She held up the front page. "The first good news since last Sunday."

"Better than *Belle*?"

Lola read, "U.S. marines hold off Japanese assault on Wake Island."

"And that's where?"

"Somewhere in the Pacific."

"Well, that narrows things down." Doris looked up. "The paper say anything about the Jews?"

A few survivors had reported mass killings in Germany, Poland, Lithuania, Ukraine—everywhere under Nazi occupation. How soon America, now technically at war with Germany, would act to save Europe's Jews remained an urgent question, if mostly in Jewish quarters.

"Enough already," Doris said. "Get *Variety*."

Lola went back to the living room and returned to display a headline— "DIZZY," DESI DAZZLE, DELIGHT. "Does this mean I am typecast as the dizzy Latin blonde singer with the crazy hats?"

"What it means is, you're bankable. A certified hot property. There's a war on, right?" People would want to escape, just like during the Depression. Like anytime. "Don't you worry. I'll find the right script for your next movie, and Irving will make the right deal." Doris's head dropped like a puppet whose strings had been severed. She buried her face in her hands.

Lola cast the newspaper aside and stepped towards her.

Doris lowered her hands and raised her chin. Her eyes glinted flamingo pink. Her lids fluttered like butterfly wings. A small, glistening stream descended from her right nostril.

Lola handed her a box of Kleenex.

"It's just that I want to keep celebrating with you," Doris said. "But in three days, you're flying back east for *Belle*'s New York opening. Then you're going on the road with the band."

Lola held her arms out.

Doris made no effort to come closer. "Wherever you go, it'll be too far. Don't *you* feel that?"

"Of course."

"No. You don't. Not now that you're a celebrity again. Everything'll be different. Your next picture, a chauffeured limo'll take you to the studio. Between movies, you'll appear on the radio with all the big stars. You'll play all the top clubs and ballrooms, too. They'll fill your dressing room with champagne and caviar. *Life* and the *Saturday Evening Post* will run stories on you. You'll be on the cover of *Photoplay*. And what about me?"

"Doris—"

"I'll be sitting home reading scripts."

Lola advanced a step.

Doris held up her hands. "Don't. Don't lie to me. All I'm asking is, don't expect me to believe you won't have lovers waiting for you all over the country. Here in L.A., too."

Lola wondered how Doris could imagine she'd freely risk being exposed, allow her career to be ruined, her very safety compromised. How Doris could dismiss the trust Lola had placed in her. How Doris never returned that trust. "I should go home," Lola said. "I will call Fernando."

Doris grasped Lola's wrists. "What will you do in New York? Who will you see? You'll be the center of attention. Everyone will want you. Who will you *fuck!*"

Lola pulled herself free. "Doris, you are having one of your episodes."

Doris grabbed the cream cheese spreader and targeted the tip of the blade just below her rib cage. "Don't think I won't."

Lola brought her palms together as if in prayer.

Doris stood motionless. Then she lowered the stubby knife and burst into laughter.

# FEBRUARY 1942

# RELEASE

Twenty minutes after the start of a fifteen-minute recess, Superior Judge A.A. Scott had yet to return from his chambers. Opposite the vacated bench, District Attorney John F. Dockweiler opened, closed and again opened the lid to his silver pocket watch. The case's joint prosecutors drummed their fingers in unison. The jury—ten men and two women—fidgeted with coat buttons and gloves. The public gallery buzzed with anticipation.

Ben Siegel, wearing a tailored navy pin-striped suit and a tan flouting his quasi-confinement, exhibited monk-like tranquility.

Lola, her hands resting demurely in her lap, sat in the gallery's third row flanked by Fernando and Heshy. Other of Ben's Hollywood friends and associates had found their business calendars full this day, but she'd made it a point to attend. She owed Ben that.

Lola had spent two days persuading Fernando that attending Ben's trial would incur minimum risk. Hardly the innocent Doris made her out to be—to her credit, Doris agreed not to accompany her—Lola calculated that events of recent weeks placed no stumbling block before her career. The press previously had run photos of her and Ben. The public saw those photos yet still made *Belle of the Tropics* big box office. As far as the industry was concerned, all that mattered was selling tickets.

Besides, the studios found that the non-romantic nature of their relationship piqued interest across the heartland rather than condemnation. The odd pairing of a Latin singer/comedienne and a Jewish gangster seemed almost as lovable as that of the lead characters in *A Long Way from Brooklyn*. Metro, at the behest of Louis B. Mayer, offered her a major film.

Top staff and contract writers were adapting a previous script set in Vienna before the Anschluss in 1938 annexed Austria to Germany. Retitled *Buenos Aires Lullaby*, it would feature new songs, including three to be written by Lola. Doris approved. Irving secured a two-picture deal.

Now, the press would take full advantage of a gift—a major homicide case. They'd focus on the jury's verdict.

If Fernando remained unconvinced, he managed for once to conceal his concerns.

Lola kept her gaze on the long oak defendant's table where Jerry Giesler whispered into Ben's ear.

Ben nodded, half rose from his chair, turned and waved at Lola.

Heads craned in her direction.

Lola waved back.

As she lowered her hand, the bailiff ordered everyone to rise.

Judge Scott entered and sat.

Officials and observers, silent in anticipation, took their seats.

The judge banged his gavel. "In the matter of the State of California versus Benjamin Hymen Siegel nee Siegelbaum, this court will respond to the motion made earlier this morning."

The law, he explained, had everything to do with evidence. Ida Greenberg, Big Greenie's still-grieving widow, had testified ten days earlier that she'd heard shots outside their apartment but not seen the assailants. Whitey Krakower, Ben's brother-in-law and one of the alleged killers, had been expected to offer testimony but could not do so. The previous July, he was found shot to death on Delancey Street on Manhattan's Lower East Side. Albert Tannenbaum, who confessed to be one of the killers, *had* testified, but this was not sufficient for conviction. California law demanded corroboration. The state anticipated that would be provided by one Abe "Kid Twist" Reles, a feared hit man for New York's Murder, Inc. Unfortunately, the jury would be denied his testimony. After Reles turned canary in New York, he was stashed away at Coney Island's Half Moon Hotel under 24-hour police guard. Alas, the canary flew out the sixth-story window. Lacking wings, he suffered a hard fall that prevented him from singing.

"Mr. Siegel," said Judge Scott, "by order of this court, you are free to go."

A murmur rose then plummeted like the unfortunate Abe Reles. The jury and observers filed out of the courtroom.

Lola rushed to Ben.

He took her in his arms. "See you tonight," he said.

The next evening, the dining room drapes closed more against prying eyes than in keeping with the blackout, Lola lit a pair of white Shabbos candles and recited the traditional blessing. She'd purchased the candles in a small shop on Fairfax Avenue, costumed and made up not as Albert but as just another Jewish housewife. After more than a dozen years since fleeing New York, she'd finally succeeded in rendering Albert a memory, albeit one mixing fondness with sorrow. She gave thanks that the two parted in peace.

Somewhat disquieting, lighting Shabbos candles in concealment reminded Lola of Doris's comment at Chateau Marmont that Lola Flores was a Marrano. How odd—how sad—that Doris's description fit an Ashkenazi Jew born in Eastern Europe. Would she have to play one role or another away from the cameras for the rest of her life?

As the flames danced, Fernando wished Lola *Gut Shabbos* and accepted *Gut Shabbos* in return. They exchanged chaste but heartfelt kisses on the cheek.

The phone rang.

Fernando answered it in the kitchen where a roast was kept warm—the oven turned off and double-checked. He returned to the dining room. "Doris," he whispered. He seemed to grimace.

Lola went to the phone.

"Are you having dinner?" Doris asked, her words slurred. Silence followed. Then sobs.

"Doris, what is it?" Lola asked.

The sobbing continued for half a minute then subsided into sniffles. "I haven't seen you all week. You don't love me."

"I have had so much to do," said Lola.

"Like go to court yesterday to see your boyfriend cleared? We know he did it."

"Doris, that is nonsense."

"Everyone knows. And you love him. You won't admit it, but you do."

"Ben is a friend. A good friend, yes. We have been over this more times than I can remember."

"You went to his house in Beverly Hills last night. It's in all the papers. There's a picture of you there in the *Examiner*. The *Mirror*, too."

"That was not his house. Virginia Hill lives there. His girlfriend. Ben and Esta are married in name only."

Ben had invited fifty associates and Hollywood notables to a private gathering at Virginia Hill's home on North Linden Drive, which he owned and leased to her. The trial's happy ending, he insisted, deserved a celebration. A small horde of photographers and reporters greeted the Rolls-Royces, Bentleys and Cadillacs that parked in the driveway and along the curb, but Ben ordered Mickey Cohen and Heshy to leave the press be. *I'm an innocent man, right? A few photos? Reminds people I didn't do nothin'.* Flashbulbs popped like Thompson submachine guns, obtaining the guests' images but failing to record their knowledge that Ben not only had organized Harry Greenberg's killing but also taken part. Inside the house, no one spoke a word about it. The police and FBI might be using their electronic wizardry to overhear. For that matter, a canary might be sipping champagne nearby.

"Doris, everything is fine," said Lola.

More sniffling followed. When it dried up, Doris countered, "No. Not fine. Nothing is fine. Not after what I just said. What I keep saying. Why? Why do I say those things? Am I unhinged?"

"You are wonderful, Doris. But you work so hard. The new script is so good because of *you*. But you must rest."

"Rest?"

"Have a good dinner. Listen to the radio. Take a bath. Go to sleep early."

"The radio? A bath? I won't sleep. I won't sleep ever again."

Lola twirled the phone cord around her finger. "Doris, have you been drinking?"

"No."

"No?"

Maybe a little."

"A little?"

"Maybe a little more than a little."

"Would you like me to come over and tuck you in? Fernando can drive me."

Doris responded with a click and a dial tone.

Twenty minutes later, Lola and Fernando arrived at Doris's home. The carport still sheltered her Oldsmobile. The house's front windows revealed only darkness. The doorbell failed to induce light, footsteps or Doris's voice. Lola rang again.

"She has probably drunk herself to sleep," Fernando said. "Cariña, we do not want Doris's neighbors to think something is wrong. You can telephone her tomorrow."

Lola knocked on the door.

"Cariña!" Fernando pleaded.

Lola cast Fernando a look laden with anger and disappointment then opened her purse and withdrew a key.

Fernando shut the door behind them.

Lola called out. Receiving no answer, she turned on a light and surveyed the living room. Everything seemed in place.

"Maybe she has gone to a neighbor," said Fernando.

Something above the fireplace caught Lola's eye. She clutched Fernando's arm.

"What?" he asked.

Lola led him to the master bedroom, reached a hand to the right of the door and flicked the light switch. Doris's bed was still made, the room tidy.

"Obviously," said Fernando, "Doris is not home."

Simultaneously, they noted lights flickering in the bathroom.

Surrounded by candles in clear glass containers of varying colors, Doris lay submerged in the half-filled tub. The handle of the *kaiken* taken from the fireplace mantel rose from her stomach like a buoy floating in an ocean turned crimson.

# OCTOBER 1945

# GHOSTS

Restless as she waited for Fernando and their unidentified guest to come up from the lobby of the Waldorf Towers—she'd occupied the same suite in 1933—Lola dropped three ice cubes into a highball glass then poured ginger ale to within half an inch of the silver rim.

She seemed to be guzzling ginger ale by the gallon. Although overwhelmed with grief following the discovery of Doris's body right after the war had begun, Lola had refused to drown herself in alcohol. What impelled her she didn't know, but she stayed dry until after the funeral at Beth Olam Cemetery adjacent to Paramount Studios then through the week of Shiva. Sober and clearheaded, Lola experienced a startling sense of relief. She'd loved Doris—or thought she had. She'd never experienced love before, never willingly surrendered herself to that most dangerous of emotions capable of sending her spirit soaring while risking exposure and a dizzying downfall. But death, she realized, had released her from the suffocating bondage of Doris's demons.

Relief proved short-lived as guilt accompanied by unspeakable pain assaulted Lola in waves. For relief, she fell back on what she knew and anesthetized herself with Scotch, bourbon, rum, anything on hand.

Fernando sent her to a clinic run by a doctor in Los Angeles referred by Dr. Gerstner. Sequestered for five weeks in a wilderness somewhere outside San Bernardino, Lola again learned to tap into her reserves of strength and dried up—more or less. A month after her return to the house on the leafy, northern end of Doheny Drive and with great fanfare, she strode onto the set at Fox.

As in the past, Lola continued to drink—she rejected asceticism—but in what she considered moderation. After the Allied landings in Normandy over a year earlier, she doubled her efforts to stay teetotal until five. If the boys driving the Germans back to Berlin could do without, so could Lola Flores.

Now, her curiosity just short of unbearable, she redirected her thoughts towards her mystery guest. At breakfast, Fernando mentioned that company was coming but refused to say who. She knew Ben Siegel was anywhere but in New York. She also ruled out Walter Winchell. She'd seen him a week earlier. Besides, arranging a social call by Walter required nothing in the way of drama, since he'd show up with or without an invitation.

Lola glanced at her watch then into the mirror of the radio-bar, the same model she'd wanted for the house in Beverly Hills. Satisfied with her blonde wig, she smoothed her dress—short-sleeved and patterned in bold red polka dots from collar to hem. At loose ends, she dropped into a tufted armchair. Rolling the chilled glass in her hand, she again wondered who her guest might be. Finding herself without a clue, she resigned herself to waiting. She'd grown used to waiting.

Six months had passed since she'd last appeared in front of a camera.

For the third time that day, she scanned the article in the *New York Times*. The previous Friday, a riot broke out at Warner Brothers' main gate. In March, more than ten thousand union workers struck to support the set decorators' walkout. The studios held fast. They had movies in the can and sent them to distributors before their planned release dates. Paramount did that with Lola's *Tropic Fever*.

Given the strike, Ben asked her to play nightclubs in the Midwest in which he and Meyer held interests. In July, she was to go down to Miami. *What with the war, the economy's boomin'. All those military bases in the Florida sunshine, right? Anyway, kid, you're Cuban. You can handle the heat. And I owe favors.* Though they'd seen little of each other over the past year, she accepted his proposal—if *proposal* was an apt word.

Not that Ben Siegel was keeping a low profile. In his mind, Lola knew, that would represent a show of cowardice. Rather, as Heshy confided, Ben was spending considerable time in Las Vegas. The desert town had grown rapidly since 'thirty-one when work began on Boulder Dam. Ben saw an opportunity to develop major resorts there. Gambling and entertainment would draw thousands of visitors—tens of thousands—from Los Angeles and cities even farther away.

Now, Lola was doing Ben's bidding with a month-long engagement at the Copacabana, famed for its Brazilian-themed décor—including huge, stylized palm trees—the Copa Girls chorus line and, for whatever reason, Chinese food. Ben made it clear that he and Meyer Lansky owed a favor to Frank Costello, Charlie Luciano's New York surrogate. Charlie—still a fan of Lola Flores—secretly owned the Copa.

Lola couldn't complain. With Germany's collapse in May and Japan announcing its surrender in August after atomic bombs devastated Hiroshima and Nagasaki, people all over the country were losing their jobs. The War Production Board was about to be abolished. The government advised it would take time to return to manufacturing refrigerators and automobiles instead of tanks and warplanes. Women had a duty to take off their welding masks and slip-on aprons. Post-war jobs belonged to the men coming home.

Lola sympathized with the millions of women who'd lost good jobs. In 1943 and again in 'forty-four, she'd reached the pinnacle as one of the highest-paid women in Hollywood. This year would not be kind. The box office for *Tropic Fever* fell far short of expectations. Perhaps Irving, lacking Doris's acumen with scripts, steered her to a project destined to fail. Or the war's end in sight, audiences wanted different kinds of movies, different kinds of stars. Still, her current run at the Copa drew houses near capacity.

As prearranged, the doorbell rang.

Lola stood.

Fernando unlocked the door and motioned someone in the hall to step forward.

Lola blanched and fell back into the chair.

Before her stood Sylvia.

Struggling to compose herself, Lola regained her feet.

Fernando smiled. Later he would explain that he believed it important to find Sylvia after arriving in New York. He hoped she could provide Lola with news of family members in Europe after the depredations—he used that word, his mastery of English grown impressive—the Nazis inflicted on the Jews. Also, the homosexuals and anyone else who was different and so determined to be unfit and threatening.

Lola gazed at her younger sister's brown hair, long and curled, then down at her matronly figure. She was attractive. Healthy. Radiant.

Sylvia, dressed in a cream blouse and plaid skirt, the hemline still raised reflecting the wartime shortage of fabric, offered a quavering smile. Her cognac-colored handbag, some of the stitching frayed, seemed a relic—or keepsake—from Papa and Uncle Mendel's business. Her hands clutched a straw sun hat. Like Fernando now, she wore eyeglasses. Stepping forward, she burst into tears.

Lola held out her arms.

Sylvia burrowed into them.

Feeling the beating of Sylvia's heart, Lola addressed three questions to herself. The first long had tormented her. Through all these years and their terrible challenges, why had she remained aloof from the family? She knew the answer even if it left her unsatisfied. Revealing herself would create too great a burden on them, the risk of an absentminded comment drawing unwanted scrutiny. During the war, Lola had seen the propaganda posters and heard the song they inspired Duke Ellington to write: "A Slip of the Lip (Can Sink a Ship)." One offhand remark could send her rejuvenated career to the bottom. But keeping her career afloat had cost her dearly! The other two questions remained unanswerable. Why would people refuse to accept Lola Flores as she was? And what could she do about it?

Lola and Sylvia sat.

Fernando brought Sylvia a glass of ginger ale.

Lola first noticed the plain gold wedding band on Sylvia's left hand accompanied by an engagement ring with a diamond that should have come with a magnifying glass. "Tell me about you, about everyone," she said, abandoning her Cuban accent.

"Well, I'm Sylvia Seligman now. Danny and me, we have two children. Phyllis, she's four. Franklin was born a month after FDR died."

"Danny. I seem to remember you mentioning him."

"He was home on leave after North Africa." She displayed an awkward grin. "They gave him a bronze star and a purple heart and sent him back to help raise war bonds while his arm healed. It did, so they shipped him to Germany." As to the children, a neighbor was watching them as she did when Sylvia went to work as an assistant manager in charge of twenty-five girls—women—at a company that reported on the credit of companies in the furniture industry. She poked at the corner of her right eye. "Danny was commanding a company of tanks in the Sixth Armored Division. Part of Patton's Third Army. His unit liberated Buchenwald. I imagine you heard about that."

Lola nodded.

Sylvia took a breath. "He won't talk about it. Anyway, he's a major now. He has enough points to come home by New Year's."

"You must have been very frightened," said Lola.

Sylvia placed her hand over her heart. "I never told him about you."

Lola touched her hand.

Sylvia took a hanky from her bag and cleaned her glasses. "Papa died last year."

Lola wheezed like an old woman.

Tosia and Eugene had three children. During the war, Gene held a position with the National War Labor Board. "Tammany Hall got it for him. It exempted him from military service. They were going to put him up for city council."

"Does anyone ever mention me?" Lola asked. "Mention Albert."

"*I* think about Albert sometimes but mostly about Lola Flores. When I saw you in *A Long Way from Brooklyn,* I knew it was you. I've seen your movies more times than I can remember. I cry every time. Walter Winchell always writes about you in his column, too. But I never—"

"Do you think I've been cruel? Running away? Tricking the family into thinking Albert was dead?"

Sylvia's eyes glistened. "Cruel?" She sighed. "It all must have been so painful for you." She pressed her lips together. "It was painful for us. I'd be lying if I said otherwise. But Albert— *You* had your reasons. I understand that, but I have to admit I still find the situation confusing." How could it not be? Here she was talking to Lola but also in a way to her brother. "Are you, I mean to some degree, also still Albert?"

Lola looked down, a response noncommittal yet revelatory.

"I guess we're talking about Albert like he's a separate person, as if any minute he might walk through the door. But he won't. I understand that." If Lola didn't mind her saying something else, she missed Albert. He was a kind, loving big brother even though he always seemed so unhappy. She never knew why. No one did. By the time it became apparent that

Albert did not think himself—herself—who the family thought he was and expected him to be, it was too late. It shouldn't have been that way. She could see that now. Hindsight and all. Papa, Mama and Tosia should have accepted Albert. Accepted Lola. Embraced her. Lola was still their own flesh and blood. And what had she herself done to persuade Papa, Mama and Tosia that their son and brother was really their daughter and sister? That it didn't matter what the rest of the world thought? She'd sympathized but in silence. "Will you ever forgive me?"

Lola kissed Sylvia on the cheek.

Sylvia sighed. "Then Fernando found me back in 'thirty-six. I remember like it was yesterday. His story about being Maribel's brother and all. Then we met at Chock full o' Nuts."

"Sylvia, I—"

"It's okay. Really. After that, it would have been selfish of me to just pop back into your life—Lola Flores's life."

"The situation has been difficult for everyone," said Lola. "I wish it could have had been different. But not me. I am who I am."

Sylvia chuckled.

"Did I say something?" Lola asked. She raised a hand to her cheek. Had her mascara run?

"Your makeup's perfect. It's just— Your accent. You sound a little like Albert might but more like a woman who grew up somewhere else. Not in New York. Not in America."

"Someone from Cuba?" Lola asked.

"When you're Lola, yes, but not now." If someone heard *this* Lola speak, they'd think she'd come to America from somewhere far away but not as a child quite young enough to sound like a native-born American."

"And where would they think I came from?"

Sylvia looked down. "Over there, I guess," she said. Her voice barely rose above a whisper.

Lola feared the worst. "Sylvia, please. You can tell me."

Sylvia stared at her toes.

"You *must*."

In a low monotone, Sylvia related the war's toll on the family. Their three American Sobel cousins all served in the armed forces. Isaac remained stateside. Julius was stationed in England and kept there right through V-E

Day. He wouldn't say what he was doing. Now he was in Germany but not near Danny. Gerald was wounded in the Pacific during the Battle of the Santa Cruz Islands. He was aboard the aircraft carrier USS *Hornet*. After it was abandoned, he was rescued at sea. Home already, he worked as a pharmacist again.

Information about relatives in Europe remained fragmentary. On Papa's side, Uncle Nosson, who'd emigrated from Warsaw to the south of France due to ill health, died long before the Germans entered Paris. Aunt Irena and her entire family perished. On Mama's side, an uncle went to London in 1938 and made it through the Blitz. Another survived Treblinka but was being held in a displaced persons camp. He planned to go to Palestine even though the British were trying to keep Jews out. The fate of an aunt and two more uncles remained unknown. The confirmed number of murdered cousins stood at five.

Lola drew a lace-bordered handkerchief from the skirt pocket of her dress, but her eyes remained dry. She'd read about the camps and the mass executions in the forests of Ukraine, Russia and elsewhere in the East, and more horrible news came out each day. But weeping came only with difficulty—when it came at all. She'd experienced so much death in her own life. "And Mama?"

Two days later, Lola and Sylvia met just off the Grand Concourse in the Bronx. They hugged on the steps of a four-story, Gothic-inspired building constructed of New Jersey brownstone. Built in 1884, it served as a home for aged and indigent Eastern European Jews.

Sylvia, on an extended lunch hour, wore an off-the-rack gray-blue suit featuring the large shoulders now the rage.

Lola chose a housewife's violet-and-gray V-striped dress, a tweed overcoat and a nondescript wig resembling the one that had been part of her cobbled-together outfit when she visited Ben Siegel in Los Angeles's Hall of Justice. What in her wardrobe, she wondered, wasn't a costume piece?

*Albert meets Maribel in the basement storage room. Deserted after dinnertime. Tonight is different from all other nights.*

*He goes out every Friday and Saturday night. Returns late. Where? Papa and Mama have no idea. No longer care. But this is a school night. Mama frets. Papa is beyond concern. Albert is seventeen. Almost a man. "In his way."*

*What Albert does weekends, he leaves unsaid. But what he does is play piano. Harlem. Times Square. Greenwich Village. Brooklyn. Mostly traditional Cuban music. Sometimes jazz. Occasionally a combination of the two. Always as Lola. Just Lola.*

*He slips into a dress. Pumps. Puts on makeup. A wig. Returns Maribel's grin.*

*They stroll to the Third Avenue El. Strap-hang north. Walk to a tenement. Begrimed brick black in dimming twilight. Climb squeaking stairs. Catch their breath at a fifth-floor walk-up shared by two sisters. Not sisters. Women who say they are. Landlords don't rent to unrelated women.*

*Isabel and Pilar greet them. Exchange kisses. Escort them into the cramped living room. Overheated. A Victrola plays son Cubano. Spanish guitar merged with African rhythms. Albert/Lola recognizes the band. The Sexteto Habanero.*

*Other women form a welcome circle. Nod heads. Sway hips. Shuffle feet.*

*Maribel introduces Lola. Just Lola.*

*Broad smiles. Greetings of ¡Mucho gusto! Strange accents. Not everyone is Cuban. Not everyone can be defined in standard terms. For tonight, Cuban names. All female. Carmen. Alejandra. Margarita. Eugénia. Gilda. Cristina. Juana. No real names. Never real names.*

*Isabel and Pilar retreat to the kitchen. The other women join hands. Dance.*

*Juana winks. Mother-like. Father-like. Tall. Broad-shouldered. Face imprinted with the map of Ireland. Long, thin nose. Square jaw. Stubbled cheeks and chin. Meaty hands. Construction worker. No. Cop.*

*Lola studies Juana's black dress. Red-and-yellow ruffled skirt. Imagines her a bruja. Witch. No. Mensajera. Messenger.*

Lola and Sylvia entered the small room Mama shared with another woman. A white curtain down the center offered an illusion of privacy, but the single bathroom occupied Mama's side. Seemingly an advantage, it required her neighbor to intrude when she sought to relieve herself. This was hourly. The neighbor's more obvious advantage consisted of adjacency to the room's single window, which offered her more light, although another equally dilapidated building restricted the view. Green linoleum covered the floor. The walls were lined with tiles the color of pee.

Mama, her oversized floral-print housedress emphasizing pink and ochre, sat in a chair near the foot of her bed. A rust-and-orange afghan covered her lap. A wooden cane rested against the chair's narrow arm. In addition to bed, nightstand and lamp, the home provided a mahogany dresser with a chipped corner and worn finish. Sylvia had decorated the top with half-a-dozen family photographs. One showed the Sobels in Central Park when Albert was ten—the only photo in which he appeared. A small pea-soup green wardrobe, one door out of plumb and perpetually ajar, completed Mama's furnishings. Above them dangled a bare lightbulb.

Lola believed Ben's cell to have been superior.

Sylvia bent down and kissed Mama's wrinkled cheek. "Mama, how are you?" she asked. Straightening, she called out to her mother's roommate, "Hello, Mrs. Weinberg."

Mrs. Weinberg responded with a small burst of gas.

Sylvia waited for Mama's eyes to acknowledge Lola's presence. "Mama doesn't speak anymore, but she hears everything. Don't you, Mama?"

Mama nodded.

Lola was taken aback by how much Mama had aged. She imagined Papa's death had much to do with her hunched posture and sallow skin.

Sylvia sat on the bed and motioned Lola to join her. "Mama," she said, "this is my friend Minna Goldstein." Sylvia had recalled a woman named Minna living in the building on 69th Street when times were flush. The name was as good as any.

"Hello, Mrs. Sobel," said Lola in the immigrant-from-anywhere accent that had replaced the New York English with which she'd grown to adulthood. "Delighted to meet you."

Mama nodded.

Lola searched Mama's eyes for a sign of recognition but found none. This left her with mixed feelings. Also, an idea. While remaining in the background, she would relocate Mama to a more cheerful place where Mama would receive the best possible care. She'd have Heshy send money to the new facility each month. As soon as they left, she'd discuss the matter with Sylvia. But reality posed a problem. What about Tosia? And her brothers-in-law? Where would they think the money came from?

For ten minutes, Sylvia filled Mama in on family matters. Her grandchildren were growing almost too fast to keep up with. Phyllis knew her alphabet. Franklin was walking. Danny would return home soon, safe and sound. New homes built for young families were popping up all over. They hoped to buy one with one of those new veterans' loans.

Mama smiled.

Whether she'd understood what Sylvia had related neither sister could determine. But a smile beat a frown.

Sylvia, her eyes watery, stood and kissed Mama goodbye. "Now say goodbye to Minna," she coaxed.

Mama's eyes brightened.

Lola took Mama's hand, mottled and bony, the knuckles swollen with arthritis. Cold at first, it grew warm. A minute passed in silence.

Mama squeezed.

# JUNE 1947

# THE FABULOUS FLAMINGO

The sun loitered above the vast western horizon as Heshy raced his dust-coated '46 Chrysler Crown Imperial northeast on US 91. Less than an hour from Las Vegas, he pulled into a Shell station, its remoteness stunning, its stucco exterior faded and cracked but offering two shiny new pumps symbolic of post-war expectations. Beneath a tattered awning, a bearded man in an oil-stained undershirt slouched in a wooden folding chair.

"I gotta— You know," Heshy told Lola and Fernando. Outside the car, he held a hand to his stomach.

Lola waited for Heshy's return before exiting the air-conditioned car. Despite the darkening hour, the southern Nevada desert seemed even hotter than since their previous stop. She walked with purpose to the bathroom, locked the door then covered the toilet seat with crinkly paper. As she sat, a cockroach crawled across the floor beneath the opposite wall. Fearless, the roach inched its way towards her. She choked off a scream. What would Ben think of her? What would Ben *do*? She crushed the roach under her shoe then used more crinkly paper to wipe it off. After peeing, she flushed but stayed seated. Her newfound courage had melted into despair. There was no way to evade the truth. Her film career was going down the toilet.

*Pecos Princess,* which followed *Tropic Fever,* barely broke even. It took months for Irving to negotiate another opportunity, this one with Universal, now reduced to making B pictures. *Havana Heartbeat* lost money. She heard the industry whispers and read the musings of columnists—Walter in New York the lone exception—who had gleefully turned on her. One wrote: *Lola Flores's shtick is old hat—pun intended.*

*Old* hat involved more than a pun. The studios remained ignorant of her age, but in three years, Lola Flores would turn forty. Producers, like white slavers, preferred girls to women.

Adding to her predicament, the House Un-American Activities Committee was poking around Hollywood in search of Communists. William Wilkerson, owner of *The Hollywood Reporter*, published "Billy's List," a roster of supposed Reds and their supporters. At the Brown Derby before the war, Walter had pointed a finger at Lucille Ball. Would Wilkerson do that? Would the committee? If so, would suspicions fall on Lucille's friends?

Lola tried to accentuate the positive. Regarding Lucille, the committee's efforts had proved fruitless. As to work, Fernando still found club dates, although for shorter runs at second-rate venues, which paid accordingly. Four months earlier, she'd appeared on the *Fitch Bandwagon* radio show, promoting dandruff-remover shampoo. She hadn't been behind a mic since.

Still, she and Fernando were comfortable. Rather than purchase a larger home higher up in the hills, they stayed in the house on Doheny. It offered all the space they needed and enabled Fernando to invest in land. He assured her that sooner or later, developers would construct homes in every corner of the San Fernando Valley and in Orange County to the south. Not only were ex-GIs building young families to make up for lost time but increasing numbers of Americans were fleeing the wintry North and East, heading west on Route 66 to claim their share of Southern California sunshine.

Sylvia and Dan stayed in New York, buying an attached house in Queens. Lola overcame her initial reservations and permitted Fernando to arrange an ongoing exchange of letters delivered to post-office boxes. For security's sake, Sylvia addressed hers to Minna Goldstein, and Lola returned semi-cryptic letters as Minna. Although Lola couldn't dismiss the danger inherent in communicating with Sylvia, the arrangement, being long distance, seemed safe enough. How could she reject Sylvia, who'd begged to stay in touch, particularly since she, like Albert, had never been close to Tosia? It was Sylvia, out of all the family, who accepted Lola for who she was. Lola found herself looking forward to news of Sylvia's growing family. A year earlier, she'd given birth to a daughter, Lenore.

With no option other than to move on, Lola stood, rearranged herself and turned on the faucet at the sink. Brownish water dribbled out. She couldn't find a towel.

As she emerged into the waning light, Fernando ducked back into the car. Lola found it infuriating that a man with what she assumed to be a woman's plumbing could cross vast distances over long periods like a camel. Of course, who knew what any individual was like inside? Fernando insisted that most doctors remained ignorant of the human body's many variations. Dr. Mortensen, who treated the two of them in Los Angeles, proved an exception.

Heshy opened the Crown Imperial's rear door.

Lola settled into the plush back seat next to Fernando.

The sun vanished beneath the horizon like a nickel swallowed by a slot machine.

A pink neon flamingo dominated the desert sky, a lodestar guiding visitors to the new oasis four miles from downtown Las Vegas. Heshy followed it and pulled up to the hotel's entrance. The night manager approached. "Welcome to The Fabulous Flamingo. Mr. Siegel asked me to take you straight to his suite."

Following dinner, plates smeared with the remnants of steak and lobster, Ben raised a bottle of 1939 Old Elgin Scotch. "Another?"

Lola and Fernando nodded their assent.

"I got a show in twenty-five minutes," said Rose Marie, the former vaudeville child star who played all the top clubs thanks to considerable talent and connections to powerful men.

"One for the road," said Ben.

Rose Marie laughed. "Why the fuck not?"

Heshy took the bottle from Ben and poured.

Ben removed a cigar from the pocket of his gold sport shirt along with a gold lighter flashing his initials in diamonds. The lighter failed. He hurled it across the living room. It shattered against the brick fireplace.

Heshy produced a black Zippo. The tip of Ben's cigar embraced the flame.

"So how do you like The Fabulous Flamingo?" Ben asked Lola. "Of course, you haven't really seen it yet."

"What's not to love?" said Rose Marie.

Ben grinned. "Smart girl."

The year before, when he and Esta finally divorced, Ben took control of The Flamingo from the Red-baiting William R. Wilkerson. Prior to New Year's Eve, he staged two openings. The showroom featured Xavier Cugat, Jimmy Durante and Rose Marie. Notables, excepting George Raft, held back. "I appreciate that your girlfriend Lucille came to the second opening," Ben said to Lola. "Sorry you had female problems."

Lola knew that Ben knew she'd lied. Also, that Ben was skating on thin ice with the mob, leaving him skittish, spooked.

During construction—under Ben's management—costs ballooned. Then came public embarrassment. When the hotel opened, the building, including guest rooms, remained unfinished. Worse, the casino staff lacked proper training. The first week alone, The Flamingo lost $300,000. Word had it that Meyer used all his powers of persuasion to keep Charlie Luciano from doing away with Ben.

Answering his wake-up call, Ben closed the place down and, with Virginia Hill's assistance, guided the resort through a major renovation. Refurbished and re-christened, the new resort opened March first. Indeed, it was fabulous. Ben had produced a lavish pool area complete with expansive lawn, date palms and cork trees from Spain, a nine-hole golf course, a stable with forty horses and striking accommodations. Keeping the odds with the house, Ben provided his owner's suite with an escape tunnel.

The Fabulous Flamingo immediately turned a profit.

Ben put down his cigar, stood and circled behind Rose Marie. "This kid? Knockin' 'em dead. And if anybody knows anything about killin' 'em, it's Ben Siegel, right?" He laughed, but the muscles around his mouth remained taut. He stepped towards Fernando and tapped his arm. "I got more big stars lined up. Lena Horne's coming. She's great. Beautiful, too. You don't even think about her bein' colored. Of course, we won't let her in the restaurant or the casino or lounge at the pool." He stepped behind Lola and rested his hands on her shoulders.

Lola remembered a story that may or may not have been true. At a banquet, the notorious Al Capone circled around three traitorous associates and beat them bloody with a baseball bat before having them shot.

"I want Lola Flores to play The Fabulous Flamingo," Ben said. "I'm headin' back to L.A. day after tomorrow, but I wanted to tell you this *here*. So, you can see this place in the flesh." He grinned. "You bet your ass we got plenty of flesh to keep the high rollers happy. Tomorrow, you'll get a tour." He glanced around the table. "Lola Flores at The Fabulous Flamingo. Has a fuckin' ring, right?" He kissed Lola's cheek. "The publicity— The studios'll be all over you again."

"Thank you, Ben," said Lola. "You are always so good to me."

Ben returned to his seat. "First, I need a favor."

That Ben needed a favor did not surprise her. Rumors had been making the rounds that Ben Siegel had lost his touch.

"Everyone's seen in the papers how the government exiled Charlie back to Sicily again," he said. "Ungrateful SOBs." In 1942, the SS *Normandie*, an ocean liner being converted into a troopship, sank in the Hudson. Panic set it. Washington tried to keep the matter hushed, but there were no secrets on the waterfront. The Big Boys called on Charlie Luciano and Meyer Lansky to keep New York's piers clear of Nazi spies. Now, Charlie and Meyer were opening a new hotel in Havana. "Before Lola Flores plays here, she plays *there*. I loan you out for maybe a month. What I hear, the Cubans still think Lola Flores is as big as the Virgin Mary. You'll get the joint off to a good start."

Lola wondered if this might be a good time to ask permission to go to the bathroom but concluded that such a request would reveal her discomfort—not physical but emotional. "I am sure Charlie and Meyer do not need *me*."

Ben cocked his head. "Havana's still hot, kid, and I'm not talkin' just the weather. Our old pal Batista's gone, sure, but he's still pullin' strings for us. The thing is, Charlie and Meyer are investin' big bucks down there. I gotta do my bit to make sure they cash in."

Lola stared into her glass.

Ben looked at Fernando. "What? You want a salary you think they won't pay?"

Fernando glanced at Lola.

Lola weighed the complications of an unexpected dilemma. Fulgencio Batista had left office in 1944 and lived in Miami. But Lola's working in Cuba still posed a grave risk. Word hinted at a coup that would put him back in the Presidential Palace. Yet even in exile, the little sergeant maintained relationships with men more than capable of carrying out the threat he'd made years earlier when she returned to play the Nacional at the behest of J. Edgar Hoover. Her defiance hadn't only assaulted Batista's authority. He'd taken it as a threat to his manhood.

Would a white knight come to her rescue? Charlie Luciano had slipped out of Sicily and snuck back to Havana only to be discovered. In April, the Cuban government bowed to Washington and deported him. Charlie conducted business with Meyer from Italy but stayed under constant police surveillance. Now, Meyer was preoccupied in Havana, looking for new profits, not trouble. If she returned to Cuba and friends of Batista sought to avenge him, Charlie and Meyer might throw her to the sharks and tote it up as just another cost of doing business. They would leave Ben no choice but to swallow his pride.

And what about J. Edgar Hoover? Everyone knew his willingness to carry a grudge for years then extract vengeance in his own sweet time. He could concoct a scheme barring Fernando and her from reentering the United States, claim irregularities in the paperwork that granted them citizenship and passports. After all these years, he'd no doubt covered up any record of his involvement in that matter.

Ben rapped the table with his knuckles. "What the fuck's wrong, kid?"

Lola wanted to say, *I am indebted to you, Ben. I will play Havana.* She could manage only, "This is not a good time, Ben."

Ben's cheeks reddened.

"Lola," said Rose Marie, "this is Ben Siegel you're talking to."

Ben held up a hand. "I'm sure Lola has her reasons. When did she ever refuse me a favor?"

Lola tried to conceal her sigh of relief.

"Only, there's one thing," he said.

"What is that, Ben?" Lola asked.

"In my business—" He made a fist, released it and made another. "In my business, there's one thing more important than anything else. Even money. One very fuckin' simple thing. You know what that is?"

Lola felt an overwhelming urge to pee.

"Do you?"

"What is that, Ben?"

His fist slammed the table. "Loyalty! Heshy'll get your fuckin' bags. In fifteen minutes, he's drivin' you and Fernando back to L.A."

Half an hour out of Las Vegas, Heshy pulled off the highway, drove down a dirt road and turned off the engine. He opened the glove compartment and removed an object Lola couldn't see. "Let's get out," he said.

Lola and Fernando followed Heshy away from the car. Neither the new moon nor the scant starlight—Lola had never seen so many stars, never imagined their existence—proved sufficient to keep them from stumbling.

Behind them, a car sped by on the way to Las Vegas. The roar of its engine died down to a hum then disappeared. The desert returned to silence.

"Okay, right here," Heshy said.

Lola suffered no illusions. Ben wasn't sending them back to Los Angeles. This is where her life would end. Where she would be buried. No rabbi. No minyan to say Kaddish for her—or for Albert. Fernando would meet his death, as well. Did he blame her for their predicament?

"Take a look. A good look."

Of course, she thought. This would be the last thing she'd ever see.

"So, what's out here anyway?" Heshy asked, as if he was making conversation over a cup of coffee. "Nothing. Out here, you're face to face with all this emptiness. Nothingness, you could call it. The stars, sure, but they're a long way off. Makes you think of eternity or wherever it is everyone goes eventually."

Lola took Fernando's hand.

"You believe in heaven?" Heshy asked.

"I do not— I do not know," said Lola.

"Me neither. Jews— Nobody's sure. It's something you find out when the time comes."

Lola squeezed Fernando's hand.

He squeezed back.

They stood in silence. They could do nothing but wait. At least, Lola thought, Heshy will bury us out here. I will die a woman.

Heshy raised his arm. A flashlight shone in the direction of the car. "Thanks for letting me stop. It's so peaceful out here. A different world. Every now and then, I get a little philosophical. My wife says I go off the deep end, but who doesn't think about these things? Anyway, we'd better get some miles on us. Those all-night gas stations? Sometimes they close."

In the distance, dry lightning flashed.

Three days later, Lola, her eyes heavy lidded, eased out of bed before sunrise. She'd stayed up reading Shakespeare and drifted off after the first murderer informed Macbeth he'd followed orders and cut Banquo's throat. An hour later, her eyes shot open. She turned on KGFJ. After the war, all major radio stations broadcast twenty-four hours. She listened to a special show, *Remember When*. It played one of her songs.

Another idyllic California day in the offing, Lola put on a robe. Taking care to leave Fernando undisturbed in his bedroom, she tiptoed to the kitchen to make coffee. Before picking up the pot, she abandoned the idea. Her nerves were shot. Coffee was the last thing she needed. She stumbled into the living room and poured a drink. Moments later, she helped herself to a refill and lay down on the sofa. Drifting off, she thought she heard someone knocking. Not wanting Fernando to be awakened, she lurched to the door.

Heshy stood before her, ashen faced, a folded newspaper under his arm.

Lola thought it ironic that rather than killing her in the solitude of the desert, Heshy would brazenly do away with her—and Fernando—right here in Beverly Hills to prove that Ben Siegel feared nothing and let no one stand in his way.

Heshy held out the newspaper, still folded. "*Herald-Examiner*," he said, breathless as if he'd run all the way from his house, miles distant. He hadn't. He couldn't run to the corner. "Someone paid someone off. Doesn't matter who. Not now. Press'll be pounding on your door before you know it."

Lola's face registered confusion.

"Last night. Virginia's house. Ben was there but Virginia, she's in Paris. Around eleven. A rifle. M1 carbine like they used in the war." As if in a scene from a movie, he revealed the front page.

A massive photo displayed Ben Siegel lying on the floor in front of a sofa upholstered in a floral fabric, his left eye shot out, and very dead.

# SAN FRANCISCO

# JULY-AUGUST 1953
# BLONDE BEAUTY

Sylvia's letter left Lola unsettled. She'd read it half-a-dozen times since Fernando retrieved it from one of their two post-office boxes. One received mail to Lola Flores and Fernando Fallon. The other, to which this latest letter arrived, had been rented under the name of Goldstein, the same name on the directory of their apartment building in San Francisco.

Lola hung her rhinestone-framed reading glasses around her neck and glanced around the living room, its walls papered in a pattern of lilacs. Her eyes drifted to the small gold-inlaid table on which she'd left a near-empty pack of Philip Morris. She'd again switched cigarette brands. This time out of loyalty. The Philip Morris ads featured Lucille Ball. Along with nearly three-quarters of American households owning a television, she and Fernando watched *I Love Lucy* every Monday night. She put the letter down, lit up, inhaled and closed her eyes.

Nicotine-soothed, Lola went to the window. The Spanish-style building perched on a hillside "out Broadway" provided a calm refuge only a moment from bustling Chinatown and North Beach thanks to the new tunnel under Russian Hill. A picture-postcard view offered the Pacific, the Golden Gate Bridge—painted orange like the sunset visible on fog-free days—the headlands of Marin County, Sausalito, the Bay, Oakland and Berkeley. Sunshine warmed her face like the touch of a lover's hands, although intimacy represented only a distant memory. She'd never found anyone to replace Doris. Never sought to. That phase of her life seemed to be over just as she put Los Angeles in her past five years earlier.

Lola and Fernando had fled to San Francisco days after the 1948 Republican convention again chose New York governor Thomas E.

Dewey—Charlie Luciano's old foe—to run against the incumbent president Harry Truman. Politics played no role in their decision.

The problem lay with Mickey Cohen. Elevated to head of the L.A. mob following Ben's murder and backed by the nation's top crime families, he purged everyone close to Ben Siegel—Bugsy, as those out from Ben's thumb and nestled under Mickey's now referred to him openly. Within weeks of Ben's funeral, attendees restricted to his brother and a rabbi, murder and, in an occasional display of malicious benevolence, exile purged the ranks.

Imposing his will, Mickey leaned on the studios and all the nightclubs in town to cut ties with anyone ever connected to Ben. Fernando fretted as Lola's already spotty schedule became skimpier with one club after another cancelling shows not only in Southern California but up and down the Coast.

Irving Shapiro encountered roadblocks halting the resurrection of Lola's movie career. *I can't buy you an audition, not even for a bit part. A cameo to get your face on screen? If I could turn lead into gold, I'd be doing that for a living.* When three important clients walked out on Irving citing "personal reasons," he shuttered the agency, sold his house in Brentwood and retreated to Palm Springs.

Heshy Kaplan's career also hit a dead end. The day of Ben's funeral, two of Mickey Cohen's minions made him an offer. He could retire standing up or lying down. Heshy moved his family to San Francisco. There, he reunited with a brother who'd come out from New York before the war and established several businesses into which Heshy invested considerable cash. Although separated by nearly 400 miles until Lola and Fernando moved north the next year, he kept in touch.

Lucille Ball, alienated from the studios but still making movies, urged Lola to hang on. Mickey Cohen had more to worry about than "some blonde Cuban dame." Besides, time healed old wounds. God knew, like Lola, she'd suffered plenty. Men would be men, but half of America was female. Hollywood would make a place for a woman who put one high-heeled foot in front of the other and refused to take no for an answer. She and Desi saw big potential in television.

Shut up in her Beverly Hills home and unable to square Lucille's advice with her world collapsed around her, Lola resumed drinking and smoking to numb her pain. Instead of relief, she experienced one bout of illness after another.

A year after Ben's murder, Albert emerged to rouse her from her self-induced stupor. In a voice deferential yet imposing, he reminded Lola of a Bible story they knew well. In Babylonia, a mysterious hand produced writing on the wall in King Belshazzar's palace. When the king's wise men failed to make sense of it, Daniel, a God-fearing exile from Judah, informed the king that the cryptic message portended the king's death, which followed that very night. Lola experienced a moment of clarity.

Fernando, while no believer in visions, supported Lola's decision to bolt Los Angeles.

Heshy welcomed the newcomers to San Francisco and found the Goldsteins an apartment blocks from his home on Vallejo Street in well-to-do Pacific Heights. If Lola Flores, ignoring Lucille Ball's assurances, went underground to avoid the long reach of the mob, who would suspect her alias would be Jewish? Minna Goldstein also enjoyed another advantage. Far from Hollywood, she found it effortless to go about unrecognized. Her gaunt face and stature, along with clothing and wigs carefully chosen by Fernando, gave her the appearance of a woman closer to fifty than forty. Without makeup, fifty stood as a compliment.

The Cuban Fanny Brice became the Cuban Greta Garbo with no pretense of a social life. She played the piano, read Shakespeare and serious novels—George Orwell's *1984* left her shaken—listened to the radio and with Fernando's assistance assembled an eclectic record collection. In time, she found herself engrossed by television. Several actors and actresses she knew had become wildly successful in the new medium, shrunken as they were on a Zenith 21-inch, black-and-white screen.

Lola's financial picture proved brighter. Fernando jested about being the "real Jew." His portfolio of Southern California real estate, some of which he held in partnership with Heshy, enjoyed impressive growth during the post-war boom.

Lola's health remained another matter. Dr. Mortenson in Los Angeles referred her to Dr. Friedman, who conducted research on gender at San Francisco's University of California Medical School and ran a private clinic. As Dr. Gerstner and Dr. Mortenson before him, Dr. Friedman periodically adjusted the levels of Lola's estrogen and reorganized her intake of other hormones.

Coming back to the present, Lola picked up Sylvia's letter, skipped the welcome news about the children and Danny's growing law practice, and re-read the heart of her sister's dispatch.

> *Anyway, what I was ~~planning~~ thinking was that Danny and the children and I might visit you in San Francisco next summer ('54). We can afford it if we arrange things with some care. The children would love to ride on a cable car (me, too), and I would tell them in advance that while we were there, we would visit a friend from my childhood, Minna Goldstein.*
>
> *Once we get together (please keep reading, please!), I could explain who you really are and why you had to hide and that it doesn't matter to me and shouldn't to anyone. The children are old enough to understand. (I really think so.) I note that next summer being a year away, they'll be older and able to understand even better. Honestly, you shouldn't have to feel all alone in this world (excepting, of course, you have Fernando).*
>
> *Because (you're not supposed to start a sentence with "because" if you remember from elementary school, but I see nothing wrong with it) I've been thinking a lot about how you've had to hide who you are. Tosia wouldn't be pleased with you being Lola (and Minna) if she knew (she doesn't!), but I think for your own sake (and for others—there must be other—many?—women like you) you should tell someone sometime. Why not start with us? (Danny still doesn't know—my hand to God!!—but I'll tell him after we arrive in San Francisco, and he'll be fine.)*
>
> *What I worry about is that if something should happen to you (keynehore—that's as good a spelling in English as any; I also just spit through my fingers; do I really believe in the evil eye?), it would be terrible if the world didn't know you for who you are. And (you're also not supposed to start a*

*sentence with "and" but to hell with the rules) I couldn't tell your story like you could.*

*By the by, have you heard (you must have, who hasn't?) about Christine Jorgensen, this man from the Bronx who had that operation in Denmark last year? Now he's a woman. He must feel so good not having to hide in the shadows (he's doing anything but).*

*Please write soon and say <u>yes</u>!*
*XOXOXOXOXO!!!*
*Sylvia*

Fernando emerged from his bedroom where he managed their investments at a small desk. "Are you ready, cariña? The taxi will be waiting."

As Lola folded the letter, she wondered if keeping their appointment represented an act of kindness or folly.

A dark-suited pianist played "Stormy Weather" as Fernando half-urged, half-pulled Lola into the dimly lit, near-deserted wood-paneled lobby bar at the Mark Hopkins Hotel atop Nob Hill. They'd dismissed taking the elevator to the Top of the Mark where countless servicemen had enjoyed a last night stateside before embarking for the far side of the Pacific to fight the Japanese and later the Red North Koreans. The lucky ones stopped off to celebrate their return. Most likely, a horde of tourists gathered there this afternoon, cocktails in hand, to enjoy sweeping views of the City and the Bay. That would never do.

As they approached a table in the far corner, Christine Jorgensen stood. She wore her blonde hair stylishly short. A green, belted dress—almost a twin to Lola's blue outfit—flattered her slim figure. Her bright red lips—the upper thin, the lower full—arced up in a pixie-like smile.

Lola experienced a touch of envy. She'd seen the photos in *Life*, *Look* and *Time*, but even without special makeup and lighting, Christine displayed unmistakable attractiveness and charm. Lola also acknowledged the strength of a woman—a sister in ways Sylvia and Tosia never could be—navigating dangerous obstacles while hiding the weariness such effort entailed.

Christine extended her hand. In a voice husky but feminine she said, "I'm so thrilled to meet you, Miss Flores."

Lola startled, although she'd made no arrangement to be addressed as Minna Goldstein. She reassured herself that their relative isolation prevented anyone but a Russian spy from eavesdropping. She feared the existence of such a possibility. If the newspapers and certain members of Congress were to be believed, Communists infested every corner of American life.

"And you, Mr. Fallon," Christine added.

Fernando ordered champagne cocktails.

Christine drew close across the table. "I hope I'm not imposing, but Walter—Mr. Winchell—called my hotel in Chicago before I flew on to Los Angeles. He suggested I call you. If I seem a little breathless, it's because I have to fly back to Los Angeles tonight and on to New York tomorrow evening. Can you imagine?" She shook her head as if to scold herself. "Of course, you can. A star like Lola Flores being so well-traveled."

"And *you*," said Lola, "have been on quite a journey these past few months." If Lola's star had plummeted over the years, Christine Jorgensen's had skyrocketed overnight.

"To be honest," Christine said, "it hasn't been all sunshine and roses." On December first, the *New York Daily News* broke her story with a huge headline: EX-GI BECOMES BLONDE BEAUTY. The Bronx's George Jorgensen had undergone two operations in Copenhagen, the second in November for the removal of his penis. On February 13, she returned to New York to be assailed by crude jokes in the press and among people who could not understand the distress experienced by a woman forced to retain a man's body and identity. "Thank God for my parents—my whole family. They've been so wonderful."

---

*Albert finishes dressing. Has plans. Why is this Saturday night different from all other Saturday nights?*

*Sylvia primps in her room. Readies herself to meet friends. A double feature. Newsreel. Cartoon. What was the world like without talkies?*

*Papa squirms in his easy chair. Refolds his newspaper. Stares. Stews. Not about Albert. Nineteen now. But Sylvia? Sixteen. A girl. Still, this is America. Still, he shouldn't be upset? Look at the headline. LONDON STOCK EXCHANGE CRASHES.*

*Albert enters the living room. Shows off a skirt and blouse. Rouged cheeks. Cherry red lips. Wig. Shiksa blonde.*

*Papa's eyes resemble half-dollars.*

*Albert bows.*

*"Rivka!" Papa shouts.*

*Mama exits the kitchen.*

*Albert reveals all. He plays piano. With a band. For money.*

*Mama shakes her head. Purim? Six months from now. Purim, you wear costumes. Halloween? A month off.*

*Albert corrects her. This is no costume.*

*Mama sighs. Albert goes out every Friday and Saturday night. This she knows. But a fellow they let play in an all-girl band?*

*Albert shakes his head. "All men. Except me."*

*Mama remembers that day in Warsaw. Nineteen-and-then-some years ago. Pain. Birth. Relief. Joy. A boy. Beautiful. Except for his little thing. Not big enough to be called little. Still, a son. Hugs herself as if chilled. "Oy, it's my fault."*

*Papa bellows like a gored ox.*

*Sylvia emerges. Face marked by trepidation. Followed by hilarity.*

*Papa reprimands. Swivels his head. Confronts Albert. Enough already. Albert will put on his clothes. His real clothes.*

*Albert/Lola holds his ground. Rejects Papa and Mama's narrow-minded views. Greenhorn views. "These are my real clothes." Lincoln emancipated the slaves over sixty years ago. Tonight, he emancipates himself. Herself.*

*Sylvia thinks Albert looks cute.*

*Papa's face turns crimson. This mishigas. This curse. His only living son. Not a son? Hurls the paper to the floor.*

*Albert/Lola steels him/herself. Knows what Papa will say. Fears Mama will agree. Tosia also when she finds out. Sylvia? Hopes she will stick up for him. No matter. He is who she is. Holds his/her arms out. Pleads. "This is me. Your child."*

*Papa delivers his verdict. "Better you was dead!"*

Christine related how Walter Winchell invited her to appear at

Madison Square Garden, a benefit for families of police and firemen who lost their lives in the line of duty. The event changed everything. Her presence drew raves from dozens of celebrities. Charlie Yates, her newly acquired manager, encouraged her to perform in nightclubs. He teamed her with Myles Bell, a veteran of the club circuit.

"We're booked into Havana in a few weeks," Christine said. "Mr. Winchell says you can tell a novice like me everything I should know about playing there, Cuba being so different."

"Walter has been very good to me," said Lola. "I am delighted to help you."

Fernando offered his agreement.

Christine's blue eyes sparkled.

Fernando ordered more champagne cocktails.

Christine launched a series of questions.

Lola thought Christine incredibly lucky. Blessed, if God raised some people's fortunes to reward their righteousness. But life had taught her a more disturbing lesson. If God played favorites, his choices reflected sheer whimsy. All she could do was make her own choices and see how they played out. That's why she'd agreed to see Christine, who in due time would learn her own lessons about the alluring and fragile nature of celebrity. As to the here and now, she advised that Christine would find Havana audiences receptive, the warm, humid climate offset by air-conditioning, the food delicious and water at the hotel perfectly safe. Regarding the political situation, Cuba remained calm after Fulgencio Batista staged last year's coup three months before elections. Yet even as she explained all this, she knew that Christine anticipated something more. She added, "I must praise your courage."

"Because of some of the comments they still make in the press?"

"For undergoing the surgeries."

Christine smiled. "I *had* to. To be *me*. And I've been so lucky. A few years ago, Dr. Hamburger wouldn't have been ready to attempt it, but with all the techniques they developed in Denmark and the female hormones— I don't know what I'd have done if I'd have been born five or ten years earlier."

Lola thought of poor Lili Elbe and their meeting in Berlin. Only one generation later, science gave Christine the life Lili had been denied. That Lola Flores, fearful of similar consequences, had been denied as well.

Christine finished her second champagne cocktail.

"Another?" Fernando asked.

"No thank you. I couldn't."

"*I* could," said Lola.

Christine took Lola's hand. "Imagine if a girl wanted a career in show business when *you* were starting out, only she was born with a man's body like me. She'd have had to disguise her true self. If she had an operation—several operations—and survived them and everyone knew what she'd done, audiences would have shunned her. I'm not sure about Europe but certainly here in America. Or maybe, if surgery wasn't an option and she was desperate enough, she'd appear as the girl—the woman—she knew herself to be. She'd be awfully brave."

Lola slipped her hands below the table, interlocked her fingers and squeezed until it hurt. Although ignorant of Lola's background—unless she possessed a sixth sense like Frida Herskovits and Fernando—Christine had outlined her story like a writer pitching a studio about a new movie. Lola took heart that Christine had the confidence to tell the world her own story and use it to build a career. But she couldn't help feeling that opposite Christine's success stood Lola Flores' pain—that Christine Jorgensen had, if unknowingly and without malice, stolen from her the life of which she'd always dreamed.

Two days later, Lola faced Dr. Friedman across the considerable expanse of his oak desk. She'd come without Fernando, who had a business appointment. Had he been free, she would have refused to let him accompany her. The matter at hand lay beyond his right to comment or object.

Dr. Friedman removed a fountain pen from a ceramic holder that appeared to have been made by a child. "I'm a bit puzzled," he said. "You told the nurse you have no symptoms."

Lola's heartbeat quickened. She reflected on that moment when she would step out onto a stage or appear on a film set, a burst of adrenalin serving as a finely honed tool for sharpening her focus. The image seemed suitable. She was here to perform. She'd rehearsed all morning, experimenting with a range of vocal tones and facial expressions. At her vanity, she'd added color to her sallow cheeks and powdered into concealment the dark, puffy flesh under her eyes and offending lines at the corners of her mouth.

Dr. Friedman held the pen poised above a pad of white paper lined in blue. "Perhaps a general feeling of ill-health?"

Lola pressed her lips together to assure her lipstick an even veneer. "My health is very good, thank you."

"Then?"

"I wish to ask you something."

"Of course."

"What I wish to know is, when do you think it can be done here in America?"

"It?"

"The surgery like Christine Jorgensen's."

Dr. Friedman offered Lola a smile weighty in expertise but light on encouragement.

"And why not?" Lola asked. During their meeting, Christine prompted a desire Lola had rejected after Lili Elbe died. Believing that medicine had made remarkable advances, Christine wanted a vagina with surgery to take place sometime during the next year—right here in the United States. Lola thought it might be time to have *her* penis removed followed by the fashioning of a vagina.

Her decision, Lola stressed to Dr. Friedman, represented far more than an impulse. "I do not expect a vagina simply to provide me with greater sexual satisfaction or, to be honest, return my desire." The issue ran far deeper. Lola Flores was a woman. Logic and a sense of longing dictated that she was entitled to the physical appearance of a woman not just above the waist but below. A vagina would enable her to go anywhere, meet anyone and never again fear discovery. It would provide a sense of peace she'd yet to experience. More—and she was not to be thought frivolous—a vagina might even encourage her to renew her career. Frank Sinatra had gone into a slump the last few years, but Columbia Pictures signed him for the plum role of Maggio in the film version of James Jones's bestseller *From Here to Eternity*. Walter Winchell and the Hollywood press touted that the movie, which would open in a month, would put Sinatra back on top.

Of course, Lola would keep her operations from the press. She had no desire to broadcast her physical transformation. Let Christine Jorgensen and the younger women who followed her present their case to the public. "I wish only for the world to see Lola Flores as the musician and actress— the woman—it has always known."

Dr. Friedman tapped his pen with his middle finger as if he was flicking a cigarette ash. "You understand," he said, "that we still have a lot to learn from Miss Jorgensen. Her long-term response to her surgeries remains to be determined, and there's no way to rush that. The same with the effectiveness of her hormone treatments which, to be clear, are different from yours. So far, so good for Miss Jorgensen, but all this is new, and the literature is far from complete. To be candid, Lola, I can't perform these surgeries on you until the government and my hospital grant their approval."

Lola wished she could smoke, but Dr. Friedman prohibited smoking in his office. What sense did that make? Doctors smoked like everyone else. She took a breath and collected her wits. She respected Dr. Friedman but saw no reason to grant him the last word. She would rely on the tenacity that had sustained her, if imperfectly, for so many years. Hadn't Vivien Leigh as Scarlett O'Hara in *Gone With the Wind* said something about tomorrow being another day? That day would come, and it would be better—but only if she willed it, shaped it to her purpose. "And approval will be granted when?"

Dr. Friedman rolled his chair closer until his stomach rested against the desk. "Lola, I know how much this means to you, but let's look at your situation from a clinical perspective. You have a history. Smoking. Trust me, not good for anyone. Drinking. Depression. These alone pose difficulties for someone facing multiple complex procedures. But when they're approved, and they will be, these procedures likely will be restricted."

"Restricted?"

"You'll be too old."

# SEPTEMBER 1953

## "ARE YOU NOW OR HAVE YOU EVER BEEN—?"

Lola hunched over the typewriter she'd purchased immediately after visiting Dr. Friedman. Her elbows propped on the living room's California Mission-style desk, she nestled her cheeks in her palms.

"Why do you spend so much time with this typewriter and not at the piano?" Fernando asked. "Can you write music this way?"

"I told you. I'm not writing music."

"Then what?"

"I told you. I'm writing what I'm writing."

Fernando furrowed his brow, mumbled something about women being puzzles never to be solved and retreated to the kitchen for a glass of water.

"Pour me a drink, will you?" Lola asked.

He reminded her that the radio-bar was in the living room, and *she* was in the living room.

"Men!" Lola muttered.

Fernando poked his head out of the kitchen doorway. "I heard that."

"It was a stage whisper. You were *meant* to hear it."

"We sound like an old married couple."

"We *are* an old married couple."

In tandem, they less laughed than snickered.

Lola poured a Scotch. She drank when it pleased her, and it pleased her often, although she insisted she could stop at will. At the end of July, she gave up drinking to celebrate the armistice in Korea. Three days later at her meeting with Christine Jorgensen, she resumed.

Fernando re-entered the living room. "I have it. You are writing a novel like your—now listen carefully—*once-upon-a-time*-friend Hemingway."

A black look dismissed Fernando's wordplay. Lola was engaged in serious work, although she *could* be another Papa given all she knew about storytelling. She'd created Lola Torres then Lola Flores. Years later, she developed Minna Goldstein. Establishing that identity required a story bold yet convincing to persuade Heshy to offer Fernando and her assistance above and beyond. On a trip to San Francisco before migrating north, she and Fernando enjoyed dinner with Heshy and his wife in their new San Francisco home and spun a masterful tale.

Fernando, Lola confided, descended from Conversos—Jews forced by the Spanish Inquisition to follow the ways of the Church. In Cuba, Fernando's grandmother married an Irish Catholic and attended Mass but made known her Jewish heritage to her son when he was a boy. Fernando's father passed down the secret but nothing in the way of traditions, lost to the family over generations. Ultimately, Fernando fell in love with Lola Flores, raised a Catholic but with no attachment to the Church or any religion. In time, he bared his soul. Lola found herself fascinated to the point of wondering whether she too had Jewish blood. Why else did they both feel kinship to Ben Siegel, Meyer Lansky, Irving Shapiro and, of course, Heshy and Rose Kaplan?

The crumbling of her film career left Lola with time to devour books on Jewish history and customs and then tutor Fernando. Their interest piqued, they began spending Friday evenings—disguised by makeup and wigs—at Reform synagogues where services were held in English. They introduced themselves as Solomon and Minna Goldstein, Cubans descended from Eastern European Jews come to the U.S. a decade earlier in flight from the uncertainties posed by the Sergeants' Revolt when Fulgencio Batista took power. All Lola asked of Heshy and Rose was compassion for their plight and acceptance of their assumed identities, which reflected the innermost desires of their neshamas—their souls.

Heshy and Rose pledged assistance and silence. After the Goldsteins established residence in San Francisco, Heshy introduced them to a nearby synagogue on California Street. He and Rose had joined *because after everything that happened in Europe, it felt like the right thing to do.*

Keeping up appearances, the Goldsteins attended occasional

Friday-night Shabbos services and those on the High Holidays. Congregants welcomed them as a delightful—and exotic—addition. Generous membership payments and fundraising gifts buttressed Solomon and Minna's status. Lola took comfort in "coming home."

Now, she placed a clean sheet of paper into the typewriter.

Fernando gazed down at Lola's hands poised above the keyboard then up into her eyes. His own eyes expressed disbelief. "You are *not!*" he said.

"But I *am*," Lola countered.

"You *cannot!*" Fernando insisted.

"I will be gone soon enough. How will this hurt me then?"

"Give up drinking and smoking, and you will live to one hundred and twenty like Moses."

"Moses never got to the Promised Land," Lola protested. "When I die, George Reuben will see that I do."

Fernando recalled how months earlier, he'd accompanied Lola to see Reuben, a lawyer recommended by Heshy. Reuben had no mob connections but being a Jew, could be trusted to keep everything within the family. They made appointments to see him on successive days. Reuben, although puzzled why a single consultation was insufficient, was agreeable.

At their first session, Lola instructed Reuben to prepare their wills. They'd brought a detailed list of their assets and specified beneficiaries to receive gifts after the first to die—the bulk of the estate would go to the survivor—and then the second.

*Were you ever a lawyer?* Reuben asked, only half jesting.

*She read a book*, Fernando answered for her.

Lola requested that Reuben accept an advance on his fee.

He told her it wasn't necessary.

She insisted.

Fernando presented a check.

Reuben took it and thanked them for their consideration.

The next day, Lola revealed to Reuben what even Heshy did not know. When Reuben recovered from his shock, she reminded him that having accepted their check the day before, the law bound him to maintain client confidentiality.

He responded that he had every intention of doing so.

Lola then detailed his additional responsibilities. Upon her death—she had no intention of entering the World to Come any time soon but had little control over the matter—Reuben was to access their safe deposit box, sparing Fernando a difficult task at a trying time. He would find instructions for her burial in the synagogue's cemetery—not as Minna Goldstein but as Lola Flores. To facilitate a delicate matter, he would find documents establishing Lola Flores' status as a Jew: a copy of Anshel's Warsaw birth registration, Albert's American passport and an affidavit from Sylvia attesting that Minna Goldstein aka Lola Flores had been born Anshel Sobel aka Albert Sobel, son of a Jewish mother.

Further, Reuben would present Heshy a letter in which Lola asked forgiveness for her deception, begged him and Rose to understand that despite the misleading nature of her body, she was a woman and requested that he offer Fernando any assistance required. "In addition, you will undertake one more task."

The safe deposit box would contain the original typewritten manuscript of Lola Flores' memoirs. She expected to complete the work before winter's end. Reuben would contact suitable literary agents, engage one and represent her estate through the book's publication in the United States and, hopefully, abroad. Lola Flores, concealed in shadow all her life would, in death, take her rightful place in the sun and help free from public scorn all men and women denied the opportunity to live as their true selves.

After exiting his reverie, Fernando asked, "And what about me? What will people say? What will I do?"

"You always said that if I die first, you will go to Europe."

Fernando nodded.

"So, everything will be resolved."

"But that will be a long time from now when I am old and gray."

Lola chuckled. "You're old and gray now."

Checkmated, Fernando went back to his room and shut the door.

Drink in hand, Lola remained at the radio-bar and studied a framed black-and-white photograph. A dozen tanned boys and girls in khaki shorts and white shirts smiled for their benefactors. They lived at a Jewish orphanage in the new State of Israel to which the Goldsteins regularly contributed in Albert's memory.

The phone pulled her away.

"A little bird tells me you spoke with Christine Jorgensen a month ago," said Walter Winchell.

"I imagine that little bird is named Christine," Lola said.

"She and I, we may be the only two people in America who know where you are. For that matter, who know Lola Flores is still alive. Like you asked, I've kept you out of the column since before you moved to San Francisco."

"You have been kind, Walter."

"*Kind* makes me uneasy. But anyway, your secret's safe with me."

"I would call it a desire for privacy."

"Have it your way. But you can't imagine how many people keep secrets these days. Anyway, I owe you one for helping Christine. Sweet kid. Works hard. Also, I thought you'd want to know it's hot as hell here in New York. Fog out your way? I bet. Summer in San Francisco's too damn cold for my taste."

"It is always such a pleasure to speak with you, Walter."

"Anyway, Christine gave me a glowing report. By the way, she killed 'em in Pittsburgh before she went down to Havana. But I'm not calling about Christine Jorgensen."

"May I ask, Walter, what you *are* calling about?"

Lola heard Walter's thoughts assemble in military ranks—if thoughts or soldiers tinkled like ice cubes.

"You remember," he said, "when Hoover asked you to go down to Havana? Before the war?"

Lola concentrated on the children. She was in no mood to reminisce, especially about J. Edgar Hoover.

Walter pushed on. "You remember, right?"

Lola held the receiver at arm's length. Walter pursuing a story or pontificating about a subject like America's security resembled a runaway train. Superman might be powerful enough to stop a speeding locomotive, but Lola Flores consisted of flesh and blood born on this war-plagued Earth. She returned the receiver to her ear. "That did not go well."

"You got that right, sister. I don't think you realize how upset that little episode made Edgar. But he let it go. As much as Edgar lets anything go. That's why I'm calling."

She heard more ice cubes tinkle.

"Hoover wants another favor."

"Walter—"

"I'm talking about what's going on right under our noses," he said, the pitch of his voice lowered to indicated that if they'd just exchanged a few pleasantries, the conversation had turned to significant matters about which he'd made a commitment and from which Lola had no right to run. A machine gun-paced narrative followed. Since V-E Day, America and the Soviet Union were engaged in a new kind of war in which neither country fired a shot. The prize was the world—free under the democratic hand of the U.S.A., enslaved under the heel of the Soviet boot. Stalin's death earlier in the year changed nothing. Communists and fellow travelers had wormed their way into every nook and cranny of American life. They infected Washington, where they schemed to ferret out dirty laundry and blackmail people useful to Moscow. "That's why in April, Ike signed that executive order forbidding homosexuals from working in the federal government."

"Walter, I have heard all this."

But America faced another Commie threat just as grave. Everybody knew, but he was saying it anyway. "Hollywood's crawling with Red serpents. Their fangs are sharp, and their poison's deadly."

"But I have not lived in Los Angeles for years."

"Sure. But what I hear, you're still close with Lucille Ball. Another little bird tells me you went down to L.A. in January after America's favorite Red—make that redhead—gave birth to Desi Jr."

Sweat formed on the palm of the hand with which Lola held the receiver.

"You must have heard things in L.A.," he said.

"Heard things? Walter, you sound like that Senator McCarthy on TV. I will have nothing to do with anything involving J. Edgar Hoover."

The tinkling of ice cubes grew lengthier and louder.

"I gotta be honest, Lola. After all I've done for your career, I take that personally."

"I appreciate everything, Walter."

"Do you? Really? I love this country. You weren't born here, but I hope *you* do, too. But like I said before—about Christine—I owe you one. So, take this to heart. Hoover says he has dirt on you."

Lola tapped her free hand against her thigh. To her knowledge, Hoover knew only about the American citizenship papers and passports he'd procured for Fernando and her. He'd get nowhere making that an issue, even if he insisted he'd never been involved, and no documents bore his signature. She considered that Walter might be bluffing. If so, he was running a fool's errand. Still, given the conversation's nasty turn, she decided to push back. The role called for considerable bravado. "If Hoover comes after me, he and I will stand together on the deck of the Titanic."

Winchell wasted no time responding. "Make it easy on yourself. You don't cooperate with Hoover, he'll send the matter to the House Un-American Activities Committee. It'd be like tossing a bone to a starving Dobermann. HUAC's already poking around San Francisco. They're looking to bust the International Longshore and Warehouse Union and hang that Commie bastard Harry Bridges, the guy who runs the show on the docks."

"I know nothing about the docks here or Communists in Hollywood, and I have nothing to say to those people."

"You think you'll have a choice? The committee can subpoena you. You'll *have* to talk."

"And if I claim my rights under the Fifth Amendment? America has a constitution, you know." Lola regretted her words as soon as they flew from her mouth. Was she admitting to Walter that she was guilty of some wrongdoing? She had nothing to hide. More, if Lola Flores had any hope of resurrecting her career—if she was even *thinking* about that—taking the Fifth would end it all.

"Trust me," Winchell said, seeming to read her mind. "Even if you're through with Hollywood, they'll make your life miserable."

"I will take my chances."

Walter softened his tone. "Listen, let's bury the hatchet. We go back a ways, right? And it's not like they want you to expose a lot of people."

"How comforting."

"Just one."

Two weeks later, with summer returned to San Francisco after its annual July-August hiatus, Fernando handed Lola a copy of the *Los Angeles Times*. A story and accompanying photo reported how the day before, Lucille Ball and Desi Arnaz held a press conference by the pool at their San Fernando Valley home. Eight days earlier—the day the United States had sought to bar Red China from being seated at the United Nations—an investigator from the House Un-American Activities Committee interviewed Lucille. With the transcript released, the press wanted to know if the star of "I Love Lucy," the country's number-one-rated TV show, was a loyal American.

Lucille reiterated that yes, back in 1936, she registered as a member of the Communist Party but only to please her grandfather, Fred Hunt. No, she knew nothing about politics then. Yes, she was a loyal American. And yes, the American people would understand.

Desi pushed back. "We're lucky this happened to us in America, where newspapermen ask the questions. In other countries, they shoot first and ask the questions later."

According to the *Times*, millions of fans who heard the news on radio and TV the night before continued to love Lucy. CBS confirmed that production for the new season would continue.

The doorbell rang. "I ordered groceries," Lola shouted to Fernando, "but I thought the market would deliver them later." She went to the door.

A small man with a sad face asked, "Are you Lola Flores?"

Lola froze. The name on the directory downstairs clearly stated Goldstein.

"I'll take that as a yes," he said. He held out an envelope. "You've been served."

Three days later, Lola sat at a table in a small, oak-paneled meeting room in San Francisco's City Hall. Her dark gray suit, chosen to make an impression of seriousness and, if she dared use the word, sobriety, belied the warmth of the season and its hydrangea-blue sky. She conceded that the setting, if not the room, helped make the inquisitors' intended impression on her. The Beaux-Arts building stood as impressive as El Capitolio in Havana. Its dome soared higher than that of the Capitol in Washington.

George Reuben sat at Lola's left. She'd been informed that an attorney would not be necessary but permitted. Reuben advised that an attorney would be an absolute necessity. Lola remembered standing up to J. Edgar Hoover and to Fulgencio Batista but feared—knew—that the strength she once possessed had deserted her.

Facing Lola at a larger oak table sat William A. Wheeler, the investigator for the House Un-American Activities Committee, who had interviewed Lucille in Los Angeles two weeks earlier. Against the wall behind him drooped the flags of the United States and the State of California. The golden eagles perched above their poles seemed anxious to take flight.

Wheeler offered a wan smile in a failed attempt to project affability then cleared his throat. "Miss Flores, on behalf of the House Un-American Activities Committee of whose staff I am a member, I thank you for your appearance at this hearing."

"I believe," Lola said, "I had no choice."

Wheeler thrust out his jaw then recomposed his face. "And you, Mr. Reuben."

"Mr. Wheeler," said Reuben, "I provided you with a note that Miss Flores is feeling ill. I ask that you postpone this interview until Miss Flores recovers her strength."

Wheeler removed his wire-rim glasses. "Duly noted, Mr. Reuben. But if Miss Flores can sit in this room erect, which she appears to be doing as we speak, it's safe to say she's fit enough to answer a few simple questions." He turned to a man on his left, whose large chin failed to divert attention from small, squinty eyes. "Let me introduce Robert Stripling, a counsel for the committee." Ignoring a functionary at Stripling's left, Wheeler shifted his weight, glanced to his right and nodded to a man in his twenties flaunting what seemed to be a permanent sneer. "And this is Roy Cohn."

Lola knew of Roy Cohn. Who didn't? In 1951, he prosecuted Julius and Ethel Rosenberg, who many people thought were railroaded, for passing atomic bomb secrets to the Russians. The past February, President Eisenhower refused to grant them clemency. In June, despite numerous protests, the Rosenbergs were electrocuted. Cohn currently served as chief counsel to the feared Joseph McCarthy, the Wisconsin Republican who chaired the Senate Permanent Subcommittee on Investigations.

"Let me make clear," said Wheeler, "that Mr. Cohn is here only as an observer. However, I've granted him permission to ask questions or comment as he sees fit." He looked further right towards a stenographer recording the morning's interview, to be sealed for at least several days, then whipped his head back to his left.

The functionary rose, instructed Lola to do the same and swore her in.

Wheeler cleaned his glasses with his navy tie then emphasized to Lola that the loyal Americans present in the room were charged with maintaining the security of the United States of America. "Now, if you and Mr. Reuben will bear with me, I'd like to save everyone time by acknowledging a few facts, such as you, Miss Flores, not having worked in Hollywood—or for that matter, New York—for the past five years."

"Longer than that," Lola said.

The functionary tittered.

Lola wondered whether his response implied sympathy or derision.

Wheeler turned to the offender, slid his glasses down to the end of his nose and stared. After repositioning them, he asked, "And you live here in San Francisco, Miss Flores?"

"Yes, your honor."

"How interesting. But I'm not a judge, Miss Flores, only a humble member of the staff of a very important committee of the United States House of Representatives."

"Yes, your honor."

Wheeler took out a handkerchief and dabbed at the right corner of his mouth. "For the record, Miss Flores, what do you do with your time?"

"I am writing a symphony."

"A woman?"

"Women can write symphonies. I also write other things."

Wheeler chuckled. "A Cuban cookbook?"

Lola refused to take the bait.

"Something political then?"

Lola placed her hands on the table and drummed her fingertips.

"Alright then. Let's get to the heart of the matter. Do you still maintain any connections with Hollywood? By which I mean the motion picture, radio and television industries."

"Very little, Mr. Wheeler."

"But some?"

"Very little."

"Would it be accurate to say, Miss Flores, that you are aware of what has transpired in Hollywood regarding the disloyalty exhibited by some individuals—"

Roy Cohn pointed a finger at Lola. "By *many* individuals."

"By many *disloyal* individuals against the United States?" Wheeler continued.

"I read the newspapers. I listen to the radio. I watch television."

Wheeler held up a sheaf of papers. "Miss Flores, I have here a list. It contains more than a hundred names of people in whom the committee has taken a deep interest. Despite your having left Hollywood, you might at some previous time have worked with some of these folks or engaged with them at some social gathering hosted by one studio or another. The studios, I point out, have been quite cooperative."

Lola leaned forward. "Mr. Wheeler, from here, I cannot read the names."

Wheeler rolled his eyes. "Miss Flores, this isn't an eye chart. What I'm going to do now is, I'm going to *read* some names. You'll say whether you know any of these people. A simple yes or no will suffice. Can you do that?"

"Yes, your honor."

"*Sir* will be fine."

"Yes, sir."

"Okay, now we're getting somewhere. I'll start with Alvah Bessie. Do you know him?"

"No."

"No?"

"No, I do not know him."

Wheeler frowned then continued, the list organized in alphabetical order: Herbert J. Biberman, Lester Cole, Edward Dmytryk—

Lola conceded that she'd met several of the nine men Wheeler mentioned. She also noted that the list contained no women.

"We'll get to that," said Wheeler. "But I'm going to ask you now, would you define any of these men as friends? People you spent time with away from the studio?"

"No," Lola answered. She saw no reason to mention that she'd kept herself isolated. Or why.

Wheeler covered his mouth and conversed with Roy Cohn in a voice that defied confidentiality and carried across the room. "No offense, but isn't it interesting how many of these fellas are Jews?"

George Reuben stood.

Wheeler motioned for him to sit then turned to the stenographer. "You get that last comment?"

"Yes, sir," she said.

"Strike it." He turned back to Lola. "One final name, Miss Flores. Do you know Dalton Trumbo?"

"Everyone knows Dalton Trumbo," Lola responded. "Who he is, I mean. But I have not had the pleasure."

Wheeler raised his hand to the knot in his tie then lowered it, sacrificing comfort for the appearance of authority. "If I have my figures correct, you are acquainted to some degree with three of the people I just mentioned."

"Hollywood is a small town," said Lola.

"That's what they say about Washington. But do you know *who* these men are? I mean, all the men whose names I just read?"

"They call them the Hollywood Ten. In 1948, they refused to name names for your committee."

Wheeler coughed. "For the record, they refused to answer the committee's lawful questions concerning Communist infiltration of the movie industry and the enormous harm that's done to this nation. They violated the law—the law of the land—and for their treachery they went to prison. Each and every one." He attempted to grin. His mouth defied him.

George Reuben again stood. "Mr. Wheeler, I see no need—"

"Mr. Reuben, I'm just leading up to the point of this meeting. Setting the stage if I may use a theatrical term. I'll instruct you to hold any objections you might fancy until we've moved along."

Reuben sat.

Wheeler again held up the list. "Miss Flores, I could read more names, but I see no need. I do wonder though, do you know what's happened to these people's careers?"

"Even those who did not go to prison cannot work. They have been blacklisted."

Wheeler placed the papers on the table. "That's such an ugly word, Miss Flores. The studios have simply chosen—of their own volition, mind you—not to hire them. And why? Because these are people with deep and dangerous relationships with the Communist Party USA. Agents of the Soviet Union intent on destroying our American way of life."

Lola's shoulders slumped. She lowered her head. She had no idea what

Wheeler was getting at but was more than aware that she was unwell and feeling worse by the minute.

Wheeler tapped his hands together. "Miss Flores, I'm proud to say that as regards Hollywood, most of this committee's work is done. But we still have a few lingering concerns. Despite our best efforts, one person remains free to continue advancing Communist treachery in varied and surreptitious ways. Have you any idea about whom I'm speaking?"

"No, sir."

Reuben raised his hand.

Wheeler dismissed him with a wave of his arm. "Miss Flores," he said, "before I continue—get to the heart of the matter—let me ask you another question. Are you now or have you ever been a member of the Communist Party USA?"

Lola leaned against Reuben's shoulder.

"Mr. Wheeler," Reuben said. "This is leading nowhere and Miss Flores—"

"Mr. Reuben, this investigation will continue on the course I've set for it come hell or high water. Do I make myself clear?"

Lola straightened up.

Reuben offered her a glass of water then turned back to Wheeler. "As Miss Flores' attorney, I have a duty to point out that she is a naturalized American citizen and a registered Democrat. That party affiliation in no way violates the interests and security of the United States. Therefore, I think it's appropriate that this interview end now."

Wheeler slammed the table with his fist. "Mr. Reuben, *I* will determine what is appropriate and when to terminate this interview." He looked at Lola. "Miss Flores, I think it best that you answer the question."

Lola swallowed. "I am not now or ever have been— You know."

Wheeler unbuttoned his suit coat then re-buttoned it. "What about in Cuba? You ever belong to the Party there?"

"I am not now—" Lola struggled to catch her breath.

Wheeler scratched his chin then shook his head. "I'll take that as a no, Miss Flores." He raised an eyebrow at Reuben then pointed at Lola. "Miss Flores, I want you to know that this hearing isn't about *you*, which I'm sure will set you at ease and, I hope, Mr. Reuben, as well." He glanced at Roy

Cohn then back at Lola. "What I'm going to do now is ask you a question about someone else, and I expect the truth. Can you give me the truth?"

"Yes," said Lola.

Wheeler smiled. "Of course. Of course, you can. So— Do you know Lucille Ball?"

As if responding to a cue, Lola said, "I love Lucy."

Wheeler's chin jutted forward. "Yes, you reference Miss Ball's television show. Very popular with a certain crowd. But I'm not talking about Lucy Ricardo which, I believe, is the character she plays. I'm talking about the actress. Do you know Lucille *Ball?*"

Lola looked towards George Reuben.

He nodded.

"Yes."

"And her husband?"

"Everyone knows Ricky Ricardo."

Wheeler scowled. "Miss Flores, you will dispense with the comedy, for which I believe you were noted once. The matter before us couldn't be more serious." He again pointed a finger at Lola as if it were the barrel of a gun and he was hard-pressed to keep from pulling the trigger. "Do you know Miss Ball's husband in real life? Desi Arnaz?"

"Yes," said Lola. "He is a Cuban, like me. A Cuban-*American.*"

Wheeler grunted and lowered his hand. "Do you know if Miss Ball is now or has ever been a member of the Communist Party?"

Lola found herself confused—more confused, as it was, than when she first took her seat. Why was Wheeler asking this when he'd interviewed Lucille two weeks earlier? Did he expect her to implicate Lucille in some Communist plot? She honestly had nothing to offer the committee. She suspected Wheeler knew she had no knowledge of Lucille's political life but believed that if he continued to hound her, she would make something up. Lie. Betray Lucille as so many in Hollywood betrayed not only acquaintances but also friends, the pressure brought to bear by men like Wheeler and Roy Cohn squeezing the life breath out of them.

Wheeler displayed what passed for a smile in anticipation of what was to follow. "The question seems to me, Miss Flores, a simple one. Shall I repeat it?"

Lola resisted shaking her head to avoid dislodging her wig. "No, that will not be necessary. I read the newspapers. Lucille told you she joined the Communist Party long ago to please her grandfather, but she had no interest in politics."

Wheeler ran a finger down his tie. "I know what Miss Ball said to *me*, Miss Flores. What I'm asking is, did she ever tell *you* about being a Communist? Confide in you about going to Party meetings. Working Commie propaganda into a film or radio show. Her TV show. Trying to undercut this nation in a way her audience—loyal Americans upholding American family values—wouldn't be aware of but would take in through what they call subliminal means."

"Subliminal?"

"They'd become sympathetic to the Kremlin without realizing it."

"No."

"No? Miss Ball never spoke about these things when you visited her last January?"

"No, sir. But I can tell you what Desi told Hedda Hopper. He said, 'The only thing red about Lucy is her hair, and even that isn't legitimate.'"

The functionary howled.

Roy Cohn looked at Wheeler.

Wheeler tapped the middle finger of his right hand against the list for what appeared to be half a minute.

Lola winced at his failure to keep adequate time but understood his power to impose all the time he wanted to pry into Lucille's life. And if he didn't like the answers she gave, into hers.

"Mr. Wheeler," said Reuben, "Miss Flores is feeling worse. She clearly has answered your questions, and I strongly request that this interview conclude."

Roy Cohn placed his left hand on Wheeler's shoulder and leaned forward. "Speaking for Mr. Wheeler, I think we've probably heard enough for today." He sat back then leaned forward again. "But don't think, Miss Flores, we're in any way finished with you."

Lola pressed her hands against her chest and attempted to take a deep breath. An audible wheeze filled the room. It approximated the grinding of gears in a failing machine.

# MARCH 1954

# FORGOTTEN AND REMEMBERED

Unrecognized, Lola gazed across the smoky, boisterous Venetian Room with near-vacant eyes. Seated ringside with Fernando, she held the stub of a cigarette in her right hand, a glass of Scotch in her left.

She'd played the club, a renowned watering hole in the Fairmont Hotel across California street from the Mark Hopkins, before the war. Her memory sketchy, she thought the columned stage even more confining, the white-clothed tables packed even closer to maximize the room's capacity to make a dollar given the booming economy under Dwight Eisenhower. Couples—men at home in boardrooms and country clubs, wives familiar with overseeing the help at dinner parties—filled the cramped dance floor where bumped shoulders and errant elbows prompted exaggerated displays of alcoholic civility. Ernie Heckscher's band played a melody Lola had heard a hundred times. A thousand. The title escaped her.

A busboy approached to take their dinner plates then hesitated. Lola had left her roast beef untouched. She motioned him to remove it, stubbed out her cigarette then lit another. She could hardly conceal her impatience for the show to begin.

Several days earlier, Christine Jorgensen had asked Lola and Fernando to attend her opening night. Christine was sure—almost, mostly—that Lola would love—at least like—the show. Her uncharacteristic angst disregarded the rave reviews she and Myles Bell had received two months earlier when they opened at New York's Latin Quarter.

Lola accepted and offered Christine encouragement but right after putting down the receiver confessed to Fernando her reluctance to attend.

Fernando insisted that Lola keep her promise. Their presence would extend Christine the opportunity to return the kindness they'd shown her before she played Havana. Christine certainly would appreciate their support. Naturally, they'd stay after the show to congratulate her and meet Myles.

Lola relented. At the same time, she swore she would never do another favor for Walter Winchell. After her interview with the pompous William Wheeler and the leering Roy Cohn—the transcript still kept from the public—his column questioned her patriotism. Fernando advised Lola to allow Walter to blow off steam. She could—*should*—win him back into her corner. He could be of great use. They had plans.

The band stopped playing. The room went silent.

Ernie Heckscher welcomed the Venetian Room's guests and introduced Christine Jorgensen. The band began an American standard from the previous century, "I Want a Girl Just Like the Girl that Married Dear Old Dad." The audience laughed. Christine and Myles bounded onto the stage. The crowd cheered.

The act met Lola's expectations. Myles sang tunes like "The Girl That I Marry" and "Daddy's Little Girl." Christine joined him occasionally but mostly used Myles as a straight man for self-deprecating quips related to each song. She also tickled the audience by affirming that she knew first-hand just what men thought about women.

At the show's conclusion, the crowd's enthusiasm left Lola with mixed emotions. She liked Christine, saluted her stage presence and wit. But Christine Jorgensen was no Lola Flores.

As dance music resumed, an ebullient Christine, Myles in hand, made her way through the admiring crowd, accepting kisses on both cheeks. A waiter wedged two additional seats around Lola and Fernando's table. After the performers sat, a photographer from the *Chronicle* appeared and urged the foursome to huddle together. After he moved to another table, Christine confided that in May, a plastic surgeon in New Jersey would provide her with a vaginal canal and female genitalia. "Isn't medicine wonderful?"

Lola shook her head, not in disagreement but to cast off the bursts of light from the flashbulbs agitating her retinas.

Fernando leaned close. "Cariña, I have respected your wishes not to make anything of your birthday, but I am feeling that a dessert with a birthday candle would be better than another drink."

Lola hoisted her glass.

Fernando interrupted Lola to read her the morning *Chronicle*'s lead story, his concern emphasized by a vocal delivery suited less to the intimacy of their living room than to the stage. The previous night on CBS's nationally televised *See It Now*, Edward R. Morrow called out Joe McCarthy for his vituperative attacks on the armed services. "This is no time for men who oppose Senator McCarthy's methods to keep silent."

Lola, eye-opener in hand, shook her head. "What about *women* who oppose that bastard? Why must women be forgotten? Treated like second-class citizens? People like *us* not even *that?*"

Fernando took Lola's question as rhetorical and continued reading Morrow's remarks concerning the impossibility of defending freedom overseas while deserting it at home.

Lola snorted and returned her attention to the entertainment section. She spotted a photo bearing an image of her she almost didn't recognize and grimaced. Its caption read: *Christine Jorgensen shares post-opening drinks at Venetian Room with co-star Myles Turner and two admirers.*

"Not that I want to frighten you," Dr. Friedman told Lola the next day, "but I'm concerned about the declining state of your health. And I won't mince words. *Very* concerned."

Fernando touched Lola's wrist. "Cariña, I know it is not the best time, but certain things can wait. Your health matters more than anything else. You *must* go back to the clinic."

After the September interview with the House Un-American Activities Committee, Dr. Friedman had informed Lola that she'd suffered a minor heart attack. *But still serious. Any heart attack is serious.* He urged her to spend several weeks at a clinic he ran, much like Dr. Sherman's in Connecticut and Dr. Mortensen's near San Bernardino. *We can wean you from tobacco and alcohol if you work with us. You'll also have the chance to put on some healthy weight.*

Lola refused.

Fernando implored.

Lola objected. Had she become an embarrassment? Did they want to put her away and keep her out of sight? Would they ever let her return?

Fernando called Heshy.

Lola's objection overruled, they drove north to the clinic in the Napa Valley. It was not lost on the three of them that this was California's wine country.

In mid-October, Fernando and Heshy returned Lola to San Francisco. She admitted that her stay had been pleasant. She'd made a dent in her reading, including Hemingway's latest novel, *The Old Man and the Sea*—the Cuban story he'd promised to write all those years ago and only his second novel published since *For Whom the Bell Tolls* in 1940. Lola found inspiration in the fisherman's brave but fruitless struggle to bring home a huge marlin. She took heart that even if she'd suffered a delay in writing her memoirs, she would eventually bring her story to the world.

She also put on ten pounds.

By Thanksgiving, Lola resumed smoking and drinking. By New Year's, she appeared near skeletal. Despite the best efforts of the clinic staff, the nervous strain provoked by the interview with William Wheeler had never abated. The committee's recent unsealing of the interview's transcript struck heavy blows against the remnants of her ego and hopes for the future. The press had declined to come to her defense. *Variety* and the *Hollywood Reporter* virtually disregarded Lola Flores, relegating their report of her testimony to three column inches buried deep within each publication. Walter Winchell denied her even a single line of print.

Wretched but relentless, Lola resumed writing.

Fernando forced upon her periods of rest. Coaxing her to eat proved less successful.

The memoir advanced. Lola's health retreated.

"There's always hope," said Dr. Friedman. "Fernando can drive you back up to Napa this afternoon."

"Yes, there is always hope," Lola agreed.

Fernando and Dr. Friedman smiled in unison.

"That is why I cannot go to the clinic," Lola said. "On Sunday, we must fly down to Los Angeles."

# MARCH 1954

# THE MAN IN THE MIRROR

Lola's hands trembled as she perched on the edge of the couch in her dressing room at Desilu Studios. Coffee sloshed up towards the rim of her mug decorated with a bright red heart. She'd gone without a drink for two days—a matter of necessity, not choice. This morning, after years away from the stage and the camera, she would sit at the first table read for a new episode of *I Love Lucy*. She gave thought not so much to triumph as disaster.

Lucille Ball had extended an invitation to appear on the show to express her gratitude for Lola's testimony rejecting William Wheeler's accusations.

Lola rebuffed her. Yes, she'd considered, if in a vague way, a comeback of sorts. No, she wasn't ready for a platform as large as Lucy and Desi's.

Lucille persisted. Lola owed it to herself—and her fans, who remembered her long after she dismissed them—to return to show business. She brought up the old saw about Lola being a fish out of water.

Lola resisted. She envisioned herself more as Jonah being swallowed by a whale. With movies and the whole studio system dying, *Lucy* represented a different kind of Hollywood, exciting but frightening. Television would put Lola in front of an audience no movie could hope to attract. On a single night, she'd enter millions of living rooms only to be exposed as a has-been and rightfully so.

Despite Lola's fears, the spark Lucille kindled grew into a small flame. Lola purchased Norman Vincent Peale's book, *The Power of Positive Thinking* and read it over the course of two days, underlining passages that spoke to her. The flame flickered. Following Peale's suggestion, she reached out to a Higher Power. She began to commune with the unknowable God from whom she'd become estranged despite Minna Goldstein's synagogue membership. The next day, flowers arrived from Lucille. God had sent a sign.

Now, minutes from meeting with the cast and director, a relentless torment plagued Lola. She'd have to maintain nerve-wracking sobriety until Friday evening when filming would take place. Further, shooting the episode offered no guarantee that this first step back would lead to another. Rather than laugh and cheer, a live audience might descend into ominous silence. The show's editors could sweeten the laugh track for the home audience, but Lucille and Desi would recognize the disaster they had on their hands. Putting business first—she couldn't blame them for that— they might re-shoot with another singer. It wasn't impossible that they would shelve the week's work, eat the cost of developing a new script and produce an unplanned episode. Lola Flores would become Hollywood's latest symbol of failure. Worse, a failure twice over.

Albert made a rare appearance. The Talmud, he reminded her, always presented the minority opinion. She owed it to herself to hear him out. Lola Flores had the opportunity to correct a terrible wrong. A self-inflicted wrong. On that morning years back when Heshy came to her door with news of Ben Siegel's death, she had slipped on self-imposed shackles and run away again, this time to San Francisco. The time had come to sever those shackles and live her life as she, and no one else, directed.

Knuckles rapped on the door. A familiar voice rang out.

Fernando let in Lucille and Desi.

After hugs and kisses, Lucille said, "I thought we'd go over the script before the table read. I don't have to tell you, you'll be terrific."

Lola found their calm troubling. Although well-intentioned— naturally, they wanted her to get off to a good start—they'd failed to acknowledge her fragile emotional state. On the other hand, she conceded, they were unlikely to know just how brittle it was.

Desi placed his hand over his heart. "I love having another Cuban on the show. We should have thought of this before." He handed updated sides to Lola and Fernando.

Lucille reviewed the premise. The legendary Lola Flores is booked to perform with Ricky Ricardo at his nightclub. Lucy, always chasing her big break in show business, insists she can sing as well as Lola Flower Hat. She hounds Ricky to give her a part in the show. Ricky reminds her that not only is Lola Flores one of a kind, she's a real Cuban. Not so Lucy McGillicuddy. But because he loves Lucy, Ricky has arranged a front-row table on opening night for her and their best friends, the Mertzes.

Lucille pointed to a key third-act scene in the Ricardos' living room.

> RICKY
>
> I tell you what. I'll introduce you at the table with a big spotlight. Fred and Ethel, too. Lola can even give you a kiss. But you can't be in the show. I'm putting my foot down.

LUCY makes a sad face.

> RICKY
>
> Listen, Lucy -- Why don't you go out and buy yourself a new hat? That always cheers you up.

> LUCY
>
> And shoes?

> RICKY
>
> (Mutters in Spanish) I put my foot down, and <u>you</u> end up putting both of yours in new shoes. This is gonna cost me a lot of money.

LUCY makes a pleading face.

> RICKY
>
> (<u>Shrugs</u>) Okay. And shoes.

(MUSIC OUT OF SCENE)

"That is wonderful," said Lola. "A perfect set-up for the finale."

Lucy Ricardo was written to be as much Ricky's teen-age daughter as his wife, a lovable but flighty child-woman consumed with daydreams and wholly dependent on the income and sage counsel of her husband. Television would have it no other way, so Lucille, Lucy's opposite, complied. In creating a sham that produced huge ratings every week, she secured a very real position of power that earned her the respect of everyone behind the camera. Still, her audience saw only Lucy. Lola wondered whether the networks would ever let Lucille pull back the curtain.

Friday afternoon, Lola practically skipped down the hallway to be readied for dress rehearsal. After, the cast and crew would break for a light supper before filming at eight.

Fernando caught up only when she paused before entering Wardrobe. "Is this really *you*, cariña?" he asked, panting, his shoulders heaving. "It is like you received the cure at Lourdes." Catching himself on the brink of a possible indiscretion, he raised a finger to his lips.

Lola kissed him on the cheek. After Monday's difficult start, the week went well. Resisting a drink proved unnerving, but each day she found renewed strength of body and spirit. She even halved her cigarette consumption. And what would prevent her from becoming teetotal again if she put her mind to it? Giving up cigarettes, too? Several times over the past days, she'd scolded herself for disregarding Dr. Friedman's advice. She felt better than she had in years.

Improved health led Lola to believe she really could revive her career and create something of a second life. No, a third. The night before, she lay awake for hours, entertaining thoughts of secretly undergoing surgery like Christine Jorgensen's. If that remained impossible in America, she'd go to Europe. Fernando often said that medicine there was more advanced. The resolve that made Lola Flores a star in Havana, New York and Hollywood would see her through. Of course, no producer would ever call upon her to play an ingenue, but as a singer and comedienne, she hardly could be considered old. For that matter, real old-timers like Sophie Tucker, another of Mama's favorites, regularly appeared on TV.

Not that she was naïve. Christine had been a nobody when she revealed her true self. Perhaps the reference to being a *nobody* was unkind. She was a person, a human being like Lola, and if unusual like Lola, still normal. And yes, also *unknown*—that term was fair—until she became a curiosity. And *curiosity* was accurate if not terribly kind because that was how the public saw her. Someday—admittedly far in the future—women like Christine Jorgensen and Lola Flores might draw notice only for their talent. Yet to her credit, Christine stood up for herself and exhibited the nerve to take advantage of her notoriety. There, Lola believed without rancor, Christine held an advantage.

Of course, one not-so-small matter put Lola Flores at a major disadvantage. She could never reveal her relationship with Albert Sobel. That would risk a nasty confrontation with the same public that hailed Christine Jorgensen for being so forthright. Millions of people knew or remembered Lola Flores only as a woman. They would take umbrage at her deception, turn on her no matter how necessary that deception had been. And what might they demand in expiation? Some people did horrible things. Violent things. As a child, she remembered Papa and Mama talking about the lynching of poor Leo Frank in Georgia, which occurred three years after the Sobels' arrival in the land of the free. Much time had passed, but their hushed tones disclosed a wound still festering among immigrants and native-born alike. *Because he was a Jew,* Papa said. *Not the crime they accused him of, which he wouldn't have done. A college man? A married man? Because he was a Jew.*

Refusing to be cowed regardless of lurking pitfalls, Lola determined to march onward. This was 1954. Despite the appearance she'd been forced to make before William Wheeler, this America was not the one in which she'd grown up. Not all that much, anyway. The role of women was changing. Lucille proved a wonderful example. With one telephone call, she could get Lola Flores a guest spot on any show on CBS. For that matter, a show on any other network.

Forty-five minutes later, Lola joined Lucille and Desi on the cavernous soundstage. The set reminded her of a cardboard diorama she'd constructed in elementary school. The living room and kitchen of the Ricardos' Manhattan apartment—mainstays of each show—connected to a third area dressed for her scene. The band, which always played live, occupied additional space just beyond. Overhead lights suspended from catwalks provided uniform illumination augmented by portable fill lights mounted above each camera. The special lighting accommodated Lucille and Desi's new approach to TV production. Three cameras filmed each scene at the same time in front of a live audience.

Lola closed her eyes and breathed deeply.

Lucille draped an arm around her. "Can I make a confession? When the writers first came up with this bit, they were thinking of Harpo Marx." She gave Lola a squeeze.

As Lola patted Lucille's hand to express her appreciation, she confronted a new bout of anxiety whetted by anger. She understood her role as Lucille's foil. She'd served as Fanny Brice's straight man—and didn't straight *man* have an ironic ring to it. In return, Fanny boosted Lola's Broadway career.

But ultimately, playing second banana to Lucille—even if she became a Phoenix risen out of the ashes—would change nothing. She'd continue to play second banana to herself. Her complete self. Albert would remain in exile, denied recognition as having been part of Lola Flores. *Still* part of her. What she desired even more than a renewed career was having her reflection seen in the mirror America held up to itself and accepted in its totality—redemption from a fragmented life.

The director, William Asher, signaled his assistant, who summoned the scene's third cast member and readied the crew. "Let's run this through," he called.

Lola and Lucy took their places.

"And *action*."

Lucy, enveloped in a floor-length beige raincoat buttoned at the neck, entered the interior of a fancy hat shop.

A matronly saleslady approached. Her skirt, jacket and blouse all met the demands of the gray scale required for broadcasting in black and white. "May I help you, madam?" she asked.

"Yes, thank you," said Lucy, her eyes darting around the shop. "I'm looking for a special hat. I'm going to the opening of Ricky Ricardo's new nightclub act tonight."

"Isn't he—"

"The Cuban bandleader who sings like a bird and talks like he has marbles in his mouth."

The saleslady smiled. "Oh yes. He's very handsome."

"And I'm *Mrs.* Ricardo."

The saleslady dismissed any hint of attraction to the dapper Ricky Ricardo while conceding that any true-blue, red-blooded American woman would find him dashing and romantic. She'd meant only to affirm her lucky customer's good fortune. "You've certainly come to the right shop, Mrs. Ricardo," she said. "Have you something particular in mind?"

Peace made, Lucy responded, "Gosh, I'm not sure. You have so many beautiful hats."

"Then please look around," said the saleslady. "I'll be right over there if you need me." She exited screen-left.

Lucy glanced at several hats and selected one fitted low to her head. A cloth and lace tie projected forward like the beak of a tropical bird. Eager to evaluate her appearance, she approached a full-length mirror—a prop consisting of an oval wooden frame lacking glass. She looked into it and startled.

The image facing Lucy Ricardo wore an identical raincoat and held an identical hat while striking the same astonished pose. But its face sported a Groucho Marx nose, mustache and eyeglasses. Lucy leaned forward and stared. Simultaneously, the man in the mirror leaned forward and stared back. Lucy stroked her nose. Without an interval, her faux double stroked his faux nose. Lucy waved her arms. The man in the mirror mimicked her. Perplexed, Lucy put on the hat. Her doppelganger did the same. Lucy tried on several more hats. The man in the mirror matched every hat, movement and expression. Finally, Lucy and her double put on huge flower hats like those made famous by Lola Flores.

Both Lucy and the man in the mirror smiled then frowned.

Bewildered, Lucy took off her hat and wailed, "Ay, ay, ay!"

The man in the mirror, leaving his hat on, pulled off his Groucho nose then ripped off his specially sewn raincoat. Before Lucy stood a woman sheathed in a brilliant red, white and blue gown of Cuban inspiration. "Ay, ay, ay!" the unmasked double sang, her voice strong and sure.

Surprised and delighted, Lucy cried out, *"Lola Flores!"*

The band began to play.

Lola, still singing, raised the bottom of her skirt, ducked her head and stepped through the mirror's frame.

The women embraced as the band played out of the scene.

"Cut!" said Asher. "Ladies, that was beautiful."

Lucille bent over with laughter.

As if still Lucy's mirror image, Lola also bent over. Unlike Lucy, she

David Perlstein

tumbled forward, ricocheted like a billiard ball off Lucille's shoulder, spun and toppled. The back of her head thudded against the floor.

Lola sensed the studio fade to black then acquired a second sight. She found herself making an unscripted exit, floating above the snaking cables and taped marks, the lights, the roof, the bleach-white clouds scudding across Los Angeles' technicolor-blue sky.

From what seemed a great distance, she heard Fernando whisper, "I'll call Dr. Mortenson. And Dr. Friedman."

Another voice, unidentifiable and as far-off, asked, "Miss Flores, can you hear me?"

Lola attempted to open her eyes. Her lids repelled the effort as if weighted down with gold coins.

"Can you wiggle your fingers?" the voice asked.

Lola's fingers remained motionless.

The anonymous voice continued its questioning. "Can you tell me where you are?"

Lola, hovering immobile in renewed darkness, could no more speak than take on ballast and descend to the studio floor. Still, if she couldn't say where she was, she knew where she was going. A faint light illuminated two paths. She intuited that the first and more distant led to the World to Come. She would follow it soon enough. The nearer path urged a brief detour to attend the brilliantly choreographed close to her own show's grand finale.

*Late-October. Lower Manhattan. Pike Slip. Opposite, sun poised to rise above Brooklyn.*

*East River. Concrete-gray mist. Thick as dry ice on a Broadway stage. Obscures boats bobbing in the water. Hushes bells, rigging, water lapping at hulls.*

*Old men gather. Early risers from the Lower East Side. Chinatown. Grasp fishing rods. Seek a meal. Scorn long odds. Oysters gone. Fish few in the poisoned estuary.*

*Albert stands on the wooden dock. Small and low. Follows Juana/John's directions. Removes jacket, shirt, trousers, shoes. Easy for Papa and Mama to identify. Into his right shoe, tucks a note. Most suicides leave notes. Juana/ John knows. A professional matter. "Keep it short. Penmanship counts. Suicides want people to know why. And don't worry. This is my precinct. By the time you're reported missing, you'll be long gone. Your folks won't push. How do they explain?"*

*Down to underwear and gooseflesh, Albert leaps into the water. Grunts. Grits his teeth. The cold familiar. Also, the filth. A nearby fisherman calls, "You nuts?" Swims on. Another shouts, "What the hell!" A second witness.*

*Albert swims farther. Thrashes arms and legs. Sends aloft white plumes. Submerges. Continues under the surface. Comes up for air. Hazy silhouettes of boats screen him from the slip. Good. Navigates around castle-size stones. The base of the near Manhattan Bridge tower. Submerges again. Breaks the surface. Gulps down air. Looks up. Peers around. Mist thicker. Listens. Locates the shore. Glides back. Silent. Stealth is all.*

*Maribel, "visiting a sick cousin," holds up a worn blanket. Throws it over Albert's shoulders. Dries him like a mother her newborn. Hands him men's clothes. Shoes. Ordinary. Worn. Unidentifiable. Combs his hair. Holds his hand as they walk towards an alley. Ducks in. Discards the blanket. Guides him to Allen and Grand. Across the street, Juana/John snaps the brim of his weather-beaten gray fedora.*

*Maribel hails a taxi. Draws Albert against her. Rests her arm around his shoulders.*

*Albert shivers all the way north.*

*They arrive at the apartment of Isabel and Pilar. Warm. Albert wolfs down fried eggs. No bacon. Toast and coffee. Much coffee. Cannot evict the chill burrowed into his bones.*

*That evening, a hearty dinner. Then Maribel helps Albert dress. Tucks his ticket and passport into his purse. Lola Torres' ticket. Lola Torres' purse. Albert's passport. Settles Lola and her luggage into a taxi. Lola and Albert must make this journey alone.*

*Penn Station. Lola/Albert seeks the platform. Stumbles into a dislocation of time and space. Autumn evening turns February morning. Penn Station yields to the icy waters of New York Harbor.*

*Lola Flores gets her bearings. The upper deck of the President Lincoln. Assumes the role of a groundling attending Shakespeare's Globe Theatre. A crowd of one. The play begins. A play within a play.*

*Papa holds up Albert. No, Anshel. Stumbles.*

*Mama's eyes widen with fear. Tosia giggles.*

*Papa regains his footing. Betrays tears of relief. Joy. Squeezes Anshel. Breathes deeply. Tastes the bitter salt air. Harbinger of a sweet new life.*

*Lola gasps as Papa points to the New Colossus. Watches Anshel blow a kiss. Lean forward. Admire the Lady's flowing robes. Spiked crown. Left hand grasping a tablet. Symbol of knowledge? Knowledge of hidden things? Right hand raising a gilt beacon of welcome.*

*Feels the chill kiss of the Malach HaMovis on her lips as Papa offers Anshel a promise. More. A blessing. The same offered by every father concluding every voyage endured by the wretched refuse, the homeless, the tempest-tossed: "In America, a man can be anything he wants."*

# ACKNOWLEDGMENTS

Numerous books and articles provided background on subjects including Cuban and Cuban-Jewish history and culture, transgender/intersex issues, gangsters (Jewish and not) and the entertainment industry.

Many historic characters appear in the book. Their words and actions reflect who they were but derive strictly from my imagination.

Many people gave of their time to review portions or all the manuscript at various stages of its development. Their comments meant a great deal to me as did their enthusiasm. Readers and advisors included Ron Eaton, Danielle Fry, Christina Jefferson, Les Kozerowitz, Jim Shay, Karen Shay and Marty Weiner. My wife Carolyn kept me on the straight-and-narrow along with my son Aaron. My writing coach Tom Parker provided indispensable guidance. Steve Sanders offered valuable advice on classical piano technique.

Above all, my son Yosi enlightened me about transgender people's attitudes towards partners and the wide variety of trans personalities we so often fail to acknowledge.

Thank you, one and all.

# AUTHOR Q&A

*Q. You have a transgender son. Did Yosi inspire you to write Lola Flores?*

A. Yes and no. Yes, my wife and I love Yosi, who made us very aware of transgender issues. We developed an understanding of the daily, often dangerous challenges faced by trans men and women. But the idea for the novel developed in an entirely different way.

*Q. What happened?*

A. I was having coffee with friends when I blurted out something off the wall, which I do with some frequency: "Did you guys know that Carmen Miranda was a man?" Carmen Miranda was a Portuguese-born Brazilian singer and actress from the 1930s to the early '50s. I have no idea what prompted this remark. Maybe, it's just that I love telling stories. I related with a straight face that Carmen Miranda obviously never could reveal she was a man. Not then. After coming to Hollywood, she worked for the FBI trying to uncover Nazi sympathizers then Communists.

*Q. They believed you?*

A. They were skeptical. So I emailed them a short bio of the Carmen Miranda I'd invented and included facts about her life. We dropped the matter, but I thought I'd come up with a concept for an exciting novel.

*Q. Why did you set Lola Flores in the first half of the Twentieth Century instead of today?*

A. That time period always has fascinated me. That's when my family established its footing in America as part of the great immigration of Eastern European Jews starting in the 1880s. I envisioned a big, sweeping story against that background, which includes the Depression, World War Two and the start of the Cold War. I could work with political volatility in Cuba, gangsters, celebrities, Broadway, Hollywood and McCarthyism. The time period established a special tension, because transgender men and women weren't thought about, let alone accepted. Lola continuously had to hide her male birth and upbringing to leverage her exceptional talents. She succeeded but at a price.

Q. *Even after meeting Lili Elbe, the "Danish Woman," in Nazi Berlin, Lola remained in the closet as it were. Why?*

A. Their situations were apples and oranges. Lili Elbe revealed herself but was European and a painter known only in limited circles. She didn't face audiences night in and night out, as well as the celebrity-hounding American press. Also, she gave up painting to abandon her male persona. Lola refused to compromise her career and found it difficult to totally separate from her male personality—Albert.

Q. *You evidently did a lot of research. Did you go to Havana?*

A. No. Havana resembles but isn't the city it was in the 1930s. Subtle changes can mislead you. For example, I described a marble fountain with dolphins in the Plaza Vieja. I found an accurately dated photo of the fountain online. Only a few years later, the plaza was renovated and the fountain replaced. If I'd taken notes in Havana, the description would have been wrong. I could have made similar mistakes with the Hotel Nacional. Fortunately, the Internet offers a seemingly endless resource of photos and films. I found the schedule of the Havana Special from New York to Key West and the breakfast menu Lola orders from. But settings should serve the story. *Lola Flores* is a novel, not a travelogue.

Q. *Lola was born Anshel Sobel, a Polish Jew who comes to America as a young child. Were you channeling your family?*

A. In a general way. My father Morris (Moishe) was two-and-a-half when he came to America in 1906 with my grandparents and two sisters. My mother was born in New York. Her parents came separately from Belorussia. *Lola Flores* is not their story. Still, I wrote my parents into a scene. On opening night for *The Ziegfeld Follies of 1936*, a red-headed woman seeks an autograph from Lola and introduces herself as Blanche and her husband as Morris. She also mentions their young daughter Kay, my sister.

*Q. The opening and closing scenes present Yankev Sobel holding Anshel up to see the Statue of Liberty. They provide quite a bit of irony regarding America as the land of opportunity. Did your grandfather do that with your father?*

A. I've always fantasized that he did. To this day, I tear up whenever I see an image of the Statue of Liberty or even think about her. The courage of immigrants leaving everything behind astounds and inspires me.

*Q. Why did you include so many real people, such as Ben "Bugsy" Siegel?*

A. Real people, like buildings, landmarks and music, heighten the reality of a novel set in the past. As to Ben Siegel, a notorious killer, I've always been fascinated by Jewish gangsters. Of course, I had to give him redeeming qualities, so he's extremely loyal to Lola and proclaims, "It ain't physical." What all the real-life characters do and say is fiction but true to the historical record. Ben shooting would-be assassins at New York's Stork Club? Fiction. Renovating the Flamingo Hotel in Las Vegas for the Mob? Truth. Meeting there with Lola? Obviously, fiction. His 1942 trial for the murder of Harry "Big Greenie" Greenberg in Los Angeles? Truth, including the names of the judge, district attorney and murdered witnesses. Meyer Lansky, the Mob's money guy, was real. Charlie "Lucky" Luciano was the boss of bosses. Leon Greenspan and Heshy Kaplan? Products of my imagination. And Fanny Brice *did* star in *The Ziegfeld Follies of 1936* then fall ill. She was a favorite of my mother's mother.

*Q. In 1953, Lola meets Christine Jorgensen. A generation had passed since Lola met Lili Elbe. Why doesn't Lola have what's now called gender reassignment surgery?*

A. Christine Jorgensen became known only following her surgery in Denmark. I remember the newspaper reports. But despite much verbal abuse, which she recounts in her autobiography, she toured the nightclub circuit and later appeared in plays. Lola's position is different. She realizes that if the public finds out that Lola Flores grew up male, they'll condemn her for defrauding them. Any hope of a comeback will be crushed. Her physical safety might even be put at risk.